BY ALYCIA CHRISTINE

SYLVAN CYCLE
Skinshifter
Dreamdrifter

SYLVAN PRELUDE
The Dryad's Sacrifice

TEMPEST MAIDEN
Thorn and Thistle

SHORT FICTION COLLECTIONS
Musings

SHORT FICTION
"The Cleaning"
"Hero's Moment"
"Paper Castles"
"The Twirling Ballerina"
"When the Medium Shatters"

Find out more at AlyciaChristine.com.

DREAMDRIFTER

BOOK TWO OF THE SYLVAN CYCLE SERIES

ALYCIA CHRISTINE

Purple Thorn Press
www.purplethornpress.com

Purple Thorn Press logo designed by Alycia Christine.
First Purple Thorn Press trade paperback edition published 2016. Printed in the United States of America by CreateSpace.

www.alyciachristine.com
www.purplethornpress.com

ISBN 978-1-941588-35-2

For my brothers, especially Derek and Ian.

CONTENTS

Extras:

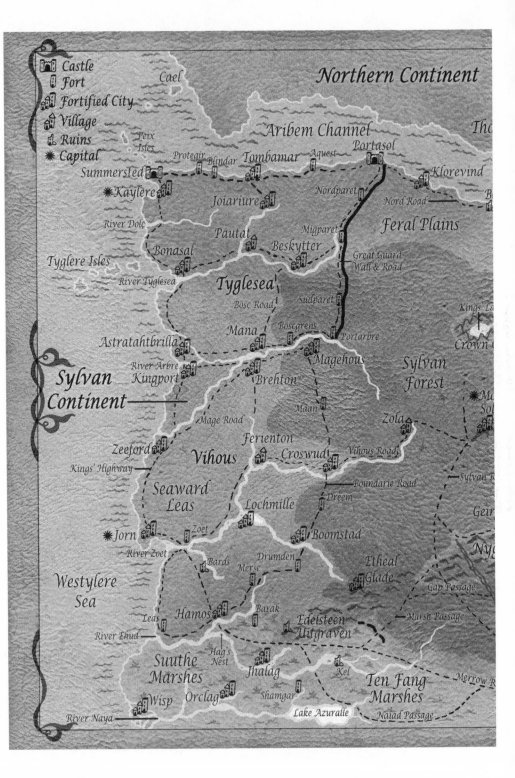

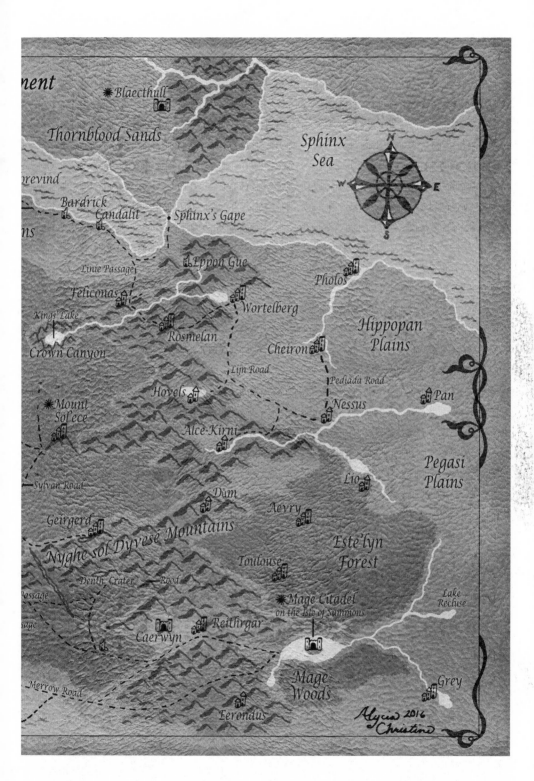

DREAMDRIFTER

BOOK TWO OF THE SYLVAN CYCLE SERIES

PROLOGUE

"My Lord Daeryn, I am sorry to keep you waiting," King Kaylor's personal envoy said, in what he hoped was an even tone of voice as they greeted each other with a bow. He was struck by how much of Marga's visage was reflected in this handsome male's appearance.

"With all due respect, Your Excellency, I had expected to meet with His Majesty this evening, not you," Daeryn said.

The ghoul Curqak suppressed the tremor of fear that coursed through him at hearing something so close to Caleb's voice after all these years. Instead the envoy affected an urbane smile—tight-lipped to hide his pointed, yellow teeth—and gestured for his guest to take a seat in a nearby chair. "Of course, my apologies, Good Sir, but I'm afraid no one sees King Kaylor without speaking with me first, as is the age-old custom of the Tyglesean Royal Court. Now, you did state that the matter in question was urgent, so shall we come to it at last?"

Daeryn narrowed his eyes, but sat nonetheless. As Curqak sat down opposite his guest, he felt sudden sweat bead up through the heavy makeup cloaking his ashen face and black-tipped ears. Would Daeryn be able to sense the decrepit state of his body underneath all the finery, just as Daeryn's mother had? If Daeryn discerned him to be a deadwalker...but no, the male was now busying himself with repositioning a chair cushion and surely couldn't smell the charnel scent masked by Curqak's heavy perfume...

"Where is my mother?" Daeryn asked.

"I beg your pardon?"

"My mother Marga disappeared over a year ago. She was last seen in this kingdom, so where…precisely…is she?"

Daeryn leaned close into Curqak's painted face and, in doing so, revealed that he too wore makeup to cover his pallid features, and had styled his long black hair to cover the black tips of his pointed ears. Could the rumors possibly be true? Was there more of the vampires' lineage than either the elves or humans in this hybrid that should have never been able to be conceived?

Curqak gulped hard, but did not break gaze with Daeryn's penetrating blue eyes. "She did of course come here to speak with the king and queen, My Sir, but it has been more than eleven months since she left our borders."

"Going where?"

"The guards told me she and her entourage rode northeast. I presumed she would return home to your family once her task here was complete."

"Why did she come here?"

Curqak feigned shock and dismay. "Well, of course to discuss ongoing negotiations between the Ring of Sorcerers and the king."

Daeryn sat back heavily in his chair, rubbing the faint stubble on his chin with a gloved hand and frowning.

"I'm sorry I can't be of more help, Master Daeryn," Curqak said consolingly. "But that is all I know."

They sat in silence as a servant placed a silver tray laden with mulled wine, mead, bread, cheese, and fruit on the table nearest them and then left the palace chamber. Curqak lazily watched her shut the large door and then turned to survey the food. Normally he made a good show of eating and drinking with guests, purging himself in privacy soon afterward. Today, however, he doubted such a show of normalcy was necessary. After all, if the rumors were true, then Daeryn likely consumed nothing but blood just as Curqak did and therefore would not touch this proffered fare.

Daeryn surprised him by walking to the table and pouring wine for himself and his host. "Forgive me, Excellency, but when did you say my mother left the country?"

"Oh, about ten or eleven months ago."

"And she was traveling which direction at the time?" Daeryn said as he turned back toward Curqak. He handed the envoy a silver goblet even as he drank from his own.

After a sip, Curqak frowned down at the liquid; it was more acrid than usual, but it gave him a nice warm tingle inside his body. He smiled and took another swig. Of course he would have to rid his stomach of it soon, but the discomfort of retching later seemed a fair trade for the comforting feeling he was enjoying just now. *I certainly must speak with the sommelier about procuring more of this particular vintage,* he thought.

Daeryn cleared his throat. "Your Excellency?"

"Hmm?"

"You said that my mother traveled southeast out of the country?"

Curqak nodded after another greedy gulp.

"You lie."

Curqak froze mid-swallow and stared at Daeryn over the rim of his cup. The hybrid had taken off his gloves and his green cloak and kicked them out of his way as he seized the emissary by his embroidered doublet. Curqak's goblet clattered to the limestone tile floor as Daeryn yanked him off of his feet. The envoy heard fabric tear and watched as two huge, pale dragon-like wings emerged from the hybrid's back. Three flaps of those membrane pinions thrust the two of them high into the air and out of the open balcony doors. Curqak shrieked as they flew beyond Castle Summersted's ramparts and on over the rolling sea.

"Scream if you wish, but none can rescue your worthless hide here, deadwalker." Daeryn's eyes were like smoldering embers. His lips parted to reveal a pair of growing white fangs as he clenched the trembling ghoul in one hand and kindled a fireforger's yellow flame with the other.

"Please, please! Spare me, I beg of you!" Curqak shouted as the wind roared passed his black-tipped ears.

"Why should I?" Daeryn shouted back as he pumped his wings, pushing them still higher into the sky.

The ghoul could feel his face begin to warm. The makeup was the only reason that the delicate skin of his cheeks and ears had not yet blistered in the dreadful sunlight. "I will tell you anything you want to know!"

"Oh, that you certainly will. I have already seen to that by drugging the wine."

"I will do anything you ask of me short of betraying my own master, which I will not do."

"Then name yourself!"

"I am called Curqak both by my former master Calais and by my current master."

"You were once my father's servant? Before he was Redeemed?"

"Yes. I was given to your father as a gift by my current master, so that he could learn how to perfect the vampire's bite of servitude. I became his first bitten and most loyal valet until our souls' tie was broken by his Redemption."

"Name your current master, ghoul."

"The Víchí High Elder Luther."

"And what assignment did Luther give to you?"

"First, to hunt down and bring to him the twelve Keystones of legend; second, to Turn or kill all suspected fulfillers of Third Age Prophesy."

"And how did you get past the enchantments protecting the Sylvan Continent from entry?"

Curqak moaned as he realized they had flown past the shore and out over the waves of the accursed sea. He retched in spite of himself. "A Tyglesean traitor smuggled me here in the bowels of his ship. It was the worst torture I have yet experienced."

"'Yet' being the operative word, ghoul." Daeryn snarled. "After the tales I've heard of your achievements during the Second War of Ages, you deserve that torture and much more." They were descending now, swooping toward a tiny island a mere league beyond the shore's jagged gray cliffs. They landed smoothly amid the dunes and then Daeryn hauled a now trembling and whimpering Curqak to the edge of the sea. Despite the power of the incoming waves, Daeryn stood firm as he held his victim over the water. Curqak winced as he felt the salty spray on his flailing legs.

"Listen to me carefully, Curqak. You will tell me everything I want to know or I will burn your face with the weakest fireforger's flame while setting your legs in the churning sea. Do you understand?"

Curqak gulped.

"Good," Daeryn almost purred. "I found the ashes and bodies of Mother's escorts and of deadwalkers not three leagues from Castle Caerwyn, but Marga's remains were not among them. So what have you done with my mother?"

"She was taken to Luther's stronghold on the Northern Continent for questioning."

"Blaecthull? Why?"

Curqak grimaced. "She is the keeper of the Keystones, but she would not tell me where she had hidden them. Luther has better ways of loosening her tongue than I."

"And he would risk the presence of a fireforger that powerful in his own fortress? He must be insane! She could lay waste to the entire keep and every deadwalker in it with ease!"

Curqak nodded. "Marga certainly tried. Fortunately, there is a water cave there, which is strong enough to subdue her. After all, she is not like you and has only fireforging magic at her beck and call."

"And so she is Luther's captive." Anguish crept into Daeryn's gaze then. "What will it take to free her?"

Curqak felt a glimmer of triumph deep within his foggy mind. Was it possible that he might ensnare this male, just as he had trapped his mother? "Master Luther will likely want a trade: either the twelve Keystones in place of Marga or another captive of equal importance."

"Do you know the whereabouts of the Keystones?"

Curqak shook his head, his eyes squinted shut with the pain of the searing sun and the swirling sea. "I discovered one—the Firesprite's Sapphire, which Marga had brought to the priesthood here to protect; she did not trust other members of the General Council of Mages. Before I could attain it, Queen Manasa's youngest brat ran off with the jewel and I cannot find her!"

Daeryn frowned. "So it must be a trade of beings then."

"Likely, but I'm uncertain who Master Luther would consider worthy of exchange."

Daeryn pursed his lips over shrinking fangs as he extinguished the flame in his clawed left hand and pulled the dangling Curqak away from the water with his right. When the hybrid released the ghoul, the deadwalker fell trembling to his knees in the dry sand. Before Curqak could think to flee, however, Daeryn shoved him onto his back and pinned him flat under his own heavier bulk. Daeryn forced the ghoul's mouth open and dripped an amber liquid from one of his claws down the back of the deadwalker's raw throat.

Heat shot through Curqak's body and every muscle felt invigorated with warmth. He smiled as he felt his inert heart begin to beat a strong, steady rhythm. How long had it been since he had truly felt warm or alive? When had he died? It must have been hundreds of winters ago, but now the ghoul could barely remember it. The full-powered serum made his mind fuzzy and his body limp, but he no longer cared as he reveled in this newfound comfort.

"Ask me anything, Master Daeryn," he whispered.

Daeryn's answering smile was cold. "Tell me *exactly* how my father successfully Turned you."

I
SHADE SHIFTING

"Felan!"

It was not a yell so much as a scream that brought the huge human male barreling half-naked into the opulent bedchamber. The full moon's eerie rays illuminated the room through its stained-glass windows, casting everything within it in a blood-tinged hue, including the screaming human now backing away from the source of her fear.

The lioness snarled at the one called Felan in warning just before a pale-skinned male and a green-skinned dryad ran into the room after him. The two nearly trod on Felan's heels when he halted just beyond the servant door.

"Katja?" Felan faltered as he gaped at the lioness.

The lioness's emerald eyes met the intruder's troubled gaze, challenging him to come closer and risk the wrath of her claws as she fought to free herself from the jumbled tunic and loincloth now restraining her. Katja yowled in frustration as she twisted and turned.

"Felan, Dayalan, do something!" Lauraisha said as she pulled on her waist-length auburn hair in agitation. The chemise-garbed human edged toward the group. "Katja's gone mad!"

Felan just continued to stare. "I didn't think it possible for her even to become a lioness—not yet, at least! She has never skinshifted into erdeling form so fully before. Until her mind gains control over her new bestial instincts, she's very dangerous."

"Really? We hadn't noticed," exclaimed Zahra. The dryad's jade-hued lips curled with her sarcasm even as her fingers wrapped more firmly around her sunsilver sickle.

"I suggest we make a slow, steady retreat," Dayalan murmured, nudging the two females protectively behind him as he raised his sunsilver staff into a defensive position.

Katja had begun to tear at the cumbersome clothing entrapping her transformed body, her curved claws and fangs shredding both linen and leather with uncanny ease. Malevolent eyes turned back toward the odd cluster of beings slowly retreating through the servants' door as she kicked off the last offending rag. Tail thumping the floor in warning, she stalked the intruders.

She smelled their foul stench all around this strange den. How dare they invade her territory! The lioness focused on the pale elf with long black head-fur. Instinct demanded that she deal with the one called Dayalan first. The breeze from the room's open window blowing the Erdeken pack's scents more strongly toward her keen nose. Katja stopped in sudden confusion, testing the new aromas. Horse blood and wolf fur as well as vegetation tickled her awareness. The scents were familiar, almost comforting, but strange to associate with the beings standing before her.

"Lauraisha, now might be a good time to use that uncanny talent of yours," said Felan. He was larger than the other male and smelled more of wolves than of humans.

How odd, the lioness thought.

"I tried!" Lauraisha whimpered.

Dayalan gripped his blood-scented staff harder even as he and the others retreated through the door. "Try again."

Katja's maw curled in a silent snarl at Dayalan's challenge and then relaxed slightly in confusion as emotions not her own brushed the edge of her awareness. Thoughts of kinship and affection floated through her thoughts in contrast to her own raw rage and frustration. The skinshifted lioness's mind dredged up a new well of memories more complex and intense than her bestial instincts could dominate.

Katja stared at Lauraisha and cocked her head, remembering the Tyglesean Princess smiling as she offered the skinshifter a fish, and then showing her the curious contraption of string and stick that she had used to catch it. She turned her gaze toward Zahra, and remembered her red hair looking almost aflame with the setting sun's rays as she strode toward Katja in the royal linen garb of her odd feminine race. Of the tallest human saturated with wolf scents, she remembered another full moon's night when Felan had comforted her after she had skinshifted beside an artificial water spring…a fountain, it was called. But the half-human who reeked of horse blood only brought forth memories of vile red eyes and crimson-streaked fangs. Flashes assaulted her mind of Dayalan's face contorted in gleeful lust as he drank his fill of blood from a horse. The lioness crouched in sudden hate and fear, her guttural growl forming a single snarled word: "Víchí!"

She roared and launched herself at the vampire fiend before he could close the door against her.

"Katja! No!"

Princess Lauraisha flung herself in front of Dayalan, a hand raised against the lioness. A blast of scarlet flame burst from her delicate fingertips, searing the lioness's golden fur. Katja felt the terrible heat even as her claws sliced skin.

"Lauraisha!" the Víchí and dryad screamed in unison.

"I'm bleeding…" the human fireforger murmured. She stared in dumb fascination at her tattered arm and chest before crumbling to the floor.

Squinting in agony, Katja roared as Dayalan knelt over Lauraisha's still body. He snarled at the werecat, his blue eyes now glowing scarlet as he watched her. Both Felan and Princess Zahra flanked him with their weapons ready so that Katja could find no opening through which to attack again.

The skinshifter roared at them in rage, her voice nearly rattling the teeth in their maws. Then she finally found words. "Turncoats!"

"Who's the traitor, Katja!" Felan, the skinshifter mage, shouted. "Look at what you've done to her!"

Katja focused on the blood-streaked human near Felan's bare feet. Cold recognition doused the lioness's ire. She had often considered this human princess to be her dearest friend and sister—when her thoughts were coherent.

Lauraisha, she thought. *No!*

She watched with sudden fear as Dayalan stripped his gloves off to reveal black claws. A strange mix of expressions washed across his pallid face as he knelt to apply pressure to the now unconscious girl's wounds—anger, fear, and a terrible hunger. His talon-like hands began to tremble as he held them against Lauraisha's slashed chest.

"Zahra…"

The dryad princess glanced at the half-breed enigma questioningly.

"Bring bandages, rags, anything so she won't bleed to death."

The dryad blanched a paler green than usual and sprinted into the neighboring bedchamber. She returned moments later with linen bed sheets, a satchel of herbs, and a dagger. As she knelt beside Dayalan to examine the damage, the rug underneath Lauraisha turned from pale green to a sickening maroon.

"There's no organ damage, just semi-deep gashes…" Zahra whispered.

Together she and Dayalan shredded the cloth and bound the princess's chest and left arm while Felan stood watch over a now mewling Katja. From somewhere in the dark recesses of the lioness's mind, a baleful voice as deep as Dayalan's began laughing.

How brave are you now, little changeling? Now that I have taught you true fear?

Katja stared, startled, at Dayalan, but he had not spoken. She looked at her victim and swallowed hard. The lioness backed away from the carnage. She was suddenly chilled even though the skin of her shoulder still felt afire. "What done?" Katja asked in broken Shrŷde.

"What indeed, Katja!" snapped Dayalan.

The lioness scooped up her own torn clothes with her maw and laid them at Felan's bare feet.

"Me…skinshift wounds close?"

"After you went to the trouble of opening them in the first place? No, absolutely not!" Felan snapped after a moment's work to comprehend her. "I'll heal her—if you can control your wretched instincts long enough for me to turn my back on you."

Katja flinched at his harsh rebuke.

"I'll watch her, Felan," Dayalan said while Zahra mixed an herb poultice to use in soaking the human's bandages. "Come quickly!"

The males exchanged places and the skinshifter mage laid his large hands on the female. After a last baleful look at Katja, Felan closed his eyes and gained an expression of profound concentration. His hands seemed to almost seep between the flesh and bone of Lauraisha's sternum. A curious scent of spicy warmth pervaded the room.

Katja perked her rounded ears and prayed silently for the Creator's aid. Her erdeling instincts still screamed at her to defend her territory, but she maintained her low crouch under Dayalan's wary eye.

A curious blue light glowed beneath Felan's palms, and suddenly Damya erupted from the amulet between his pressed fingers. Without a word, the firesprite also laid her tiny hands in healing upon Lauraisha's ravaged chest and arm. Together they closed the gashes, lacing the female's small body with skinshifting and fireforging magic.

The Mage Citadel's bell tolled once as they finished their work. Zahra unwound the seasoned bandages and added fresh poultice to the angry red scabs. Although the healing seemed to have succeeded, Lauraisha still did not wake.

"She has lost too much blood," the little blue firesprite whispered, gently smoothing the female's hair out of her ashen face. "Best to get her to the Healing Ward now that you can safely move her."

"Will she live?" Katja asked and suddenly felt four sets of scornful eyes upon her.

Damya surveyed Katja with a cold glare as Felan began to move the human princess. "She will need time to fully heal, and time is a luxury we do not have. Her body must remake the blood that she lost tonight thanks to you. That is no easy task. She may yet come down with sickness before this is finished. At the very least, we will have to once again postpone the upcoming mission to Tyglesea until she heals, and thus risk even more lives in the process."

Katja mewled. "I am sorry, so sorry."

"Zahra, call the guards!" Dayalan's flames flared. "Tell

them to get this changeling out of my sight or I will finish the scorching that Lauraisha began!"

The whimpering lioness pushed past Zahra as she opened the bedchamber door to yell for aid and dashed down the granite corridor—evading guardians and mage pupils alike as Daeryn's triumphant laughter echoed through her thoughts.

* * *

Katja Escari stared across the cold waters of the moonlit lake and wished with all her being that she could cry. Her worthless lioness body allowed no tears to be shed, however, so she simply lay in the cold mud, voicing her misery with soft, shuddering moans. For the past two hours, she had watched the Citadel's guardian squads hunt for her from her hiding place under a shelf of rock near the lakeshore. The stench of rotting vegetation had masked her scent while her golden-furred body was easily blended among the yellowed stalks of the pond reeds. Occasionally she heard the guardians' nearby whispers and considered surrendering herself, but feared to communicate with anyone while under Daeryn's influence. Even now, she could feel the faint echoes of his laughter in the corner of her mind.

"Katja?"

She screeched when his deep voice penetrated her thoughts again—this time not mentally but audibly.

"I'm sorry. I did not wish to frighten you."

The tone was too kind to be Daeryn's. Katja released a sigh of relief mixed with grief as Dayalan cautiously approached her hiding place.

"Is Lauraisha...?"

"The harmhealers think she'll live."

"Are you here to imprison me then?" she asked as he stopped several body-lengths away, peering at her warily through the plants as she lay before him.

"You despise me," she said.

"I—"

"Don't try to deny it. I know you do! How could you not after what I've done?" Her rounded ears drooped further in defeat.

Dayalan hesitated, and then crawled to sit beside her—

his black boots sliding in the stinking, gray muck. "Actually, I came to beg your forgiveness."

The lioness shifted and looked up at him in surprise. His countenance was both sincere and somber. "For what? Do you think what I did is somehow your fault?"

Dayalan shook his head. "No, I suppose not, although my presence tonight certainly worsened the situation."

Katja snorted at the hybrid. "I would have mauled Lauraisha whether you were present or not. You, at the least, distracted me long enough for her to try to reason with me, for all the good that did. And you were able to protect her from further harm."

Dayalan shifted uneasily. "I offer my apologies not for my actions, but for my attitude. I treated you abysmally tonight when I, of all beings, should be able to empathize with your lapse of sanity."

"I deserve no empathy." Katja laid her head back on her paws. "My behavior nearly cost my dearest friend her life!"

"I did not say that I condoned your loss of control, Katja, only that I understand it."

Katja peered at him in sudden curiosity. "How did you find me?"

Dayalan tapped the sunsilver spearhead hanging from his neck with his black-gloved right hand. Katja squinted down at her own spearhead. Despite being caked in mud, the broken spearhead's center mirror shard still clearly reflected her bestial face within its scarlet depths.

"Yours has been whispering to mine ever since you fled the Citadel," he added.

Katja felt her shard pull toward Dayalan's, sliding the spearhead point through the muck. She closed her eyes and let out a breath between clenched fangs. "I heard Daeryn's laughter in my mind after I attacked Lauraisha."

Dayalan's body stiffened at the mention of his twin brother's name. "Did Verdagon come to you, then?"

The lioness shook her head.

Dayalan was silent, but his brow was creased with worry. "I thought you were cured of Daeryn's influence."

"So did I. Apparently, our bond flows much deeper than I had imagined." She shuddered.

"More than anything else, his presence would help explain your behavior tonight. Does he still manipulate your thoughts?"

Katja shook her head. "He's gone...for now."

"You must explain this to the dragon, Katja. Surely Verdagon will know how to mend this."

"Maybe." Katja sighed and looked away.

They sat in silence until Dayalan finally spoke again. "Regardless of anything else, Lauraisha is alive and that is what matters."

The catch in Dayalan's voice made her glance sidelong at his haggard face. Unshed tears stood in the corners of his azure eyes. Surprised at his sudden display of emotion, the lioness quickly averted her gaze. She resumed her study of the cold lake to give Dayalan some privacy as he wept. They sat quietly together for a long while before Katja finally gathered enough resolve to speak on the issue weighing down her mood.

"You do know that Lauraisha is very fond of you, don't you?" she asked.

Dayalan's sniff was barely perceptible. "I admire her as well. She's quite a courageous female...highly intelligent, kind, a skilled warrior..."

"I know your sentiment for her runs deeper than simple admiration, Dayalan." Katja's green eyes stared unblinking at the male's now guarded façade.

"Of course I deeply value her friendship, Katja. She has stood loyal to me, as have you, during some of my worst moods. A rare number of beings are fearless enough—or foolish enough—to show such loyalty to a blood-drinker like me."

"We do so because we know your true worth, Dayalan, even if others do not...even if you do not."

"My true worth..." The hybrid gazed at her a moment. "You consider me worth your loyalty even after the way you reacted to me tonight? When you finally recognized my face, your expression was the same look of fear and hatred that you had given me the moment we met at Caerwyn Castle. You thought me a vampire then; you saw me tonight as the same."

"That wasn't me, Dayalan. How could it be after I nearly

killed...?"

"That was my basic point earlier, Katja," the fireforger hybrid said gently. "You were no more in your right mind than I am when I thirst..."

He cleared his throat then and rubbed a trembling hand over his pale brow.

She stared at him. "Are you well?"

He shook his head. "I must visit Tyron tonight."

The skinshifter lioness watched him a moment. His admission told her more than she wanted to know. The horse Tyron was Dayalan's bloodmate—the erdeling beast from whom he gained his main sustenance. When Daeryn had killed the wolf Bren, Tyron was the only beast who could survive Dayalan's need for nourishment. The memory of that first feeding still made Katja shudder. The fact that Dayalan needed to visit the horse tonight told her that his seeing Lauraisha's bloody condition had affected the hybrid more deeply than he cared to admit.

"I saw the way you looked at Lauraisha tonight, Dayalan—as if you might lose everything if she..." She shook herself out of her sudden melancholy and persevered to her point. "You love her, don't you?" She asked as she watched him with narrowed eyes.

"I beg your pardon?"

"You heard me."

Dayalan abruptly stood. "Katja, I hardly think this is the time for an attempt at matchmaking."

Katja's tail thumped the ground hard in warning, but Dayalan had already turned his back to her and began to stride away.

"Ah, so you do care for her very deeply, then," she called after his retreating form. "Perhaps far more than you think you should."

Dayalan stopped and whirled to face her, his look venomous. "If you inform anyone of this—"

"Don't threaten me, Dayalan," she snarled while bounding to his side. "Her actions tonight—as foolish as they were—no doubt proved her love for you. I had once feared that my dearest friend's soul might be torn by unreturned love. However, I see now that will not be the case."

"No, instead her soul will be tarnished by something far worse." he whispered, almost to himself. Dayalan shook his head and said, "Her feelings for me are but the whims of a youth and will soon pass to a more fitting suitor."

Katja shook her head. "You are wrong, Dayalan," she said gently. "Lauraisha's affinity for you will do nothing if not grow. She may be young, but she has an old soul. She has seen you in her dreams since before she knew me. We both saw you battle your brother through the Ott vre Caerwyn mirror. She saw your true nobility then and she understands you better than any other being—including yourself."

"I know the dreams you speak of; Lauraisha showed them to me when we first met. It makes no difference." His tone was flat. "Lauraisha has seen barely sixteen winters whilst this winter is my thirty-sixth. If I chose to love a female, I would choose someone closer to my own age. Even so, I can never allow myself to be so vulnerable with another—that is far too dangerous a temptation. I should have thought that you, of all beings, would understand this."

Katja watched his hardened gaze in sadness. "I understand it, but I don't agree with it. You are not your brother."

Dayalan's eyes flashed scarlet as he turned and extended his dragon-like wings from beneath his wool cloak. "Besides a single arm scar, how can you even tell the pair of us apart?" He growled and launched himself into the night sky.

Katja sat watching his fleeing figure until Dayalan was no more than the merest dark speck among the low winter clouds. Once again she wished she could cry.

"You, there! Halt!" Katja spun in surprise at the centaur's voice. Her conversation with Dayalan had caused her to momentarily forget that the Citadel guardians were hunting her. The centaur stopped a safe distance away with his fighting staff leveled at her tawny chest.

Katja stared at the male and blinked in sudden recognition. It was rare to see her sparring partner in his guardian uniform. "Garret?"

"Katja Escari, you are commanded to attend an audience with the High Pyrekin, Dragon Prince Verdagon. You must return to the Citadel with me at once."

Katja's ears twitched in annoyance. "Calm down, Garret.

I am my sane self once again and I'm not going to fight an arrest, especially when you're the one making it."

Garret looked visibly relieved, but still stood his ground. She walked slowly toward him and then sat on her haunches in the least threatening posture she could hold while in the form of a lioness. "You do realize that Verdagon isn't a prince."

Garret grimaced. "Sorry. Verdagon doesn't seem to prefer titles, so it was the best one I could think up at the moment."

Katja cocked her head. "I guess a Pyrekin could be considered regal even if he doesn't hold the title. May I make myself somewhat presentable before you take me to him?"

The centaur nodded his head once in consent. Katja sighed, pushed herself into the lake, and rinsed the stinking silt out of her fur. After the water had washed away the worst of the filth, Katja quickly shook herself free of moisture and hurried back to Garret. As the cold air whipped around her, the skinshifter was quite certain she would never be warm again.

The centaur led her along the beach toward the Mage Citadel's tallest tower where the hidden entrance to the lower dwarf-mined cavern existed. Garret and Katja searched out the cave's staircase and then wordlessly descended into its craggy depths.

The winding labyrinth eventually opened into an antechamber adjacent to the ancient Hatching Cavern. The chamber was large enough to accommodate hundreds of eggs hardening on its volcanic-heated sands. Katja's eyes focused on the various carvings of each egg-bearing Sylvan race: accipions, griffins, harpies, hippogriffs, lamia, sercaps, and the much-maligned girtab. The early part of the Second Age had seen almost every female from all the land-walking Sylvan races hatch their young in the safety of the Isle of Summons. Now, however, the Hatching Cavern stood empty, with the exception of Verdagon. He was the first dragon to be hatched in the cavern in a millennium.

How long had it been since a Sylvan or Pyrekin had been hatched on these grounds? Four centuries? Five? The werecat's thoughts wandered to Aria and the rest of the Forgotten Races holed up behind the protective ramparts of Caerwyn Castle under the protection of Dayalan and Daeryn's father

Caleb. Would the girtab ever be able to lay her egg-bound young here in solace? Would King Canuche ever see his all-but-extinct griffin race return to their former splendor? Katja fervently hoped such would be the case, but only the Creator knew these answers.

"Katja, come!"

The dragon's booming voice rocked the lioness out of her reverie. She broke into a run—bounding ahead of Garret across the warm black dunes until she pushed past the crackling magic barrier of the Ring Spells, past the observation stands, and onto the Hatching Chamber's main grounds. She stopped when she saw the green-scaled dragon in all his iridescent majesty and bowed low, touching her head to her outstretched front paws. Verdagon had almost tripled in size since his hatching barely a moon-cycle before and would very soon be large enough to bear the weight of his chosen steward—her.

"What troubles you, Katja?"

For a moment she said nothing as she saw the elf Vraelth appear around Verdagon's bulk and bow to her. He was holding a scrub brush. She returned the bow and then looked at him, puzzled.

"My herald was kind enough to relieve some of my more terrible itches this evening," Verdagon said in answer to Katja's unspoken question.

If Katja had had the ability to blush in her present lioness form, she would have done so. Keeping the growing dragon's hide free of sloughed-off skin and scales was a steward's job, not a herald's.

"I am so sorry, Verdagon. I have failed."

She meant the phrase as all-encompassing, and indicated such to the dragon through their mental link. The dragon, however, gave her as gentle of a smile as he could around his long white fangs.

"Nonsense, Steward, you couldn't very well take care of all my itching in your current form. After all, you have no thumbs with which to grip the brush!" Dragon's booming laughter made the jagged cave roof shudder.

Vraelth meanwhile set the brush down and stepped from the Pyrekin's side. "I believe I should take my leave, My

Lord."

"As should I, My Lord," Garret said. "If my services are no longer needed, that is."

The dragon dipped his angular head toward the elf once in agreement. "Go see to Lauraisha's well-being, please. Katja and I have much to discuss. And, Garret, your services are always needed, but at present they are not required. I hear your stomach grumbling, so go find something for yourself in the kitchens."

"Thank you, My Lord." Garret said, smiling. The centaur bowed deeply and then trotted up the main steps leading out of the Hatching Cavern.

Once Garret was gone, Vraelth bowed. "Thank you for our time together, My Sir."

Verdagon smiled again and touched the hard tip of his snout to Vraelth's outstretched fingers in an affectionate farewell. The dragon watched as his chosen elf herald followed the centaur across the grounds and did not turn to gaze at his steward until the charmchanter mage and Citadel guardian had disappeared up the steep interior stairs.

"I chose well. He is an excellent herald and will prove an asset to our fellowship."

Katja bowed her head and waited.

"Katja, how badly did Lauraisha burn you?"

Katja felt sick. "I suppose Damya conveyed to you what happened tonight, My Sir?"

"She did." Verdagon's answering expression was grim. "We must see to those wounds soon. First, however, I need to examine your mind again. I must delve deeper than I have before and it will likely cause you some pain."

Katja nodded glumly. "I deserve it, My Sir."

Verdagon shook his reptilian head, concern flashing in his eyes. "No, I'm fairly certain you do not. This is meant for your protection, not your punishment. Come and sit quietly before me, close your eyes, and breathe deep breaths. My work will go faster if you can calm your thoughts."

The lioness obeyed. The dragon bent close to her until his snout almost touched her forehead. White fire arced between Katja's forehead and Verdagon's nose as the dragon's consciousness brushed the skinshifter's awareness.

Neither the light nor the blue-white fire actually harmed her, but they did hurt. Instead of fighting the piercing pain, the skinshifter tried to allow the pain to find a concentrated point in the front of her mind. As the pain culminated, she ground her fangs together and drew the light into the core of her mental awareness, creating a sort of doorway through which Verdagon could enter.

The tendrils of his thoughts wove into the familiar places at the center of her awareness, and then wound their way outward from there, seeking to reveal all that was hidden. Katja felt the darkest edges of her existence lit by the being's fire and felt sudden shame at the memories and thoughts lurking there. Mistakes and wrongs and revolting ideas shrank away from the Pyrekin's purity, and yet were held captive to his power. A sudden desire overwhelmed Katja to purge the spiritual dross thus illuminated within her, and yet Katja knew she was powerless to do so alone. Despair gripped her as she watched her most recent atrocity against Lauraisha once again unfold before Verdagon's mental eye, and she began to mewl.

She was suddenly aware of another presence linked to her mind—a ruined crimson darkness in contrast to Verdagon's white light. Daeryn's darkness. It grew faint as Verdagon neared it—diminishing to a single thread. Yet it would not completely recede, no matter how the dragon fought it. Instead, a chilling laughter echoed in her thoughts.

"Verdagon, what is happening to me?" A paralyzing fear traveled through her body and she felt a simultaneous shudder run its course through Verdagon.

Verdagon's countenance was grave. "This is troubling indeed. Your wraithwalker training must be intensified immediately. Otherwise you cannot hope to protect yourself or others from the evil that has beset you."

Katja huddled close to the ground as she fought to control the tremors now coursing through her. "What do you mean?"

The dragon growled low and then asked, "Katja, would you show me what you remember of the night that you fought Daeryn?"

Katja recalled her memory of the night of the full moon when Daeryn's attacked the packmates' camp. She shuddered as she remembered him slaughtering the white wolf Bren, before he had almost killed Felan and herself...

*

"No! I will not go to Luther!" Katja had screamed.

She struggled wildly, trying to break Daeryn's grasp as they flew high over the forest. She would rather fall to her death than be Turned and forced to serve evil like her brother Kayten.

The vampire snarled and wrapped his arms even tighter around his prey. "Then perhaps you would do well to bond with me instead."

Katja snarled her defiance and then shrieked as Daeryn's fangs pierced her throat. Incomprehensible pain penetrated her senses as his Taint pervaded her body and then invaded her brain through the blood feeding it. The screams of her packmates echoed distantly in her ears until a cold darkness expelled all external awareness. She felt her soul writhe in protest as a new voice spoke inside the depths of her mind.

Bond with me, Katja.

The voice compelled her obedience and yet a part of her soul felt something innately wrong with its entreaties.

Turn, Katja, Turn... Bond with me and Turn...

The voice was seductive—his words so tempting, like honey on the lips of a lover. The cold darkness deepened and she felt her soul sink with unfathomable weight. In the depths of that darkness, an unquenchable thirst she had never known was unleashed and raw power ravaged her being. She was changing, awakening, and hungering for more...

"Katja, come back to me!"

Felan? A vision flashed before her of Felan still in the form of a full wolf lying in a bloody heap at the base of a tree. The vision changed to show Dayalan as he shattered the Ott vre Caerwyn bearing Daeryn's laughing face with his sunsilver staff.

Katja, break his hold! Break Daeryn's hold over you!

Dayalan's deep voice resonated through her mind, but then hideous laughter drowned it out. Daeryn's triumphant pleasure echoed in her mind. He was changing her not into a zombie soul slave or a nemean soul servant, but into the very thing she loathed most—a vampire like himself.

Yes, Katja. Feed me more. More! Let me drain you dry…

Katja tried to push back Daeryn's voice, to fight the cold hunger raging within her, but she was too overwhelmed to prevent the change now consuming her. And the darkest part of her soul craved more. In desperation she cried out to the heavens, "Creator, I love you! I cannot save myself! Save me!"

Daeryn's cold laughter continued to ring in her mind, but a sudden warmth seeped back into her bones. The darkness weighing down her soul began to waver and then it cracked as a soothing blue-white light—Verdagon's fire—blazed against its barrier. As the hunger died, situational awareness flooded back into her mind. The darkness finally shattered—dispersed by the light. She felt Daeryn's claws still clutching her tightly, but discovered that his fangs no longer pierced her neck. She tentatively opened her eyes and found herself hovering just above the treetops. Her captor was trembling and she heard his mental voice suddenly scream as their souls' connection broke. Daeryn's grip loosened and Katja instinctively knew her moment had come.

She writhed against his grip with all her strength and plunged the sunsilver-and-mirror-shard spearhead into the chest wound made by Zahra's earlier arrow. Daeryn convulsed and instinctively flew backward—breaking off the spear tip in the process. When he did so, Katja wrenched the remainder of her spear point out of his jerkin. Then she had fallen toward the safety of the trees below her…

*

"Thank you, Katja."

The trembling skinshifter pushed her mind away from the abominable memory and gazed at the dragon once more. "Why did you make me relive that?"

"Your memory clarifies a few things that mine cannot. I was still bound inside the egg when I helped you escape Daeryn's bite, so I had no knowledge of the spearhead breaking off in Daeryn's chest; I only knew about Daeryn's attempt to Turn you into a deadwalker vampire like himself."

"How is the spearhead significant?"

"The spearhead was forged long ago from one of my

predecessors' sunsilver hoards. Dragons are some of the few Pyrekin who take on a fully physical form when we enter the Erde Realm, and so our bones have long been used as a catalyst to intensify magic. The same, of course, can be said of sunsilver and of bloodstones. My belief is that when you stabbed Dayalan's brother with your sunsilver-and-mirror-shard spearhead, you did so before I had managed to completely sever the ties between the two of you. With some help from your innate wraithwalking magic, I was able to keep Daeryn from Turning you. However, you must have inadvertently intensified the aftereffects of his bonding spell when you stabbed him. The mirror shard created an unusual mental link between you—a lasting tendril of the Blood Bond that Daeryn was trying to establish. This would explain why I, in all my power, can only temporarily cleanse the dark link between your minds, but I cannot destroy it."

"You can't?"

Verdagon shook his head.

"But vampires, like all deadwalkers, cannot withstand a Pyrekin's fire any more than they can endure a fireforger mage's flames."

Verdagon nodded. "It's true that fire destroys all of Luther's spawn…all but one."

Katja swallowed hard. "Caleb."

The dragon nodded again. "The vampire once known as Calais was not destroyed by the fireforger Marga's flame. He was transformed by it—Redeemed, as the legends say. It's possible that Daeryn has somehow kept his father's miraculous tolerance to fire even though he has now Turned into a full vampire. If that is the case, then nothing I know can destroy him and we are all in grave peril."

"What do we do then?" she said in utter panic.

The dragon frowned and scratched a dry spot on his cheek. "*You* are to continue training, of course…just as I have already said. You will decrease your skinshifting studies in favor of training more as a wraithwalker mage."

"But I nearly killed Lauraisha tonight because of my lack of skinshifting skill!"

The Pyrekin snorted. "No, you wounded her tonight because Daeryn was experimenting with the bestial part of your brain. Now that he has successfully discovered a way to manipulate your instincts, I'm certain he will attempt it again. This poses a far worse threat than a simple case of skinshifting madness.

"If left unhindered, Daeryn could continue to plant suggestions in your mind during each new skinshift and then eventually make himself a strong enough presence to dominate all of your thoughts. You would become slave to his every whim with no independent identity or will of your own."

"I'd be a zombie?"

"Essentially, yes. However, we will not allow that to happen—that I promise you. As long as you are bonded with me as my steward, I can help you fight Daeryn's domination. And there are others who may be able to help us as well." Verdagon put a huge talon on her shoulder. His gentle touch helped Katja cease her shivering. "I will contact the Ring of Sorcerers immediately. Doubtless they already know of tonight's events, but I need to inform them of Daeryn's destructive influence so that Joce'lynn, especially, may take the proper precautions."

"What must I do now then, My Sir?"

Sorrow tinged his smile. "You need healing, rest, and forgiveness. While I cannot aid you in the last, I can certainly help you with the former two."

Katja felt a surge of pleasant warmth spread from the dragon's talon into her aching shoulder. Then she sank into the soft sand beneath her paws as he curled his huge body protectively around her. Her last conscious feeling was her surprise that Verdagon's reptilian hide felt so soft against her tawny fur.

II
WRAITH FIRE

Katja awoke from a dreamless sleep and frowned. The world around her was green—scaly green. She awkwardly pushed herself into a sitting position and realized that Verdagon's bulk still enveloped her body. The skinshifter squirmed free from between the snoring dragon's forearm and chest only to find herself fending off the emerald expanse of a wing as he rolled to one side. With a slight screech, she dropped to the sand below him and scrambled away from Verdagon's bone-crushing weight as he shifted positions.

"Jierira, that went well," she growled sarcastically. Meanwhile, the dragon settled on his side and began to snore all the louder.

She checked her body for injuries and, after finding none, was shocked to discover that she was her normal werecat self once again. She must have skinshifted back to her true form in her sleep. With a sigh of relief, she stood upright on her back paws and double-checked the areas where Lauraisha had scorched her shoulder. Thanks to Verdagon's attention and her own skinshifting abilities, Katja's skin and muscle had fully mended; however, several bare patches mottled her usually thick golden fur where the worst burns had occurred. She was also naked. Katja flushed in embarrassment and quickly searched the cavern. The cave was empty of both beings and garments. This would never do. She needed at least a loincloth and more preferably a full robe to cover her current shame, but she found neither.

She looked around again and spied Verdagon's broken eggshell near the edge of the sands closest to the thermal vent that heated the cave. She sprinted over to it and ducked inside the cracked casing, hoping to find something useful. There was nothing but long-dried membrane and shell fragments. She sighed in disappointment.

"Finding anything interesting in there?" Verdagon was watching her in bemusement.

She yelped and hid herself in the shell's shadow. "No, My Sir. Now that I am a werecat once again, I need proper clothes and there aren't any in this cave."

He chuckled. "Stay hidden a moment more and I'll see to that."

The dragon lifted his head and gave a stone-shaking bugle. Soon a plum-skinned elf came bounding down the nearest set of steps and bowed low as soon as his boots touched the sands.

Verdagon cocked his head at the elf. "Oeled, I thought that you would be helping Neha'lyn with Princess Lauraisha's care."

The Aevry Clan elf nodded. "I was, My Lord, but he sent me to you with a formal inquiry."

"Which is?"

"He humbly requests a vial of tears from you to help aid in Her Highness's healing."

The dragon sighed, and then shed his pearlescent tears into the messenger's proffered container. "Warn Neha'lyn that He will need to extract the salt from my tears and use that directly on his patients for this to be any help at all. Dragons' tears are far less effective healers without phoenix tears to catalyze their strength, and such elixirs are meant to treat Tainted wounds, not natural injuries."

The harmhealer mage nodded and bowed his thanks.

"In the meantime, I require clothes for my steward. Would you please bring me proper garments befitting Katja's rank?"

"Yes, My Sir."

Once Oeled had returned with a tan mage robe, a dark orange skinshifter rank sash, and a burgundy wraithwalker sash, he told Verdagon, "Mistress Joce'lynn wishes to see your steward as soon as she is presentable."

"Of course, please inform her that Katja and I will meet her in the courtyard nearest her study tower."

* * *

Joce'lynn's study was located at the top of the second tallest tower in the Citadel on the Isle of Summons above nearly five hundred rather steep steps. Fortunately, Katja was not required to climb those stairs today, but staring up at the tower gave the werecat a new appreciation of why the Sorceress was so fit and healthy despite having seen over 300 winters in her lifetime.

As the werecat and dragon waited in the misty courtyard below Joce'lynn's tower, the morning bell tolled ten times throughout the Citadel. On the ninth peal, the tower's ground-level door banged open and Joce'lynn burst forth—shouting even before Katja finished her bow of greeting toward the elder.

"Katja Kevrosa Escari, what in the bloody fangs happened last night? Magistrate Aver'lyn and half of the Ring are demanding that I place you in irons this instant!"

Katja instinctively crouched into a defensive stance as Joce'lynn berated her. Never had she seen the Ring of Sorcerers member so irate.

"I believe I am better able to answer that question, Mistress Joce'lynn," Verdagon said, coming to the stunned werecat's rescue.

"With all due respect, My Lord Verdagon, you weren't even there—"

"No, I wasn't. But I am one of the few beings besides the currently infirm Lauraisha who can delve deep within Katja's thoughts—an act that I performed last night as soon as Garret brought her to me. I saw everything from her point of view and I have much to discuss with you."

The human wraithwalker gestured to a nearby cluster of carved benches near the courtyard's west wall away from the icy wind. "Fine, then, let us discuss it!"

Joce'lynn and Katja sat on opposite benches while Verdagon crouched beside them. Even prone, the dragon had to hunch his angular head to be eye-level with the females. He spread his wings to shield the three from the winter drizzle and any prying eyes before saying, "My Madam, I understand you to be a student of prophesy as proficient as the dryad Queen Mother."

Katja frowned at him as Joce'lynn nodded. "Zahlathra and I often correspond about our individual findings. I sorely miss her advice, especially now that the war with the Asheken deadwalkers has cut off most of the communication between us."

"What can you remember from the Sylvan Prophecies about the Third Great Darkness?" the dragon asked.

Joce'lynn began to recite: "'Then there will come a day when a forger will Fall to the Tainted Thirst of the First Turned. This Fallen Forger will betray the Sphinx and open wide her Gape to the First Turned and his allies. Together they will march against all those living and spread their Taint over the face of the world. In the midst of this Third Great Darkness, the Seer, the Arbitrator, the Sower, the Guardian, the Pariah, the Discerner, and the Renewed shall unite in common purpose. They shall search the whole of the world to bring together the scattered Keystones. When the Keystones unlock the Gateway, the final battle for freedom will begin.'"

Verdagon nodded as she finished. "A good translation, although I should note that "the final battle" can also be translated as 'the greatest battle.'"

Joce'lynn took a breath. "Zahlathra believes that her daughter Zahra is the Sower. Is she correct?"

"She is indeed."

"But wouldn't that also mean that Lauraisha is the Seer and Katja is the—"

"Discerner," Verdagon finished. "Yes, it would."

"I admit that when I first met her and realized that she too was a wraithwalker, I had hoped as much, but how can Katja be the prophesied Discerner after she tried to kill Lauraisha? Murder is one of the worst acts of betrayal. Wraithwalkers must be truthful and pure of soul. How can any Sylvans hope to trust Katja if she is a mere breath away from becoming a Fallen necromancer like Luther?"

"Joce'lynn, Katja is pure of soul. The madness that drove her to attack Lauraisha was not within her soul but without."

Joce'lynn shook her head. "I don't understand."

Verdagon described how Daeryn's mental manipulation had caused Katja to lash out at her packmates. He explained Daeryn's and Katja's continued mental bond and his own powerlessness to permanently destroy it.

Joce'lynn nibbled her lip, her expression troubled. "What of the scarlet shard imbedded in the broken spearhead? What is its role in all of this?"

Katja looked down at her three sunsilver spearheads and picked up the one with the broken tip. "The mirror shards were once part of the Ott vre Caerwyn. Caleb gave them to me after I inadvertently mended his shattered mirror."

Joce'lynn sucked in a breath. "That means that the shards hanging around your neck and the necks of your companions are pieces of vampires' *bloodstones!* What was Caleb thinking?"

"Actually, Damya was responsible for distributing the mirror's shards to the packmates. Despite its dangerous origin, Joce'lynn, the Ott vre Caerwyn was purified by Marga's fire long ago. In and of themselves, these shards pose no threat to Katja or to her allies," the dragon reassured her. "In fact, they've proven invaluable as a means of communication in times of trouble."

"Until now. Now this bloodstone shard has given Daeryn a way into Katja's mind and a path to her soul. That is beyond dangerous."

Verdagon nodded his angular head. "Yes, it is. If Daeryn can find a way to corrupt the shard, he could turn the shard into a bloodstone once again. If that happens, it will strengthen his and Katja's bond even more—eventually trapping and enslaving her soul to his will."

Joce'lynn shook her head. "This is grim news indeed. Will increasing her wraithwalker training be enough to reverse the damage he has already done?"

"I doubt it, My Madam. Even with you shepherding her night and day, Katja will have to battle him through her worst instincts during every full moon until the spear-and-mirror shard is removed from the vampire's possession."

"What shall we do in the meantime then? Lock her away?"

Katja's furry ears drooped in deep sadness as she held out her paws to be bound. "I don't wish to lose my freedom, but I could not bear it if another to be harmed because of me."

The expression that stole across Joce'lynn's face was one matching Katja's sorrow. Gently the human wraithwalker mage pushed the werecat's paws down. "A pure soul indeed. Would training with Dayalan help her?"

The dragon nodded. "I believe so. Mind you, nothing at this point would mean a cure, but Dayalan knows how his brother thinks. They share the same bloodlust, which Daeryn will try to instill in Katja and which Dayalan is very adept at thwarting. It would be a good therapy at least."

"If Dayalan is willing," Katja murmured.

"Oh, he will be willing, Katja," Verdagon said soothingly. "Do not worry; I will discuss it with him."

Joce'lynn rubbed her forehead. "Very well, then. What do we do in the meantime?"

Verdagon frowned. "Let Lauraisha heal. When she is strong enough, I can teach her how to facilitate a mental bond between Katja and Dayalan. Until then, I will need to oversee Katja's and Dayalan's training—together and separate. I should be able to establish and protect a working mental bond between them to help speed the training process."

"Good," Joce'lynn said. "I'll see to it that they keep their current teaching schedule, but meet on the Hatching Sands as well as the Ring Room. The spells in the caverns should be more than sufficient to contain any wayward magic. Plus it will better if you train Dayalan anyway, since he is quickly outpacing any fireforger sent to instruct him."

Verdagon gave the Ring member a knowing smile. "Agreed."

* * *

As expected, Dayalan's attitude was less than amiable during his and Katja's principle instruction session under Verdagon.

"Verdagon, I am not pleased by this arrangement—at all. We are taking an enormous risk having you build a mental bond between Katja and me. If Daeryn realizes what we're doing before we've had enough time to shield the bond, he could ensnare us both."

"I am aware of that, Dayalan," the dragon replied. "Would you rather leave Katja undefended against your brother?"

"Fangs, no!"

"Then please stand facing each other," Verdagon said, "and let us begin."

When Dayalan and Katja did as instructed, Verdagon bent close enough to touch each of their brows with the tip of his snout. The shock of connection nearly flung Katja off of her back paws. Only the dragon's wing against her back kept her upright. She could feel her blood pulse in her ears and saw its powerful color wash over her vision until the world around her looked devoid of color and shape.

Verdagon? her mind whispered in the blackness.

I am here.

Dayalan?

Yes, I'm here, Katja.

Good, but where is here?

Images smote her mind. Katja looked around and saw skeletal trees loom above her—their stark white trunks stabbing the murky sky. Where was the Citadel cavern? The Hatching Sands and carved dwarven runes were nowhere to be found. All she saw instead was the inverted decay of the world as if she were under Curqak's and his allied revenant's influence once again. She looked down and screeched in surprise as she saw the blood-red river rushing beneath her perch. She was sitting on the same fallen tree that Curqak had trapped her on when she had fled her village!

Dayalan and Verdagon appeared beside her, just as ashen as the rest of this uncanny realm. Their presence was at once reassuring and unsettling to her. They neither moved nor talked, but she felt their thoughts within her mind as powerfully as her own awareness.

Katja, what do you see? Verdagon prompted her.

Trees. Dead trees. It looks like the riverbank where Curqak trapped me just days after he and his fellow deadwalkers slaughtered my clan. Can't you see it?

We cannot.

Katja looked at her companions and yowled in consternation. Their eyes were milky with blindness. *What is wrong with you!*

My brother does not wish us to help you. He isn't strong enough yet to break or block our bond, but he can still thwart our connection to your visions, Dayalan replied, his voice reflecting a forced calm.

How is he able to block you?

He has the aid of other deadwalkers, Katja. Do not worry, though, Verdagon replied. *We are blind, but we are by no means helpless. Describe to us what you see.*

She did.

Can you think of a reason why Daeryn would want you to remember this place?

Before she could reply, Katja's vision changed to show her slaughtered kinsmen as she and Kayten burned their bodies and buried their ashes in the Feliconas village's amphitheater. She screamed as each of their faces paraded before her mind's eye, taunting her with their silence.

Stay with us, Katja, Dayalan's thought cut through the terrible torrent.

Curqak's grinning face assaulted her next. "Your brother is dead…" he whispered.

Then the ghoul's cracked voice changed into her own. "No. No! You were dead!" Katja screamed as she stared at a nemean deadwalker bound with chains in the keep of Caerwyn Castle. "They could not have Turned you! You were already dead!"

Kayten's voice cackled as the Turned werecat watched her. "Join us, Katja. Join me and share in true freedom…"

"You are not my brother!" she screeched, but the face shifted again into one of incredible beauty, like the alabaster visage of an elf noble with broad shoulders and sleek, black hair swept back from his oval face and pointed ears. The male's eyes were as pale blue as sea ice, but then they changed to bloody crimson as he watched her.

Come to me, Katja, he whispered through her mind. They were now in the clearing of a frost-bitten forest with moonlight illuminating the small space between them. It was the same clearing where Dayalan's brother had attacked and had almost Turned her. It was the same night that the wolf Bren had died trying to save her.

Daeryn, she whispered.

And now I have you, Katja, the vampire hissed through fully exposed fangs as he walked toward her.

What do you want of me?

Your blood loyalty, of course.

Katja felt her hackles rise in spite of her effort to keep calm. She felt Dayalan's anger through their connected minds and unleashed it against her fear. *How dare you use me to attack Lauraisha!*

Oh, no, my little changeling, *I'm afraid you did that yourself,* the male replied, emphasizing the name used for a Turned skinshifter mage with a smug purr in his voice.

Katja could feel the power of his magic swirl around her like a dangerous undercurrent—far more like a shade's murky grasp than a shadowshaper's nebulous touch. As a full vampire and a corrupted mage, Daeryn was the most dangerous kind of deadwalker. She shuddered under the sheer weight of his power. *Don't ever call me that!*

Why not, changeling? The title suits you. They were back among the corpse-white trees near the riverbank and Dayalan's and Verdagon's images were gone.

I am not *a deadwalker mage!* she screamed.

Daeryn's half-smile was that of a pure predator. *Are you so certain of that? I've known ghouls far less prone to destruction.*

Katja snorted. *Your ally, Curqak, doesn't fit that description.*

The fanged smile faltered. *He did what he was commanded, certainly, but the killing of your kin would not have been necessary if you had come to us willingly.*

That is a lie worse than a grim's tale, she spat. *I was never given that opportunity...*

You were, Katja. You were given the choice the day your parents died in that unfortunate rockslide. You chose to flee the shadow instead of embrace it and you have been fleeing for your miserable life ever since. Haven't you?

Unbidden, she saw a vision of her parents' graves, and then saw the boulders that had killed them crashing toward her.

Stop it! she screamed through clenched fangs, and tried to shut her eyes against the vision.

You condemn your companions to suffering and death every time you resist my calling, Katja. Why make them suffer more? Do you delight in their torture?

Silence, villain!

The boulders evaporated and the moonlit walls of a bedchamber took their place. Katja whimpered as she saw Lauraisha lying bloody and broken on the rug in front of her.

Who is the real villain, Katja? I merely wanted the world rid of Dayalan's infectious presence and you *decided that Lauraisha was in our way. I give full tribute to you for your ruthlessness, but it was unwarranted. I would have preferred that she live, so that I could add her to our ranks...*

She felt the crimson tendril of Daeryn's mind wrap tighter around her own like a serpent squeezing its prey. Her vision changed again as the shade's mind overwhelmed hers. Daeryn now held her in his arms as they stood together on the riverbank under the corpselike trees, his drake-like wings extended to shield both of them from the chill wind whistling through the dead forest. She could almost feel Daeryn's yellow fangs pressing once more against the scared skin of her neck as he pressed her trembling body against his.

Bond with me...

No!

Daeryn made a flicking gesture and Katja watched in horror as her scarred right paw flexed and unsheathed her claws of its own accord. *Did you forget the potency of my mind's sway over yours? Bond with me or become the instrument of your packmates' destruction.*

Never!

As had happened once before, Katja's rage boiled up inside of her soul at the deadwalker's threat to her loved ones and then found its release through her voice. What issued from her maw, however, was not only a wraithwalker's illusion-shattering roar, but also Dayalan's purging fire. Katja felt the fireforger's flames burn throughout her being and then released the fire straight at Daeryn's horrified face. The vision of Daeryn evaporated as the flames engulfed him. The corpse trees melted into the vision of a castle courtyard with stone archways that overlooked the rolling sea. Daeryn lay writhing in pain on the sandy stones. Then that vision also dissolved and Katja's awareness was suddenly thrown back into the solidness of reality.

She stared at the monolith pillars surrounding the Hatching Cavern. Then she collapsed panting against

Verdagon's quivering flank. She thrust her paws into the sand, savoring the gritty texture beneath her pads. Daeryn was gone and so were his twisted visions! She couldn't feel even the slightest tendril of his presence in her mind.

Dayalan sank to his knees beside her. She starred at him in wonder as the two caught their breath. "Did I really just… burn Daeryn…with your mage fire?"

Dayalan raised a brow at Verdagon. The dragon shook his head and smiled. "It may have appeared that way, but no. What you did was use the spiritual essence of Dayalan's fire to sear and cleanse the mental connection between you and Daeryn."

"Does that mean that I'm free of him?"

"For the moment. The core problem of the two shards' link still remains, but I'm hopeful that your mind was cleansed well enough that it will require Daeryn a vast amount of time and effort to rebuild the bond. It's still possible for him to contact you mind, but he should have little sway over you for a little while."

"How much time?"

"Two moon-cycles, maybe three. I'm not certain."

Dayalan shook his head and growled. "I will kill him for this."

The dragon gazed at the fireforger male a long moment before he replied. "While I understand your sentiment, Dayalan, killing out of hatred makes you no better than him."

"But Katja and Lauraisha. Why should they suffer his evil? He should be punished for his crimes—"

"And he will be, Dayalan, but not out of revenge. After all, what sets you apart from your brother?"

Dayalan crossed his arms and did not reply.

"A single drop of a being's blood, Dayalan," Verdagon said more gently. "The choice to drink or to abstain from the blood of beings is all that separates you from damnation alongside the Abomination, Luther, your brother, and the rest of the deadwalkers. Vengeance brings you ever closer to the wrong side of that choice because hatred drives it. Love is your responsibility; vengeance is the Creator's. Is it not bad enough that your brother walks as one enslaved to death now? That he will be tortured for eternity beyond the shores of Edgewater when his body is destroyed? Do not try to carry the Creator's burdens; they are too vast for you."

Dayalan sighed and absently rubbed the place on his forehead where Verdagon had touched it. Katja watched him mutely, wondering if Verdagon's message was meant more for her ears than for Dayalan's. She had wrestled with her anger and hatred toward the ghoul Curqak for his massacre of her family and her clan for several moon-cycles now. While she knew that it had been the Víchí Elder Luther who had ordered their slaughter, Curqak was the one who oversaw the village's destruction. And now she hated Daeryn just as much for Turning her own brother Kayten into a nemean deadwalker, nearly killing Felan, murdering Bren, manipulating her, and his part in what had happened to Lauraisha. As much as she respected Verdagon, she could not and would not put aside her hatred for these two insidious monsters!

In answer to her unspoken vow, Verdagon added, "Hatred is a slow poison—killing the heart one thought at a time. If given free reign, hatred will quell every emotion save rage and bitterness—leaving a being bereft of all love, joy, or hope. Such a being is a deadwalker in mind, even if not in body. Thus it is the one who murders, not the one who is murdered, who suffers the cruelest death."

Katja swallowed hard at the warning. "So how does a being fight against hatred?"

The dragon shrugged. "You must choose to love that which you think you should hate."

Katja growled. "So you would have us admire a monster?"

"Did I say admire or even trust? No. I said love. Beings can love and forgive one another without trusting each other. Love is life; love is of the Creator. Hatred is of the Abomination and he gives only death. I would not see either of you so easily ensnared."

Dayalan cleared his throat. "What you demand, Verdagon, is no easy task."

The Pyrekin nodded. "The simplest tasks often aren't easy, but will the two of you do this for me anyway?"

Dayalan and Katja both looked at each other a moment and then bowed toward the dragon. "We will try," said Dayalan.

"Good."

Katja frowned. "What happens now?"

"Dayalan and I need to work together on a few fireforger techniques before we part ways. As for you, Katja, I believe a lesson in forgiveness would do well to round out your lessons for today. I suggest you visit Lauraisha in the Healing Ward since I know you cannot understand my teaching about hatred without first learning about forgiveness."

Katja looked at him in helplessness. "What could I even say to her?"

The Pyrekin's smile toward her was gentle. "The truth. She knows you well enough to know when you speak truth and when you lie. She will likely listen to you even if the others are not yet ready to hear your apologies."

The dragon lifted his head in the direction of the main stairwell and gave a quick bellow. An elf descended the stairs in response.

"Lauraisha should be awake now. Have Vraelth take you to her. Off you go."

The werecat bowed and slowly ascended the stairs, dreading the meeting to come.

* * *

"How dare you come near her after the harm you've caused! Get out!" Zahra's screams thundered down the corridors of the Healing Ward.

Neither Vraelth's presence nor Katja's normalized appearance seemed to reassure the dryad that Lauraisha was in no danger. The green-skinned female guarded the human princess's sickroom with her fighting sickles unsheathed — daring the golden-furred werecat to test her resolve.

"Quiet your voice or you'll wake the sick!" Katja hissed.

"I don't care how loud I am. You have no right to see her, changeling!"

Katja's rounded, tuft-tipped ears flattened against her head at the insult. "You go too far, dryad. I am no deadwalker traitor and I *never* will be!"

Creator willing, she thought.

"You are already marred by a vampire! Look no further than the scars on your neck for the proof of that."

As the dryad princess spoke, Katja's paw involuntarily moved to cover the fang marks where Daeryn had bitten her on the night of Bren's death. Before the werecat could ask if Zahra knew that Daeryn had manipulated her or think of a way to defend herself, a new voice added itself to the fray.

"Will the two of you cease this infernal squabble at once? I have a Healing Ward to run and I can't do so when your shouting is upsetting my patients!"

Master Neha'lyn, came sprinting down the hall, the harmhealer elf's usually calm face flushed deep purple with his anger. "Will someone explain to me what lunacy has taken hold of you? Zahra, I can hear your voice behind my warded office door!"

Katja looked startled at the exasperated elf and quickly looked away, smirking. Even under the serious circumstances, Katja couldn't help herself. The utter ridiculousness of Neha'lyn's frazzled appearance caused her maw to quirk with a smile. She glanced at Zahra and the dryad's look of utter astonishment caused her last bit of self-control to slip. Beside her, Vraelth's mouth working furiously to stifle a chuckle of his own as the werecat burst out laughing.

Neha'lyn cleared his throat as the packmates fought and failed to keep their composure. "I am waiting."

"Sorry, My Sir," Zahra finally murmured. "Katja wants to speak privately with Princess Lauraisha. Given the fact that Katja was the one responsible for Lauraisha being in the Healing Ward in the first place, I told the changeling that I'll see the sun go black before I ever give her access to Lauraisha in such a weakened state. "

Neha'lyn looked at Katja, Zahra, and Vraelth in solemn silence before reaching into his tan robe's front pocket. He pulled out a square of parchment and unfolded it to reveal Joce'lynn's handwriting. "As it happens, I know about your present situation, Katja. Joce'lynn has instructed most of the mage masters concerning your odd predicament. Tell me, did you and Dayalan meet with Verdagon this morning?"

"Yes, My Sir, we did."

Neha'lyn nodded and reached into his pocket once more. He pulled out a curious looking flat stone the size of his fist. It was as smooth as a stone from a riverbed and had a hole worn through its center. "Do you know what this is?" he asked.

She shook her head.

"This is a Discerning Stone. Joce'lynn, Si'lyn, and Mori'lyn made it for me a long time ago before Mori'lyn Fell to Peha'lyn's evil. It shows the truth in a being's countenance. As you can imagine, it is quite useful when I deal with patients." He sighed then. "I'm just sorry I didn't think to use it on Peha'lyn when he returned from his journeys abroad."

The harmhealer held the stone up to his eye and peered through at Katja through its hole.

"Was your training session with Dayalan and Verdagon successful?"

Katja nodded as Zahra glared at her. "It was."

"Are you feeling any strange numbness in your limbs or chest?"

"No."

"Are your thoughts based on rational resolve or on bestial instinct right now?"

"Rational."

"Are you sure?"

Katja nodded her head vigorously. "Yes."

"Do you hold any thoughts right now of harm to yourself or toward any other?"

"Just to Daeryn." The werecat growled.

"Understandable, but even that sentiment can be dangerous to you."

The werecat nodded. "So Verdagon told me."

Neha'lyn nodded and put a gentle hand on her furry shoulder. "I see that you have told me the truth and that, for now, you pose no threat to Lauraisha. However, I am deeply sorry for the burden that Daeryn has placed on you as it means that confrontations like this will happen often to you until his influence is finally purged."

Katja swallowed and nodded while Zahra looked at the two of them in baffled silence. "May I see her then?"

Neha'lyn sighed. "Yes, I suppose so. As a precaution, though, I want Vraelth outside the room while you are with her."

He looked over at the elf. "Listen to them carefully. If you hear anything unusual or alarming, distance Katja from others immediately and call for me."

Vraelth nodded.

"Thank you, My Sir." Katja bowed to him and turned expectantly toward Zahra, who was still blocking Lauraisha's door.

The dryad's jaw tightened, but she moved to one side nonetheless.

As Katja pushed the heavy wooden door open, she caught Zahra's whispered promise to Neha'lyn that she would also remain at guard just in case the worst should happen. Katja's ears drooped a little as Vraelth shut the door behind her.

III
OF GRIEF AND FORGIVENESS

The air that rushed to her nose was slightly warmer than the corridor air had been. Pungent herbs seasoned each breath enough to make Katja sneeze.

"Oh, good. I'm glad it's not just me. I've been doing that all morning."

Katja turned to find Lauraisha sitting up in bed, wrinkling her nose.

"Lauraisha! You're awake!"

The Tyglesean princess grimaced. "How could I sleep with all the yelling outside my door?"

Katja winced and sneezed again. "Sorry."

"It's not your fault. Zahra should learn to steady her voice when she gets angry and Neha'lyn should curb his use of aromatherapy." Lauraisha gestured to the hundred or so plants hanging from the exposed rafters above them.

"No, I mean I'm sorry for putting you here in the first place." Katja felt tears well up in her eyes as she moved to kneel before Lauraisha's bedside. "I have no notion of how you could forgive me, but I hope that someday—"

Lauraisha groaned and held up her scarred left hand in protest. "Of course, I forgive you! You and I both know that the real reason I have these wounds is because you were not yourself last night. I saw the drives of a beast in you, not the thoughts of a being." She shuddered. "I felt deadwalker evil tinging your thoughts as well."

Katja blinked. "Have you conversed with Verdagon

then?"

Lauraisha frowned. "No, why?"

Katja quickly explained the dragon's discovery of her mental link with Daeryn and then shared her memory of the morning's expulsion session with Verdagon and Dayalan.

Lauraisha shuddered as the experience faded. "So Verdagon and Dayalan helped you expel Daeryn, but Verdagon cannot completely destroy your mental bond?"

The werecat shook her head. "Apparently, the spearhead that I stabbed Daeryn with has kept a small part of the bonding spell that Daeryn cast on me during his Turning Bite intact. As long as Daeryn has that shard, he can manipulate me."

Lauraisha was alert. "Are you in danger now?"

The skinshifter shook her head. "Verdagon thinks that they've bought me three safe skinshifts—at most. It gives me time to continue my wraithwalker training and strengthen my mind against Daeryn's attacks before he tries to possess me again."

"What happens then?"

"If I can't resist him…" Katja paused and let out a shaky breath. "If I can't resist him, Daeryn's claim over my thoughts will grow stronger with each skinshift. I'll become even more bestial than before until I'm utterly ruled by him."

"Then no amount of training will be enough," Lauraisha said. "We need another solution."

"There is none!"

Lauraisha shook her head. "There is one: hunt down Daeryn and take back the shard."

Katja stared at her. "I will call Neha'lyn immediately! You must be running a high fever."

"Oh, relax. I'm fine—well, I'll be healthy soon enough. Anyway, since Daeryn's possession of the mirror's shard is the reason the two of you are mentally bonded, the obvious solution to the problem is for us to take back the shard!"

"The shard in his shoulder is laced with my blood and my magic, so it will respond to no one besides me—not even Verdagon. The only way to remove such a magic-linked artifact is for me to physically fight Daeryn! Since I was the one who stabbed him with it in the first place, I must the one who has to pull it back out!"

"Agreed."

"You are just as insane as the dragon."

Lauraisha cocked a brow. "Am I? Well, let's consider for a moment that not even a Pyrekin dragon can break the link between the two of you. And Verdagon is the most powerful being we know! That leaves you with very few options. Whether or not you wish it, you will have to face Daeryn again, Katja, just as you will have to face Curqak again. They are both responsible for the deaths and enslavement of your clan and kin. They must answer for their evil."

"Verdagon said that vengeance is the Creator's burden, not ours."

Lauraisha shrugged. "Perhaps that is true, but even if vengeance isn't your burden, justice is. You yourself swore that you would find a way to bring justice to your clan's murderers not three days after you burned and buried your slaughtered kin. You cannot allow other Sylvans to suffer the same evil that was done to them or to you. Not when you have the power to prevent it."

"He's far more powerful than me physically and magically. How can I possibly have the strength to do what is necessary?"

"Necessity breeds ingenuity," the human said. "Besides, none of your packmates will let you face him alone."

Katja shook her head. "There is no way I'm putting you all in mortal danger again. Even so, how could I find him? There have been no reports of his whereabouts since the night he attacked Felan and me and killed Bren."

Lauraisha's eyes shut against her sudden tears at the mention of the wolf's name. "I know where Daeryn is."

Katja stared at her. "What? How?"

She grimaced. "The last image I saw in your memory before you broke ties with Daeryn's mind was of him fainting in the upper courtyard of Castle Summersted in Tyglesea."

Katja stared at the Tyglesean princess. "Your former home? Are you certain?"

Lauraisha nodded. "Trust me, Katja, I know those sandstone archways. During his interrogation, the dullahan Perefaris said that a deadwalker spy had claimed Tyglesea as his territory. He had no knowledge of the spy's identity, but what if Daeryn is actually that spy?"

Katja thought about that a moment. It seemed to make sense, but a suspicion still nagged at her. "If he is the deadwalkers' principal spy in Tyglesea, what was he doing attacking me on the road outside of Caerwyn Castle?"

The human frowned before answering. "Perhaps he isn't the main spy, then. Maybe he's just well-associated with him. Regardless, we need to go to Tyglesea. We need to find out why he is in Castle Summersted at all."

Katja hissed. "Absolutely not! The journey is too long! If you go to Tyglesea, you risk your safety by being near me during at least four full moons, and you will have to face your father again. I would never wish you such danger or pain!"

Lauraisha wiped the sweat away from her pallid face— her resolve overruling her present feebleness. "Katja, you will need my help against Daeryn. Joce'lynn has already commanded that I train with you and Dayalan to help weave your minds together so that you can combine your talents. All that aside, though, I would still go to Tyglesea without you. If my father is allied with deadwalkers, then I have to do something. As a dreamdrifter and a fireforger, I might finally have the power to free my country and my family from King Kaylor's despotism! Even so, I doubt that I can do this without your help. Katja, I need you with me. I doubt I can do what I must without your courage bolstering my own."

Katja stared at her dearest friend and finally sighed. "I doubt I can do what I must without you either."

Lauraisha reached out her arms in invitation and Katja obliged her gratefully. The two females hugged each other and, somehow, all the world seemed right just then.

* * *

A knock echoed on Lauraisha's healing chamber door and the hulking, black-and-gray-furred werewolf that was Felan in his usual form walked into the room. Katja's ears perked as he sat down on a nearby stool with his back paws perched on the lowest rung, his huge clawed paws balled into fists in his lap as he stared at the floor.

"Lauraisha, Katja, I need to talk with you..." He looked at the human princess with gentle worry. "If you are up to it."

With a grimace, Lauraisha sat a little straighter on her prop of pillows. "Of course, Felan. What is it?"

Felan fidgeted for a moment—crossing and uncrossing his arms and legs before he sighed. "It's Zahra. I just found her at the end of the hall sobbing."

"Is she still upset with Katja?"

"Yes, but this is something else." Felan's look of sadness was profound. "Qenethala sent word through the trees. She's dying."

"What! How?" the females said in unison.

Felan shook his head. "I only know that she was somehow ambushed on her way back through enemy lines to the Glen. She...she chose to Merge rather than allow the deadwalkers to Turn and use her against us."

Katja paw covered her maw even as hot tears stung the corners of her eyes. Qenethala was Zahra's half-sister and one of the most battle-hardened dryads that Katja had ever encountered. The only reason she would ever have chosen to Merge herself with a tree other than her birth oak was if there was no other way to escape her captors. "I was too harsh with Zahra this morning. She had a right to be angry with me—you all do, but had I known what had happened to Qenethala... I'm sorry. I never meant for any of this to happen."

"Katja, you can hardly blame yourself for Daeryn's assaults," Lauraisha broke in. Quickly she filled Felan in on Verdagon's discovery and its confirmation of her own suspicions. "I told you that Katja had gone mad. I just didn't realize its true cause until now," she concluded.

Felan's eyes met Katja's for the first time since he had entered the room. "This was Daeryn?" He gestured to Lauraisha's bandaged body.

Katja nodded.

They watched each other for an eternity before Katja murmured again, "I'm sorry."

The hulking werewolf sighed. "No, Katja, I'm the one who should apologize. I knew that you had the potential power, but I never really expected that you would make the full transformation into a lioness so soon after learning to control your regular skinshifts. If I were a better teacher, I would have prepared you for such a difficulty. I could have helped you guard against any potential madness…maybe if I had, you could have mentally held your ground against Daeryn… Maybe then you wouldn't have attacked…" The skinshifter male hung his head. "I am sorry to have failed you, both of you, so utterly."

Lauraisha shook her head. "It's impossible for either of you to blame yourselves successfully," she said. "Daeryn's role in this complicates the situation tremendously. I'll gladly accept your requests for forgiveness if it makes you feel better, but let's lay blame at the feet of the monster actually responsible for my injury."

Felan's curved fangs flashed as he snarled. "I will eviscerate that vampire if it is my last act in this world."

"You will have some competition for that opportunity," Dayalan said as he opened the door. The hybrid's boots pounded the stone floor like hammers as he stalked into the room. His dark green hunter's cloak billowed out as he sat down on the last empty stool. He looked straight at Lauraisha.

"How are you feeling?" he asked, and his deep voice cracked.

Lauraisha grimaced. "Felan knows his skinshifting skills. Neha'lyn said that he was able to mend the tissue well enough before you brought me here that I've sustained no permanent damage. Neha'lyn believes I will recoup enough of my lost blood to be able to move freely in a week or two. I won't be rid of all of the scars, but that is a small price to pay for cheating death."

Dayalan nodded, his blue eyes glinting red. She watched him in silence for a moment before asking, "Are you content enough to be here? The smell of my blood on these bandages can't be comfortable for you…"

"I visited Tyron last night, so I'm well-sated," Dayalan said, referring to his main source of blood sustenance, which also happened to be Lauraisha's horse. "Otherwise I would have never strayed near the Healing Ward in the first place, much less to your room."

"Oh."

Felan crossed his arms across his massive furred chest. "Well, packmates," he said, breaking the tense silence. "Now what do we do?"

Lauraisha looked over Katja and pursed her lips in speculation. "Well, I had suggested to Katja that we track down Daeryn to retrieve the spear shard that has caused so much of our current crisis—"

"No." The werecat shook her head. "I will not let you come with me on such a dangerous mission. Besides" — Katja shifted her gaze around the room— "we need to help Qenethala and Zahra first."

"Do we even know when and where Qenethala decided to Merge?" Dayalan asked.

Felan shook his head.

Lauraisha's deep blue eyes grew distant and glassy as she suddenly slumped against the pillows.

"Lauraisha!" the other three cried in unison.

The human held up a hand in reassurance and continued her dreamdrifting trance. After a few tense moments she spoke. "I can't find her...or anyone for that matter. The minds of Sylvans feel...foggy beyond the shore of this island." She frowned.

"Then it has begun," Dayalan whispered.

"What has?"

"The deadwalker psychics have commenced their assault on the minds of Sylvan dreamdrifters just as they did in the early days of the Second War of Ages. They'll try to disrupt any conventional methods of magical communications, including your own awareness of other beings' minds."

Lauraisha made a sour face. "Well, it's working."

"We need to inform Joce'lynn of all of this," the werecat said.

Dayalan bobbed his head. "She has already sent a summons for you to join her in her study, Katja. She needs to discuss your new training schedule."

Katja sighed and gave Lauraisha's hand a gentle squeeze. "You'll be well?"

The human smiled. "I will. Go, Katja. Time is all important now."

The werecat skinshifter bowed her head and turned for the door which Felan was already opening. "I think I'll go with you since I know the details of Qenethala's predicament."

Katja nodded to him and let him usher her into the

hallway. Once he had closed the door, the werecat then turned to him. "How are you? As dear as Zahra is to you, knowing Qenethala's fate can't be easy to bear."

Felan sighed and rubbed his furry forehead. "Yes and no. We were close friends once, but that was long ago. Much has changed since our youth."

Katja watched him for a moment. "She scorned you once she discovered that you were a skinshifter, didn't she?"

He nodded.

"But Zahra never did?"

The werewolf shook his head. "Never. She has remained loyal to me no matter the circumstances. I can only hope to be as true of a friend to her in return."

"I see."

They walked on in silence.

"Are you still angry with me?" the werecat asked.

Felan looked down at her. "Because of Lauraisha?"

She nodded once.

The huge werewolf passed a clawed paw over his maw. "I'm frustrated and confused and afraid. In light of our conversation about Daeryn, I have no idea if I have a right to be angry with you even though I was. I was beyond enraged."

"You have that right, Felan."

He sighed and shook his head. "No, I don't. The beast that I met under the light of the full moon wasn't really you. Daeryn manipulated you, and so this wasn't your fault."

Her green eyes stared down the stone corridor without really seeing it. "I was still the one who carried out his evil. I was the werecat that Curqak wanted when he killed my parents and again when he massacred my clan. I was the one Daeryn was hunting when he killed Bren and nearly killed you." She blinked away tears and continued. "No matter what I might wish, evil constantly haunts me and destroys anyone around me. I am so weary of fighting this…and yet what else can I do but try to protect those I love?"

Felan's paw slipped onto her shoulder and he pulled her into a cautious embrace. "I know. Katja, I love you and you are worth the risk." His grip tightened on her shoulders and he nudged her away. "Yet I know I can't fully trust you until we find a way to rid you of Daeryn's influence."

Katja swallowed. His words wounded her, but she knew he spoke the truth. "I hope Joce'lynn can guide me to a solution…for all our sakes."

"So do I."

＊ ＊ ＊

"I was about to hunt down some much needed sustenance," the human said kindly once Katja and Felan had hiked up the spiraled stairs to her study. "Would you care to join me?"

Katja sat down quickly before her wobbly knees buckled and Felan did the same. "If you could give us…a few moments to…catch our breath first…please, Your Honor."

"And what is so important that you felt you must run up the tower steps to see me?"

Felan held up his huge clawed paw in a beseeching gesture. Joce'lynn's lips twitched in humor, presumably at the sight of the fit male's hard panting. "I'll wait in my study for your explanation then. Join me once you are recovered."

Katja nodded, grateful for the reprieve. When she and the werewolf finally did begin to explain themselves to the Mage Magistrate, Joce'lynn's relaxed mood shifted. She sat chewing her lip throughout the conversation and did not speak until long after the skinshifter mages had finished recounting their news.

"This is my fault. I was the one who sent her on this quest. When Qenethala ceased her communications over a week ago, I feared that she'd been killed or Turned…" Joce'lynn passed a hand over her age-worn face—her worry evident in every line. "This is grim indeed. Even more so as it comes right on the heels of two new deadwalker sightings. I received word from the harpies this morning that enemy scouts were seen near Reithrgar Pass and along Vihous's eastern border. Zahlathra just sent word through the trees that her dryads cannot sustain the Glen's First Tier's defenses much longer. She expects a retreat to the Second Tier in two weeks unless reinforcements arrive. I have sent word to the ogres in Jhalag and at Barak Fort via sprite carriers. I can only hope that they can arrive in time."

Katja frowned. "Wouldn't it be simpler to have a

dreamdrifter broadcast the dryads' need for assistance to all available allies?"

Joce'lynn shook her head, dislodging a few silver ringlets from her bun. "The Asheken have several high-level shades and psychics within their ranks now. Those Turned shadowshapers and dreamdrifters are disrupting our dreamdrifters' efforts. Only the most basic messages can be pushed through right now."

Katja looked at Felan. "So Dayalan was right about the psychic attacks."

Felan's furred fist slammed against Joce'lynn's aged oak desk. "There must be something we can do!"

Joce'lynn looked at him intently and then inclined her head. "There is. I am declaring an Inquisition."

Katja stared at her. The only time in history that an Inquisitor had ever roamed Sylvan soil had been when the first fireforger Aribem had named himself Inquisitor, and fought against the vampire High Elder Luther himself during the First War of Ages. Such was Aribem's power that his sacrificial death had caused a worldwide quake, one which had split apart the Northern and Sylvan Continents. It had been the only thing that saved the remaining Sylvan Order races from being Turned.

"Surely the circumstances aren't that dire!" the werecat said.

Joce'lynn nodded. "Never have I known a fireforger to Turn into a deadwalker! It has always been impossible. Every fireforger who has ever felt a vampire's Tainted bite has been destroyed by his own fire during his Turning, yet Daeryn wasn't. He is a vampire and a shade. A shade who has managed to attack a wraithwalker mage on the mages' very island of refuge. And not even a dragon can stand against him! This may be unwise of me to say to you now, but I fear him more than even Luther. I fear what Daeryn may become if his power grows. And I am not alone in my assessment. Meanwhile Luther's deadwalkers spread across our lands, casting all of our lives into the deepest darkness. Katja, Felan, I have not seen such destruction since I was a youth!"

She balled her fists as her jaw tightened. "I will not be caught in another deadwalker noose as we were during the

Eppon Gue Battle. We Sylvans became far too entangled in their snares mere weeks ago with Peha'lyn's betrayal. We need an Inquisitor. There are too few bureaucrats left on this island to oppose me, so I will use my vote as the ranking Ring of Sorcerers' Judge and wraithwalker mage master to name an Inquisitor."

Joce'lynn's declarations shook Katja to the marrow and she saw her fear reflected in Felan's eyes as well. "But who could be powerful enough to take up Aribem's mantle?" he whispered. "Yourself? Nicho'lyn?"

Barely restrained triumph crept into the mage's face. "Dayalan."

"Dayalan?" both Katja and Felan were slack-mawed.

Joce'lynn's smile was smugness in its purest form. "Dayalan is the most powerful fireforger mage since Aribem. He is also the only being I know besides you, Katja, who can still thwart Daeryn's attacks. The two of you did so this morning, did you not?"

Katja nodded numbly. "But, My Madam, what of Dayalan's thirst? He still craves the blood of beasts just as his brother once did. If the hybrid Falls to temptation and drinks the blood of a being—"

"If he drinks the blood of a being and successfully Turns into a vampire like Daeryn, then all hope is lost. Fire and those that wield it are our last line of defense against the deadwalkers and it will mean nothing to either of them."

"You're desperate," Felan murmured.

"I'm desperate," she agreed. "That being said, I don't believe my hope is misplaced. Dayalan's experience with deadwalkers and his intimate knowledge of their history will be invaluable in the act of rooting out evil. He may hate the idea, but Dayalan is the natural choice for the title. The Inquisitor is autonomous in his authority, so he and his retainers hold political invulnerability. They can journey to any Sylvan Order kingdom, territory, or township on the Southern Continent in search of Asheken with the full authority of the Ring of Sorcerers supporting them. No laws save those governing the Ring can bind them."

Katja's ears perked. "Who would be his retainers?"

"Lauraisha and yourself as a start. The Sylvan mages

desperately need to reestablish a presence in Tyglesea and discover the veracity of Perefaris's claims that the royal court plays host to a deadwalker spy. From what I know of your morning's visions, our Turned sproutsinger instructor was telling the truth. The question is how deep does the deception run? If Princess Lauraisha is named one of the Inquisitor's retainers, she'll give us a good reason to find out. I want you to go along as well, Katja. Dayalan will need your skills as a wraithwalker mage to help him in his task."

"And if I meet Daeryn while in Tyglesea?"

"Have the good sense to relieve him of the spear-shard bonding your minds before he uses it against you."

For the third time that day, Katja's maw hung open in her shock. "After all that you've just told us, you still want me to confront him?"

Joce'lynn nodded. "The three of you allied hold the best chance of winning any fight against him."

"What about me, My Madam? I want to go with them."

She shook her head. "Unfortunately, Felan, I must send you with Zahra and Vraelth on another mission."

Felan growled. "No disrespect intended, My Madam, but I don't think it's wise to split up our pack."

Joce'lynn frowned. "I understand your concerns and, of course, I'll consult Verdagon and my fellow Ring of Sorcerers members about this, but I'm sure that they'll all agree with my choice."

"Where are you sending us, if I may ask?"

"You and the others will be traveling to the Sacrificial Pines at the cratered remains of Mount Denth sol Dyvesé. I need whatever information you can glean from Qenethala before her mind is lost to her Merging tree. I cannot stress the importance of this enough."

Felan stared at her. "She's trapped in a tree in the shadow of Aribem's sacred mountain?"

Joce'lynn nodded.

Katja and Felan's ears flattened at the implied danger.

"From what you've just told us, deadwalkers have completely overrun that entire region!" Katja said.

"I know. Trust me, I would not ask you—any of you—to undertake such dangerous errands if they weren't absolutely vital to Sylvan survival. Before she Merged, Qenethala sent me a message through the trees. She knows where the Ursa Agate lies hidden and how to retrieve it. She Merged with that pine tree so that she would not have to give up the Keystone's location to our enemies. "

"But you could send someone else besides Zahra to retrieve it," Katja reasoned. "Why would you ask Zahra to face her dying sister?"

"A strong sproutsinger mage like Zahra is one of the few beings who can still communicate with a Merged dryad. Besides, Qenethala trusts her." The female elder frowned. "Is it wrong for me to offer family members a chance to say farewell?"

Felan's gaze was defiant. "Does Zahra really have any choice in the matter?"

"I will not order her to do this, Felan, but I *will* strongly implore her to go."

Felan bowed his head. "Very well, then. I will go with her so long as she agrees."

Joce'lynn nodded in satisfaction. Katja, however, flattened her ears and growled. The likelihood that any of her packmates would return alive from such a task was minimal at best.

"With all due respect, Joce'lynn," she interrupted. "How wise is it to send me along with the others to Tyglesea—given my recent behavior?"

The sorceress peered at the werecat a moment and the skinshifter felt the mage master's power brush her soul. Katja forced herself to lower her own defenses as Joce'lynn examined her innermost being.

"I can feel Daeryn's darkness in you, Katja, as the barest wisp of crimson Taint anchored to your mind and soul. That is beyond dangerous for a wraithwalker mage because you walk the very edges our Erde Realm of Existence every time you delve into your abilities. If the Taint causes you to stray even a little and you could die. Even so, I also glimpse the smoldering markers where Dayalan, Verdagon, and yourself have destroyed his Tainted influence. Those markers will help guide you away from the darkness. There is hope for you yet—even if it is small."

A memory sparked in Katja's mind. The werecat shivered

as she remembered her brother Kayten's pallid face after he had been Turned. Dayalan's fire had destroyed him, but not before her own loving brother had tried to murder her. She swallowed hard. "If Daeryn has his way, will I become a…a nemean like Kayten?" she asked, whispering the name for a Turned werecat.

Joce'lynn frowned. "It's possible, but I doubt that is Daeryn's intention. If left unchecked, Daeryn's corruption will certainly affect you more with each skinshift until it eventually Turns you into a zombie or nemean. However, you would be of far better use to the deadwalkers as a full vampire."

"Why?"

Joce'lynn frowned. "When wraithwalkers are Turned into full vampires, they become necromancers. I could be wrong, but my assumption is that Luther wants another necromancer like himself and such Fallen mages are very rare. Daeryn has already tried to Turn you into a Víchí at his master's orders. I've no doubt that he'll attempt it again."

"What can we do to stop him?" Felan asked.

The sorceress pursed her lips in thought. "Damya's, Dayalan's, and Lauraisha's combined talents should help protect Katja once in the field. That is, of course, if Dayalan accepts the duties of Inquisitor.

"Truthfully, Felan, I would prefer you, Vraelth, and Verdagon to accompany her as well, but I cannot leave Zahra so lightly guarded on her mission and, thanks to the war, I can spare no other mages. If the dryad princess is to have any hope of success, you three must accompany her. Once you have recovered the Ursa Agate, you must reunite with the Inquisition before they journey inside Tyglesea. If Daeryn is there just as Lauraisha suspects, it will likely take all of your combined strength to destroy him."

"How can we hope to join forces before the Inquisitor and his retainers are due at court?" the werewolf asked. "Tyglesea is across the continent from here and we must travel north before moving south and then west again, all while Dayalan's entourage will journey almost due west from the outset."

"Felan, you will have Verdagon with you and he can fly."

"Yes, but can he bear all three of us at once?"

"Not now, but he'll be large enough in two months' time to fly short distances while carrying the three of you."

Felan scowled, but finally nodded.

Katja, however, was still frowning. "Joce'lynn, how can Dayalan be made an Inquisitor when he has not been given the name-change due a mage master?"

Joce'lynn smiled again. "Not to worry. I will see to it that Dayalan tests for his master-level rank by the end of the week. He is ready. However, I expect the two of you to keep your confidence in this matter until the official announcement. Will you protect my secret?"

Felan and Katja bowed their consent.

"Good." She stood up from her chair and the two skinshifters followed suit. "Now, if all of your inquiries are settled momentarily, I suggest we go find food before the servants run out of anything warm. I believe lamb is today's meat selection."

O f course I will go, Felan!" Zahra exclaimed. "It's my last chance to speak with her! How could I refuse?"

The packmates, with the exception of Lauraisha, were all hurrying to the Ring Room training chamber for their afternoon drills.

"Look, even Verdagon believes this is a wise venture despite the risks of deadwalker capture and worse. I am going to the Sacrificial Pines whether you agree to come or not."

"Of course I'm coming with you. I'd never abandon you to the wilds!"

Katja flicked her ears in annoyance. *Of course Felan will follow Zahra anywhere she chooses to go!* she thought in annoyance and jealousy. *He'll never question her judgement, but he'll keep a wary distance from me.*

"Jierira to all males," she muttered under her breath and kept running.

Vraelth, who was close enough to hear her, frowned but said nothing as she pulled out to run just ahead of the group.

Joce'lynn was waiting for them. "All right then, apprentices will split into different groups. Dayalan will work under Master Nicho'lyn with Master Si'lyn's supervision. Katja stays with me. Felan, Vraelth, and Zahra are together in the far corner's mage circle. I want the three of you to practice two-on-one attack and defense strategies at seventy percent strength. Dayalan, you will undergo advanced skills testing. Katja, you and I will further your perception skills. Everyone, go to your proper training places."

When the others moved away, Felan looked at Joce'lynn. "My Madam, may I also take the advance skills test? I believe I'm ready for the responsibilities of a mage master."

Joce'lynn pursed her lips as she stared from him to Katja and back. "Given the current political climate, I doubt that announcing a new skinshifter master to the world would be prudent, Felan." She frowned. "That being said, I have no right to hinder you from undergoing the test. I will make the necessary arrangements in two days' time, but I expect you to keep this secret. No one besides Katja may know what you are doing. Now go continue your practice sessions with Zahra and Vraelth."

Felan bowed his thanks and then joined the others. Katja meanwhile watched as Dayalan followed the two mage masters into the heavily-warded center circle with seeming calmness. She turned to follow Joce'lynn into the room's third mage ring just as the fireforger male summoned a tiny golden flame in his hand and then rapidly enlarged it as he went through each more powerful color phase.

"Joce'lynn, is my skinshifting madness the reason that you don't want Felan to take the skinshifter mage master test?" she asked as Dayalan's glowing violet fireball grew to the size of his own head.

Joce'lynn shook her head. "My pushing Dayalan as the candidate for Inquisitor will be difficult enough without trying to convince others that we also need to instate a skinshifter master for the first time in a few centuries. Our allies' forbearance can only stretch so far.

"Now, Katja, let us work on your awareness of the world and realms around you. When you sense the Erde Realm around you, you only use your five physical senses: touch, taste, smell, sight, and hearing. As I believe we have discussed before, wraithwalkers use modified versions of these physical senses to detect the Wraith Realm. Do you remember my description of them?"

Katja nodded. "Senses without essence: smell without scent, vision without sight, hearing without sound, feeling without touch, taste without flavor."

"Very good. The easiest way to detect the Wraith Realm is

to look for its elements that are tied into this world."

"You spoke before of moving shadows."

Joce'lynn nodded in affirmation. "Shadows which move independent of any casting object are the first Wraith Realm elements that most fledgling wraithwalkers notice. You will also find that many Erdeken will also notice them in the earliest stages of youth."

"Why?"

"No one knows for certain, although I suspect that youths' minds are both more innocent and more flexible than those of adults, so they tend to be more aware of spiritual elements than their more narrow-minded seniors..."

Katja frowned. "It does make logical sense based on my own experiences as a kit." She explained to Joce'lynn the vast number of times her elders had complimented her for her imagination whenever she saw eyes in a shadow or felt that she was being watched when she seemed to be alone. Her father was the only one who had ever believed her visions, and so he had taught her several simple prayers to help keep the darkness at bay—including the one she had used when Perefaris attacked the packmates. Even after his death, Kevros had helped his daughter survive.

"Now you know that it was not just your imagination, or even a simple nightmare." Joce'lynn's lips were a thin line. "I promise to prove the point further today. Kneel there, if you please."

Katja knelt in the circle's center. Joce'lynn rearranged her robes and knelt in front of her toward the circle's edge and instructed her to focus on a single point in the floor.

"What should I do? Clear my mind of all thought?"

"Absolutely not!" Joce'lynn said. "To push aside thought and open your mind to nothingness is an invitation to anyone with nefarious intent to invade your awareness. Warriors don't protect a country by abandoning its borders, do they?"

"Well, no."

"The same principle applies in the mental realm." Joce'lynn explained that the mind's best protection against another is its ability to focus on a particular idea or strategy. "Confrontation is one of the mind's simplest and best strategies because a possessor is less likely to carry out an act of invasion if he or she finds you willing to fight him no matter the consequences. It is far better if you catch a would-be possessor quickly and can mentally strike him before all of his own defenses are in place."

"In other words, gain the advantage by striking first."

"Exactly. Now, there are several first strikes you can use, but one of the most effective is truth."

"Truth?"

Joce'lynn grinned. "Truth. Deadwalkers, in general, and shades, in particular, hate truth, because it leaves no room for Deception to wriggle around their victims' defenses."

Katja frowned at her. "You use the word Deception as if you're naming a being."

Joce'lynn nodded. "Correct. Deception is a being—a Darkkyn prince of vast power much like the Abomination who first Turned Luther. No one knows what Deception's true name is, so we call him by his function. His influence is often used by nefarious spell-casters to ensnare others."

"Can we see Darkkyn and Drosskin?"

"They most often appear as twisted shadows of creatures swathed in crimson light."

Katja gulped.

Joce'lynn stared at her. "You have already seen them? In full shape?"

The werecat bobbed her head and shuddered at the vile memory. "When Kayten was destroyed, I glimpsed three of them clinging to him."

"His possessors." Joce'lynn let out a slow breath. "Good, that solves the first problem of your education in truth. After all, I cannot and will not summon a Drosskin for you to discern since this isle is constantly cleansed to ensure minimal contact with them.

"If you have seen Drosskin in full shape then you already have a basic understanding of their existence. They are ruined creatures, twisted by their own evil into hideousness as unnatural and unbalanced as can exist. The deadwalkers are their physical allies, able to do the things in the Erde Realm that the Wraith Realm dwelling Drosskin cannot. However, Drosskin can possess and control their victims without the need for initial physical contact. This is why deadwalkers are a lesser evil compared to the Drosskin. If you want to know the finer details, ask Master Caleb. He is the only living Sylvan expert on the subject."

Katja shivered.

"Do not fear them. When you fear them, you give them a way to control you. Likewise, do not curse them, because profane language and attitudes only weaken you against them. Most importantly, remember their natures are to destroy whatever good they can find in you. Do not hesitate to deal with them and do not doubt your ability to do so no matter the situation or the beings involved. When Aribem sacrificed himself to save all Sylvans, he left us the ultimate weapon against Drosskin or Asheken deadwalker: fire. By Aribem's fire, we are purged of evil and therefore saved."

"But I do not wield the fire!"

"No, Katja, but you can perceive those who do and awaken their gifts if they are dormant, just as you did with Lauraisha shortly after you both first met."

Katja blinked. "What?"

"When Lauraisha was injured by the basal snake, you introduced her to the fireball still alight in Canuche's cavern."

"How did you know—?"

"Your touch in combination with the fire's touch helped to heal her of the venom and awaken her fireforger mage abilities. This is one of our most vital roles as wraithwalkers. If there is the merest trace of talent, we will sense it and pull it forth. But, we must be able to discern the true nature of each being to correctly perform this service."

"How do we accomplish that?"

"I'll show you. Focus on that spot in the floor and then keep its image in your mind once you shut your eyes."

Katja did so.

"Good. Now try to form a mental image of each being in this room, remembering all of the details that make up their physical appearance. Keep your breathing deep and even while you perform the exercise so that you don't faint."

Startled, Katja checked her breathing and then focused even more on the mental portraits of her friends and allies. She used a technique that Si'lyn had taught Lauraisha, where the mage pushes her mind toward the intended target to gain more perspective.

"Once you have each of them firmly fixed in your mind, I want you to layer each of their personalities, drives, wants, and needs into your mental image of each being."

Katja pictured Zahra with her aspen-leaf-shaped ears, root-like toes, pale-green skin, and vine-like strands of scarlet hair. She thought of the dryad's remorse for her lost sister, her determination to see things through to the end, and her hope for peace. She added these things to the twenty-one-winter-old dryad's image and then added the female's admiration for her sister dryads, her twisted little smile, her rich voice, her esteem for her mother, and her tenderness toward all plant life. Katja filled Zahra's image with these things until her visage seemed about to burst with life.

Katja envisioned Felan's towering, muscular frame covered with his thick, silky fur. The fur was mostly black, yet he bore pure white along his maw and around his uncanny blue-green eyes. Gray ears crowned his dark head and streaks of gray and white fur also raced down his neck to pool upon his massively-muscled chest and stomach. She included Felan's indomitable courage, his loyalty, his gentle guidance, his relaxed attitude, his tremendous healing abilities, and his raw warrior's spirit in the werewolf's appearance. For some reason, she could not envision the twenty-one-winter-old male without his father's war axe, so she explored the axe's features in depth. She traced its ancient runes and battle scars and the curious spear tip above the double blade with its inset red gemstone.

Next the wraithwalker imagined Vraelth's elegant, willowy frame. The elf's skin was as dark as an eggplant's peel and he always kept his lavender locks pristine and swept back from his angular face in an intricate braid. She noted twenty-four-winter-old male's beautiful tenor voice, his sophisticated charm, and his zeal for life's goodness. She added charmchanter's audacious pranks, his otherwise perfect manners, and his keen intelligence into the elf's representation.

Dayalan was more difficult to comprehend even though his striking physical features were easy to visualize. He was as pale as new snow and unbelievably beautiful with broad shoulders, a strong physique, and blue eyes as intense as a hot inner flame. His sleek, waist-long hair was as dark as a moonless night and he kept it tied back away from his oval face and over his pointed, black-tipped ears in a half-ponytail style. Dayalan did his best to hide his black-clawed hands and feet with gloves and boots at all times yet he could never conceal the pair of white fangs that always protruded from his upper lip and caused him such shame. His desperate desire to do what was right, his defiance toward his father's family's evil, as well as his hatred toward his Fallen brother were obvious. However, Katja had to concentrate for a time before she noted his lingering grief over his mother's and Bren's deaths, his sense of betrayal toward Daeryn, and his conflicted care for Lauraisha. Dayalan, she sensed, was more honor-bound than anyone else in the room, even Felan. This was his true strength, but also his greatest frustration because it warred against the darker parts of his nature.

The dwarf Si'lyn and the liopion Nicho'lyn were enigmas to her. Katja tried and failed to discern each of their subtle qualities, but could only add their proficiency in teaching and using each of their mage abilities to their respective likenesses.

Katja found Joce'lynn somewhat easier to understand because she had worked with the mage far more often. Into the Sorceress's image, Katja poured Joce'lynn's admiration and respect for Caleb, her genuine care for others, her candor, her tenacity, and her stalwart wisdom.

"Keep each being's characteristics firmly fixed before your mental eye," Joce'lynn instructed. "After each being becomes whole, you can then strip away their physical appearances and discern only their true natures, unchecked by the container of their flesh."

Katja worked to keep the mages' qualities secure in her mind while letting their images melt away.

"Open your eyes."

Katja did and yelped in surprise. Her packmates and mentors were still in the room with her, but their appearances had changed dramatically. Each being was inundated by light of a vastly different color, and within each brilliant hue pulsed a translucent outline of each being's physical form, perfected to reveal the utmost uniqueness and beauty. Dayalan was himself without fangs or clawed talons, and he radiated a golden fire that was almost blinding within his refined features. His outstretched wings were those of a dragon and his blue eyes burned with a yearning to protect life above all else. Zahra appeared leaner than even her physical form allowed, with scarlet oak leaves crowning her head and glowing green willow branches for arms. Her voice echoed within her like the joyful peal of bells on a gentle breeze. Vraelth's usually lithe form was bulked with devastating power. His quiet voice was wrapped with a low hum of suggestion and his now glowing brown features constantly shifted between attitudes as a river shifts between currents. Katja's eyes widened in surprise as she sensed a deep longing flowing under the surface of the elf's other emotions—a longing, it seemed, for Zahra. Si'lyn and Nicho'lyn were still solid, but each male was wrapped in the color indicated by their mage rank-denoting sashes. Felan was the most astonishing of all. He bore refined features like the others, but the werewolf appeared as such only in body, while his head was that of his human form and his broad back bore the feathered wings of a great eagle. He held the axe of his family as if it were a royal scepter, its orange light bathing him in authority.

Katja stared at him and mouthed "sphinx" in utter confusion and then looked back at Joce'lynn, who was now pervaded by scarlet light and wearing a crown of woven thistles on her brow.

Katja watched as Joce'lynn's physical lips smiled gently amidst all of her scarlet authority. "Welcome to the true reality beneath our physical perception, Katja."

The little wraithwalker looked down at herself and noted the same scarlet power flowing amidst the stronger orange of her skinshifting magic underneath her now translucent skin. Then she realized her tail looked more like the girtab Aria's than her own. She felt her head begin to throb and let go of the vision. As she did so, she felt a black tendril of fear weaving its way into recesses of her mind.

"No!" she shouted in defiance as she recognized Daeryn's presence.

"Katja, what's wrong?" Joce'lynn said.

"Daeryn is trying to break through!" Katja said aloud.

"Already? Fight him, Katja. Deliver the first strike."

Katja nodded and calmed herself—focusing on discerning his true nature as she had just done with the others now gathering around her to help her overcome her fear. Her focus ensnared Daeryn a moment, and she was able to discern his deep loyalty to his mother Marga and his hatred toward his father Caleb and his brother Dayalan. Daeryn snarled as she pushed her mind against his, striking out at his defenses. Then a stray attitude shocked her. Instead of seeing his loyalty to Luther, Katja witnessed Daeryn's bleak loathing for the Víchí High Elder. Her realization of this surprising truth caught Daeryn off-guard and the deadwalker cut his ties to the werecat's mind and fled.

Katja sank panting to her knees on the training chamber floor. Then the golden and violet light of Lauraisha's awareness touched her own.

"Are you well? Did he hurt you?" came the human's scared mental whisper.

"He's gone for now. We're safe," Katja told her. Then blackness consumed her vision and she knew nothing more.

* * *

Katja's head was too heavy to lift from her pillow once she awoke. In fact, her entire body was completely unresponsive. She did manage to open her eyes and see the healing chamber surrounding her, but was otherwise unable to move. She let out a roar of frustration within her mind.

Then Verdagon's presence entered her mind. *Calm yourself!*

I can't move!

Do not panic, that will only make it worse. Your body and mind would need some time to reconnect once you regained consciousness.

What? Why?

You fainted while fighting Daeryn. Your mind was working somewhat disconnected from your body and the two did not have a chance to reconnect before you lost consciousness, so you are going through the process now.

How long will I stay like this?

I'm not certain. You've been asleep for three days thanks to Neha'lyn's potions. He wanted you to find strength and movement quickly when you did regain consciousness so he drugged your sleep. Did you dream at all?

Katja tried to shake her head and then growled in frustration. *No. Where are you?*

In the Hatching Cavern. I am sending Lauraisha to you.

A moment later, Katja heard her door creak open and saw Lauraisha walk into her field of view. The Tyglesean princess was garbed in her tan mage robes and her arm no longer bore bandages. Instead jagged, red scars encircled the forearm and elbow areas of her right arm. Katja eyed it and gulped at the knowledge that a worse wound was hidden under the dreamdrifter's clothing.

Lauraisha followed the werecat's stare to look at her arm. *Oh, yes, I will finish with my treatments and be released from the ward tomorrow.* she said through their mental bond.

The scars—

"Will not fade, just as expected," Lauraisha said aloud as she slumped into a chair. "Felan and Neha'lyn could not counteract all of the magic you put into your attack, so I will have these for life."

Katja tried without success to groan.

"It seems that we will share scars caused by Daeryn just as we seem to share everything else. This will be a good reminder for me to be ever on guard."

"Yes, and to stop trying to save the life of a male who neither needs nor wants your help." Zahra walked into the room.

Lauraisha met the dryad's look of disdain with a gaze as sharp as a werecat's fehg'lig dagger. "What business is it of yours?"

"Oh, none, I'm sure, but someone needs to remind you how to use some common sense. Anyway, I just came to remind both of you that the ceremony is tomorrow after the midday meal."

Lauraisha nodded curtly.

Zahra watched her a moment longer and then turned to Katja. "I suppose I should apologize for thinking you would purposely attack one of your own packmates. I saw you fight against Daeryn during our lessons. I know that you are trying to break his hold. For all of our sakes, I hope you do. I can't put full trust in you until you conquer him."

With that, the dryad left the room.

Lauraisha waited until the dryad slammed the door before shaking her head. "What a faithless skut!"

Katja stared wide-eyed at the princess's sudden use of profanity.

"Well, I'm sorry, but she *is* a coward."

She has a point, the werecat replied.

"I don't care! We all knew the risks involved when we resolved to fight the deadwalkers. If she can't deal with it, then perhaps she should have stayed at home and hidden under her birth tree's roots."

That is not fair, Lauraisha. She just lost her sister right after we nearly lost you! Did you expect her to be cheerful with me?

"I cannot believe that you are defending her when you are the one she just insulted so pointedly!"

Katja tried to shrug and then gave up with a disgruntled sigh.

"Your voice is coming back. Good!"

Katja rolled her eyes and changed the subject. *What is this ceremony that she mentioned anyway?*

"Oh, I forgot. You were asleep, so you haven't heard. Joce'lynn announced that Dayalan has passed his master's skills test. He'll receive his sunsilver mage eye pendant and formal name change tomorrow!"

Katja's excitement for Dayalan was overwhelming. Then a not-so-encouraging thought emerged, and she wondered privately what had gone wrong with Felan's test.

* * *

The packmates devoured their food at the midday eat and then hurried to the central Mage Council Assembly Chamber for Dayalan's Renaming Ceremony. Vraelth once again met the other packmates outside the chamber's massive doors as he had on that fateful day mere months ago when the companions first sought the aid of the General Council of Mages.

The charmchanter mage bowed toward them once and then turned to the doors. His rich tenor voice sang out a single word in a high clear note and the doors began to shake. They swung outward and Vraelth calmly stepped between them with his allies just behind. He led them again to the large circular floor of the huge amphitheater with walls that tiered up around the circle. Seated mages of all ranks and races were scattered throughout the three tiers. The business of war now employed more than two-thirds of the island's number, with the remainder largely too old or infirm to fight.

The metal doors groaned shut and the resulting clang caused a sweeping silence throughout the room as Katja and her packmates took seats north of the podium and dais.

"May it please the General Council of Mages, I have brought the individuals so summoned by this body!" Vraelth intoned. He bowed and strode off the floor.

The mages commenced their meeting with a clang of the large gong located on the triple-tiered dais on the Northern end of the floor—an act which left Katja's ears throbbing far longer than she would have preferred.

"Who comes to the Council and the Ring seeking the rank of mage master?" Si'lyn's voice boomed.

"I seek the honor," the hybrid Dayalan replied.

"I seek the honor," a centaur harmhealer named Prisca replied.

"Then step forward and kneel to receive denotation of your achievement."

The two mages obeyed. With crisp new sashes and mage eye crests draped over his left arm, Si'lyn stepped down from the raised dais toward the two kneeling mages. He removed the Third Adept mage rank sashes from each of the seekers. Si'lyn began to recite an ancient Draigas prayer.

"Dayalan, you will forever more be called Daya'lyn, as is the proper address for a mage master."

"I thank the Ring for this rare honor. I swear to bring honor to my fellow masters and to conduct myself properly as a guide and protector to all Sylvans."

Si'lyn nodded his approval as he slipped Dayalan's bright yellow Sun Sash with its white embroidered emblem over the fireforger's head. "Then please accept this sash as a symbol of your rank and this sunsilver crest denoting your talents."

Daya'lyn bowed low as the mage master slipped the crest around his neck and then watched in silence as Si'lyn and the female Prisca went through the Naming Ritual together.

"Prisca, you will forever more be called Pris'lynn, as is the proper address for a mage master."

After Pris'lynn swore to uphold her duties, Si'lyn asked the pair of new mage masters to present themselves to the assembly. Each mage master stood and bowed to the scant number of council members—all of which stood and bowed in unison to their newest members. Katja found the whole scene touching and rather ironic given their previous experiences with the Council. She felt Lauraisha's agreement resonate inside her mind and glanced at the human dreamdrifter. Lauraisha was sitting perfectly straight on her bench with her delicate hands folded in her lap. Her entire demeanor was regal to the point of aloofness, yet her eyes burned with a mixture of pride, fear, hope, and concentration. The werecat suddenly realized the dreamdrifter was on the hunt—searching the thoughts of the crowd members seated around them. Katja frowned and involuntarily readied herself for an attack. Lauraisha's presence was barely perceptible in the wraithwalker's mind and she doubted most other minds would notice the dreamdrifter at all without the added help a mental bond. For what, precisely, was she searching?

Katja blew out her breath slowly and waited for Si'lyn to finish his speech, her emerald eyes darting from each packmate to each of the eleven Ring of Sorcerers and back. Then it happened. The exchange was so subtle that Katja almost missed it. Joce'lynn's eyes met Lauraisha's for a moment and, with the dreamdrifter's slight head-bob, returned their attention to the proceedings. Joce'lynn then caught Nicho'lyn's attention and blinked at him thrice. The male Ring Sorcerer's mood seemed to lighten then as his eyes turned back to Si'lyn.

"May the merciful Creator bless your every endeavor!" Si'lyn's deep voice said in conclusion, and he bowed to the two mage masters one last time before relinquishing the podium to Nicho'lyn.

"Thank you, Master Si'lyn, for that rousing welcome of the Citadel's newest mage masters," the fireforger mage master said as Daya'lyn and Pris'lynn took their seats among their new peers on the first tier. "I am sure that I speak for all present when I say that we wish you the best blessings along with your new ranks."

The liopion paused, his black eyes scanning the crowd. "Now, fellow mages, we come to the less-than-pleasant portion of our session. As you are all keenly aware, the ongoing war with our northern enemies has grown grim indeed. News abounds every day of the horrors facing our Sylvan Order allies beyond the Nyghe sol Dyvesé Mountains. Many of our number have already sacrificed themselves while carrying out the duties of protection which lay so heavily upon all of our shoulders. Because of these facts, we members of the Ring of Sorcerers do beseech you to pass the legislation of Inquisition brought before you today."

The crowd's combined voices were a roar in Katja's ears. She couldn't discern a comment from the general din.

Magistrate Aver'lyn banged the gong to renew order before Nicho'lyn continued. "Mages, please, I need a vote yea or nay."

"Not since the days of Master Aribem has an Inquisition been called!" a satyr said.

Nicho'lyn's scorpion-like tail twitched even as the liopion narrowed his black eyes in annoyance. "And can you think of a more desperate time than what has befallen us, Master Hem'lyn?"

The elder sproutsinger satyr scratched his scraggly gray beard and then firmly shook his head. "In truth, I cannot."

Murmurs of general agreement met his concession.

"Very well, then. Are there any other pertinent statements or objections before the vote is cast?" The lion-like fireforger looked around.

A few other complaints were aired, but nothing of consequence. Finally, the assembly came to total silence.

"Good, then let us proceed. Those in favor of enacting an Inquisition, please stand."

In one fluid wave of motion, the assenting mages stood. The companions' gazes swept the assembly as members continued standing while each mage council section leader tallied their count with marks on scraps of parchment with graphite sticks. They then dropped their section's vote parchments into a slit-topped box as it was passed between tiers by ushers. Once every vote was collected for the record, the assenting mages sat. Then the head usher took the box to a table on the chamber floor and counted the votes.

"All opposed, show your dissent."

Nearly one hundred mages stood and were counted. A second usher tallied the dissenting votes, and then the pair of ushers confirmed and scribed the final counts on a record scroll. Aver'lyn called out the final count. It stood confirmed at 178 to 92 mages in favor of enacting an Inquisition.

Nicho'lyn bobbed his head at the announcement. "Very good, then. The Ring of Sorcerers will convene forthwith to choose the Inquisitor. Please present any recommended candidates' names by ballot to Si'lyn or myself before you leave the meeting.

"Now, what other business needs to be discussed during this council session?" Silence met Aver'lyn's question. "None? Very well, the Council of Mages is dismissed, then. May the Creator bless and keep you."

Aver'lyn beat the gong twice and the assembly adjourned. The council members all stood and bowed before dispersing. A few gave folded ballots with candidate names to the Ring members, but most departed in whispering clusters through the chamber's upper doors.

Katja found herself in such a cluster of her own packmates and the two new mage masters. The packmates all properly introduced themselves to Pris'lynn and then discussed the prospects for the position of Inquisitor. Only Katja and Felan seemed to know the true politics behind today's events. Katja was content to keep the information to herself and she judged Felan also quite willing to let others talk without his opinions. In fact, the werewolf had been unusually quiet during the past few days and he wouldn't tell Katja—or anyone, for that matter—why. The werecat frowned at his sullen visage. Had he not been allowed to take the mage master test after all?

"They need to choose someone both wise and powerful," Lauraisha said from her riding place in Felan's arms, breaking Katja's flow of thoughts. The werewolf had elected to carry the human princess since she had yet to fully regain her strength.

"I would agree," Vraelth said as he caught up to the group. "I'd also prefer someone spry enough for the duty.

As wonderful as Nicho'lyn and the other Ring members are, most are well past fighting age."

"Indeed, after all, the task is terribly demanding on the Inquisitor's physical, mental, and magical abilities," Pris'lynn agreed.

"And, certainly, it must be a fireforger mage," Daya'lyn added.

Lauraisha twisted in Felan's gentle grip to give the male hybrid a mock frown. "Why? Are you hoping for the privilege?"

Katja's ears twitched uncomfortably at Lauraisha's jest and she quietly bulwarked her mind to keep the dreamdrifter from accidentally stumbling upon her knowledge of Joce'lynn's secret.

"Certainly not!" Daya'lyn exclaimed. "The last Inquisitor had to sacrifice himself in a torturous explosion of fire and rock to protect the Sylvan continent! I have no ambition to be another daft martyr!"

"Aribem was not daft!" Pris'lynn said. "Without his sacrifice, Sylvans would not be free today!"

Daya'lyn shook his head. "I don't disagree with you about either the necessity or the greatness of Aribem's deed; however, I will say that no one in such an impossible position could be completely sane and still split the continents as Aribem did. The mage would not accept defeat when completely at the mercy of his enemies and so, for that act of bravery, he is a legend long after his demise."

"With a mountain range like the Nyghe sol Dyvesé as your legacy, how could anyone forget you?" Zahra pushed her fiery tresses back from her jade face.

Katja snorted. "It would be impossible, I think."

"Agreed," Lauraisha added, her eyes a little wide.

Katja considered the Tyglesean. "You do know the story, don't you?"

She nodded. "During the First War of Ages, Aribem and his closest followers traveled to the Northern Continent intent on confronting Luther and ending the war between Sylvans and Asheken deadwalkers once and for all. On their way to the fortress, however, the Sylvans were ambushed. Aribem was captured and his followers were scattered. He was brought before Luther in water chains. To save the lives of his allies and the rest of the Sylvans, Aribem sacrificed himself."

Daya'lyn nodded his head. "Correct. Aribem, the first and most powerful of all fireforgers, chose to release the core of his soul's flame and incinerate himself and everything around him rather than let the deadwalkers hunt down the other Sylvans. His heroic act of self-sacrifice destroyed half of the deadwalker army, smote Luther so badly that the Víchí High Elder could no longer fly, and set off an earthquake strong enough to destroy the land connecting the two continents, create the Nyghe sol Dyvesé mountain range, and carve out the Sphinx Gape and the Aribem Channel."

"How does a fireforger set off an earthquake?" Lauraisha asked. "I thought only charmchanter mages could do such a thing, and very rarely at that."

Vraelth grimaced. "No one is really sure. It's a matter of passionate debate among the more philosophical of our mages as to whether he also had charmchanter abilities. Others question whether it was the Creator's divine act of interference that led to the land's upheaval. Hence the historical name of Nyghe sol Dyvesé—Line of the Divine."

"Still others question whether Aribem himself was in fact divine," Katja added, remembering an old conversation with her father on the subject. The sudden memory of Kevros sent a sharp pang of anguish down her throat and she averted her gaze, lest the others see the sudden tears collecting there. She swallowed back her grief.

Vraelth rolled his dark brown eyes. "That is such a grim's tale! Aribem was a prophet and nothing more!"

"How would you know? Did you ever meet him?" Katja countered.

"Of course not! He is dead!"

"And what if the rumors of his resurrection from death are true? Would that not make him divine, having triumphed over both death and undeath?"

"It would if he had, but he didn't, so that argument is moot."

Katja flicked her ears. "I should know better than to talk either politics or religion with an elf."

"What is that supposed to mean?"

"You two, quiet!" Daya'lyn snapped. "We began with history and then spiraled out into mythology. The point is that the first Inquisitor gave up his life and the next Inquisitor will likely need to do the same to end this war."

Katja watched him a moment. "Why are you so certain of this?"

Daya'lyn looked down at her, his pale-blue eyes gloomy. "Because an Inquisitor knows no boundaries either on Sylvan soil or abroad. He or she will go wherever necessary to stamp out evil and restore peace. Eventually we must confront and defeat the inhabitants of Blaecthull. As long as one vampire remains, all Sylvans remain in danger of being bitten and Turned into deadwalkers. If we Sylvans don't destroy every last deadwalker while they are here on Sylvan soil, then the Inquisition will be forced to destroy the remnant on the Northern Continent in order to end this abysmal war."

"Well, then," Felan said, and shifted Lauraisha's weight on his massive chest. "We had better be sure to lure every last one of them here and hunt them down, so that the Inquisition stays domestic."

"An excellent plan—simple, ruthless, and insane!" Daya'lyn's smile was full of fang.

Felan returned the hybrid's smile with a chuckle, his own eyes glinting in anticipation.

V

A BROLAGHAN'S REVENGE

Two weeks of quiet anticipation passed over the Isle of Summons before the Ring of Sorcerers announced their decision of Daya'lyn as their chosen Inquisitor. The declaration sent waves of shock throughout the entire island, but no being's surprise surpassed that of Daya'lyn himself.

"They are all insane!" the male yelled as he and the other packmates sat in the privacy of Felan's chambers with a meal that the werewolf had confiscated from the Citadel kitchens.

"Actually, it's genius," Vraelth said after swallowing a bite of dried fig. "The Ring members have been looking for a legal excuse to investigate the suspicious incidents in Tyglesea and here are the two of you. Lauraisha, the estranged princess, is now a member of the Inquisitor Daya'lyn's entourage. No doors can be barred against either of you without risking war and everyone knows it. Pure political genius, I say. Oh, I almost wish I could be there to join in the fun!"

Katja growled. "Instinct tells me this will not be fun at all, although I do expect some very dark games."

"Agreed," Daya'lyn said.

The dryad frowned. "You two have to be some of the most morose beings I have ever met."

Katja shrugged at the dryad and ripped another bite off the lamb shank she was holding. They were on somewhat better speaking terms for now. However, Katja doubted the truce would last long.

"But you will accept the position, won't you?" Lauraisha

asked Daya'lyn.

The fireforger scowled at her. "Why should I?"

"Because there is no other fireforger as powerful or as fit for battle as you, Daya'lyn," Felan said. "There is no one else who can do this."

Daya'lyn's blue eyes flashed red as he stood. "And if I Fall...if I follow my brother's foolish footsteps past the grave and become what I most loath, what then?" He regarded the werewolf and balled his gloved fists to keep his hands from shaking. "You know what nearly happened when I lost Bren. If I become a vampire immune to fire, who will be able to withstand me then?"

Felan stood and observed Daya'lyn's enraged face with a calm that Katja found awe-inspiring. When in his normal dark-furred form, the hulking werewolf was a good head taller than the fireforger. Yet Daya'lyn had bested him in a fight during their first encounter while wielding nothing more than a staff against Felan's battle axe. Felan gripped the other male's shoulder with a gentle paw. "No one," he said simply.

"How can Joce'lynn and the other Ring members dare ask me to do this?"

"She knows the dangers, Daya'lyn."

"How do you know that?"

"Because she told them to us," Katja supplied.

Daya'lyn stared at her. "You both knew of this?"

Katja and Felan nodded while the others stared at them in shock.

"And you didn't think to inform me?"

"Joce'lynn swore us to secrecy until the announcement, Daya'lyn," the werecat explained. "We could not break her trust."

Daya'lyn went very still. "And so instead you broke mine?"

Katja licked her lips even as Felan's paw fell from Daya'lyn's shoulder. "We are sorry."

The fireforger's eyes glowed an eerie red as he stormed out of the room.

"Not yet you aren't, but you will be," were the last words he uttered to either of them until after Joce'lynn, Verdagon, and Damya had appointed Daya'lyn as Sylvan Inquisitor during the Ceremony of Blessings.

* * *

The morning after the ceremony dawned crisp and mostly clear. The lands beyond the Isle of Summons were cloaked in deep drifts of snow while the island itself felt as cool as an early autumn day thanks to the constant volcanic heat warming its shores. Even the lake was warmer than it ought to be and steam rolled off of the waves in misty tendrils, cloaking the isle from view of the shoreline.

"Perfect weather for flying, I would say." Verdagon sniffed the air in anticipation, his leathery wings stretching.

Katja stood petrified beside him. "Perfect by whose estimation?"

The dragon turned to her. "You know that I prefer to try this now with you on my back rather than later without you beside me. It will be some months before I join you in Tyglesea, after all."

Katja gulped. "And you know that I would much prefer to keep my paws on firm ground."

"As a dragon rider, you do not have that luxury, Dear One. Do not fear the sky or the trek to meet her."

"Greeting the sky isn't my main concern," Katja replied through clenched teeth. "What I take issue with are the different ways you keep discovering of leaving her."

The dragon had been steadily practicing his dubious aerial skill for almost a fortnight now. Even with Daya'lyn's instructions, the dragon had only shown marginal improvement after his first flight's tumbling crash.

Verdagon ducked his huge angular head to lick a recently earned bruise. "A few minor accidents due to a sudden change in wind direction shouldn't worry you. I can easily avoid such problems now that I can identify the warning signs."

Katja hid her tawny-furred face with her paws. "Jierira."

"Come now, no more arguments. Climb into the saddle and let us be off."

Against her better judgment, Katja climbed up the dragon's thick scales to perch lightly upon his ridged back. She then scooted herself into the leather saddle tucked between two spines and buckled herself into the riding harness. Once the werecat was secure near his massive wings, Verdagon rushed down the island shoreline toward the water—pumping his wings rapidly as he sprinted. The dragon lurched into the air as his wings caught the wind and then the two launched into the scattering mists high enough to lose sight of the land and water below them.

Katja whimpered as she clung to Verdagon's back and fought to keep the contents of her stomach precisely where it belonged. She searched for a steady place on Verdagon's back where she fix her gaze and thus regain her sense of balance, but that proved futile as the dragon's strong wing beats carried them still higher upon the morning breeze.

"I hate this!" she screeched.

"That is only because you have yet to see the true beauty of the sky!"

Verdagon let out a triumphant roar as they flew up through the mists and then rode an updraft toward the tops of the few wispy clouds. Cool gray gave way to cold white. The dragon and his beleaguered rider leveled out just above the frothy white waves of winter clouds under a bright sun and jewel-blue sky.

Katja stared about her in awe. "This is…beautiful."

Verdagon's lips parted in a fang-ringed smile. "That it is."

Katja gazed along the snow-like fields toward the granite teeth of the Nyghe sol Dyvesé, which loomed large enough even at this height that they seemed beguilingly close. Katja felt as if she could lean out and touch them from Verdagon's back. "Incredible."

"Yes, but dangerous. The wind currents shift wildly around the rocks. I dare not attempt to follow them without more flying experience. Let us go back now. I should like to try flying low over the lake today."

Verdagon began to dip into the clouds when Katja tugged his reins, signaling him to level out.

"What is it?"

"Another winged creature approaches us," Katja exclaimed. "I can see it over your left shoulder, but I cannot discern its race."

Verdagon squinted in the direction Katja indicated. "A harpy."

Katja stared at him and then at the fast flying creature in astonishment when she drew near. "Hail, Verdagon, honored Pyrekin," the harpy said.

"I and my steward Katja Escari greet you, harpy," Verdagon replied with formality.

The harpy was slender and short—only half a body-length tall. Her golden-brown wings stretched to thrice the length of her lean-muscled body. Soft white and brown feathers cascaded down the harpy's human-shaped torso and back and flowed into a magnificent brown-and-white banded tail fan. Her human-like arms and bird-like legs were also covered in fine feathers. Her large golden eyes had an eagle-like essence, even though they were perched in a very human face.

She moved almost without sound and seemed to simply float in midair as she flew, giving her an almost delicate demeanor. Two things, however, made Katja very wary of this soft-spoken creature: her deadly sharp talons and the sharp curves of the venomous fangs jutting from her otherwise dainty mouth.

"My Sir, I am Otwenia and I bring news from my aerie. My clan, the Clan Eerondus, has joined the fray at Reithrgar and our combined forces have driven the deadwalkers back past the western foothills!"

"This is excellent news indeed!" Verdagon exclaimed.

"What of the inhabitants of Caerwyn Castle?" Katja asked.

"They suffered some casualties, but Master Caleb and his fellows fought valiantly and are on the whole unharmed."

"What of the girtab Aria? Have you seen her?"

Otwenia blinked in seeming confusion. "There is a girtab still alive? If she was at the battle, I have no knowledge of her. Take heart, the battlefield is large and I am merely a messenger. I was not privy to much of the actual fighting."

"Thank you, Otwenia." Verdagon lurched as he spoke. "Please present your full report to the Ring members at once!"

"Yes, My Sir!" The harpy dove beneath the blanket of clouds and was gone.

"Katja, I grow tired."

"I know; I can feel the tremors of your muscles. Descend, now!"

Verdagon folded his wings and dropped like a stone beneath the cloud-cover, leaving the sky's bright beauty and Katja's momentary elation behind. The pair dove through the misty darkness faster than either of their night-vision could adjust. Then they finally comprehended the land rushing toward them.

"Pull up!" Katja screamed as they hurtled dangerously close to a small lake's outer bank.

Verdagon wrenched open his wings to catch as much wind as possible. He managed to slow their descent, but it was not enough to avoid hurtling headlong into the icy bank. The dragon swept his wings forward and flattened his tail straight out to keep them from tumbling head over paws, but the maneuver cost him. Katja's ears flattened at the sounds of scraping scales and cracking bone as they skidded into the lake's icy shallows. The frigid water parted and then crashed over them as the dragon's body finally lost its forward momentum and began sinking into the mud.

"Verdagon!" Katja roared.

The dragon didn't move. Instead, his head stayed beneath the water and only bubbles broke the surface of the dark waves.

"Verdagon!" she shouted again. She scrambled desperately out of her harness and jumped into the cold waters now stained with dragon blood. She pushed herself into the mud under his head to try to raise his snout above the liquid swirling around her chest. He was so heavy!

"*Lauraisha!*" Katja shouted the human dreamdrifter's name with her voice and with her mind. She had no idea where they had landed, but she hoped that the Ott vre Caerwyn mirror's shard embedded in the broken spearhead around her neck would amplify her words well enough for the dreamdrifter to hear her.

Katja? What's wrong?

Help me! Verdagon has been gravely injured and I do not know how long I can keep him from drowning! Katja felt hot tears flowing down her cheeks.

Hold on, Katja! Help is coming!

Katja groaned under the dragon's weight and butted her head against the soft part of his jaw to wake him. Her attempt failed. All the while, the water around her was becoming redder and the bank's mists' grew darker.

Lauraisha, hurry, please hurry! She begged. The mists congealed around her then, and her terrified scream froze in her raw throat. She sniffed the air and smelled a terrifyingly familiar stench. One of musty, salty decay.

"No. No!" Katja whispered. "It cannot be! Not here!"

Her nose never lied and neither did her ears, which now heard nothing, not even the lapping of the waves against her soaked fur. The unnatural darkness enveloped her. Katja watched as the world around her flipped color. The gloomy sky became as black as it was during a new moon, the lake shore looked like the white of crushed bones, and the bloody waters swirled higher around her shivering body. The mists clawed at her and then she screamed as she realized that this time she was chest deep in the brolaghan's favorite element—water.

"Creator, keep us. We should not die like this," she whispered. Terror gripped at her as the water edged its way up her torso to her shoulders.

Then, in midst of the fog, a dark figure cloaked in gray appeared. It hovered just above the water without the aid of wings and drifted toward the werecat and dragon. It had four limbs with webbed feet and hands. It seemed to walk upon only the back two legs just as humans, werecats, and werewolves. Its face, however, resembled none of those races. Instead the brolaghan bore a head like that of a horse with a cruelly fanged maw and deep orange eyes. A faint glow emanated from them, giving off the only light available in the foggy darkness.

Katja stared at the waterweaver and shadowshaper mage aghast. "Brolaghans have a bodily form?"

Yes, but one only seen by one such as you, discerner. Why have you entered my domain? his thought came to her.

I deeply apologize for the intrusion. The dragon was learning to fly. We stayed aloft too long and crashed into this part of the lake. I cannot wake the dragon, nor can I move him on my own, so I have called for aid.

The brolaghan's soundless mouth curled in a snarl. *No being is allowed into my territory without my permission, werecat, which I did not give to you. I will destroy all who interfere!*

Katja felt sick as the cold current tugged her torso and threatened to drag her under. She edged onto the dragon's forearm and grabbed one of Verdagon's horns to steady his head as she climbed on top of his back and used the reins to keep his head above the swirling waves. The dragon's head lurched dangerously to one side, almost throwing her off balance and into the frigid water.

"You would threaten the life of a Pyrekin and his steward?" she shouted in desperation.

I would. The brolaghan's thought was laced with the darkest hatred.

Shivering, Katja hauled the head by the horns and reins to rest on Verdagon's left shoulder out of the water. The brolaghan meanwhile drifted closer, his misty tendrils wrapping around the werecat's and dragon's necks, choking them. With her last unrestricted breath Katja roared at him in defiance, causing him to flinch.

"I would know the name of my murderer!" she gasped around the loosened tendrils.

The fiend actually smiled. *Greyman Rubero, brother of Greyman Ruthero, murdered by you! Yes, it was your filthy voice, discerner, who shredded his existence. His essence still clings to your memories!*

Katja stared at him, incredulous. "I killed a revenant after he helped deadwalkers massacre my clan, Turn my brother, and capture me! And you want revenge against me for an act of justice and self-defense?"

The notion was laughable and yet still the monster pressed his attack.

Lies, lies! he hissed.

Using the techniques that Joce'lynn had taught her, Katja sought Rubero's mind with her own and bombarded him with the memories in every wretched detail, from the moment she and her two brothers Kumos and Kayten had first noticed the revenant's smoky haze drifting through the forest, to the mutilated bodies of her clansmen, to her near capture by the ghoul Curqak and his deadwalker allies on the river.

Cease this torment, witch! His stranglehold loosened even more.

No. You know that I show you the truth and that you have no grounds to justly execute me. I am innocent of murder. You, however, will not be, and your crime will cause great harm to all Sylvans. Katja's memories of Verdagon choosing her as his steward and his blessings of Daya'lyn as Inquisitor pummeled Rubero. *By killing me or harming the dragon, you endanger the Inquisition and the lives of all Sylvans. Do you choose to ally yourself with the hope of Sylvan freedom or with the deadwalkers' enslavement?*

Rubero snarled again, but Katja could sense his fear and continued her barrage of thoughts. She showed him the deadwalkers' atrocities at every encounter in contrast with the warmth and friendship she knew from her family and packmates.

"Choose your side, brolaghan!" she shouted.

"Yes, choose, brolaghan."

Katja's stream of thoughts abruptly stopped when she heard Daya'lyn's deep voice behind her. Rubero followed her gaze and spied the crest of Aribem that Daya'lyn had been given during the Ceremony of Blessings now hanging from the fireforger master's neck.

Inquisitor! came the mental hiss.

"I am he, and I will protect my own."

As Katja felt the incredible heat of the fireforger's flame build behind her, the mist tendrils lifted from around her and Verdagon. Then the world's hues became normal once again.

The werecat turned to look at Daya'lyn over her shoulder. The fireforger held twin flames in his ungloved hands—their light adding a luminous glow to his pale skin. His dragon-like wings were half-extended and his blue eyes burned with an expression as intense as the heat of the blue flames blazing above his palms.

"Release my allies, brolaghan, or so help me I will transform your lake into a scorched crater!"

Rubero pulled his misty shroud about him and vanished with one last echoing shriek of fear and loathing.

"Katja, are you well?" Daya'lyn asked.

The werecat shook her head. "He won't wake! I can't move him!"

"Let me examine him," Neha'lyn said from behind the fireforger.

The werecat turned to blink at Daya'lyn in surprise, and then realized that he had flown Neha'lyn to attend Verdagon.

"What's wrong with him?" she asked.

Neha'lyn was silent until he finished his inspection. "Aside from multiple contusions and a concussion, Verdagon has a broken limb, a broken wing, four cracked ribs, and at least three fractured vertebrae in his tail. If there are internal injuries, I can't locate them. How far did the two of you fall?"

Katja squinted in thought. "He tried to level out of a free-fall dive at roughly a spruce-length above the ground. He was only partially successful."

"So I see." Neha'lyn cleared his throat. "Daya'lyn, would you be good enough to bathe him with as intense a flame as you can maintain?"

Daya'lyn frowned. "Do you think it will help to heal him?"

"Possibly. At the least, we need to cauterize his outward injuries to stave off infection and then hope that the fire can penetrate deep enough to help the Pyrekin heal any internal injuries. The mending of bones will take a great deal longer, but we have far more pressing concerns right now."

"What of the brolaghan?" Daya'lyn asked as he searched the retreating mists.

"I'll help you move Verdagon out of the water and then stand watch against the brolaghan." The harmhealer mage gestured for Katja to let go of the dragon's head and slide down from his back. Together the three managed to push and turn Verdagon up the muddy incline so that his head, at least, was above the lapping waves.

"Hurry now. Katja helped keep the gash in his neck pinched closed while she was holding his head above water, but he'll bleed to death if you don't cauterize the wound."

Daya'lyn nodded, took a deep breath, and went to work. The harmhealer and skinshifter hurried behind the fireforger as he gently touched an incandescent blue flame to the dragon's neck. Fire licked among the green scales and then seeped into Verdagon's inert body. As Daya'lyn continued his treatment, the fireforger's flames enveloped all but the submerged parts of the Pyrekin's body.

"Where are we?" Katja asked Neha'lyn.

"You landed down the river about a few leagues southwest of Lake Summons," he replied. "There have been unconfirmed reports of deadwalkers roaming this area, so when Princess Lauraisha received your cry for help, we feared…"

Katja shook her head. Neha'lyn nodded and took a seat on a nearby fallen log to sort through his bag of medicines while Daya'lyn continued his ministrations. Katja used the intervening time to skinshift some of her cuts closed and otherwise clean the muck out of her tangled fur.

The sun was almost at its zenith when Verdagon's tail finally twitched—his first sign of life since his and Katja's fall. The dragon's eyelids rolled open and he sneezed a great spray of water out of his nostrils, once again drenching Katja in water and muck. The werecat cringed. She looked forward to the day when her adventures didn't include her being dunked in some form of grimy liquid.

"Good to see you awake again, My Sir."

Verdagon squinted at Daya'lyn in surprise. "What happened?"

"We crashed and you were badly injured," Katja volunteered. When the dragon squinted at her, Katja explained the encounter with the brolaghan and Verdagon's subsequent injuries.

"You're well?" the dragon asked Katja.

She nodded even as she began rinsing her fur again. "You took the brunt of the fall and saved me from any great injury."

Verdagon let out a relieved sigh.

"Daya'lyn is working to mend you," Neha'lyn added. "You have been unconscious for most of the morning."

Verdagon nodded and then winced. "I see."

"We had to see to your worst injuries before we could hazard moving you. I hope the transport barge arrives soon. I want to be well rid of this place before nightfall."

"Are you worried that the brolaghan will attack us in the darkness while Verdagon is still vulnerable?" Daya'lyn asked.

"Him or something worse," the elf said as he surveyed the tall trees. None of them had seen deadwalkers since Verdagon's crash but that didn't mean that the monsters weren't lurking somewhere in the shadows.

"Forgive me, My Sir…but I need…a moment…" Daya'lyn

said through rapid breaths.

"Not at all. Rest while Katja assists me."

Daya'lyn extinguished his fire and seated himself beside Neha'lyn on the log—hanging his head in exhaustion.

"What can I do?" the werecat asked.

"I need you to skinshift the cauterized wounds closed."

"Master Verdagon, wouldn't my gifts be better suited for such a task?" Neha'lyn interjected.

The dragon nodded and then winced. "True, but I wish Katja to refine her healing procedures since she must act as healer for the other members of the Inquisition during their journey together."

The werecat grinned and went to work while the others kept watch. With her paws pressed against the scales of Verdagon's shoulder, Katja closed her eyes and began to explore the intricacies of the dragon's muscles and bones. Through the touch of her magic, the skinshifter delved beneath the damaged tissue—feeling the broken bones.

"This will hurt," she murmured.

Verdagon stifled a roar of pain as Katja shifted each of his bones back into their correct positions. Droplets of sweat began to drip down her furry forehead as she encouraged bits of jagged bone to reconnect along the breaks. She could not completely meld the bone back together, but she could at least spur its healing.

Once she had reset each bone so that Neha'lyn could splint them, Katja pulled her concentration back to the wounds that Daya'lyn had cauterized closed. Adding her touch to his, she helped to stitch healthy skin along the worst of Verdagon's gashes. "I'm sorry," she panted. "But I don't have the strength or skill to do more."

"You've done more than enough, Katja." Verdagon's deep voice was gentle.

Neha'lyn looked up at the late afternoon sky as he wrapped poultice-laced cloths and splints around the dragon's injured limbs and tail. "It grows late and the transport barge still has not arrived."

Katja and Daya'lyn followed the harmhealer's gaze across the lake, noting that Rubero's dark mists were gathering once again. "We're too exposed here," the fireforger said. "Can you move?"

Verdagon grunted as he pushed himself to a stand, using his remaining good wing to keep as much weight off of his broken left foreleg as possible. "I will do what I must."

"What's your plan?" Katja asked.

Daya'lyn pulled his gloves back over his black-clawed hands and pointed to the mouth of the river where it emptied into the lake. "We need to follow the river as far upstream as we can get in an effort to meet the barge."

"The brolaghan can easily follow us if we do that."

"True, but the alternative is to try to find a path back through the forest leading to the Island of Summons and that assumes that there is a trail through the trees wide enough to accommodate Verdagon's size. In either case, the riverbank should afford us a more defensible position."

Katja bowed her head in concession to his point.

"We will follow the river then," the dragon said as he limped forward.

Together the four of them labored across the semi-frozen ground around the lake. They reached the river's mouth and followed it northeast for several spruce-lengths before discovering what had delayed the barge. A huge pair of trees had fallen across the main channel, forcing the barge crew to anchor while they worked to clear the blockade.

"More of Greyman Rubero's maliciousness?" Katja asked.

Daya'lyn snarled as he nodded. "I should have scorched him black when I had the chance."

Verdagon shook his head. "It is of no consequence now. Let us leave him to his petty hatred and depart this accursed place."

Together the three mages helped the Pyrekin hobble onto the barge and then continued their vigil against the brolaghan and the gathering night as the barge's crew propelled them upriver toward the safety of the Isle of Summons. As the sun dipped below the trees and gave way to the waxing quarter moon, Katja sat down beside Daya'lyn on the wooden foredeck.

"Thank you for coming to save me," she said simply.

He nodded once, but did not speak.

"Are you still angry with me?" she ventured.

He glanced at her and arched a black eyebrow. "Can you give me a compelling reason why I shouldn't be?"

She frowned.

Daya'lyn sighed. "You and Lauraisha and I are about to go on a journey together where we must rely solely on one another for survival and yet you would withhold a decision as important as my being named Inquisitor from me?"

"I had no choice. I was—"

"Sworn to secrecy. Yes, I know. But from this moment forward, I cannot afford for you keep secrets from me ever again. The wellbeing of our lives and our souls depend upon your capacity as a wraithwalker to be truthful and pure. Remember that. I know you did not keep your silence out of malice, but my being ill-prepared is dangerous..." He sighed and hung his head.

"Ever since Bren's death, you have doubted yourself."

He nodded. "I felt the darkness well up inside myself. The terrible Thirst that the white wolf's blood kept at bay is barely quenched when I feed from Tyron, and if that horse fails me... There will be no escape—not for me, not for anyone."

Daya'lyn picked up the crest of Aribem resting on his tunic and traced his gloved fingers over the lamb and lion insignias on the sunsilver disk and stopped when they reached the fireforger's mage eye engraving. He laughed then and the bitterness in his voice stung Katja's ears like frostbite. "How ironic is it that the grand hero whom the Ring and the Pyrekin would send to follow Aribem's path to rid the world of the fanged vampires and their bitten deadwalker spawn is himself a blood-drinker?"

He dropped the medallion. It swung heavy against his chest as he hid his pale face behind shaking gloved hands.

VI

PAINFUL PROMISES

"Will Verdagon completely heal?" Lauraisha asked as she and Katja packed saddlebags with the kitchen's supply of hard cheese and dried meats for their journey tomorrow.

Katja sighed and stretched her knotted muscles. She had endured the previous night's full moon without any interference from Daeryn. Yet her anxiety over him coupled with her fatigue after dealing with Verdagon's wounds had made her skinshift into her human form a grueling event.

"He should be fine in a few weeks. Thank the Creator that he was able to pull himself onto the enclave's barge when we found it. I have no idea how we would have moved him back to the isle's safety without it."

Lauraisha nodded absently. "I'm just relieved that you are all relatively well considering the circumstances."

Katja fussed with the neckline her gray-green dress robes and stubbornly adjusted her loincloth and winter leggings before answering. "Neha'lyn, Daya'lyn, and I are still exhausted from all of our work. I think you will have to be Daya'lyn's and my main defense for the journey's first few days until we can finish recovering our strength."

Lauraisha grimaced. "I think I'm well enough now to do that. Still, I think it's almost cruel for the Ring to order us away from the isle just days after Verdagon's crash. I would have liked a few more weeks training before we began the Inquisition Quest."

Katja nodded. "The harpies' latest war reports give them

ample reason to send us now. I'd rather risk the road now that we know that the deadwalkers have been pushed back from Reithrgar Pass and the surrounding mountains. Yet I also can't help but worry given the fact that the next full moon may well be my last sane—"

A knock on Katja's room's door interrupted her.

"That is Felan," Lauraisha said without looking up from her work.

Katja frowned and walked through the servant's door adjoining Lauraisha's and her own room. Katja opened her chamber's front door and noted without surprise that Lauraisha's prediction was accurate. The werewolf inclined his head toward her and stepped inside the room without a word. She watched him a moment before she shut the door. She could tell by the tense set of his shoulders that he was anxious, and he said as much.

"I'm worried about our upcoming journeys, I suppose."

Katja nodded and awkwardly gestured toward a chair.

Felan shook his head and stood staring at her, his arms cradling a pair of age-worn books.

"Katja, I... I have something to give you before you leave." Felan's eyes were unreadable as he pressed the books into the werecat's paws. "The librarian was kind enough to loan them to me indefinitely since I am as close to a skinshifter mage master as we have on this island..." Bitter disappointment added an edge to his voice.

"What happened during your rank examination, Felan? Why did you fail?" she asked.

"To be honest, I'm not certain. Every part of the test went well until I had to skinshift into a human." He frowned. "I still have no idea what happened. My body would not respond the way it should have. Try as I might, I could not make a complete transformation.

"The first time I tried, I could not eliminate my tail. The second attempt left me with a werewolf's snout on an otherwise human face. The third and final attempt was even worse." He shook his head. "That lack of control has not occurred since I was fifteen winters old."

"Perhaps it was an accident?"

"Perhaps. I was certainly worried enough for my anxiety

to cause problems. In any event, I will try to sort it out during the next full moon or two."

"I hope you do." The werecat looked down at the books. "Thank you for these."

"You're very welcome." He smiled. "The book on top is the most in-depth study I could find on advanced skinshifting. I have added quite a few extra notes in the margins dealing with my own experiences and more recent training that I hope you will find helpful. The other is the library's only book on the subject of wraithwalking. It includes several prayers of protection as well as quite a few mental defense techniques. Joce'lynn was kind enough to add her notes inside it as well."

Katja rubbed a paw down the cracked leather spines. "Felan, these are wonderful! I can't thank you enough..."

Felan pulled her into a crushing embrace. "Swear to me that you will guard yourself, Katja. Stay safe. I cannot bear to lose you! Swear to me that we will see each other again."

She looked into his beautiful eyes and visually traced the blue and green swirls and flecks surrounding his pupils. "I wish we had more time together."

"As do I, Katja. Oh, how I wish..."

Katja could not help herself. She pushed high on her hind feet and touched her nose against his. It was cold, wet, and perfect. She felt the softness of his muzzle touch her maw and the warmth of his lips as they brushed hers. Her head spun and her heart sang. His strong arms kept her upright as she started to sway. Hot tears from two sets of eyes flowed through the golden fur of her cheeks. Felan's embrace tightened in desperation.

"Katja, I'm so sorry...for doubting you. I—"

"We will see each other again, Felan. I promise. I swear to you, we will see each other again. I love you!"

Felan nodded his head and sniffed away his tears. "I love you too. I have to go, before I cannot bear to let you out of my embrace."

She hugged and kissed him one last time, and then he turned toward the door.

"Creator, keep you, myn liebte...my love," she said as her tears puddled in her fur.

"And also you, mith vil perle."

Katja's ears drooped as the heavy door shut between them. She hugged the werewolf's gifts to her chest as the meaning of Felan's words rang in her ears and in her heart long after the sound of the male had retreated down the corridor. *Mith vil perle. My life's treasure.* It was the first time that the werewolf tongue of Jakkle had meant something beautiful to her.

* * *

As dawn lit the next morning in muted gray hues, all of the packmates met with the Ring of Sorcerers at the Isle of Summons's main dock. The same boat which had ferried Bren to his watery grave now waited to transport the Inquisitor, his entourage, and their belongings to the south side of the lake so they could then travel across the southernmost pass of the Nyghe sol Dyvesé on horseback. Under the best circumstances, the mainly human kingdom of Vihous would be a month and a half's trek across the continent. Yet, since they were crossing the mountains during the last of winter, unpredictable weather would likely make it much longer.

"Well met, Inquisitor Daya'lyn!" the boat's captain called as his crew helped haul provisions onboard.

Daya'lyn smiled as he bowed with a gloved hand held out, palm up in greeting. "Thank you, Captain Nascius. You're looking well."

The captain returned the smile. "I feel well. I must say, you're looking better than the last time I saw you."

Daya'lyn's smile turned rueful. "One can only hope. Are you ready for us to board?"

When the captain nodded, Katja, Lauraisha, and Daya'lyn all led their mounts onto the boat and tied their reigns to the foredeck railing. Tyron seemed finicky near the water, but the other two mounts gazed placidly at the lake. Katja studied them a while, still uncertain what to think of their peculiarities. These nacken looked and smelled like horses, but they bore thick, reed-like hair in their manes and tails, and had sharp fangs for eating meat just like the kelpies who raised them. As strange as they were, the sleek white steeds were excellent runners and even better swimmers. Since the three packmates would be traversing swampy country, the Ring of Sorcerers had insisted that Katja and Lauraisha take them.

Katja thanked Joce'lynn and Si'lyn for the rare mounts when they stepped aboard.

"Not at all, Katja. The members of the Inquisition need the best steeds possible and Calder and Glashtin are two of the finest. You find two more intelligent stallions. And they're well-tempered, even around werecats," Si'lyn said with a smile.

Katja nodded and then bowed formally to all of them. Lauraisha and Daya'lyn followed suit and then each gave more personal farewells to their packmates. Katja noticed that Vraelth was far less stiff or formal than either Zahra or Felan was toward her. Felan was his public self, shy and reserved. Zahra was downright aloof, although she did at least clasp Katja's paw in parting.

"I will miss you, all of you," Felan murmured.

"I will miss you, too," replied Lauraisha who then threw aside all formality and convention by hugging the huge werewolf. He stiffened in surprise, and then smiled as he embraced her in return.

"As will I," Katja added and gave him a fierce hug.

She turned back to the dryad and dug a paw into the depths of her knapsack to retrieve Durhrigg's small vial of Pyrekin Panacea that had saved her life when the deadwalker Perefaris had poisoned her a few moon-cycles before.

"Take this," Katja said, placing the troll's golden vial into the dryad's trembling hands. "If there is a way to restore your sister, use it."

Zahra stared at her. "Katja, I... Thank you...I am sorry for the things that I—"

The werecat raised a paw. "You were right to say them. In any event, it doesn't matter now. Just promise me that you'll be safe and keep Felan, Vraelth, and Verdagon out of danger as well as you can."

Zahra nodded, and then gave Katja a hug in thanks. "I will. I promise."

"We know you will," Daya'lyn said as he embraced her. He bowed to Vraelth and then clasped Felan's forearm as the werewolf clasped his in return. The two males searched each other's eyes a moment before either spoke.

"Swear to me that you'll protect them as well as you can,"

Felan murmured.

"I swear it, Felan."

The werewolf nodded. "You can do this, Daya'lyn. Just remember not to carry your burdens alone."

The hybrid nodded. "Stay safe. I'll see you in Vihous soon."

Embraces, bows, and arm clasps ran the length of all Ring members and packmates present. Then the others left the three members of the Inquisition onboard Nascius's boat and waved as the vessel steered out of the harbor and headed south. Katja stared at the dock until its occupants seemed the size of gnats.

Lauraisha stood beside Katja at the railing, but said nothing until the skinshifter sighed and looked away at last. The dreamdrifter gripped her shoulder in comfort. "You will see him again."

"I hope so." Katja bowed her head. "The Creator knows how much I hope."

Lauraisha smiled but said nothing more. The two stood in companionable silence on the upper deck as the boat rolled on through the white fog. Daya'lyn eventually joined them and pulled the leather map out of its protective sheath.

"I need to show you the route I have in mind before we make landfall."

The three of them sat down on the planked deck with the map showing the entire Sylvan Continent spread between them.

"I had thought to take the pass here." Daya'lyn pointed to the jagged angles indicating the the Nyghe sol Dyvesé mountain range road just north of the Clan Eerondus aeries. "We can then use the Merrow Road to journey to Vihous..." He traced his finger along a narrow line stretching overland to the border road of the southern coastal kingdom. "Once in Vihous, we can book passage on a ship to the Tyglesean capital city of Kaylere and proceed from there."

Lauraisha glared at him. "Proceed from there? You make it seem so simple. Of course I like the idea of moving ourselves up through Vihous, as it will offer a safer passage west and should prove less confrontational than pushing into Tyglesea straight from the Sylvan Forest, but the credibility we will need to do this will cost an exorbitant amount of time, money, and contacts."

Daya'lyn frowned at her. "I am the Sylvan Inquisitor; what more credibility could we possibly need?"

She shook her head. "You forget that while the Ring of Sorcerers' edicts are law to most clans and kingdoms associated with the Sylvan Orders, they hold little to no sway in Tyglesea. My father broke ties with the rest of the Sylvan Orders once he became king. He oversaw the construction of the Guard Wall and border watchtowers to ensure that Tyglesea would remain autonomous and separated from all other Sylvans—especially magic users. Tyglesea remains friendly with Vihous only because the country is mainly human in its population and because those humans provide the only source of regular trade that Tygleseans recognize."

Daya'lyn arched a black eyebrow. "So King Kaylor won't allow trade with anyone other than Vihous, and yet most of the goods and services that he acquires from Vihous actually come from elsewhere on this continent."

The princess nodded. "Such is the hypocrisy inherent to Tyglesean politics. It isn't convenient to admit the impracticality of cutting ties with all other countries and clans, so instead they just lie about it.

"In any event, Vihous is the far safer route into Tyglesea and the leaders there are far more likely to aid us in our mission. That is, if we can gain access to them. With the ongoing war, I have no idea how much effort that will require."

"I think Holis's vow will prove useful to us in that regard," Katja said, studying the map. "After all, the shadowshaper mage is a high-ranking member of the Vihous Embassy in Kaylere."

Lauraisha blinked. "He is?"

"That is what Joce'lynn told me."

"Well, then…it will certainly help. I assume you want to find the nearest of Vihous's port cities and sail from there to Kaylere to save, Daya'lyn."

"That would be preferable."

"It should be doable. What do you think, Katja? Do you know the road to which Daya'lyn is referring?"

Katja studied the map. She clicked her tongue against the

roof of her maw and traced the line over and over again. "No. I don't know this way, but I know its legends. The Merrow Road is the most direct way to travel to the Vihous capital city from here, but it is also very dangerous. If we use it, we will cross through swampy terrain and will be forced through both ogre and naiad territories." She scanned the other roads with increasing frustration. "Yet, if we take any of the other more northern roads, we will likely run afoul of deadwalkers and the war. The last that I heard, the dryad and werewolf territories are overrun with the monsters, although Otwenia did mention that Reithrgar Pass is back under Sylvan control."

Daya'lyn nodded. "True, but I wouldn't risk that pass and stray so close to Caerwyn lands. Daeryn and his allies will likely expect us to pass through that area and seek shelter with my father along our journey. One encounter with Daeryn on that road is enough."

"How do you know that Daeryn knows we're taking this journey at all?" asked Lauraisha.

He watched her a moment. "Since my brother holds a mental bond with Katja through his possession of part of her spearhead, he could also know when and where she moves. As long as we stay well within the guardianship of allies, he cannot attack. That is one of the few advantages we have against him now."

Katja's ears flattened against her tawny-furred head. "I do not like this, Daya'lyn. The Merrow Road is teeming with lakes, bogs, and marshes. At the least, we'll likely have to deal with brolaghans, basals, and wasp willows. At the worst, we'll be ambushed by Turned deadwalkers like nixies or oni."

"I believe that is the true reason that the Ring of Sorcerers' members gave us the nacken, Katja. Besides Tyron, I can think of no better steeds to have in such country... Besides, the naiads and the ogres will not easily give up any of their number to Luther's forces."

"I still do not like this."

"I don't either, but I fear we have no alternative."

Lauraisha peered over the werecat's shoulder. "Daya'lyn, what if we took this road here for part of the journey? The map shows it running just south of the Merrow Road on the edge of the wetlands before looping back to merge with the

Merrow Road just before Vihous."

Daya'lyn and Katja studied the map again, visually tracing the thread that was Lauraisha's prescribed path. "I know nothing of this road, but it does appear at least a little safer if a bit longer than the Merrow Road. What do you think, Katja?"

The werecat frowned. "It will cut even further through the heart of naiad territory, but I prefer dealing with them than more brolaghans."

"Agreed," Daya'lyn said. "We will follow the Merrow Road until it meets the Naiad Passage, and then take the passage west until it loops back toward Vihous. There, we can use the last part of the Merrow Road to cross into Vihous."

The male carefully rolled up the hide map and slid it back into its tube before capping the case and looping its strap over his shoulder.

"Land, ho!" Captain Nascius shouted from the tiller less than half of an hour later.

The fog parted around the boat and they could see the lake's Southern Mooring platform and its adjacent snow-strewn sandbar. Two sailors came up the ladder from below deck and jumped to the dock as the vessel pulled alongside it. They deftly tied the ship to the platform with frost white ropes and waited as three other crew members moved the wooden ramp into place so the members of the Inquisition could disembark.

Katja pulled her robes and heavy cloak more tightly around her before helping Lauraisha and the deck-hands with their mounts and supplies as Daya'lyn paid the captain for his services.

"Thank you, Nascius, for your assistance." Daya'lyn retrieved two gold runelings from his belt purse and passed them to the male.

"Gladly, Inquisitor. Creator's blessings and protection to you on your journey." Nascius bowed and Daya'lyn returned the gesture.

"May His gracious hand guide you, My Sir."

Katja and Lauraisha also bowed before checking their saddles' girths and mounting their steeds. Daya'lyn climbed onto Tyron's back and took the lead—trotting down the platform to the snow-strewn road beyond with the two mounted females and two pack steeds in close pursuit. The party's steeds held a brisk trot until the flat lands surrounding the lake gave way to the rolling foothills of the mountains west of the Southern Mooring. The five mounts' gait became a quick walk as the party ascended the hills; a speed set more for the comfort of the unaccustomed riders than their stalwart steeds.

The snow deepened as they ascended the trail. At several points, Lauraisha was forced to melt the heavier drifts before they could continue. Katja meanwhile kept her cloak hood pulled away from her ears so that she could continually survey their surroundings with all her senses. She hated snow almost as much as she hated rain. Snow often muffled sound, and the cold weather that often instigated it made her nose numb and therefore less sensitive.

The weather stayed relatively calm until they began their ascent of the first mountain. By the time they made camp early that evening, the wildly swirling snow had made sights, sounds, and smells all but impossible to discern. Katja found the group a sheltered alcove of rock on the northern side of the road just big enough for three grown beings to huddle inside. They tied off the four nacken and one horse to a gnarled tree growing in the cleft of a leeward facing cliff, removed their tack, and brushed them down before draping each in a clean, waterproof blanket. Katja fed the nacken with the meat supplies and gave Tyron a portion of grain while Daya'lyn and Lauraisha gathered tinder for a campfire.

When the werecat finally sat down by Daya'lyn's newly constructed fire, Lauraisha had already set a pot of stewed vegetables to boil on the hot stones near the flames. Daya'lyn tossed a piece of the unused dried meat to the werecat, who devoured it greedily.

She shifted her weight and growled. "Three moon-cycles of sleeping on a cushion have made me soft. Jierira, I hate this. One day's ride and I'm already sore."

Lauraisha bobbed her head. "I feel a little ridiculous because even I am somewhat stiff!"

Daya'lyn said nothing; he simply stared at the campfire's flames. After a moment, he rose slowly from his sitting position and walked over to Tyron, who was tied slightly apart from the nacken. He patted the huge sorrel stallion and seemed to whisper something in the beast's perked ear. The horse whinnied and moved so that his neck was extended toward the mage. With his back to the females, Daya'lyn bent close to the horse. Katja heard the horse's soft grunt as the hybrid's fangs sliced through fur and flesh, then the rhythmic succession of sucks and swallows as Daya'lyn drank his evening meal.

Lauraisha gritted her teeth and turned away. Katja watched as her closest friend tried to ignore the soft sounds of Daya'lyn's quenching his thirst from her horse. The human's delicate hands shook as she stirred her meat and tuber stew. Katja squeezed her other hand with her only somewhat steadier paw.

The Ring and our two Pyrekin must have known what they were doing when they gave him the rank of Inquisitor, Katja murmured through their minds' bond. *No one else among the mages could ever come so near to evil and still resist it as he does every day.*

Lauraisha nodded, but her expression was still troubled. *I know but, what if he fails?*

Katja sighed and answered ruefully. "Then he is no worse than me."

The human looked at her with sorrow in her sky blue eyes. "Oh, Katja." She hugged the werecat.

* * *

The next morning dawned clear and white. The three huddled packmates awoke stiff and cold to find snow piled up against the canvas tarp that Katja had tied across the entrance of their alcove. The winds had shifted enough during the night to bury them despite Katja's and Daya'lyn's best efforts.

Katja growled at the wall of white after she pulled the tarp away. "Perfect."

"Are we trapped?" Lauraisha asked in between yawns.

Katja stopped clawing and kicking at the packed snow long enough to look over her shoulder as the human stood. "Jierira, really? You, a fireforger, are going to ask me whether we're trapped by *snow*?"

"Be kind to her, Katja; she is barely awake," Daya'lyn murmured as he stood from his crouched sleeping position.

He stretched and then touched a gloved hand to one of their unused torches and held it to the upper area where the werecat had dug a hole. Katja grabbed their water skins, uncorked them, and shoved them under the new stream of water Daya'lyn was making with the heat from the torch.

Lauraisha frowned. "Wouldn't it be easier just to melt it with conjured flame?"

He raised an eyebrow at her. "I'd rather just light the torch; that takes less of my energy than melting the entire wall myself. Always conserve your strength when you can."

"Oh."

She nodded when all three of them had filled. By that point, half of the blockage was gone, so Katja was able to climb out and reconnoiter the rest of their campsite. She waved to the others when she had found no fresh tracks of anything other than a hare and no other signs of danger.

She wrapped her robes more securely around her furry torso for added warmth and then went to work brushing and feeding the horses while Daya'lyn stoked the campfire embers back to life and thawed what was left of Lauraisha's stew from the previous night.

After the morning eat, the three packed up the camp. Once the princess had doused the campfire and Katja had washed their cups in the snow, the group set off into the clear morning at an easy trot. Katja contemplated the deceptive softness of the white world as they trotted through it and sniffed the crisp, clean air. Winter was an arduous season, but it did have its beauty.

"How long do you expect us to be in the mountains, Daya'lyn?" Lauraisha asked as they walked their steeds up a steep incline.

"It will likely take us the better part of two weeks if the road stays this choked with snow."

Katja growled as she leaned forward in the saddle. "You anticipate that much hindrance to our pace? I thought Si'lyn marked these mounts as conditioned for traveling up to seventeen leagues a day."

"He did...on flat land. With the terrain as buckled at it is, we will be lucky to cover five leagues at most. Besides, our steeds might have the endurance to travel great distances without excessive fatigue or soreness, but we riders do not—at least not yet. I hope to speed our course once we reach more level ground."

To save time, the three beings and their beasts had their midday eat while on the move. Even with relief stops as their only breaks, the trio still set evening camp only five and a half leagues west of their morning position.

"Jierira, this is frustrating," Katja growled as she tied a canvas cloth between two intersecting fallen pines. The result was a weatherproof shelter that stayed secure and fairly warm even in high winds.

"I know," Daya'lyn responded at he lit his pile of tinder with a small flame. "I promise the pace will improve."

Lauraisha sighed as she wiped down the mounts. "At least I have plenty of time to plan my defense."

"Defense?" The werecat asked as she hammered a stubborn iron stake into tree wood. She then crawled under the canvas and began to plug dry pine needles into any drafty holes.

"Defense for my trial," Lauraisha said as she put their sleeping furs outside the cross-shaped tent.

"What trial?" she said as she unrolled a fur.

"Katja, upon my return to Tyglesea, I will be charged and tried for sedition."

Daya'lyn looked up from where he sat stoking the fire. "What!"

"My father wants me dead, remember? My 'stealing' Damya's Keystone from the country is a perfect excuse for King Kaylor to execute me."

Daya'lyn sighed. "Lauraisha, you cannot be charged with any crimes now that you are a part of the Inquisition. You are immune to all authorities other than myself and members of the Ring of Sorcerers, all of whom are very glad you took the sacred jewel and helped awaken its inhabitant in the first place. None outside our circle can detain you without instigating an act of war."

The Tyglesean princess gave him an exasperated sigh. "As I've told you before, Tyglesea's government will not recognize the Ring's authority, because they hate Sylvan mages. And Tyglesea may well be at war with the Ring already. If Perefaris's ravings were accurate, the kingdom has already been infiltrated by deadwalkers. Whether or not they are posing as humans, we don't know."

"Were they when you fled?"

"I never saw a deadwalker while I was still living in Castle Summersted. However, the kingdom's politics were drastically changing. Kaylor was allowing some true brigands to serve in the Tyglesean Regiments. He had increased unprovoked searches and seizures for mages, magical artifacts, and other 'weapons' all over Tyglesea—even among the Kaylere priesthood. Our citizens were ready to take up arms over the whole thing, but of course that would have been an impossible fight since it's been illegal for ordinary citizens to keep or bear arms for the entirety of my father's reign.

"I was at least protected from the impromptu searches by my title as princess, but after I heard the rumors, I never went anywhere without having Damya's Sapphire hidden on my person—and even that was dangerous. If my father had ever found it when he—" she swallowed and changed the subject. "Mother had told me that the gem was linked to powerful magic even though she never spoke of its true purpose, so I took it with me when I fled the country."

Daya'lyn considered her as he dropped oil and herbs into a pan and set it to warm on the stones ringing the campfire. "Lauraisha, why did your mother give you the Sapphire Keystone in the first place?"

"She told me that she knew I had mage blood running through my veins and that if someone must guard that stone, it should be me."

"How did she come by it?" Katja asked.

The princess shook her head. "She only told me that a woman of some importance had given it to her in secret. I have no idea how my father found out about its existence, but the flogging he gave my mother for losing me and the stone when I fled Castle Summersted was one of the worst I have ever witnessed."

"You saw it? How?"

Tears stood in her eyes. "In my dreams, I have seen it many times."

A fragment of memory surfaced in Katja's mind of a

human female tied to a pole, agony lacing her face as each whiplash bit into the pale skin of her back. Katja put a paw on her shoulder. "I am so sorry," she whispered.

Lauraisha's jaw was firm as she wiped a tear away. "So am I."

Daya'lyn cleared his throat. "Lauraisha...did you ever see the woman who gave your mother Damya's Keystone?"

"I know her face only from my mother's dreams."

"What did she look like?" Katja asked.

"She was human with long black hair and fiery blue eyes like yours," Lauraisha said as she and Katja sat across the fire from Daya'lyn. "She looked to be of Vihous heritage...tall with dark olive-toned skin and a curvy figure."

Unbidden, another memory came to Katja's mind. This one was of a blood-smeared human female hiding between a thorn bush and the ruin of a caravan wagon. A single orange flame whispered into view in the female fireforger's palm before it guttered and died. The Víchí stalking her hissed in triumph as she slid into unconsciousness.

"Creator, help me!" Katja whispered involuntarily.

"Katja?" Daya'lyn put a gloved hand on her shoulder and gently shook her. "Are you well?"

Katja shook her head and sent the fragment of memory to Lauraisha through their bond with an unspoken question.

Lauraisha frowned at her then gazed at the male. "Yes, that is the same female. I thought she looked familiar! Daya'lyn, is the dark-haired female in both of these memories your mother?"

He gave her a sad smile as he nodded. "She must have given your mother, Manasa, the Sapphire Keystone during her journey to Tyglesea before she died." Daya'lyn groaned and rubbed a gloved hand over his pale face. "Fangs, was that really how my father looked before he was Redeemed?"

Katja looked at Lauraisha and then back at the hybrid. "You tell us. Lauraisha and I experienced that memory several weeks before Felan and Zahra accidentally led us to Caerwyn Castle and we met you and your father. It hasn't surfaced again until now."

Daya'lyn frowned. "That must be my father. It is strange that the memory isn't from either of their points of view, though."

Katja nodded. "There must have been another being present, one whom neither of them noticed."

Daya'lyn's eyes narrowed. "Or whom he chose to ignore."

"How exactly was Caleb Redeemed?"

The male looked at Katja as he handed her a raw piece of meat to eat. "You really have been lax in her education, haven't you?"

Katja shrugged. "I have done my best, but not even I know the full account of this tale."

Daya'lyn opened his mouth, glanced at Lauraisha, and then shook his head. "I would do you a disservice if I tried to explain it. You both really should ask my father."

She watched him a moment. "Why are you so reluctant to discuss this?"

He studied her a moment. "Why are you so reluctant to discuss certain things about your father?"

She matched his stare. "I asked you first."

A deep sadness filled Daya'lyn's eyes and Katja knew that his grief over his mother's death was pushing the male to tears. "Lauraisha, let it go."

The human looked from one to the other and sighed. "Fine."

"In any event, Lauraisha," Katja said, changing the subject, "if you can't rely on diplomatic immunity, how do you plan to avoid the charges of sedition?"

"I don't."

"What?" Daya'lyn nearly dropped his cooking pan into the fire.

"Look, if I am put on trial, that will provide the best distraction to allow you, Daya'lyn, to do your investigating as Inquisitor while Katja sneaks around sniffing out any deadwalker trouble. If the three of us go into Tyglesea brandishing our status as mage diplomats, we will be politically blocked at every turn and likely killed in a damp alleyway long before we can discover anything of use. However, if the Sylvan Inquisitor himself brings me back to Tyglesea to be tried for my crimes by my own people as a show of good faith, Kaylor will see you as an ally and open the entire kingdom to you."

Daya'lyn glared at her. "I am not sacrificing you for *any* reason, nor will I *ever* ally myself with that villain!"

"You won't sacrifice me, Daya'lyn. My charges will be dismissed for lack of evidence. After all, Damya's Keystone can be slipped to my mother or one of my brothers during the very first throne room audience."

Katja's ears were flat. "And if you're still found to be a traitor, you'll burn at the stake!"

Lauraisha frowned and looked at Daya'lyn. "Can I even die by fire since I'm a fireforger?"

He shook his head. "No, not unless you commit sacrificial suicide through the rite of Crawhmongue like Aribem did during the First War of Ages or the Kirni Kingdom griffins did during the Second. However, you aren't a high-ranking fireforger yet, so a hot fire will still prove very painful for you to endure."

"But you would rescue me long before my burning at the stake came to fruition."

Daya'lyn pinched his eyebrows together with his gloved fingers in exasperation. "That is beside the point. There is still too much risk! If something goes wrong—"

"Oh, like our ship being fired upon before we even reach Kaylere? If Kaylor discovers that a mage Inquisitor is on board, you can bet the entire Tyglesean treasury that he will have the offending ship rammed to the sandy bottom of the sea rather than see it anchored in his own harbor."

"That is such a pleasant thought." Katja growled sarcastically.

"Look, the point is that my way works better than yours. Therefore logic suggests that we follow my plan first and resort to an open investigation only in the grimmest circumstance."

Daya'lyn sighed and passed the cooking pan to her before taking a drink from his own blood-and-wine skin. "We will see what Holis suggests when we meet with him and the other leaders of Vihous. For now, I will make no decisions. We might as well get some nourishment and sleep. We have a long road to travel yet."

Katja nodded and then looked down forlornly at the pan. Its meat was charred as black as a cinder.

VII
THE NAIAD PASSAGE

True to Daya'lyn's word, their trek across the buckled terrain of the Nyghe sol Dyvesé mountain range took a day less than a fortnight. By the time they reached the western foothills, the three riders and their mounts were traveling barely seven or eight leagues a day. On the relatively flat country along the Merrow Road east of the marches, however, the weather improved and the leagues crossed stretched to fifteen a day. Daya'lyn kept the group on a relatively hard pace with each midday eat always taken in the saddle. Katja learned how to take occasional short naps while riding to boost her energy, but otherwise she kept her ears perked and her eyes moving for any dangers. She spent half of her time either riding with her packmates or running and scouting ahead of them. They met a few refugees along the road, but little else. She smelled no indications of deadwalkers, nor could she find any signs of battle in these lands, but once in a while a streak of crimson would flash at the bare edge of Katja's vision and cause her hackles to rise. She knew that they were being watched, but she could never discern how or by whom.

On the fourteenth day, the group deviated south from the main Merrow Road and followed the Naiad Passage into the marshlands—setting up their overnight camps on the solid ground alongside the main roadway. Setting camp so close to the open highway was a dangerous gamble since it afforded them little in the way of concealing cover, but Katja and Daya'lyn reasoned that it was far worse for the group to camp on the softer ground near the bogs and risk the possibility of trapping their steeds, supplies, or themselves in a quagmire. To make matters worse, winter's snow had finally yielded to spring rains, and the members of the Inquisition found themselves soaked and chilled more often than they were warm and dry. As they made camp each night, the werecat desperately missed having Zahra along since the dryad's sproutsinging abilities would be invaluable in aiding the group find safer, drier places to shelter.

Even so, having the nacken proved quite useful. The strange water horses seemed to be natural deterrents to many of the larger predators dwelling in this part of the continent, so while the group's nightly camps were wet, they also proved far safer than Katja had expected. The steeds' nimble agility in water also helped the group ford streams with a fair amount of ease. Despite her unease around horses in general and these in particular, Katja found herself actually enjoying her ride with Glashtin each day.

On their tenth day following the Naiad Passage and twenty-ninth day of travel, the weather improved and the Inquisition came to a curious sight. The roadway curved and then sloped downward into a thicket of pale green trees whose whip-like branches blanketed the roadway.

Daya'lyn halted the party and dismounted, tossing Tyron's reigns to Lauraisha. "We can go no further."

"What? Why?"

"These trees mark the boundary where Naiad Territory crosses this road. We will need the naiads' permission to cross."

Lauraisha frowned. "Couldn't you just demand passage for us since you are the Inquisitor?"

"I could, but I would rather observe proper manners. Besides, I need some information and these naiads may know the whereabouts of what I seek."

Katja looked at him. "What are you seeking?"

Daya'lyn's azure eyes met hers, but he said nothing. Instead, he turned to the edge of the trees on the northern roadside and bowed deeply. "I am Daya'lyn Calebson of Caerwyn Castle, fireforger mage master and newly appointed Inquisitor of the Ring of Sorcerers. I and my entourage seek an audience with your Naya on a matter most urgent. Please convey our greetings to her."

Katja perked her ears for a response and heard nothing. Then a low-pitched thrum vibrated from the trees' trunks. It vibrated the ground beneath them and then rippled through the brackish puddles of water in the roadway ditches. Then all was once again still.

"They have heard us," Daya'lyn said as he took the reins from Lauraisha and stood beside his steed.

"How do you know that and how do you know the naiads' rituals?" the princess asked.

"Mother taught me some of their customs."

Katja swiveled her eyes and ears in all directions. She heard the gentle sound of water meandering past plants, but saw no ponds—only the wall of trees with green trunks so pale that they seemed to glow incandescently. The trees were the likeness of willows in shape, yet held not a scrap of wood on their stubby trunks and lank branches. The seemingly languid limbs would twitch to life when so much as a leaf would pass by—unsheathing the pink venomous barbs hidden within each translucent tentacle—and strike with appallingly fatal precision.

"An apt defense," Katja said while watching the swift demise of a particularly foolish sparrow.

"Truly!" Lauraisha shuddered. "What are these things?"

"They are called Wasp Willows," Daya'lyn answered while ogling the plants with reverent fear. "The naiads call them that at any rate, but I have been told that these are not really willows at all. In point of fact, they aren't even plants. When the naiads settled the Azuralle Lake long ago, it is said they did so by swamping the land between here and the sea with water and—through their peculiar magic—somehow transporting many of their sea creatures with them. These strange 'trees' are one of the creatures that survived the transition between environments."

Lauraisha looked at Daya'lyn in confusion. "You mean these Wasp Willows are…erdeling beasts?"

His head bowed. "They are certainly not beings."

Lauraisha looked intently at the Wasp Willows, narrowing her eyes as she watched their movements. "They remind me of...oh, how do I translate this...the sea-stingers that sometimes wash up on our beaches at home."

The hybrid smiled. "I believe the Wasp Willows are actually descended from your sea-stingers, which is why they look somewhat similar. The legend is that the naiads somehow changed sea-stingers so that they could live outside of water. As long as the willows can still soak their lower tentacles in water, they can survive."

"And so the naiads have a perfect land-based system of defense built right into their lake home shores," Katja supplied.

"Wonderful," said the human. "Now how do we get past them?"

Daya'lyn shook his head. "We don't."

Moments later, the wind shifted and Katja caught the scent of clean water as it drifted through the Wasp Willow branches. The curious tentacles pulled back to reveal a narrow path winding between the road and the southern shore of Azuralle Lake.

Katja's ears flattened as a dreamy voice echoed from the lake. "Come, weary travelers, come and rest with us."

"Do we dare comply?" Lauraisha whispered.

Daya'lyn stared resolutely at the narrow passage. He pulled the Inquisitor's and Fireforger's Crests out from under his tunic and then led Tyron forward on foot by the reins. The females followed his example and together they trekked single-file through the thicket of death toward the calm waters of the lake. Not one Wasp Willow unsheathed a barb as they passed; however, the tree-like beasts did shift their iridescent white limbs to cover the trail behind the party as they moved closer toward the naiads' sheltered home.

When the trio finally stood on the sandy shore overlooking the lake, Katja saw for the first time that its clear surface was strewn with lily pads of all different types. The largest lily pads were each a body-length across—as wide as Katja was tall. Their golden-green surfaces looked wrinkled and leathery while their curled crimson edges were tipped with curved, yellow thorns. The smaller lily pads ranged from light to darkest green in hue and the plants featured a variety of yellow, violet, scarlet, and pale pink lotus blossoms in full bloom despite the cool weather. Tiny minnows and perch swam in the water tracing rippling circles between the leaves.

Katja sniffed the air and frowned. She crouched down, skimmed her paw through the surprisingly warm water lapping at her feet, and sniffed the liquid.

"Katja, what are you doing?" Daya'lyn asked in alarm.

Satisfied, she poured the remaining liquid back into the sand by the lake and stood. "This lake is freshwater, not saltwater."

"What is the significance of that?" Lauraisha asked.

Katja flicked her ears. "The significance is that the naiads have adapted themselves and their transported sea creatures to a freshwater environment. I had no idea that any sea dwelling beings could do that. This is incredible!"

"We think so as well."

Katja's head jerked in the direction of the newcomer's voice and saw a naiad's translucent blue figure rising out of the water as she waded ashore to greet them.

"Welcome, weary travelers, to our home," she said as she raised a webbed-fingered hand to her chest in formal greeting. "I am Neamyntha, Chief Naya and Mistress of this lake's naiad community."

Daya'lyn, Lauraisha, and Katja all bowed with their palms raised in respect, and then introduced themselves in turn as other naiads watched them curiously from just below the lake water's surface. So transparent were they that Katja had barely noticed those floating under the water until their iridescent white hair broke the lake's surface, casting dreamy ripples in all directions. Curiosity flitted behind their gazes and leisure ruled their movements.

"Such lovely names," Neamyntha whispered as she watched them with eyes which glowed like the flickers from a dying candle. She raised a gentle hand to touch Daya'lyn's cheek. "Daya'lyn Calebson, you hold your father's bearing, but you have your mother's eyes. Do you harbor her spark as well?"

Daya'lyn's smile was tight as he produced a single white flame for her inspection.

The smile that Neamyntha gave him in return was sincere. "Thank you for humoring my request, Inquisitor. In times of war, we can take few things for granted, even a fireforger's crest. Know that today we sighted deadwalkers hunting in the Ten Fang Marshes northeast of our lake. They seek you, but they cannot circumvent the Wasp Willows."

"Some deadwalkers can fly, My Madam," he reminded her.

"Yes, but none of these can. For now, we are safe. Come, leave your steeds in the care of my fellow naiads and come dine in the shallows with us this eve. We will make certain that you and your allies feed on the finest fish and the most wholesome vegetation during our evening meal."

Lauraisha cleared her throat. "With all due respect, My Madam, we are air breathers and cannot hope to hold air in our lungs long enough to sustain a meal in the watery depths as you suggest."

"Of course you can, my dear. We will simply lend you larger lungs for the occasion."

The naiad flicked her translucent, webbed fingers and three naiads swam out of the water holding three inflated bubbles made from a strong clear substance for which Katja had no name. Neamyntha took the bubbles, checked their attached breathing tubes, and then gave one to each of the three packmates.

"These should last you for an evening at least."

The three bowed in thanks and proceeded to shed their bulkier outer garments for added ease when swimming. Katja did not like the notion of submerging herself underwater for so long, but she kept her grumblings to herself. The last thing she wished to do was insult their hostess, particularly when a mere twitch of Neamyntha's fins could signal their deaths.

"Do you trust them?" she asked Daya'lyn in an undertone once Neamyntha had slid back into the water.

"Yes." Daya'lyn politely turned his back to her while she and Lauraisha stripped and readjusted their undergarments. "They were close allies of my mother's long ago, and she always spoke of their generous hospitality."

"Let us hope that their blessings toward Marga extend to her son, then," the werecat growled before shortening the lengths of the necklaces holding her three spearheads and Feliconas Clan signet crest so that they could not float off over her head in the water. She stepped back to the lake garbed only in her customary loincloth while Lauraisha favored a short, wrapped skirt, under-leggings, and a linen cloth that she wrapped tight around her torso and tied much like the tourniquet she had worn after Katja had mauled her a moon-cycle ago.

Katja shuddered and turned to the water lapping against the stone outcropping on which they stood. Once Daya'lyn had stripped down to a pair of breeches, all three waded into the naiads' watery world. Naiads pulled them deeper into the water and held onto their lower limbs to anchor them while Neamyntha instructed them how to use their air bubbles to breathe. Once all three packmates felt comfortable with their new apparatuses, Neamyntha led them between the twining roots of the giant lily pads to the naiad city residing along the lake's sandy bottom.

The naiad world was one of bubbles. Root-bound bubbles formed the main structures of their dwellings and luminescent algae bubbles formed their main sources of light. Even their furnishings were composed of hundreds of tiny, round bubbles, which looked to be made of the same clear substance holding Katja's supply of air. The werecat marveled at the sight as she and the others swam after Neamyntha toward the city's center and the largest bubble of all. They swam into the bubble through a large, unfilled gap between roots and found seats among the carved shell benches adhered to the inside of the bubble's clear walls at all elevations. A large number of naiads also sat inside the bubble chamber. Most were curious onlookers, although a few appeared to be rather important members of the community; or at least Katja assumed as much, based on the large number of shells and beads adorning their delicate necks and heads.

Bubbly laughter and excited chatter filled the chamber. Since the packmates had no education in the language of Napune ven Asterai, most of the naiads' conversations meant nothing to them. They simply sat in polite silence and bowed to the curious.

Soon naiads laden with thin spears packed with skewered fish swam out of an adjacent bubble and offered food to those seated. The servers went from bench to bench allowing beings to pull their choice meal straight off of spears. There were even spears laden with different pond plants, of which Lauraisha delightedly sampled even if Katja and Daya'lyn could not. After a few moments, Katja successfully tested a system of timing that allowed her to eat and breathe in quick succession without the fear of choking on her food. The fish was wonderful and raw, yet fresh enough that even Lauraisha could consume it without fear of stomach sickness.

After the naiads and their guests had finished their eat and deposited the remaining bones in the woven reed basket hooked to their bench, Neamyntha and two heavily adorned naiads swam over to sit with them. She taught them how to use the air bubble nozzle's release to talk and then introduced the two naiads beside her as Eureshra of the Ten Fang Marshes and Helerha of the Suuthe Marshes.

"You traveled this way, Inquisitor, for a specific purpose, did you not?" Neamyntha said.

"We did."

"Tell us of your quest, then."

"We seek safe passage through the marshes to the western kingdom of Vihous, then on to Tyglesea. I also seek information on a more personal level about my mother's mission to this part of the Sylvan Continent many winters ago."

"Of the first, I can certainly help. Of the second, I can make no promises."

Daya'lyn bobbed his head. "Understood. I had hoped that you could tell me some of the locations where my mother stopped on her journey to hide the twelve legendary Keystones."

"Marga has told you nothing?"

"I know the locations of two, but she died before she told me where she had hidden the others. By chance—or perhaps fate—we have discovered and awakened two others. One is the green dragon Verdagon, who was awakened through the Emerald; the other is the firesprite Damya, who was awakened through the Sapphire. Both have expressed an urgent plea that we seek out the other ten Keystones during the course of our mission to Tyglesea, so that we can awaken them all when the time is right."

Neamyntha blinked her lash-less eyelids. "You speak

truly?"

"He does, Neamyntha," Damya's voice echoed from Lauraisha's Sapphire Keystone. "I, Damya, confirm his request."

Neamyntha's sad eyes swiveled to the glowing blue gem as it floated before Lauraisha's wrapped chest. The naiad bowed toward it and murmured, "A Pyrekin's wish is my joy to fulfill."

The gem twinkled with Damya's thanks and then ceased to glow. All was sudden silence within the chamber.

Neamyntha pushed away from the bench. "Please come with me, then."

She and her two allies swam out of the huge chamber bubble with Katja, Lauraisha, and Daya'lyn. Neamyntha led the five across the underwater city to her private chamber bubble and bade them to make themselves comfortable while she fetched a curious metal box from beneath the sand comprising her bubble's flat floor. She pressed it into Daya'lyn's grip. "This has been in my possession since your mother's second visit. I believe it is now yours by right of succession."

Daya'lyn frowned and opened the sunsilver case—pristine even after many years of underwater storage—and pulled out a sunsilver chain and mount holding a round opal the size of a walnut.

"The Unicorn's Opal," he said in excitement and awe.

"We were instructed to guard it in secret until the times were dire enough to reveal it. With deadwalkers at our northern borders and a pair of Pyrekin awakened, that time has come."

"Thank you," Daya'lyn whispered as he opened the chain's clasp and slipped the necklace around his neck.

Neamyntha inclined her head. "Master Daya'lyn, I know the whereabouts of only one other Keystone, the Chrysoberyl of Cabrica. Your mother—Creator, keep her—visited many places while in possession of the Keystones. I know for a fact that she delivered the Chrysoberyl of Cabrica to the Apotharni Clan of centaurs at Cheiron before she brought the White Opal of Azmar to us. I have heard rumors that she deposited Keystones with the High Priest of Tyglesea, the Vizier of

Vihous, and the Feliconas Clan of werecats. These are only rumors, mind you. I have no way to confirm them."

"Well, the one in Tyglesea is certainly confirmed," Lauraisha said holding up the Sapphire of Damya.

"Indeed."

"Can you remember any other place that my mother may have gone with the sacred stones?"

Neamyntha frowned. "Are there no stones left at Caerwyn Castle?"

Daya'lyn shook his head. "Father told me that she had successfully hidden all of the gems from the Mage Council traitors before he had even met her. She was traveling back from Mount Sol'ece when he and his deadwalkers attacked her caravan. They found no Keystones and so Father never possessed one—either before or after he was Redeemed."

"Then perhaps Queen Mother Zahlathra knows the whereabouts of one. You should also contact the Aevry elves, and the Silenus of each of the satyr clans. She had frequent dealings with all three races."

Daya'lyn bowed his head. "Thank you."

Neamyntha smiled. "Gladly would I help you, Daya'lyn. Your mother was very dear to me and I mourn her passing even now."

"As do I and my father."

"What of your brother Daeryn?"

Daya'lyn's eyes and mouth hardened. "He has Fallen to the Víchí."

Neamyntha and the other two naiads bowed their heads. "We are truly sorry for your family's loss—of your mother and of your brother."

Daya'lyn inclined his head curtly. "Thank you for your kindness."

"Always." Neamyntha watched him a moment more and then gazed at his partially deflated air bubble. "I believe it is time for the three of you to leave our tranquil waters and breathe once again under your own sky. Come, I will lead you back to the shore."

The sun had begun to set and the full moon had already commenced its ascent when the three packmates climbed onto the lake shore. Neamyntha and her fellows encouraged their guests to sleep on the lake's large lily pads and then bid them goodnight. Katja forced her body to remain in its current form until their hostess departed and then helped Lauraisha set up the canvas tent on shore for some privacy. The three took turns using the tent to change into warmer clothing. Lauraisha then climbed onto a floating lily pad and pushed it away from the shore with the naiads' provided paddle. She curled up under a fur to sleep upon the gentle waves while Daya'lyn drank his fill of Tyron's blood and Katja began her skinshift into her human form.

The skinshifter's transformation into a human was more painful than usual. The werecat lay on a pile of furs inside the tent and did her best to endure the metamorphosis. The hardest part she had to cope with emotionally was the loss of her fur, which was always the first to go. Before her mage training, her skin would itch in a thousand places simultaneously as the fur came out tuft by tuft, minute by minute, until all of it was out save the hair on the crown and back of her head. Felan had taught her how to meld the fur into her body in the same way she had learned to meld her bones into the shapes needed for human hands and feet. This melding meant for less itching or bone aching most of the time. Tonight, however, Katja's prehensile tail throbbed and itched as it thickened and elongated—the exact opposite of its normal behavior during a skinshift. Her paws also stayed as they were rather than transforming into the long-fingered, clawless hands to which she had grown accustomed. They were therefore little use in the subtle work of scratching her tingling tail.

Next, Katja's eyes, ears and nose all lost their sensitivity and she suddenly felt like she had been thrust once again under the surface of the naiads' lake. Then, rather than keeping her dulled senses, her environmental awareness grew sharper than she had ever before experienced it. It felt like her wraithwalking abilities were reinforcing her physical senses. Such a merging of awareness had never occurred before and so Katja cried out in shock.

"Katja, are you well?" Daya'lyn's voice echoed with worry from outside the tent.

"Sorry, Daya'lyn, I'm fine. It's just that this particular

skinshift isn't going well."

"Is your mind—?"

"No, I have not taken leave of my senses. In point of fact, they are more attuned than ever. It is just that my tail and paws...I have no idea how to describe this. Perhaps I had better just show you the change when it is complete."

"Very well, I will be waiting."

"Thank you," she said, simultaneously grateful for Daya'lyn's aid and wishing Felan was here to assess the strange situation. She missed his warm touch and gentle voice now more than ever.

"He would know what was happening to me and would go through his own skinshift along with me," she whispered to herself.

Then the worst of Katja's metamorphosis occurred. Her two top fangs elongated out of the gums of her mouth so that their sharp tips were just visible outside her lips. Her ears were pulled down against her head so that she could not swivel them to listen, and then a new set emerged on the sides of her face near her neck.

The metamorphosis was all wrong. Katja kept her tail, which was now covered in splotchy-skinned armored plates and curled vertically over her back. Her hind limbs and hind paws never changed their contour. Her forelimbs had changed, but her furless paws including her opposable, clawed thumbs had not.

Katja finally finished her skinshift when the full moon had already begun its descent from center sky. She readjusted her loincloth around her cumbersome tail and bound scraps of linen around her now exposed breasts. Slowly she crawled out of the tent on aching limbs. Daya'lyn's gloved hand was immediately there to help her.

"Are you well enough to stand?" he asked as she clung to him.

Katja tried to flick her ears in annoyance. She had to settle for narrowing her green eyes instead. "It will take more than a few aches to keep me off my back paws, Daya'lyn."

He stared at her wide-eyed. "They are still paws!"

Katja's human head nodded. "My tail grew thicker rather than shrinking away, and my forepaws are still paws despite the fact that the rest of my body is now basically human. My senses are better than they have ever been in my life, and I now have fangs long enough to rival yours! What is wrong with me?"

Daya'lyn eyed her in complete bafflement. "How should I know? Felan is the expert, not me."

"I know," she growled. "I wish he were here now."

"Believe me, I do as well. How is your mind? Has Daeryn visited you?"

She shook her head. "I can't sense him, and I feel fine. Although the increased senses are making me a little dizzy. I feel like I can see, hear, smell…well, everything. It's like I'm seeing the world around me with my wraithwalking abilities, not just my physical senses. Since I first began wraithwalker training, I have learned how to turn the added senses on and off. Tonight I cannot and it's beyond unnerving."

Daya'lyn hugged her in sympathy. "I know of only one course of action, then." He gripped the mirror shard embedded in the sunsilver spearhead around his neck and called Lauraisha's name as he looked into it.

Katja heard the dreamdrifter shift on her drifting lily pad and murmur Daya'lyn's name in response.

"Please do not wake, Lauraisha. Katja and I need you to dreamdrift," Daya'lyn said. "Contact Felan through your shard, if you can. Katja has urgent questions for the werewolf and you are the only one of us who can likely communicate with him over the considerable distance."

Lauraisha's dreamy presence wafted into Katja's mind. The wraithwalker's awareness suddenly sharpened and she was sharing Daya'lyn's mind with the dreamdrifter. Katja and Daya'lyn stared at each other as their thoughts traveled freely through Lauraisha's link to each other.

Oh, this is uncanny! Katja thought and Daya'lyn wholeheartedly agreed.

They felt Lauraisha's awareness leap across the lake north in search of Felan. She eventually found not only him, but Zahra and Vraelth as well. The three were in a pine-needle-strewn hollow west of the Nyghe sol Dyvesé Mountains.

Packmates, hear me! Her vibrant voice echoed in all six minds.

Lauraisha? Felan's and Zahra's answering thoughts were simultaneous.

Vraelth was slower to respond, but Katja felt the familiar sense of nobility coupled with a stale bitterness once he finally lowered his mental defenses.

The distance is taxing my strength. Katja, reinforce the bond if you can and then quickly ask your questions.

The wraithwalker added her strength to Lauraisha and felt the others do the same. *Felan, are you well from your skinshifting this night?*

I am. His groggy voice echoed both in Katja's mind.

I am not.

Daeryn?

No, something different. She explained her predicament and then asked for his advice.

Thank the Creator that your mind has remained intact! I'm unfamiliar with the changes that you described—especially the tail. There is a chapter in the skinshifter book that I gave you, which details focusing techniques to aid the changes. Reading that may help. Other than that, I'm unsure what to suggest.

We have discovered Zahra's sister's final resting place and have found a Keystone—the Ursa Agate, Vraelth added. *Qenethala had it with her when she was caught. That is why she sacrificed herself; she took the stone into the pine when she performed the Merge so that the deadwalkers would have no knowledge of it. As of now, we have yet to discover a way to free it from Qenethala's chosen Merging tree without destroying what is left of her in the process.*

She is a true heroine then, Katja responded with profound respect. *I hope you free the stone soon!*

So do we.

We have also obtained a Keystone, Daya'lyn informed them. *The Azuralle Lake naiads graciously gave us the White Opal of Azmar when they offered us safe haven this evening.*

Wait, Daya'lyn, does that mean that you are on the Merrow Road? Zahra asked.

Not at the moment. We took the Naiad Passage south and west out of the Nyghe sol Dyvesé foothills. We will use the Merrow Road during the latter part of the trek to Vihous. Why do you ask?

We heard a pack of ghouls discussing their allies' movements. When the deadwalkers were routed at Reithrgar Pass, one of the factions was pushed south along the Merrow Road. Please find another course!

I am sorry, Zahra, but there is none.

If they find your scents, they will hunt you and there will be no way of escape through those marshlands!

I know.

Then please be cautious!

Always.

There is something else you three should know, the dryad continued. *My sister revealed to me a grave danger in Tyglesea. She overheard several ghouls talking about the fact that their 'mistress' has infiltrated the royal court in Kaylere…she may even have the ear of King Kaylor himself. Daya'lyn, these deadwalkers were from Luther's own coven.*

So the spy isn't Daeryn? he asked.

Qenethala doesn't believe so. While Daeryn may indeed be at the Tyglesean Royal Court, he is not the deadwalker spy of whom they spoke. The spy in question is female.

Do the ghouls actually belong to Luther or do they belong to one of the vampires in his blood lineage?

She is not certain.

Thank you, Zahra. I will put that *information to good use.* Loathing edged the hybrid's shared thoughts.

I am losing my hold on the link. If there is anything else any of you wish to say, do it now. Lauraisha's thoughts were clipped with strain.

Katja, try not to worry about your skinshifting. Try to explore the changes and discover their source. I am sorry I cannot — Felan's thought faded as the link between all six minds collapsed.

"I am sorry." Lauraisha sat awake and panting on her lily pad. Her voice was a strained whisper through their shards. "I could not hold it any longer."

"Not to worry. You did well." Daya'lyn responded. "Thank you."

"You're welcome," she said, and then fell back against the pad again in new exhaustion.

Katja watched Daya'lyn a moment, seeing the subtle anxiety in his eyes as if it were a lit beacon on a high tower. "What are you so worried about? The Merrow Road?"

The male looked at her startled and then shifted his

worried gaze to the slumbering sixteen-winter-old on the lily pad. "Creator, keep us, if I am right," he whispered.

"About what?"

He slowly shook his head. "Not tonight. I need to explain my thoughts when Lauraisha is coherent enough understand them and I'll not further trouble her dreams tonight. Creator knows how many dangerous visions already plague her sleep now." Daya'lyn looked back at Katja. "I think we should find our beds. We need to be well rested for our journey tomorrow."

The skinshifter nodded, bid him goodnight, and made her way to a waiting lily pad. She crawled onto the velvety pad—which was tied to a stake along the lake shore by one of the plant's roots—and freed it of its bonds. As she lay drifting upon the gentle waves cuddled beneath her sleeping furs, she stared up at the starry expanse of sky and thought of Felan. This had been the first full moon in months that she had endured without his gentle guidance, and she missed him even more now than she had thus far on their journey. The fact that she had fallen in love with a werewolf still shocked her, and yet she couldn't deny that during his absence, nothing felt right. She held the fur of her sleeping covers to her cheek and imagined that it was the back of his large paw caressing her face. As the water rocked her to sleep, Katja's last conscious thought was a prayer to the Creator that she would see Felan again.

VIII

A BRIDGE OF SKY

Sometime during the night, Katja awoke to the night's peaceful sounds and saw the nacken conversing with Neamyntha. Her vision then faded into the haunting image of a sphinx and a manticore. The pair stood in the midst of a corpse-strewn battlefield. The red sun rose behind them, illuminating the dismembered carcasses and casting the victors' faces in sinister shadow as dark blood dripped from their claws. When the two began to skinshift into a pair of humans, Katja awoke with a scream.

"Katja, what's wrong!" Lauraisha called.

The skinshifter opened her eyes to see the first rays of sun's light filter through the Wasp Willow tentacles. She answered with a second panicked screech as her limbs and tail spasmed and she tumbled off of her lily pad into the lake. Sheer terror consumed her as the muscles of her body bulged and then shifted back into those of a werecat. The process was the swiftest and most excruciating metamorphosis that Katja had ever experienced, and it left her unable to breathe or swim. Water invaded her lungs as she thrashed below the lake's surface.

Katja! Lauraisha was swimming toward her, advancing under the water with expert strokes. Together the human and one of the naiads caught hold of the werecat's wayward limbs and pushed Katja's head above the waves. The female coughed and sputtered as the two kept her afloat and then helped her swim to shore. Daya'lyn and Lauraisha hauled her onto the bank and deposited her inside the tent so that she could dry off and change out of her drenched garments.

She nodded. "Jierira, I hate this," she said between pants. "Don't frighten us like that!"

The sore werecat looked at the human. "I'll be happy not to do so ever again…as soon as I can regain control over my own body and stop scaring myself."

* * *

By the time the sun had burned the last mists off of the lake and the rest of the naiads had come to the surface to greet them, the skinshifter was her dry, golden-furred werecat self once more. Katja watched in awe as the naiads hoisted gifts of staked fish, pond weed, and colorful beaded strings onto the lily pads. One was even kind enough to offer Lauraisha a beautiful set of reed pipes. The human gleefully experimented with these after she finished her morning eat, much to the delight of all her listeners.

Katja was humbled by her gifts of beads, most of which were made from jade, pearl, sea ivory, and jasper. She thanked her attendants many times over the precious gifts. Daya'lyn, meanwhile, dried as much of the fish and vegetation as he could and then packed the food and his own gift of sunsilver beads into the nackens' saddlebags.

With Neamyntha's blessings, the three packmates rode between the Wasp Willows along the Naiad Passage under the midday sun. Evening found them camped near Eureshra's submerged home along the Ten Fang Marshes. As with Neamyntha, they slept on lily pads that drifted atop the rippling waters and ate with the naiads—this time above water—during their evening eat. After the following day's morning eat, the members of the Inquisition once again gathered their belongings and rode off among the Wasp Willows. The Ten Fang Marsh naiads gave them a slightly mournful farewell as they departed, and Eureshra echoed Zahra's warning of deadwalkers being seen on the Merrow Road.

"Is there any other way we might go?" Daya'lyn asked her.

Eureshra shook her head. "I can offer only the Bridge

of Sky as a different course, but you still must traverse the Merrow Road, ultimately. Mind you, if you choose this second path, it could prove no safer than the first."

Daya'lyn nodded. "Even so, we must try. How do we find it?"

"Your mounts know the way. If Calder is willing, he can guide you to it." She looked at Lauraisha's steed. "Are you willing?"

Calder turned to stare at her for a long moment and then nodded his head ever so slightly.

"Very well, then," she said while Lauraisha repositioned the reins. "Lead them on."

When Calder nodded again, Katja gaped at him. Not even Tyron did that and he was more attuned to the emotions of his riders than any horse she had ever met.

"I wish you all well on your journey. May the Creator guide and favor you," Eureshra said by way of farewell. The three riders bowed their heads to her, and then the members of the Inquisition departed the naiads' safety and trudged on toward the dangers ahead.

* * *

"Oh, how I wish I could sleep on those lily pads every night," Lauraisha exclaimed that afternoon.

"They really do help ease your aches after a hard day's ride," Katja agreed.

"Indeed," Daya'lyn said and then fell silent while the two females laughed and joked.

After a time, Katja looked at him quizzically. "Daya'lyn, what is wrong?"

The male said nothing and kept his eyes on the road before them.

Lauraisha frowned. "Why are you worried about Zahra's and Eureshra's warnings about the Merrow Road and the trouble we face in Tyglesea? There is nothing we can do about either until we come to those respective crossroads."

"I wish you would not do that," he snapped. "It is difficult enough for me to mind my own thoughts without your interference."

"You thank her for her mage ability in the dead of

night and today you snarl at her for the same?" Katja was incredulous. "That is beyond unfair."

He turned on her. "Did I ask for your opinion? No! So let it alone!"

Katja flattened her ears and hissed at him.

"You know that I cannot always control the ability. Besides, your mind was practically shouting your worries. So who is this 'Mistress' that Zahra overheard the deadwalkers discussing?"

"That is not your concern."

She crossed her arms in stubbornness and continued to steer her mount using her knees. "If it is troubling you, then, of course it is my concern, and Katja's. As friends and packmates, Katja and I will have to deal with the same problems you do, so we might as well all discuss it rather than individually brood about it."

Daya'lyn crossed his own arms and tried to stare her down. When his attempt failed, he snarled, exposing his white fangs. "Oh, very well, then. As Zahra's information was rather vague, I can only speculate at the moment. But, from what she said, I have a suspicion of who we might meet Tyglesea."

"What is the worst possible scenario?" Katja asked.

"We could meet the Víchí mistress Naraka—Luther's bloodmate and lifemate. She is one of the oldest vampires and a powerful shade. When Luther first Turned my father into a vampire, Naraka acted as Calais's dam—nurturing him and teaching him much about Víchí society. When Caleb was Redeemed and abandoned that shadowed lineage, Naraka was the first to hunt him. She has caused my family nothing but strife."

Katja shuddered. "If Naraka is there, then this is truly grave indeed."

Lauraisha frowned. "Why have I heard that name before?"

"Among the Víchí, a dam is a female vampire who rears a youth to adulthood before Turning him," Daya'lyn explained. "Since they are walking corpses by definition, vampires and all other deadwalkers have no ability to sire young when they mate. They can only proliferate through biting and Turning living beings. Some Víchí prefer to steal babies or young children and raise them into full adults before Turning them.

They seem to think it makes those who are eventually Turned much more powerful.

"My father was one of Luther and Naraka's earliest attempts at such a delayed Turning. He had lived only eight winters when Luther ravaged his village and introduced him into the covens. It wasn't until he had lived twenty-five winters that my father was Turned. The few memories that Father has shared with me of Naraka and of Luther are… unsettling."

The Tyglesean princess frowned. "I know that deadwalkers can't sire young. That fact is why you and Daeryn are called sons of the Impossible Union. No one ever expected that Caleb would ever be able to have children even after he was Redeemed. What I meant was that I've heard the name Naraka before now. I just wish I could remember where."

Daya'lyn sat even straighter in his saddle. "Did you hear her name while on the Isle of Summons or in Tyglesea?"

"I cannot remember. Ugh, what a horrible monster! No wonder you didn't wish to discuss her!"

Daya'lyn arched a black eyebrow. "I didn't wish to discuss it because I have no proof that she is the spy—just a terrifying notion that I didn't want to upset you with until I could affirm it. Now perhaps you'll be good enough not to pry into my thoughts unless I give you permission."

He trotted Tyron ahead and they all rode on in uncomfortable silence until that evening's eat.

"We need to make a decision," he said as he spread out the map on the dark grass and weighed its curling corners down with stones. "What shall we do about the Merrow Road?"

"How far off are we from the crossing?" Lauraisha asked, sitting down beside him with her steaming bowl of porridge balanced in one hand.

"We have a day, perhaps two of travel before we come to the roads' intersection."

Katja bent over Lauraisha's slender shoulder to study the map in the campfire's light. "I'm sorry, Daya'lyn, but I see no useful alternative to that road. Under normal circumstances I would say that we could take our chances cutting across country, but such an act could prove quite fatal in these marshlands."

"I agree," Lauraisha said. "Better to be caught with firm ground under our feet rather than trapped in the treacheries of a bog."

Daya'lyn sighed. "Very well, then. I had assumed as much, but I could not make this decision without both of your consent. I am sorry to put you in such danger."

Lauraisha squeezed his shoulder in comfort. "It is better that we go to face the danger rather than let it catch us unaware. At least this way we might even be able to surprise them."

Daya'lyn shook the map free of dust and rolled it up once more. "Let us hope so. Either way, I will do as much aerial scouting as I can. I will also need you both to continue subtle mental sweeps searching for ill intent set against us."

They nodded.

"Master Daya'lyn."

Katja and Daya'lyn whirled toward the sound of the new voice and saw only their steeds snuffling at the vegetation on the edge of the campsite. Lauraisha put a comforting hand on each of their shoulders. "What is it, Calder?" she asked.

The nacken untied his reins from around the limb of a shrub and trotted over to the three. "Forgive the intrusion, but we have a solution to your current dilemma."

"You can talk?" Katja blurted out and then immediately regretted her outcry.

The stallion nodded. "Forgive the subterfuge, but Glashtin and I thought it best to remain observant rather than to meddle in your daily lives."

"You were sent to spy on us!" There was a dangerous edge to Daya'lyn's voice.

"Admittedly, My Sir, we were," Glashtin said after he also untied his reins and stood beside Calder.

"The two of you had better have a good explanation for your misdeeds," Daya'lyn said before whirling around to face Lauraisha. "And *you* had better tell me why you kept your silence about the fact that these two were kelpie beings not nacken beasts!"

The princess gave him an arch look. "I did not want to worry you until I had confirmed my suspicions and I only had such suspicions when Eureshra addressed the steeds this morning."

The fireforger's mouth worked furiously—opening and closing without a sound—as bafflement and anger wared across his pale face.

Katja groaned and shook her head. "I should have guessed. I saw the two of you communicating with Neamyntha on the night of the full moon, but I thought I was dreaming. I should have realized then that you were kelpies, not nacken."

"We do deeply apologize for our deception, My Sir and Madams, but we were sworn to secrecy by the Ring of Sorcerers," Calder said.

"Why?" Daya'lyn demanded.

"The Ring members wanted at least two of our kind to accompany you since you would have to traverse the naiad and ogre territories," Glashtin explained. "They thought that our assistance would open political doors to you that might otherwise remain sealed."

"He was, of course, correct." Calder added. "Without us, Neamyntha would have been far more reluctant to allow a blood-drinker or Tyglesean human near her lake, let alone a werecat skinshifter."

Lauraisha and Daya'lyn scowled at them.

"No offence intended, My Sir and Madams," Glashtin said. "It's just that naiads and Tygleseans have never been on the friendliest of terms and no one in three hundred years has trusted a skinshifter until now."

"We know," Daya'lyn said. "Now, why did you hide your identity from us in the first place?"

"And why reveal yourselves now?" Lauraisha added.

"We were meant to be your primary test to prove yourselves worthy of your posts as Inquisitor and entourage," Calder replied.

Glashtin continued. "You were meant to believe that we were beasts rather than beings. How you treated beasts under your charge would help us determine if the Ring of Sorcerers had chosen the right Inquisitor."

"Which they obviously have. Your integrity of character, your self-control, and your caring toward others—be they beast or being—all speak well of you."

"To be honest, you have all proven your merit and we were tired of the subterfuge," Calder add. "Of course, Neamyntha realized what we were the moment she welcomed you to the lake. She counselled us to reveal the truth soon since the deadwalkers now pose such a direct threat to all of us."

Daya'lyn crossed his muscular arms. "Were Si'lyn and Joce'lynn among those who devised this idiotic plan?"

Calder shook his head. "They were staunchly against it, but Aver'lyn and the others overruled their objections."

The Inquisitor's eyes flashed red. "And what would you have done if I had tried to feed from one of you while mistaking you as beasts?"

"We probably would have kicked you across the camp," Glashtin said.

"Thus injuring your Inquisitor and likely yourselves on an already perilous journey. As always, Aver'lyn plays the misguided fool. He and I will have words about this completely pointless subterfuge later. For now, though, how do you hope to prove *your* merit to us since we have already proven ourselves to you?"

Calder looked expectantly at Glashtin, who stamped a hoof, tossed his mane, and then whistled a silvery note through his fangs. A low rumble like the sound of distant thunder shook the stones beneath their hooves while the air vibrated above their heads. With a slight crackle, a rainbow burst out of the ground behind the kelpies and arced far over their heads toward the west.

Calder whinnied in triumph. "By revealing the Bridge of Sky."

* * *

The trio's crossing of the Bridge of Sky may have occurred without incident, but it did not happen without considerable cringing on Katja's part. The bridge itself was not a physical bridge at all, but was made of Ring Spells similar to those that allowed passage into Crown Canyon and Caerwyn Castle. The path was multihued and almost as narrow as the Naiad Passage between the Wasp Willows had been. The company members trooped single-file along the bridge's length and tried to keep their gaze averted from the ground far below them. They camped three nights on the bridge without the light or warmth of campfires.

"I fear we'll have to do without fires from now until we cross the Vihous border," Daya'lyn said as they huddled under furs and ate dried fish and hard cheese the second night.

Katja stared at the swamp below her through the Bridge of Sky's translucent surface. She noted unnatural movement twice and watched as groups of deadwalkers patrolled the area along a copse of cypress trees. "I've seen three zombie packs, four dullahan, and an imp hunting the marshes so far tonight. What are we going to do?"

"Calder, are you sure that they cannot see us up here?" Lauraisha asked in apprehension.

The kelpie shook his head from where he stood on the rainbow-hued archway. "The Ring Spells of this bridge hide us from evil eyes and keep us from tumbling into midday. Even so, we must leave their shelter tomorrow."

Daya'lyn pulled the map out of its leather case and spread it flat. "How familiar are you with the ogres of this area, Calder?"

"Unfortunately, we've had very few dealings with them, but Jhalag should be well within a day's travel of the Bridge of Sky's northern foundation."

"Is the city secure?"

"If the naiad territories are still safe from deadwalkers, then I have no doubt that Jhalag will be as well. It could be under siege, but the ogres will have an easy time defending the city since the entire thing is built on platforms rising above the marsh waters."

Daya'lyn nodded and continued to study the map with furrowed brows. "I think I will take wing tomorrow and follow you from the air. Having eyes surveying everything from aloft might be useful."

Lauraisha stared at him with slight panic on her face. "What happens if we get ambushed while you're still flying?"

"Not to worry, Lauraisha; I can swoop to your location within moments if there is trouble."

"And if you lose sight of us through the foliage?"

"You can keep a mental bond open with me, can you not?"

The human nodded. "I can, but the last time I formed a bond with you, you snarled at me."

He grimaced, and then spoke gently. "I'm sorry. I would

just like some warning when you plan to do it, so that I'm prepared."

"Prepared for what!" she suddenly snapped. "I'm not trying to delve into your deepest, darkest secrets!"

He shook his head. "No, I know you're not. Nonetheless they seem to reveal themselves to you anyway, and that is more than a little unnerving for me."

"It wouldn't be so unnerving if you would learn to trust me!" she said.

"I do trust you! Even so, though, I need to protect you."

"I'm not an infant!" She gave him a strangled scream of frustration, and then stomped down the bridge to sit huddled in her sleeping furs several body-lengths away from the group.

Daya'lyn watched the princess's huddled form in bafflement. "Katja, what did I do?"

The werecat sighed before also standing and wrapping her robes and cloak more tightly around her torso. "You patronized her. You put a condition on your trust of her after you made the explicit point that she and I need to be completely honest with you. That isn't fair."

He glared at her. "Fair enough, but do you let her rove around in your thoughts unannounced and uninvited?"

"Yes, as a matter of fact, I do. Her presence is one reason I have stayed fairly sane since the death of my family. You should try it. Contrary to what you apparently believe, Lauraisha is a very considerate respecter of privacy. She knows, for example, that there are certain memories of my father and mother that are private and she has never delved into them. She also keeps others' confidences without question and tries to only delve into others' memories when they are conscious of what she is doing. No, she cannot always control her gift, but she does at least try."

"I...I'm sorry."

Katja gave him a quizzical look. "Don't apologize to me. I'm not the one you slighted."

He looked at Lauraisha's hunched form with sudden apprehension playing across his face. "Should I apologize to her now then?"

She sighed. "Only if you want her to speak to you at any

point during the rest of our lives, which could be shorter than we all hope, judging from the enemy movements I've seen during the last few days."

Daya'lyn let out a strangled breath of frustration that mirrored Lauraisha's before striding to where the Tyglesean sat. Katja watched him sit down just as Lauraisha shifted to put her back toward him. The werecat flicked her ears. "Jierira, males!"

"I beg your pardon!" Glashtin said.

Katja winced. "Sorry, Calder and Glashtin, I mean no insult to the two of you. Those two just frustrate me sometimes. That is all."

Calder snorted derisively. "Too true."

Katja sighed and looked toward the bejeweled night sky. While the moon was still too bright to see all of the constellations, the werecat's sharp eyes traced the stars' patterns of the dragon, hippopyre, and phoenix until she at last gazed upon the more-central symbol of creation.

Katja stared at it and sighed, suddenly feeling very small, weary, and lonely. The last time she had been star-gazing had been with her brothers Kumos and Kayten barely a fortnight before the Feliconas Clan Massacre. Now they and all others of her race were either Turned or dead. And, despite her best efforts, Katja might well join them tomorrow.

* * *

Despite Katja's misgivings, the trio's crossing from the narrow Bridge of Sky onto the wider Merrow Road occurred without incident. In fact, they met no one on the main highway at all. They had passed a few Sylvan refugees during their journey through the Nyghe sol Dyvesé Mountains, but not even those were present now. Far from calming Katja's sense of unease, however, the dearth of traffic along the roadway only served to heighten her apprehension. The fur on the back of the werecat's neck stood straight out and she twisted her rounded ears this way and that on the top of her head even while she sat hunched in her saddle in an imitation of a deadwalker nemean, just as Glashtin had suggested to do during that morning's eat.

Lauraisha whispered through their mental link as their

steeds trotted along the Merrow Road. *This makes me nervous.*

What? Katja asked.

Pretending that Daya'lyn has switched allegiances and that we are now his hostages.

I am not comfortable with it either, Lauraisha. Unfortunately, though, we don't have any better options at this point, Daya'lyn replied sullenly.

Lauraisha almost fell out of her saddle in surprise.

What are you doing *down there? You opened the link to all five of us, remember? So please stop speaking about me as if I'm not present,* the male growled.

Sorry, I'm not used to this open of communication, especially when one of my companions isn't even close enough for me to see.

You were the one who grumbled at me for not being close-minded with you.

You two, quit snarling at each other so that I can scout! Katja silently snapped.

Sorry, came the simultaneous apology.

They trotted on in silence with Daya'lyn flying somewhere overhead, Katja and Glashtin in the lead, and Lauraisha and Calder bringing up the rear with Tyron and the pack nacken. Lauraisha wore false bonds made to mimic water-chains and Katja wore willow ash worked into the skin around her eyes, nose, and ears to make her look like she was in the beginning stages of Turning into a nemean deadwalker. The effect was convincing enough so long as she avoided sneezing, which was no easy feat of self-control with this much dust caked around her nose.

Daya'lyn, she whispered through their bond.

What?

We are being watched.

I know. I sighted some twenty deadwalkers north of your position. Just make sure you look like you are leading Lauraisha as a prisoner and keep moving.

Katja caught a glimpse of Daya'lyn flying high above the trees and cringed. Daya'lyn's long, black hair was swept up to reveal his pointed, black-tipped ears in the customary high ponytail and twin side braids of a Víchí male rather than his normal half-ponytail. The expanse of his pale, dragon-like wings coupled the odd hairstyle and the absence of the leather gloves that usually covered his black-tipped talons mimicked a vampire so well that Katja could barely tell the difference between Daya'lyn and his Fallen brother.

"Daeryn's scarred left arm and particular scent are all that differentiates them now," she whispered to herself. She shuddered at the memory of Daeryn's spicy scent mixed with her own when he bit her. The ghastly vision of his attack gave way as another familiar stench tickled her nose. Katja's eyes went wide and she immediately gave a low hiss.

Lauraisha's mind immediately brushed the werecat's awareness. *What is it?*

Curqak is here!

What! Lauraisha and the kelpies' simultaneously reply.

Daya'lyn must be out of range of my thoughts. Warn him that the ghoul is among those watching, Lauraisha. Do it now!

The dreamdrifter's mind drifted away from Katja's thoughts. The wind shifted and a stench of death rolled past Katja's nostrils. She almost gagged. Sudden darkness swept over them as a revenant spread its protective shadow upon the road. As Katja's eyes adjusted to the Turned brolaghan's strange darkness, she noted hunched shapes encircle them upon the roadside.

"This path is death." The zombies' hollow voices rattled like a chorus of rattling bones. "We dead tend it; you living will feed it."

Katja made a haughty show of flanking Lauraisha on the left. "I will speak with your master, sklaaven."

Katja felt Lauraisha shiver beside her and then felt an odd sensation as her own upper fangs lengthened, seemingly of their own accord. She hissed and noticed in satisfaction that some of the closest zombies backed away. She continued to stare down the soul slaves, while her ears constantly flicked, listening all around her for sounds of attack. Lauraisha, meanwhile, kept her seemingly bound hands on the saddle horn and her posture in a submissive hunch. Katja could feel the human's mind drifting from one deadwalker to the next weaving subtle suggestions of confusion.

"Hello, little changeling."

Katja steeled herself and turned to face Curqak as the ghoul walked toward her. "Go scorch yourself, hunza."

Curqak whistled. "Such ire from one pretending to be a deadwalker just will not do. If you really were Turned, you would show due respect for your superiors."

"Turning didn't rob me of my hatred toward you, Curqak. If anything, it added a good dose of contempt for your miserable carcass."

Curqak stared at her in sudden confusion—taking note of her lengthened fangs. Her snarl caused him to step back. Then her snarl turned into a sneeze.

Curqak's black eyes narrowed. "Liar! You're no more Turned than I am an elf!" He started toward her.

"Touch them and burn." Daya'lyn's deep voice was a simmering hiss as Lauraisha relayed his message through every mind. Guided by Katja's and Lauraisha's minds, the fireforger had pushed his way through the revenant's illusions. He landed in a bent tree just off of the road behind the sklaaven, poised to swoop in and attack anything foolish enough to defy him. Katja silently congratulated Lauraisha on her subtle mental amplification of the male's voice.

Curqak turned to glower at him. "You dare to—"

"Silence, ghoul." Daya'lyn's face lit up in the unnatural gloom from a blue fireball he conjured in his right talon. "This group is under my protection. Therefore, if you interfere with their safety, I will incinerate your entire entourage and torch the entire marsh if I must just to destroy every last member of your miserable alliance."

Katja felt a prick of pain in her lower limb. She looked down and realized the nearest sklaaf zombie had edged close enough during the shouting match to cut her with a claw. It was all she could do to hold her posture and not rip out his throat as she felt the gash begin to fester with deadwalker Taint.

"Master," the zombie's guttural voice called to Curqak. "This werecat still bleeds red. There is no trace of black blood in her veins."

"So you *are* still among the living." Curqak turned to glower at Daya'lyn. "You will pay for your would-be deceit and your threats! Take them now; subdue them!"

Daya'lyn's roar of rage matched Katja's in ferocity as he launched himself from the tree. She and Glashtin turned to face outward. Lauraisha was already at work with orange flames spiraling out of her raised fingers to hit two deadwalkers full in each of their chests. Daya'lyn was launching flame in every direction to frighten and maim the revenant controlling the unnatural darkness while Tyron and the kelpies all put their teeth and hooves to good use. Katja grabbed the short staff that Durhrigg had given her and speared her enemies with its sunsilver spear ends even as her kelpie bit and flailed his hooves at anything foolish enough to come too close. The five mounts and three riders remained in a loose defensive circle with their backsides toward each other so that no attacker could sneak past the Sylvans' defenses. At least that was the plan until Glashtin accidentally bucked Katja off his back and into the circle of her enemies.

The deadwalkers were on her before she could find her staff or her sunsilver daggers or even refill her deflated lungs, dragging her by her flailing limbs away from her packmates' fiery protection.

"Katja! No!" Lauraisha's scream reverberated in the cold air as a dozen zombies pulled her toward the marshlands north of the road. Daya'lyn's and Lauraisha's fireballs crackled past their heads as they hurried. Katja roared in rage and fear and felt the revenant's spells weaken from her voice, but not shatter. His mists clouded her sight as he shielded his allies from the eyes of her friends. With a vengeful hiss, Curqak bound her maw and then he and his mob moved into the screen of twisted trees and high grasses flanking the main road.

"Kalawan gancang," he hissed. "Quickly!"

The group scurried through the underbrush with Katja in tow. Curqak led the way to what looked like a bear's den, hollowed out of the ground from under a fallen log. As he ran headlong down into its darkness, however, Katja realized that it was the narrow entrance to a sizable cave.

"Strap her down," the ghoul ordered as his slaves sealed the entrance from the inside.

The werecat flailed madly as zombies and imps tied her limbs to one of the stone platforms jutting out of the cave walls. Katja hissed at Curqak through her gag.

"You will tell me what your mission is, changeling."

Curqak smirked as he pulled the gag free. She roared with little result. The spongy, black ichor on the cavern's thick walls muffled even the loudest noise.

"Tell me what I want to know and I will spare you from being Turned."

Katja spit into the scarred face of the being who had led the attacks on her clansmen and her family. "Liar."

"You have grown bold since last we met," the ghoul crooned as he dug a venomous claw into her upper arm. "I will enjoy breaking your newfound courage."

IX
THE GHOUL'S LAMENT

K atja bit back a scream. Curqak pulled his black claw back and stabbed a pressure point on her shoulder. The shock of the pain caused Katja to gasp and then snarl at him.

"Tell me what I want to know, Katja. Tell me where you and your allies are traveling."

She laughed in a harsh voice. "Get singed!"

The ghoul's Tainted touch was excruciating. In desperation, Katja delved into her soul and pulled forth her wraithwalking abilities. She used the remaining pain to focus on her tormentor. When she closed her eyes, Katja felt the pain pulsing in her wounds suddenly subside. Time seemed to slow as she sought Curqak's true nature. It was a quest that brought her impressions of shame, longing, frustration, awe, and a crippling fear toward the ghoul's blood master Luther and other members of the Víchí elder's defiled race.

She saw Curqak's overwhelming lust for power and his deep desire to be one of the vampire elite. He had vainly desired this for centuries and would do anything to gain the favor of those who could grant his wish, but time and again his request had been denied.

Curqak's next piercing proved far less painful while she considered him as a wraithwalker and not simply as a Sylvan. Her mind shifted from a quest of truth to a need to purge the Tainted dross from her target. Her awareness grew as sharp as a spear and she pierced his mind even as his claws once more stabbed her skin. Both roared in pain, but she felt Curqak's discomfort was far worse than her own.

"In the name of our holy Creator, be cleansed!" she shouted, and cast the light of her thoughts deep into the shadowed recesses of his mind. His skewed sanity scurried away from her purity even as his claws wrenched themselves free of her flesh. Katja felt her skinshifting talents take control of her body then, expelling the toxins out of her wounds and then mending the damage caused in moments. Katja opened her eyes to find Curqak staring at her in abject terror.

"How? How could you possibly fight the Taint and heal so quickly?" The black orbs of the ghoul's eyes traveled to Katja's neck, then, and widened even more when he saw her bite scars. "So the rumors are true… Daeryn has marked you, but he failed to Turn you. How?"

Outside Katja could hear heavy steps running in her direction and Daya'lyn's muffled yells. She intensified her attack.

"Kill her," Curqak wailed to his cohorts as he clutched his shuddering head. "Please kill her now!"

Neither the zombies nor the imps moved. Whether or not they understood Curqak's order, Katja could not discern. However, they trembled just as their master did and cowered away from her as if afraid of an oncoming whip. Quickly, Katja began slicing through her leather bonds with her claws even as her mind lunged deeper into the ghoul's awareness— searing him with his own shame and power lust.

Katja's mind shifted slightly as the zombies finally broke through their fear and came at her. She lashed out at the primitive cognition that they used instead of fully functioning brains. She pushed Curqak's shame onto them and watched as they fell to their bony knees wailing in the keenest misery and confusion.

"You have no hope, Curqak. Be free of this!"

"No! Never! I will not forsake my masters!"

"You will forsake evil, Curqak, and so will your cohorts!"

"Never! Oh, Abomination, make it stop!"

A loud crash shook the cave and the boulder blocking the cave mouth cracked. Katja lost her mental focus even as she gained a free paw. The zombies came at her again and then staggered back moaning as a second shudder swept through the stone, sending a sliver of daylight slicing into the darkness. Katja wrenched her second limb free even as the recovering deadwalkers tumbled onto their knees and backs again.

The third strike split the rock clean through and flooded the gloom with light. A towering figure tossed the stone fragments aside as if they were stray twigs. The brown-furred creature was twice Katja's height and wielded a massive war hammer. Felan's hulking form would be dwarfed compared to the muscled frame of this colossus. He had an almost feline face set in a large, round head with hard, gray horns curving around his goat-like ears.

"Ogre!" she whispered in awe and fear.

And then Daya'lyn and Lauraisha were there—burning through darkness and deadwalker alike with their fire. With her last limbs finally free, Katja leapt past her captors to the safety of her packmates.

"Katja Kevrosa Escari of the Feliconas Clan of werecats, meet Borgar, son of Borlag and ranking Brute of the Shamgar Clan of ogres." Lauraisha's tone was formal and cheerful as she shot a fireball at Curqak's face. The ghoul lunged just fast enough to evade the blast and then scrambled on all fours past his flaming underlings and into the cavern's back tunnel.

"Katja, did he hurt you?" Daya'lyn asked as Lauraisha handed the werecat her lost spearheads and staff.

She nodded. "I'm fine."

"Come then! We must not lose him. Leave the others for the ogres and follow me!"

A ball of flame lit in Daya'lyn's hand as he sprinted into the tunnel with the human and werecat close on his heels. The tunnel opened out into a natural limestone cavern roughly three body-lengths tall and six body-lengths across which had been partially widened by excavations at some point in ancient times. There were eight tunnels carved out in the far side of the chamber and Curqak could be hiding in any one of them.

"Which way, Katja?"

She sniffed the cool air, her ears flicking this way and that. The fiend's stench was mixed with other deadwalkers and so Katja took her time discerning between the rancid scents. "Curqak was not the only Asheken to wander through this place. Be on your guard," she whispered before investigating each tunnel opening.

Finally her nose focused on a fresh scent in the tunnel second to the left. Katja picked up a chalky white rock and marked the stone floor and ceiling of the tunnel.

"This way," she said, and slunk into the entrance. She kept her pace quick but cautious as she moved just ahead of her packmates. The werecat heard drips and ripples of water as the tunnel widened out into a stone gallery replete with rocky spikes growing from the walls, floor, and ceiling. The smell of diluted limestone and silica made her nose itch.

"Daya'lyn, would you light the world a bit more for us?" she whispered.

The fireforger threw his fiery globe into the room and it alighted on a stone spike spiraling down from the vaulted ceiling. A shower of golden sparks emanated from the stone as the hot flames burned away its clinging moisture. The sparks drifted into a shallow pool seven body-lengths under the spike and bathed its liquid with orange flame. The entire cavern exploded in color as the light radiated from the pool to expose glittering piles of polished agates, opals, and carnelians littering the floor, while brightly hued crystals of amethyst and rose quartz ornamented the walls.

"What is this place?" Lauraisha asked in awe.

"It must be Edelsteen Uitgraven," Katja whispered with equal awe. "The source of the ancient dwarves' wealth. This mine was one of their most closely guarded secrets. Many Sylvans sought this place after the Dwarven Plague decimated most of the race, but no records I have read from my clan's archives or at the Mage Citadel Library ever suggested that it was this far south. No wonder none of the searchers have ever found it!"

"That they reported, at least," Daya'lyn added as he nudged a chisel with the toe of his brown leather boot. Despite looking quite new, the tool didn't appear to be from any Sylvan clan or order that Katja knew.

"The deadwalkers are mining this place?" she asked.

Daya'lyn nodded. "I think so. I cannot fathom why."

Lauraisha stooped to pick up a pair of opals. "Wars are expensive. Even if Sylvans themselves provide a ready food source, the deadwalkers will still need to trade for tools, equipment, and weapons that they cannot make for themselves."

"Yes, but who among the Sylvans would be foolish enough to trade with them?"

"Any beings unscrupulous enough to be bought with such trinkets." Lauraisha said, as she held the opals up to the light of Daya'lyn's fire, studying their sparkling play. "And gems as exquisite as these would make such brigands joyfully ransom half of the continent!"

Katja heard scuttling sounds to her immediate right and instinctively rolled out of range as Curqak's short sword struck toward her ribs. She snarled as he sprang back into the shadows between two huge floor spikes and disappeared into the gloom of a tunnel just as Daya'lyn hurled a fireball after him. They heard a pained screech in the darkness as Katja pushed herself onto her back paws, growling.

"Come," Daya'lyn murmured. Again Katja marked the stone floor and ceiling of the tunnel with the chalky white rock and they moved forward.

Daya'lyn's fist-sized conflagration lit the wider tunnel's precious mineral veins and showed twice the amount of light as it had in the previous tunnel. There was no sign of Curqak, although Katja could still smell his lingering stench.

In the radiance of Daya'lyn's blaze, Katja saw a huge paw protruding from around the tunnel's bend. At first, she thought it was Curqak's, and then realized it was the wrong shape and size to be one of his. Then a new stench registered in her nostrils—that of death and ogres. She held up a paw to signal the others to halt and then cautiously moved forward with her recovered bone staff held at the ready.

The sight that met her eyes pierced her soul. An adult ogress lay crumpled against the stone wall, her heavily furred hide split open from sternum to navel with her half-eaten entrails bulging out. The ogress's magnificent curled horns had been hewn off and stabbed into her chest while her skull had been split and her brain plucked out and presumably eaten. Katja gasped at the deadwalkers' favored execution method and felt the memories of her own clan mates' similar deaths overwhelm her. A soft mewl escaped her maw as

Daya'lyn and Lauraisha came up beside her. Lauraisha stifled a whimper of her own before pulling the Feliconian into a fierce embrace. Behind them, Katja heard a sniffling and pushed Lauraisha behind her as she spun with staff and claws ready.

In a shallow alcove, well-hidden from general view, huddled an ogress youngling. The tiny female sat staring at her mother's corpse in wide-eyed terror. The werecat sniffed the air around them for Curqak's scent, but the smells were too muddled. Cautiously, she edged her way toward the youngling.

"What is your name?"

The ogress did not respond, but instead kept her golden eyes fixed on her dead mother.

"All will be well, I promise." Katja reached a paw palm up toward the female.

"Katja!" Lauraisha screamed.

Katja saw the shadow move just behind the youngling and felt Curqak's blade pierce her chest before she could react. The ghoul pulled the sword free and hot blood flowed from the werecat's wound. Curqak licked his lips as he huddled behind the frightened ogress.

"Daya'lyn!" Lauraisha's yell shook the tunnel as her fireball flared with new purpose.

"Anyone attacks me and she dies!" Curqak hissed at the Inquisitor as he forced his captive to stand. Even so young, she stood nearly as tall as the ghoul. The Turned elf's fangs were poised above the pulsing artery of her brown-furred neck even as he held his bloody sword before the two of them.

Daya'lyn's narrowed eyes glinted scarlet with rage and his fangs once again reached their full length. Katja's own were lengthening as she crouched with her hackles raised and her right paw pressed tight against her bloody gash. Curqak's blade was laced with the same caustic toxin found in his own skin, but by good fortune it had not penetrated deep. Katja struggled to draw out the Taint, but she finally was able to isolate and expel it through the blood seeping from her wound. She felt a sudden surge of energy and used it to skinshift her wound closed—repairing the damaged tissue.

"I have had enough of your abominable brutality, ghoul,"

she hissed as she lowered her still bloody paw from her newly-healed skin. She delved deep into her soul and brought forth her wraithwalker's sight. "By the Creator and Aribem, I will ensure you never harm another living being ever again."

For the first time during any of their encounters, Katja saw fear—raw and overwhelming—creep into Curqak's coal-black eyes as he stared at her healed wound. It was the same fear he had shown for Luther during her and Lauraisha's dreams of the ghoul's torture. Katja was his sole fear, not Daya'lyn or Lauraisha. She felt it paralyze him as her awareness touched his.

Manticore's Daughter! His mind shuddered. *Oh, mage, have mercy on me!* he screamed as his tarnished essence tried and failed to hide itself away from her mental scrutiny.

You gave my family and my clan none and yet you dare ask it for yourself? She pressed his soul with the power of her words—the truth of her voice—and heard him scream aloud. His hold on the ogress loosened as he trembled.

Lauraisha, grab the female when I tell you, she whispered inside the human's mind.

Curqak's mind groveled before hers as a whipped slave before his master.

You will receive mercy only if you are completely truthful with me. I need information.

Of course, of course, mistress.

Katja's stomach turned at the title. "Tell me who Luther sent to Summersted Castle in the Tyglesean capital city of Kaylere," she asked aloud for Daya'lyn's benefit.

"I cannot betray my master!"

"You can and you will." The strength of her wraithwalker's voice enveloped his soul, severing the tendrils that bound him to his master's will. "Answer me!"

"Luther sent his mate, the vampire Naraka."

Katja hissed. "What is her purpose for being there?"

"She was to gather intelligence for Luther and sway King Kaylor to ally with the deadwalkers against the Sylvans."

"Why?"

"Tyglesea boasts technology far superior to the rest of the Sylvan Orders and it is therefore useful to Luther."

"Why does Luther want me captured and brought to

him?"

"I cannot, I cannot... Mangga eureun!"

"You will tell me or I will squeeze your wretched soul right out of existence," she said between clenched fangs.

"No, I... He wants you alive so he can Turn you himself."

"Why?"

Tears streamed down Curqak's pallid cheeks. "You are a wraithwalker and a skinshifter. It has been foretold for centuries by Luther's augurs and oracles that the birth of one such as you will herald the beginning of the Fourth and Final Age. You could well be the courier of our destruction if you are not Turned. Your allies are among the strongest we have faced and we Asheken could well stand on the brink of destruction should we fail to sway your loyalties."

"So you were sent to find me and destroy my clan before I and my allies could rise against Luther."

"Yes."

"You were responsible for my parents' deaths, then; were you not?"

"I was."

"Why did you hunt them?"

"I hunted the beings who I thought were the last powerful skinshifter and wraithwalker mages outside of the Ring of Sorcerers so that they could not produce any offspring who could wield both abilities. If I had realized that such offspring already existed, I would have never let you live!" His snarl turned into a whimper as she watched him.

"Was my father a wraithwalker?"

"Yes. He never officially trained at the Isle of Summons or at the Magehous settlement so it took me years to identify him and hunt him down."

"And my mother?"

"A skinshifter. Most beings assumed that she was a harmhealer because she could skinshift her own and others' wounds closed, but she had no mastery of the ancient healing tongue and could never be one of its wielders. Even so, it was far safer for her to pretend to be a harmhealer after the skinshifter betrayals during the Second War of Ages condemned so many of her kind as traitors."

"What of Marga?" Daya'lyn interrupted. "Were you

involved in her death as well?"

Curqak looked at him with a depth of loathing matching his fear toward Katja. She jerked his mind's attention back toward her. "Were you?"

"No. I only aided in her abduction."

"Who killed her, then?"

Curqak frowned in confusion. "Marga lives."

"What! That cannot be. Where is she, then?"

"Blaecthull."

"She, a fireforger, is being held in Luther's fortress? How? Why?"

Curqak bobbed his head. "She is the keeper of the Keystones, which Luther wants. Her release was Daeryn's original motivation to serve Luther. She remains trapped in a water dungeon until Luther recovers all of the Keystones. Then she will die."

Daya'lyn began cursing.

From somewhere in the depths of Katja's mind, triumphant laughter began echoing through her thoughts. She and Curqak froze as this new voice gained strength.

Lauraisha, grab the ogress!

Lauraisha yanked the trembling female out of the ghoul's wavering grip while Katja pressed the fiend's mind still harder.

"Daya'lyn, Daeryn has found his way into my mind again. You must do what is necessary if I fail," she hissed.

With Lauraisha's help, Katja gripped Curqak's mind once more and began sifting through his memories as swiftly as she could so that she could glean as much information from the ghoul as possible. They were both drawn deep into his memories of Luther and Caleb when Daeryn struck.

The two females felt a blinding pain inside their skulls. Katja tumbled out of Curqak's awareness into a mind much younger and even darker.

Moarns ljocht en ehre, Katja. I've missed you. Shall we continue our previous discussion?

Katja growled low in her throat. She reacted quickly before the shade could plunge her mind into any of his illusions. She cast Curqak's memory of Marga in water-chains around Daeryn like a net. *Where is she, Daeryn? You have strayed too far from your mother's nobility. How can she be proud of a male who has done such harm to so many beings? You have betrayed her and your father, Daeryn. You have betrayed your brother and all Sylvans.*

How dare you use my own mother against me! You are no better than Luther, changeling!

Daeryn, Lauraisha's voice echoed in Katja's and Daeryn's minds. *Repent or face your destruction!*

From whom, human? Do you think your pitiful talents can harm me?

Katja felt Lauraisha pull Daya'lyn into their mental bond and together they channeled a burst of energy into the werecat's mind, and at once Katja understood the fireforger's intent. Half afraid of being singed herself, Katja grimly took Lauraisha's and Daya'lyn's soul fire into her mind and wrapped her own wraithwalker's discernment around it. The result was a wraith fire much like the power she felt whenever she was mentally linked with Verdagon. She held and built the uncanny power inside her soul until it was barely contained, and then released it through her link to Daeryn's mind. He shrieked as it exploded against his tarnished consciousness.

Daya'lyn's mind flooded the four-fold bond with heat and light. *Daeryn, you once fought the bloodlust and its evil valiantly. Fight it again and help us free Mother.*

Dayalan, you do not understand, Daeryn whispered, his voice nearly strangled with pain and regret as the first shock waves seared his awareness. *You will never understand. Mother's bondage could well unlock all of our freedom!*

With a last desperate hiss, Daeryn cut his ties to their minds and vanished just as quickly as he had come. As the link faded, Katja looked her shaking body over, noted no burns, and then stared at Lauraisha and Daya'lyn in awe.

She sighed in weary relief. "He's gone."

Lauraisha's smile was smug. "I did warn him."

Katja's laugh was a hoarse hiss. She stretched her sore shoulders and felt some of her tension expel itself. With Daeryn's threat stymied for the moment, she focused her keen eyes back on Curqak. The ghoul looked much more singed than he had the last instant that she had laid eyes on him. Katja frowned and looked over her shoulder at Daya'lyn.

The muscular fireforger shrugged. "He tried to bolt while we were occupied with Daeryn. I had a little fireball ready for the occasion—nothing too destructive, but enough of a blaze to help him reconsider leaving." The male's smile was full of fang.

Katja smirked. "Thank you for being so considerate."

"I am, aren't I?" he said, mirroring her sarcastic smile. His expression then became grim. "In all sincerity, Katja, what is your wish regarding Curqak's continued existence?"

She sighed and looked at Lauraisha, who was busy comforting the weeping youngling ogress now huddled in her arms. "Did you see all that you needed to see?"

The human shuddered and nodded. "I doubt there is anything left of importance."

"I agree," Katja replied and then turned back to the cowering deadwalker. "You have asked me, the daughter of two murdered parents, sister to three dead siblings, and lone survivor of an entire massacred clan and race to treat you with mercy. On what grounds do you expect me to give such latitude?"

"I was only serving my master." Curqak's answering whine was piteous.

Katja shook her head. "Even a slave whose master orders him to murder another must rebel against such evil. Yet I saw you, a servant, laugh in delight as you carried out your master's demands. This damns you more than if you had committed the acts solely by your own ambition because you willingly aided someone else in the destruction of others."

"Curqak, as sole survivor of my clan and family, I hold the right to punish you for your many crimes under the ancient Sylvan Code. I therefore decree that you will undergo full soul cleansing and bodily destruction as retribution for your crimes."

Curqak stared at her in horror. She stared at his black eyes and swallowed hard at the thought that her last link to her family and clan was about to be severed. She then set her jaw in determination.

"Daya'lyn, will you help me? I cannot do this alone."

The hybrid nodded.

"I'll also help," Lauraisha said while stroking the ogress's fur.

"Very well. Would you please help Katja maintain a blockade of Curqak's mind so that he cannot turn himself into a phantom after I destroy his body?"

The human dreamdrifter bowed her head and joined her hand with Katja's paw for added comfort and closeness even as their minds touched once again. Lauraisha struck Curqak's quivering consciousness first, pinning him until Katja could muster her strength. Together she and Katja bound Curqak's awareness with their own as Joce'lynn had taught them to do. Lauraisha kept the ogress's head turned away to shield the youngling from the sight and smell of Daya'lyn's blue-white fire burning the ghoul to death.

"Do it quickly, Daya'lyn. I will give him that much mercy even if he showed none to me or my kin."

As the Cleansing began, the two female mages felt Curqak's mind move from one part of their blockade to another, searching frantically for an escape. They gave him none. Slowly they tightened their mental noose and then Katja channeled her purity into the Asheken's mind, rapidly purging it and by extension his soul of the Víchí's corruption. Katja felt the memory of the ghoul's Turning bite well up as Curqak's undead experiences were seared away.

She saw him as he once was—an elf male of perhaps twenty-five winters who had stopped to help a stranded traveler along the road. That traveler was Luther. He had feigned a limb injury so that his intended victim would have to come close to help prop up the leg, so that no weight rested on the injury. Once the male was close enough to him, Luther attacked. He dragged the male down on the ground and pulled him behind a tangle of brambles where a younger Víchí male waited—the same Víchí whom Katja had seen stalking Marga as she lay bleeding beside the broken wagons of her ambushed caravan.

"Father, no!" Daya'lyn had whispered as he, Lauraisha, and Katja all watched the memory play through in horror...

*

"Now, Calais, just as I taught you." Luther almost purred. Calais bent to the helpless elf's neck and drained his life-flow almost entirely. Once Calais had gorged himself, he propped the corpse on a nearby tree trunk and sighed.

"Not a bad meal, Father. Elven blood really does have a majestic flavor to it."

"Yes, but this one is not meant to be your equal, but merely your servant, Calais."

"When, Father? When may I add a full Víchí to our ranks?"

Luther cuffed the younger vampire across his blood-smeared cheek and licked his own fingers clean. "Too hasty, Calais. Finish your Turning bite quickly or you will lose his soul to the Wraith Realm. Soon we will find a female for you to take as your bloodmate. Then you can practice your fangs properly on her."

Calais nodded before piercing his own bottom lip with an upper fang. He sucked a single drop of his own blood into his mouth and then spit the blood and saliva mixture into the corpse's mouth. That one drop of the vampire's blood meant the difference between a mindless soul slave and a self-sufficient but eternally dependent servant. Calais breathed thrice into the corpse's mouth and then cleaned his own face. He finished licking his fangs clean just as the corpse began to stir.

"What is your name, servant?" Calais asked.

"I am called Solomos, master."

"No longer," Calais said. "Now you will be known as Curqak, and all the world shall fear you because you bear my bite scar. Go now and feed, and when you have slaked your thirst, come back to me, for I have much I wish you to do."

"Yes, My Sire," Solomos, who was now Curqak, answered, and ran in search of his first victim.

*

Katja's voice echoed her disgust. "How many have you murdered as Curqak?"

The ghoul was weeping. "Hundreds, My Madam. I have lost count over the centuries."

"And what were you in life as Solomos?"

"A simple tanner, My Madam, with a beautiful wife and two precious daughters. I slaughtered my own family to feed my first Thirst as a ghoul."

Katja felt hot tears roll down her cheeks. For the first time, she recognized that the villain had also been a victim — that the evil done to him had twisted him into the wretched monster that he had become.

"Please destroy Master Luther, Katja Escari. Please end his evil, as I cannot."

"I swear to you by the Creator I will see Luther's end, Solomos, or I will die trying."

"Thank you, My Madam. Now I beg you to be merciful and end me so that I bear this cursed body no longer."

"As you wish. Depart this realm, Solomos." Katja focused the full power of her and Lauraisha's combined strength at the ghoul even as Daya'lyn's blue flames incinerated his broken body. She watched with wraithwalker's vision as the deadwalker's body was burnt to ash and his blackened soul was restored. The white outline of his true elf form floated before her and bowed deeply before vanishing into a shaft of light too brilliant to describe.

"In peace, Solomos," she whispered as he departed beyond the Erde Realm. And then she wept.

X

THE JEWELED MANTICORE

What did Daeryn mean by 'Mother's bondage will gain our freedom'?" Lauraisha asked as Daya'lyn led her, Katja, and the ogress youngling out of the mining tunnels and into the wider cavern.

The male shook his head. "I'm not certain."

"But you have a notion?"

"Several." Daya'lyn sighed. "None of them are pleasant... especially near young ears." He shot Lauraisha a meaningful look.

"I wish we could contact your father," Katja said as she hefted the sack holding the dead ogress's ashes onto her other shoulder. The stench of burned flesh and fur was heavy in her nostrils, but she had to admit that the revolting odor was better than the ogress Turning into an undead oni and assaulting them from behind. "Caleb needs to know about your mother's situation."

"So you trust Daeryn's truthfulness?" Lauraisha asked her.

"No, but I do trust Curqak's...or rather Solomos's memory."

Daya'lyn nodded. "On that I do agree."

"Would the ogres have a special mirror that we can use to contact your father?" Lauraisha asked.

Daya'lyn looked at her and frowned. "No. The Ott vre Caerwyn and those mirrors like it were forged of vampires' bloodstones. They are exceedingly rare. As far as I know, only three have ever existed. However, you've given me another idea."

"What?"

"We can try using our mirror shards to contact the Ott vre Caerwyn and leave a message for Father through it."

"Wouldn't it be simpler to try contacting him directly through my dreamdrifting?" Lauraisha asked.

"There is too much distance and deadwalker interference between us now, as you well know from your failed attempts to contact Joce'lynn. In all honesty, I was rather shocked that your communication with Felan and the rest of our packmates actually succeeded. I am certain that the attempt was only productive because of our mirror shards' odd connection with one other."

"An oddity that you hope will aid us again," Katja surmised.

The male nodded.

"It's worth the effort," Lauraisha agreed as they entered the central mining cavern. "Now, what do we do in the meantime with all this wealth?"

Daya'lyn chuckled at her wide-eyed examination of an uncut amethyst. "Surely a princess has little need for more baubles?"

Lauraisha frowned at him. "Do you think my life at Castle Summersted was lavish?"

Daya'lyn's smile slid off his face in favor of a frown of confusion. "It wasn't?"

Lauraisha's eyes and mouth hardened. "I ate and dressed somewhat better than my subjects, but that was only to flaunt Father's wealth and power, not to dignify me. As a child, I had few personal possessions and even less comforts. I didn't even have a bed of my own until I had seen twelve winters—and that wasn't even for my personal comfort."

"Oh," was all the male seemed able to say.

"What do we do with these?" Katja interjected as she picked up a paw's fill of gems.

"Take them with us, I suppose," Daya'lyn replied. "Borgar told me this cave system isn't currently claimed as part of anyone's territory, so its riches will be considered fair use. I say that we fill the ogress's supply sack with as many of the loose stones as Katja can comfortably carry so that we can give them to the ogress's family as compensation for the monetary burdens incurred by her death."

Katja and Lauraisha nodded and set to work adding what they could to the ogress's sack of belongings, which Katja now carried while Daya'lyn continued to comfort the youngling and guard against enemies. After they had filled the ogress's knapsack, the two females gathered many of the jewels in their own cloaks for later use in trade with Vihouset and Tyglesean merchants.

They followed Katja's chalk marks through the tunnels and found their way into the entry cave once more. Then the ogre Borgar ran toward Daya'lyn with his massive arms outstretched.

"Sorsha! You're alive! Thank the Creator!" He scooped his beloved daughter from Daya'lyn's care and hugged her close to him. "But where is your mother? Where is Kulgra?"

Sorsha peered up to her father through tear-filled eyes. "Mama was killed."

Borgar held the youngling and gazed at Daya'lyn. "Inquisitor, is this true?"

The male sighed and nodded. "I am sorry, My Sir, but Curqak murdered her before we could destroy him."

The ogre's eyes narrowed. "But he has been brought to justice?"

Daya'lyn's jaw hardened. "He has. Thanks to Katja's quick thinking and our combined mage skills, Curqak had only one last death to account for before he perished instead of two."

Borgar nodded and then hugged his daughter even tighter. He openly wept as Katja presented the bundle of Kulgra's belongings to him, including her broken horns, her ashes, and the jewels the three had collected for her family.

"You shall be honored as high guests of the Clan Shamgar. Master Daya'lyn, Katja Escari, and Princess Lauraisha, you all have done my family a great service by destroying my lifemate's murderer and saving my daughter from deadwalker evil. Please come. Eat and sleep within the protection of Jhalag tonight."

Daya'lyn and the others nodded their heads in appreciation.

"What of Edelsteen Uitgraven?" the werecat asked. "We cannot afford to allow the deadwalkers access to it now that we have rediscovered it."

The ogre frowned. "True. Since you, Katja Escari, were the first living Sylvan being to set paw in the mine in several centuries, you and you alone hold ownership of it according to Sylvan law. This mine lies along a disputed boundary-line between ogres and naiads, so none of us can lay claim to it."

"Can you form a coalition of both races to protect the mine?"

The ogre frowned. "I will send word to Neamyntha and Eureshra about that possibility. In the meantime, I am humbled by your gift of rare stones. I fear that I cannot accept such items from a neutral territory; I can only add them to the clan treasury until such a time as you find a use for them."

Katja frowned as she thought through the political risks involved with giving such a gift. "Very well, since these are my jewels to keep or to give to whom I wish, I bequeath half of the value of this gift to you and the rest of the ogres living in Jhalag and half of the value to the naiads of Azuralle Lake in gratitude for the aid you all have given the Inquisitor and his entourage. Is this acceptable?"

The enormous ogre nodded and bowed low to her with both of his paws outstretched in deference. "It is. Thank you, My Madam. Now, come, let us lead you to safety and rest."

Together Borgar and his fellow ogres led the packmates and their allied kelpies along a secret dry path through the marshlands south of the Merrow Road to the Shamgar Clan's city of Jhalag. The ogre's stone city itself was built on an artificial island which rose out of the swamp on a foundation of wooden pilings held together with clay-based mud. Katja ogled the sturdy construction as Borgar led them along a stone causeway between the central city and its surrounding marshlands. Giant cypress trees rose out of the mud to shade the buildings, which were made from stacked stone ascending as steps to the main living chambers perched atop. The result was magnificent.

"If I may, My Sir, why do you build your dens atop so much stone? Is it to reduce the risk of flood damage to your homes?" Katja inquired.

Borgar grinned. "That is the practical reason for it, yes. Although in recent years, flooding has proved less of a problem since our naiad neighbors rerouted part of the river. In any event, the main reason for the design of our buildings is actually to honor the Creator. Each ogre is bound with an oath at speaking-age to serve the Creator with the best of his or her talents. This is symbolized by each being giving an offering of his or her best work to the Creator as a daily sacrifice upon the altar at the highest point of their family's edhuklo—that is, their home."

The ogre took a deep sniff of the smoky evening air and smiled. "The sacrificial fires are already being lit as we speak. Come and see."

Borgar and Sorsha led the Inquisition members to the second largest edhuklo, which the Inquisition and their allies ascended once the packhorses were secured under a nearby cypress tree. As they toured Borgar's family's home, Katja marveled its efficiency. The squared stone compound at the top of the step-style platform was comprised of an inner courtyard open to the sky and several outer buildings all connected by covered porches. The inner courtyard consisted of a central cistern designed to catch rainwater runoff from the surrounding slanted roofs. Several reed baskets growing herbs hung from hooks beneath the eaves surrounded the opening to let stray drops nurture the plants. One of the smallest buildings housed a stone water basin large enough for a full-grown ogre to sit inside, and a covered waste-disposal pipe. The waste from that pipe was mixed with the waste from the ogres' livestock and cultured into fertilizer for their herbs and crops. Nothing was wasted.

Borgar led the companions to the conical kitchen building next to the ogre bathhouse, which held wooden shelves filled with ceramic bowls and jugs as well as a large fire pit and two large tables. Katja, Daya'lyn, Lauraisha, Calder, and Glashtin ate with Borgar and his relatives. Then all present followed Borgar up the stairs to the roof of the main sleeping quarters and sang prayers as each family member laid a portion of his or her best work onto the Altar of Supplication. Finally, the mighty ogre emptied his beloved lifemate's ashes onto the altar and prayed for the Creator's favor toward Kulgra in the afterlife and toward her family in their current life. Borgar then set fire to the altar's contents with a ceremonial torch and stepped away bowing.

Once the conflagration had ceased, a mighty wind stirred from the east and swept every last speck of ash away toward the distant western sea. Watching the ash dissipate gave Katja a strange peace. She felt her soul stir and heard a gentle whisper call her name. Without thinking, the werecat took her meager pouch of gold and the pouch of gems she had collected that afternoon and flung both onto the altar. Before anyone could restrain her or retrieve her gift, fire spontaneously arched between the torch and the altar. It consumed the bags and their contents, leaving only the now fused gold and the dazzling gems in their original state.

Katja closed her eyes to the dying embers and turned to feel the east wind ruffle her tawny fur. "I know that I am not perfect. Nevertheless, I give to you who created me all that I have, all that I am," she whispered.

Again she felt the calm whisper in her soul, saying, *Before your heart began its first beat, I knew you. I love you and I am with you, Katja, always.*

Katja fell to her knees in tears of overwhelming joy. A sense of peace and grace—one that she had never known—washed over her. From somewhere in the direction of the largest edhuklo a deep bell tolled in slow cadence over the marsh city and the uncanny wind fell silent once more. Katja felt a huge paw's tentative touch of her shoulder and looked up into Borgar's amber eyes—eyes that reminded her so much of her brother Kayten's. With the ogre's aid, she rose into her weary, hind paws.

"Never has anyone outside my own family members successfully sacrificed their works on this altar," Borgar said.

"I'm sorr—"

"Hold, Katja, do not apologize for showing an act of love and supplication toward the Creator, especially when He has so readily accepted your offer. You are divinely favored, Katja Escari of the Feliconas Clan. Or should I say Feliconas-Shamgar? We cannot allow an exception to the sacrificial law. What say you, Father, is there any reason she should not be made an honorary member of our family and our clan?"

The wizened figure of Borlag sat with a staff crooked under his withered right shoulder and stroked his goat-like beard with his left paw. "Her humility is unmatched. I have no objections to the compromise, but as always I will defer to your decision as ranking Brute."

Borgar bowed his huge head and then stroked a curled horn while in thought, his amber eyes darting to the other faces of his family. All met his gaze and either nodded or shook their heads. "Very well, Katja Kevrosa Escari, you have violated the law stating that only Shamgar blood-kin may offer supplication at the altar of their family's edhuklo. The usual punishment for such a desecration is permanent expulsion from the Clan Shamgar and its territories. However, the Creator accepted your supplication and has therefore ordained you and your sacrifice pleasing to Him. His rule is law above all else, and so we must defer to him."

Borgar knelt and placed his right paw on the stunned werecat's brow. "By my right as Brute of this family and an elder of the Clan Shamgar, I accept you as my own kin and swear protection over you and your allies even unto death. Will you accept our act of fidelity?"

Katja nodded at him in awe. To be so freely accepted by another race and culture was unheard of in her experience, particularly as a skinshifter. She glanced at her packmates and saw tears standing in Lauraisha's and Daya'lyn's eyes as they smiled at her.

"Thank you," were the only words she could manage in response. He smiled gently at the werecat, and then reverently scooped up the remainder of Katja's gift to the Creator from the sunsilver altar.

"These you must keep with you always as a sign of the Creator's favor." He gave her the jewel-studded gold plate forged from Katja's gift of coins and gems. She held up the crescent-moon-shaped plate and noted how the jewels' placement at its center bore a striking resemblance to an etching of the legendary manticore which she had studied long ago as a kit. Borgar filled a small bag with the remaining gems and gave that to her as well. He then studied the plate over her shoulder. "I suggest you wear it upon your upper chest as a broadcollar. It certainly will bring you protection.

I will have a smith make you a proper chain for it as well as fasteners for your other neck pieces on this broadcollar's backing."

Katja bowed and submitted the piece to him before staring at the altar and then the rest of her honorary ogre family in mixed trepidation and hope. As one, the ogres stood and welcomed her as their kin.

* * *

The Shamgar Clan's impromptu family celebration lasted well into the dark hours before morning. Whatever else could be said about ogres, Katja was grateful to be in the company of a group that truly welcomed others as family even if their method of acceptance was much rowdier than she had expected. By the time Katja had finally found her sleeping furs, her head had already begun to ache from too much mead. As she closed her swimming vision, Katja clutched the broken spearhead and the Feliconas Clan seal that Felan had given her seven moon-cycles ago. She wished with all of her being that she could see the werewolf again. She imagined him with his paws wrapped around her shoulders as she lay there, and the thought had made her smile in her dreams…

*

Felan dug his forepaws into the craggy edge and peered over the precipice, sniffing the sour air above the corpse-strewn battlefield. It was all he could do not to retch from the vile stench invading his nostrils and maw.

Turning his snout to the leeward side of the wind, the large black-and-gray wolf sneezed and then turned his gaze back to the grisly meadow. He searched for any movement among the bodies of elves, dryads, werewolves, zombies, ghouls, imps, and dullahan, but spied none. Filled with regret, he turned from the slaughter and loped back to his companions' hidden camp—hoping his wolf form would continue to help him avoid deadwalker detection.

He pushed through Zahra's protective ring of tangled vegetation and leaped into the small grove of Sacrificial Pines on the outskirts of Denth Crater. Zahra greeted him, holding a bowl of cold rabbit stew.

"What news?" she asked as he shifted back into his normal werewolf form.

"Thank you." He took the bowl from her and drank deeply before answering. "No survivors on either side that I can see, and the fireforgers have not yet returned to burn the corpses. The stench of death is unbearable!"

The dryad nodded, tears glistening in her brown eyes.

"It was a terrible fate that we came late to the battle. We could have aided the Sylvan cause," Vraelth said as he offered a cup of tea to the newcomer.

Felan accepted the elf's gift with a head bow. The elf gave him a brief smile, and then his face turned somber. "What now?"

"I can't be sure. We have at least acquired the Ursa Agate, so I suppose we should keep trekking east as quickly as possible to join the others. Thanks to Lauraisha's Sharing Sleep we know that they've yet to reach Vihous. What are your thoughts, Verdagon?"

The green dragon sat staring at the Agate Keystone he held through half-closed eyes. His features were etched in a deep frown of concentration.

"Verdagon?" Felan repeated.

The reptilian head did not move when his gaze finally met the werewolf's.

"What of our present circumstances?" the skinshifter asked. "Should we make haste to Vihous and join Katja, Daya'lyn, and Lauraisha or do we have another task yet before us?"

"Several tasks, actually…although you will perform those along the way to the western coast." The dragon murmured. "For now, thought I must fire the field and burn all remaining corpses since the fireforgers have not returned to honor the dead."

"But, Master Verdagon, such an act would expose us to the deadwalkers. Is this task worth such a great risk?"

Verdagon bowed his head and kissed the jewel in his left talon. "It is. No deadwalker may rise again to feast on more Sylvans on my watch. Not while there is yet fire in my lungs. Do not trouble yourselves. I will incinerate the corpses while the three of you guard against ambush. No straggler Asheken could withstand my fire and no Víchí master can hope to match my speed in flight.

"Even so, we will use caution. Vraelth, you will ride the winds with me and chant your spells to add protection to my armored scales. Felan, you will scout ahead in wolf form and alert us to any dangers on the ground. Zahra, you will stay in constant communication with the trees to discern the movements of our enemies when Felan cannot.

"Are we all agreed?"

The three packmates bowed their heads.

"Good. Let us set to work cleaning up camp in preparation for a rapid departure."

"Verdagon, what of Qenethala?" Zahra asked quietly.

"I am sorry, Zahra, but there is little I can do for her besides thank her for the selflessness of her sacrifice."

Tears stood in the dryad's eyes. "But…you are a dragon. Surely your tears can heal her!"

Verdagon shook his head. "Neither my tears nor those shed by any of the Pyrekin can free her. The Pyrekin Panacea is meant to fight the corruption of deadwalker Taint and other such venoms. It cannot undo the natural magic of Merging."

"Then what can I do?"

"Speak your final words to her."

Zahra closed her eyes against her tears.

"Do you want me to go with you?" Felan asked.

She nodded. The werewolf nodded and laid a gentle paw on the dryad's shoulders as they walked away from the camp into a more secluded part of the grove. He stopped at the edge of the trees and watched with twitching ears as the dryad moved on without him. She stopped at the base of an ancient pine—one of only two with bark tinged a strange shade of green.

"Qenethala?" Zahra's query seemed almost timid.

"I am here, sister," came the pine's quiet response.

"Sister, I…have to… Verdagon has called us to move on from this place and continue our fight against the deadwalkers. I must leave."

"You will leave and not return," Qenethala whispered through the pine's rustlings.

"Of course, I will come—"

"No. You must not."

"Why? Why would you forbid such a thing?" Zahra asked.

"Because, sister, you love me."

"Yes, of course, I do. I don't understand what that—"

"Zahra, if you come here again before the war's end, the deadwalkers will trap and Turn you. Your love and loyalty to me will mean your destruction. The trees remind me of this constantly. Your fate is not mine. Do not pity me."

"I want to free you!"

"I know you do. I love you, too," Qenethala replied. "But you cannot, so you must say farewell."

"No, there must be some way to free you!"

"Death is my only path to freedom now, Zahra, and my time here in our realm is not yet finished. Go with my and Eliza's blessings. Go with our gift of Mainmangi's Keystone. Find happiness again." The green pine next to Qenethala's twitched its needles in response to its name.

"How can I find happiness where none exists?"

Tears flooded down Zahra's face as her hands touched the rough bark of her half-sister's Merging Tree. The pine's surface began to glow under the sproutsinger's contact. With one hand, Zahra pulled the Pyrekin Panacea from its case on her belt, opened it, and doused the tree's roots with the restorative. For a moment the tree glowed even greener and then a dryad's face appeared in the bark under Zahra's hands.

"Sister!" she gasped as her fingers caressed Qenethala's cheek.

The face stared her in horror. "Why did you waste something so precious? Didn't the dragon tell you it would not work?"

"But your face…" But, even as Zahra said it, Qenethala's visage slid back beneath the wood.

"No!" she screamed.

"I love you… Goodbye…"

"No! No! No! It can't end this way! I won't let you go! I can't!" Zahra cried. The glow intensified around Zahra's fingers and then darkened.

The wind shifted and Felan was suddenly alert. The scents being blown toward him from Zahra and her half-sister's tree had somehow mingled. Something was very wrong.

Felan sprinted toward them in alarm. "Zahra, what are you doing?"

"Sister, do not do this!" Qenethala suddenly wailed. "It will be an abomination to my sacrifice! Felan, pull her back!"

"Leave me, Felan!" Zahra shoved him back with a surprising amount of brutality.

Zahra's fingertips slipped beneath the bark even as the werewolf threw his massive arms around her waist and pulled. "Zahra! Zahra, don't do this! Verdagon, Vraelth, help!"

"Let go, Felan! I can bring her back. I can pull her out!"

"No, you can't! All you're doing is Merging into the tree with her!"

The dryad gazed at the tree through her tears, and then her eyes widened in sudden recognition of what was happening. Instead of trying to wrench out of the tree, though, she pressed herself further inside it.

"Zahra, no!"

"Why shouldn't I Merge, Felan? There is nothing left for me here!" the dryad tried to kick him free even as her hands sank deeper into the tree trunk.

"You have your mother and your other sisters who are fighting for survival," the male said as he dug his back claws into the ground for added traction. "You would just leave them here? You would leave *me* here?"

"Felan, you are my dearest friend, but you don't love me—"

"Yes, I do! Now cease this madness!"

"—Not the way you love Katja, Felan. Admit it. You have never desired me the way you long for her. I can't compete with her for your affection, so why should I continue to try? It's hopeless." She was now Merged up to her elbows with the pine.

Tears were standing in Felan's eyes even as his strong grasp began to slip. "Please, don't do this! Don't leave me!"

"You'll survive," she replied in a hollow voice. "Katja will make you happy, you will see."

"Zahra, I can't lose you!" Felan roared as Vraelth and Verdagon sprinted to his side.

"Zahra!" Vraelth screamed as he pushed his lean frame

between her and the tree.

"Vraelth, don't, or you'll Merge, too!"

Vraelth wriggled into her grasp until their faces were less than a paw-width apart. He gasped as the backs of his legs began to settle into the wood.

Before she could reply, Vraelth reached around her shoulders and pulled her head toward his. Their lips met and locked even as they melded further with the tree. Zahra pulled back, breathless. "What are you—?"

"I love you and you're blind to it! If this is what it takes for you to see me for who I truly am, then so be it. I will Merge instead of you."

She stared at him with shock as Vraelth pushed her back against Felan. Her eyes went even wider as Vraelth's legs slid completely beneath the bark. "I can't stop the Merge! Vraelth! Oh, Creator, what have I done!"

Vraelth desperately tried to push her out of the tree even as she clung to his Merging body and Felan held onto her with all of his strength. The werewolf's back paws were slowly sliding through the dirt when Verdagon's tail wrapped around his hips and began to pull backward. Even the dragon's tremendous strength could not pull any part of the elf or dryad free from the wood.

"Qenethala, help!" Felan cried.

The pine rustled again. "Set flame to us, Verdagon."

The dragon flipped his angular head back to stare at the tree. "Are you daft! That will kill you!"

"And set all of us free. Do it!"

"Qenethala, no!" Zahra screamed.

"It must be done or they will perish, too! Do it, Verdagon, please!"

The dragon looked questioningly from Qenethala's tree to the green pine next to it. "Eliza?"

The strange green pine rustled and whispered, "I have fulfilled my task of guarding Mainmangi's Keystone until the appointed time, Verdagon. Now let me finally see my sister Ella and the rest of my family beyond the Dyvesé Gateway."

With a roar of anguish, the dragon launched a single fireball into the tangled upper branches of the two trees. A pair of muffled screams came from within the two pines as a deep crack rent each of their lengths from top to bottom. The two Sacrificial Pines split in two. Qenethala's tree expelled Vraelth and Zahra from its depths, and then both pines' halves toppled to the east and the west. Their fires extinguished as soon as they hit the ground. As the packmates watched, twin tendrils of white mist billowed up from the bottom of the split trunks. The pair of mists bobbed a farewell, and then vanished into the sky.

"Sister! No!" Zahra had wailed…

*

"No!" Katja gasped and sat up with the dryad's scream echoing from her own throat. She kicked off her sweat-soaked sleeping furs and clutched her roiling stomach. All around her was quiet except for the steady breathing of her fellow sleepers, none of whom seemed in the least bit roused by the werecat's sudden outcry—not even Lauraisha.

Katja frowned at the human, confused. Lauraisha always shared the werecat's dreams and almost always was startled awake by them at the exact moment Katja regained consciousness. Tonight, however, the human only murmured in her sleep and rolled in the other direction.

The werecat cringed as her stomach churned again and she lurched to her shaky paws. With one paw on her belly and the other on her aching head, the female stumbled out of the sleeping chamber toward the bathhouse building. She made it there just in time to vomit down the waste hole. Then she did it again and again. Once her stomach was thoroughly purged of its contents and Katja felt more dead than alive, the werecat washed her paws and face in the small water basin and crawled out to sit on the cool stone bench near the central cistern.

"Difficult night?"

Katja jerked her head in the direction of Daya'lyn's voice. The hybrid stood on the rooftop across from her near the offerings altar, his cloak wrapped tight around his body to ward off the damp chill.

"Too much mead and too many foul dreams," she replied through clenched fangs. Suddenly she wished for her own cloak as the night air chilled the warm sweat clinging to her body.

"Would you welcome some company?" he asked.

She watched him a moment before bobbing her head. "Please."

He jumped down to land neatly on the narrow wall of the cistern before walking around its edge to sit beside her. "Aren't you cold?"

She nodded and felt part of the male's cloak envelop her shivering shoulders. The muscular male leaned back against a column and gestured her close to his side. Gratefully, she curled up under his cloak and shut her eyes against the pain raging in her head.

"What troubles you, Katja?" Daya'lyn's deep voice was unusually gentle.

"Zahra and Felan."

"What of them?"

She huddled against Daya'lyn's linen shirt for warmth and comfort. He held her trembling form as she explained her dream in hushed tones.

"Normally Lauraisha dreams with me…normally I feel her presence when I dream. But she didn't so much as twitch when I screamed myself awake. Why wasn't she with me during this one?"

Daya'lyn shook his head. "I don't know. You will have to ask her once she wakes. Is that what has you so upset?"

Katja grunted. "No. It's the fact that Zahra is still in love with Felan and neither of them bothered to tell me."

"Do you love him?"

She shut her eyes against her sudden tears and nodded.

"Have you told him?"

She nodded again. "He told me that he loved me too. We kissed. It was perfect…and then I asked him who would marry us—a werecat and a werewolf—and he had no answer."

"Do you believe that Felan knew of Zahra's true feelings?"

Katja shook her head. "I don't know. The dream didn't seem to indicate that he did, but he certainly knows her feelings now. And the way he roared for her when he thought he was losing her… What do I do? I want him happy and perhaps he would be happier courting a dryad than a werecat. His sire and dam at least approve of that interracial match, as it has the chance of producing viable young. But I... Maybe I'm selfish, but I want him for my own lifemate and not as someone else's. Is that wrong?"

Daya'lyn shook his head. "I have no idea. Thirty-six winters I've survived in this world, and I have yet to understand any of you females."

Katja's ears drooped and she moaned softly as she clutched her wayward belly.

"Are you going to retch on me?"

She grimaced. "If I do, it's of no consequence. There is nothing left for my sad stomach to expel. How can the ogres possibly drink that much mead and not get drunk or sick?"

"Well, they are a little larger than you." Daya'lyn's pale lips twisted into a smirk.

Katja snorted and then whimpered. "I am *never* drinking that much again!"

Daya'lyn rubbed her back. "I'm sorry I cannot give you advice about Lauraisha since dreams are not my specialty. But, as to the matter with Felan, I suggest you not brood about his feelings until you see him again. From all I know of the male, Felan is both honest and loyal. After all, he originally annulled his betrothal with Zahra before all of you journeyed to the Isle of Summons together because he did not return her affections and refused to mislead her. For a being like him who is driven by honor, hypocrisy is not an option. If his feelings toward her have changed, he will tell you his true feelings when you ask. Besides, from what you've just told me, Vraelth will give Felan some competition for Zahra's affections."

Katja moved to dip water from the cistern into a clean cup and rinsed the bile out of her maw.

"Don't be too harsh with Felan or with Zahra," Daya'lyn said as Katja curled up against his broad chest once more. "After all, grief can thrust beings' minds down some very dangerous paths—as you and I well know."

She closed her aching eyes against the wrinkled fabric of his tunic. "I'll try my best."

They stayed silent for a while and watched the stars wheel overhead as Katja slowly sipped water and pondered the hybrid's advice. Eventually the fresh water helped to settle Katja's stomach and ease the throbbing in her head. Wrapped in the protective comfort of Daya'lyn's cloak and presence, she began to feel drowsy.

"What of your brother's comment?" Her voice was a bare whisper.

Daya'lyn stirred beside her. "What?" He also sounded drowsy.

"What did Daeryn mean when he told you that 'Mother's bondage will gain our freedom'?"

"It means that he will likely try to Turn her."

That roused her. "What!"

Daya'lyn shut his eyes against the world. "Cruel, isn't it …that I should discover that my own mother is alive, only to realize that she'll suffer a fate far worse than death."

"How do you know?"

"My father wanted to Turn my mother when they first met as a means to obtain true immortality."

Katja frowned at him.

Daya'lyn rubbed a gloved hand over his weary face. "Father will have to tell the full story to you, but I can at least describe the essentials."

Daya'lyn explained that by the time Caleb had survived for two-hundred winters as the vampire Calais, he began to search for a way to become more powerful than his blood sire Luther so that he could seize control of the Víchí Covens for himself. Spurred by his power lust, Calais began attacking and Turning Sylvans of all different races—experimenting with the vampire bite techniques to find a way to make himself invulnerable to the one thing all vampires fear: a fireforger's flame.

"When he discovered my mother, Marga, almost dead in the wreckage of her caravan, Father brought her to Caerwyn Castle to try to Turn her. Instead, however, she Redeemed him."

"How?"

Daya'lyn shrugged. "Love. My mother fell in love with Calais and he with her. He came to her one night after she had regained full health and asked that she destroy him because the alternative would be him trying to Turn her. The flame-laced kiss that she gave him in response purged him of his soul's corruption and restored his dead body instead of destroying both of them. Her love is what ultimately saved them. And so my brother must think that our mother's love is the key to finding the power that my father once sought to wield against fireforgers.

"As you know, no vampire can Turn a fireforger. Instead both will die during the Turning process as the mage's soul's fire consumes and destroys the corruption in each. That was the law of nature until my mother and father met. Then they broke that law with the vampire Calais's Redemption into the dhampir Caleb. My brother and I, through our conception and birth, then destroyed the natural law that states that all deadwalkers are barren and, therefore, cannot sire children of their own. Now Daeryn has Fallen and thus abolished the natural law that claims that no fireforger can become a deadwalker. Every law that the Creator set up for the Sylvans' protection against the deadwalkers have all been abolished — save one."

Katja frowned. "The one which claims that all vampires can be destroyed by fire?"

"Correct."

"But since Daeryn is a fireforger who successfully Turned into a vampire, doesn't that mean that he is already invulnerable to fire?"

"Apparently not, otherwise he wouldn't still flee my flames every time we meet."

"But why wouldn't he be able to withstand you fire now?"

Daya'lyn shook his head. "I'm not certain. It may be that he can tolerate weak flames, but that my power is still too intense for him to endure. That was the case in our youth before he Turned. Daeryn could never forge more than a golden flame and anything more than that would leave him in agony."

"So what do we do?"

"Hope, pray, and continue to look for the Keystones. If my brother discovers how to make himself invincible to all levels of fireforger flame, then only the combined strength of the twelve Pyrekin will be able to raze him — and that might not even be enough."

Katja shivered. "And I'm bonded with him."

The male nodded. "Now you know why I'm so worried."

"Have you been able to contact your father through your

mirror shard and tell him any of this?"

He shook his head.

"So that is why you were awake tonight?"

He nodded.

She hugged him. "I'm sorry."

"I am sorry too. I wish that none of this had ever happened. My family has been at the center of so much pain and torment. I'm sick of it, and I will see it end one way or another."

They sat in silence for a while until Daya'lyn turned to her again. "Swear to me that you will tell no one what we have discussed this night dealing with my family. Not even Lauraisha. She has enough to burden her mind and I cannot bear for her to have to carry any more."

Katja sighed, thinking of the dangerous road ahead. "Daya'lyn, you shouldn't keep secrets from her—especially not something this important."

He shut his eyes. "I know, but if she knows how I came to be... I fear that it will taint her decision."

Katja frowned at him. "What decision?"

He shook his head. There were tears now standing in his blue eyes. "Katja, do you trust me?"

Katja searched his face. "Yes, I do."

"Then, I beg of you. Keep my family's secret."

Finally, she sighed and nodded. "I swear it."

XI

IRKLINGS

The members of the Inquisition rested a few days in Jhalag before departing the ogre city. On the eve of their travel, Borgar met with Daya'lyn to discuss the dangers they would face on their way to Vihous.

"I see no alternative but to traverse the remainder of the Merrow Road until we reach Vihous," Daya'lyn told the Clan Shamgar Brute as the two spread the map over the clean eating table. The fireforger traced the route with a gloved finger.

"What of the kelpies? Surely, they can help you cross the marsh waters in safety."

"I discussed the journey with Calder this morning and he made it quite clear to me that, while he and Glashtin can likely keep us clear of any deadwalker ambushes, these are still strange waters to them and he cannot promise our safety from sawtooths, swamp basals, or some of the other natural predators that lurk in these marshes."

Borgar rubbed his furry jaw with a paw and squinted at the map. Katja watched him out of the corner of her eye in fascination. True to the stories of his muddled ancestry, Borgar looked like a strange cross between a Rosmelan Clan werecat, a satyr, and a giant. He bore the shaggy brown fur of a satyr over most of his massive body, yet his paws held retractable claws and his face was almost leopard-like in its structure and coloring. Two curled ram horns crowned the brute's head and Katja could see thick gray skin in the interim where they merged into his fur. She wondered whether the ogre's hide was as stone-hard as a giant's like the Feliconas Clan legends said.

"Hmf."

The werecat glanced over in time to catch Lauraisha scowling at her before the human crossed her arms and turned back to look at the two conversing males.

Katja flicked her ears. The human had been distant to the point of rudeness ever since the Offerings Ceremony and the werecat had yet to understand why. Try as they might, neither Katja nor Daya'lyn could elicit more than a one-word response from Lauraisha when they asked her about anything. Katja wondered if the princess was somehow envious of the ogres' adoption of the werecat, yet she had no way to discover such a truth when the human wouldn't talk to her.

What bothered the werecat even more, however, was the fact that the dreamdrifter had blocked their shared mental bond. Not only was that act uncharacteristic, it was also potentially dangerous. If Daeryn rewove his mind's bond with Katja and found the skinshifter alone without the defensive aid of either Lauraisha or Daya'lyn, the thought of what might happen made the werecat shudder.

Daya'lyn looked up from the map to stare at the werecat. "Katja, are you well?"

She met his troubled gaze and glanced at the human. Daya'lyn's eyes flicked from hers to Lauraisha's. He considered the glowering human, shook his head, and went back to the map.

"What if we cut through the marshes here, just south of the Merrow Road? Will that help us save time and avoid detection?" Daya'lyn asked as he pointed to a pathway which paralleled the River Ehud south of the main road's crossing.

Borgar shook his head as his furry finger tapped the river island just north of the pathway. "You'll stray too close to the Hag's Nest. That is a perilous place even during the most peaceful of times. My scouts tell me that it's being used as an Asheken fortress and currently plays host to a whole mob of irklings. Not the strongest deadwalker foes you could face, but best to avoid without decent ear coverings—their cries can drive any being insane. The island itself has grown and so has its influence because of the additional deadwalkers now in this territory. It poses the main threat to the Merrow Road."

"How can an island grow?" asked Lauraisha.

"By collecting corpses. The Hag's Nest is called such because a powerful sproutsinger dryad once resided there. She was Turned into a hag by a powerful vampire who was later defeated during the Second War of Ages. Even though he was destroyed, his bloodstone was never recovered. Rumor has it that the hag Alqama somehow stole it just before her master's end and has been hoarding it on the island ever since then."

Katja was aghast. "No one has been able to kill her in over three hundred winters?"

Borgar shook his head. "Keep in mind, neither ogres nor naiads have birthed a fireforger mage in well over two centuries. The gift is very rare in this part of the continent."

"Hence why the deadwalkers have been able to invade and overtake this area of Sylvan soil so swiftly," Daya'lyn surmised.

"Correct."

"But surely the Council of Mages or the Ring of Sorcerers would have sent one of their fireforgers to help you deal with the problem?"

Borgar shook his shaggy head. "We have asked others to come; but, Master Daya'lyn, you are the first fireforger to travel these marshes since your own mother visited the naiads over three hundred winters ago."

Katja looked at Daya'lyn. "That makes no sense. The Council and the Ring are sworn to protect and defend all Sylvans from deadwalkers. Why would they not intervene?"

Daya'lyn's eyes narrowed. "It could be that the Mage Council's corruption runs deeper than we thought. I know that their depravity was the original reason that Mother hid the Keystones in the first place. She did not trust those in power to protect the sacred gems and so she stole and hid them."

"Yes, but most of those mages are long dead! Surely things would have changed in three centuries!"

Daya'lyn cocked a brow at her. "After what we've endured on the Isle of Summons during the past three moon-cycles, do you really believe that things have changed all that much?"

Slowly Katja shook her head.

"In any event," said Borgar, "Alqama now has her former master's bloodstone, which means that she has access to any magic he stored within it plus any magic that she has added to it. Alqama's evil attracts other evils. Basals often attend her, seeking out Sylvan beings to capture and bring as sacrifices to her. She'll drain their souls' life and magic into her bloodstone and then give the corpses to her pets for food. Any remains are piled onto the outer banks of her island fortress, thus making the island grow in size and complexity. Most of the time, Alqama keeps to herself and only abducts one or two beings during each moon-cycle. Recently though, I've heard reports of seven or eight beings taken during the past fortnight."

"If she has become so bold, then she must have a strong deadwalker ally," Daya'lyn concluded.

When he said this, an image came unbidden to Katja's mind…

*

An island emerged out of the mists of the river as she approached. The isle was bare of all vegetation save the cruelest of thorny brambles. A tall tower rose out of its center—its walls made of cut stones held in strict formation by crushed bone mortar. The ground surrounding the tower was littered with layer upon layer of skeletons of every shape and size. At the bottom of the tower stood a small wooden door guarded by two huge coiled basal snakes. The door was adorned with a single tiny skeleton—that of a gnome baby with its body curved into the fetal position.

As Katja watched, a ghoul approached the door while several dozen Turned gnomes trooped in behind him. The door opened at his knock and a gray-skinned dryad smirked when she saw the irklings trailing behind him

"My gift to you, My Madam," Curqak had said…

*

Katja hissed at the memory. "It was Curqak. He needed an ally in this territory, so he befriended Alqama and Turned a village of gnomes into irklings at her request."

"You're certain?"

She nodded. "I saw their exchange in his memories before Curqak's end."

"I am so glad you destroyed that fiend when you did," the ogre growled.

"It wasn't soon enough," Katja said.

Daya'lyn's arm slid gently around her shoulders even as the princess stood and stormed out. Daya'lyn said nothing as he watched her go, but his grip on Katja's shoulder threatened to crush bone.

"Inquisitor."

Daya'lyn turned toward Borgar and his hand fell away.

"I know that you all have a long journey ahead of you, but I must ask: will you and your entourage help us fight against Alqama and her allies? I fear what she will do if she is left unscathed much longer."

"As do I." Daya'lyn said. "Do you have enough warriors to lead a proper assault?"

Borgar hesitated, rubbing his scruffy chin in thought. "Not here. There is an ogre fortress not far from the Hag's Nest. It should provide us with decent protection against Alqama's allies and may also give us an eager supply of warriors should you choose to battle her. However, the fort does not belong to Shamgar. It belongs to our rivals—Clan Barak. If you wish to attack the island, we'll need the strength of both clans—if they are willing."

Daya'lyn nodded. "Tell them that the Sylvan Inquisitor calls all able-bodied warriors to fight alongside him as he and his allies wage war against our oppressors. Hopefully that will stir the passion of more than a few brave souls."

* * *

The next morning, under the combined protection of their kelpie mounts and the ogre warriors of Clan Shamgar, the members of the Inquisition progressed northwestward through the marshes toward Fort Barak. After three days, half of their ogre escort broke off to aid a clan of gnomes who were fighting against deadwalkers along the edge of their shared territories. Heeding Borgar's warnings, the remaining party used several game trails to skirt the edge of the Merrow Road. Their progress was slow, but largely unhindered as they trekked through the wetland wilds.

Throughout it all, Lauraisha stayed silent in speech and mind toward the others—her mood growing fouler with each passing league. On the third night of their journey from Jhalag, Katja had had enough of the human's poor attitude. After the evening eat, the werecat excused herself from the others and stalked beyond the camp circle in search of the human, who had strode off just as soon as her own chores were finished. Katja found her quarry sitting alone at the base of a cypress near the water's edge stabbing the mud between her boots with a dagger.

"Lauraisha?"

The human looked up at her with uninterested eyes and then lowered her gaze to her lytzahn-etched patterns once again.

Katja gazed around the hollow in the gathering gloom and shivered in the damp chill. The relative quiet of this murky marsh made her uneasy. "You leave the safety of the camp without even bothering to tell us where you're going or when you will return? What are you thinking?"

The dagger continued its muddy assault and Lauraisha said nothing.

Katja flattened her ears and glared at the female. "You haven't so much as said 'fangs' to me since the celebration... or to Daya'lyn. Why are you mad at us? Are you jealous of me?"

Lauraisha gaped at her, disbelief, anger, and genuine hurt shining in her blue eyes. "How dare you!" she whispered as tears slid down her face.

Katja cocked her head in confusion, her ears flicking in agitation. "What did I do?"

"First you have the gall to chastise me for leaving the two of you alone like you wished in the first place and you rebuke me for being jealous of you! Oh, forgive me if I just can't cope with the sight of you and Daya'lyn together right now." Lauraisha's voice dripped with sarcasm.

Katja frowned at her. "What is wrong with you?"

"Wrong? There is nothing wrong with me other than I have a treacherous whore for my dearest friend!"

The muddy dagger whistled through the air and landed

blade-first in the grass between Katja's paws. The werecat's maw fell open in shock and the rhythm of the werecat's heartbeat echoed loud in her ears. Tail twitching, she backed away.

"Did you really think that I wouldn't catch the two of you in your lie? That I wouldn't see the way you look at each other? Or realize that you were keeping secrets from me? I love him, you lecherous little changeling! But, no, you wanted him for yourself. You couldn't allow me one moment of happiness, one grain of contentment. Better the 'innocent' orphan win her prize than the sullied noble. You don't think I'm good enough for anyone, do you?" Lauraisha's blue eyes were smoldering with hatred, as she drew her sword.

"Daya'lyn!"

"That's right, call for your lover, you worthless tramp. It won't avail you this time!"

Katja stared in panic at the advancing princess. The werecat's frantic heart hammered in her ears as if it were muttering its own language. "Lauraisha, we didn't do anything! We don't love each other—not in that way. He's like a brother—"

"A brother! Hah! You named me lytzsibba, Katja! You named me a younger sister when you had none! And now you go to him when my back is turned—" Tears were streaming down the human's face now. She was waving the sword almost drunkenly as she staggered toward her retreating rival. "I heard the two of you whispering together under the offerings altar after your Celebration Ceremony! I saw what you did with him!"

Katja feinted away from Lauraisha's sword swing, and then shoved her sword arm aside with one paw even as she clawed the female's arm with the other. The wound was purposely shallow, but it was enough of a painful distraction for the werecat to scale the nearest stout tree and put some distance between herself and the bellowing human.

From her heightened perspective, the wraithwalker suddenly became aware of a faint chittering flowing along with the cold night air. Its subtle rhythm matched her heart beat and the blood rushing through her veins; the words were undiscernible, but they caused a clammy claw of dread to scrape the back of her mind. And then Katja noticed the crimson haze assaulting the edges of her vision. Deadwalkers were close. *No wonder Lauraisha is acting insane!*

"Irklings! Lauraisha, cover your ears!" Katja yelled even as she flattened her ears back against the muffling fur of her head. The human was yelling incomprehensibly at the base of the werecat's tree, a semicircle of Turned gnomes creeping through the undergrowth behind her. Katja pointed in panic and shouted again for the human to cover her ears and look behind her. Lauraisha refused.

"Daya'lyn, we need you! Irklings have us! Where are you?" Katja screeched into her scarlet spear shard. She discerned no reply through her muffled hearing nor did she see the muscular male anywhere.

"Katja…we're surrounded. We'll come when we can!" Daya'lyn answered. A panicked gasp issued from the shard and then it was silent.

At once the world slowed down. She saw her dead family members' faces parade before her and then watched as her packmates added themselves to the list of the dead.

"No!" she gasped.

Katja's allies' panic and rage buffeted against her own fear and grief—an icy pool of emotions threatening to drown her. Then a curious warmth spread across her chest, its source coming from the Feliconas Clan signet crest resting over her throbbing heart. Sudden peace flooded her being and washed away her turmoil. Katja looked at Lauraisha and saw Damya's Sapphire glowing faintly beneath her robes even as the irklings stalked closer. Among the trees in the distance, she saw a glimmer of white—the Opal of Azmar. The gems twinkled their message and Katja understood. The wraithwalker drew all of the peace held deep within her being, raised her head to the night, and roared.

It was not a roar of defiance, anger, or grief as it had been when she first encountered Curqak and discovered his role in her family's destruction. Instead the sound now issuing from the wraithwalker's maw was one of overwhelming hope— the same hope Katja had felt when Verdagon had hatched and named her his steward on the Isle of Summons. Her roar reverberated through the gloom and sent the irklings tumbling into the murky waters surrounding them. Lauraisha lay where she had landed—flat on her back on the muddy, gray-green moss.

She gazed up at Katja in complete bewilderment. "What just happened?"

The werecat hunted for their enemies and found the little monsters silently retreating back through the swamp. Then she looked back at the human. "You tried to kill me in a jealous rage while under the influence of irklings."

Lauraisha blinked at her, and then her lower lip began to tremble. "Did I harm you?"

Katja shook her head. She slid down from her perch in the top of the tree and pulled the female to her feet.

"Do you even remember our conversation?" she asked as she examined the wound she had given the human. Lauraisha's guilty contemplation of her own boots confirmed that she did. Katja sighed in sudden weariness as she rinsed the muck out of the gash she had given the human. "I am *not* in love with Daya'lyn, Lauraisha."

"I—I believe you... It's just..." Fear and frustration played across Lauraisha's face as she watched the werecat skinshift her wound closed. "He seems to get on better with you than he ever does with me."

"We have similar temperaments and our souls bear similar scars. We understand each other, but we don't steady each other the way that soulmates should. You provide a better balance for him. You are what he needs...if you're willing to be."

There were tears in the human's eyes. "I thought love would be so much easier."

Katja gave her a sad smile as she removed her paws from Lauraisha's healed arm. "Nothing worth so much can ever come so cheap. Now, come. We need to find Daya'lyn and make sure he and the others are well."

"Never mind that; I'm fine."

Katja whirled around at the sound of the male's deep voice, and then gaped at him in shock. The male's face was cut up, his tunic was torn, and his wings were exposed—one of which was folded halfway behind his back at a strange angle.

"Daya'lyn?"

"I'm well," he said wearily as he slumped against a tree trunk.

"He's lying," Lauraisha said.

The male cocked a dark eyebrow at her.

"Well, you are!" she retorted.

Katja frowned. "You're bleeding and your wing is injured!"

Daya'lyn shook his head. "The blood is more from the others than from me. We can worry about my wing later. Come quickly! The others are in grave need of your skills."

The females followed him through the underbrush back toward camp. They found Calder leaning against a stand of cypress trees while Glashtin lay still at his hooves. Katja covered her maw with a paw when she saw him. The prone male's hindquarters had been ripped open and flies were already congregating around the gaping, rotting wound despite Calder's efforts to swat them away with his tail. The rest of the prone kelpie's body was peppered with cuts—some of which were fizzing with deadwalker Taint and some of which had been cauterized closed by Daya'lyn's fire. Calder gently nuzzled Glashtin, neighing softly.

"What of the others?" Lauraisha asked Daya'lyn even as Katja sank to the ground and put a paw on Glashtin's neck—feeling the fluttering of his weak heartbeat.

"Two ogres are dead; one nacken is dead," the fireforger answered quietly. "Borgar and Tyron are badly injured. If it hadn't been for Katja's wraithwalking roar, we probably would have lost them as well."

Katja shut her eyes against sudden tears. "How long do you think it will take for our enemies return?"

Daya'lyn licked his shrinking fangs with his tongue—something he did only when he was nervous—and stared off into the darkness. "The cleansing magic that you unleashed is still strong in this place, but will it hold until dawn?"

Katja shook her head. "As this was my first attempt using wraithwalking magic in this way, I have no idea."

"Assuming that it does not hold, the deadwalkers will need to regroup and attack again before sunrise if they want any chance at us before the wounding glare of daylight once again inhibits their movements. That means that we will see less than ten hours pass before they come again."

"Precious little time to waste, then. Lauraisha, would you please see to the others while I work to heal Glashtin?"

The human nodded and strode toward the medical pack. After digging through its contents, she produced a bottle of saltwater, a tin of mixed herbs, and a fistful of rags and gave them to Katja. Lauraisha then hoisted the medical pack onto her shoulders and followed Daya'lyn out of the camp clearing in search of the others.

"Katja?" Calder asked once the werecat had finished her preliminary examination of the kelpie.

Katja shook her head. "The Taint is deep. We need the Pyrekin Panacea."

"You gave that to Zahra so that she could use it to help Qenethala Emerge from her pine prison."

The werecat nodded, remembering with a sudden pang of guilt how much of the dragon and phoenix tears compote she'd had to consume after her disastrous encounter with a dullahan and his deadwalker allies three full moons ago during the Isle of Summons Ambush. She doubted that even the whole vial would have made a difference in Qenethala's situation, but, then, her guilt never troubled itself with logic. "I know I did, but without it I doubt... I will do everything I can."

Katja pulled out the bottle's stopper and poured liberal amounts of the saltwater into Glashtin's wounds—disinfecting as many as she could before she tried to skinshift them closed. The deadwalker Taint made the process all the more difficult. Try as she might, Katja could not draw the toxins out of the kelpie's body like she had for herself when Curqak had attacked her. She growled in frustration.

"Is there any hope for him?" Calder asked her after she finally succeeded in closing the largest and second-largest gashes.

"I...don't know," she said between panted breaths. "This is all very new to me. I'm not a harmhealer, so I can't do much more than knit skin or bone together in another being. I've had some success drawing Taint out of my own body, but drawing it out of another...ordinarily only a master harmhealer or a Pyrekin can do that."

Calder bowed his head and said nothing more as Katja tried and failed to close the fourth wound. She looked forlornly at Glashtin's broken body. What more could she do? She had no contact with Verdagon and he had been the only one to help her fully heal another. She winced at the memory of Felan's near-death and rubbed her face with the back of a bloody paw.

"I'm sorry…I've used too much strength," the skinshifter panted. "I'll have to suture the others closed…without magic."

"With what? Lauraisha took all of that material with her."

Katja frowned as she looked around the dark hollow. Night had long since descended and the crescent moon and stars had been her only source of light for a few hours now. In the wan light, Katja spied a curtain of curly moss. She picked up a willow branch and used it to gather the moss into a bundle around her stick.

She set to work cutting away the dead tissue from each of Glashtin's lesions. Once a wound was stripped and cleaned with saltwater, she packed it with saltwater-dowsed moss and herbs to help absorb as much Taint and infection as possible. As she finished packing a cut, she covered it with more moss and wrapped the wound with bits of cloth torn from one of her winter robes. The smaller wounds she simply cleaned with saltwater and left open to try to let the toxins drain. She was just finishing her makeshift bandages and sutures on the last foaming gash when Lauraisha led a hobbling Tyron and a pack nacken back into the camp clearing. Daya'lyn followed closely behind as he helped Borgar limp over to a fallen tree and sit down.

"You were beginning to worry me. What kept you?" Katja asked.

"A few remaining deadwalker scouts," Daya'lyn replied grimly. "They are cinders now."

"This is my fault," Borgar lamented. "I led us too close to the Hag's Nest."

Lauraisha shook her head with tears in her eyes. "No, this is my fault for being so foolish and leaving the safety of our camp."

The cold night wore on slowly as the Sylvans waited for the second deadwalker attack. Daya'lyn and Katja dug a shallow trench around the clearing and lit peat fires within it to help deter irklings while Lauraisha fashioned earplugs from scraps of cloth. Once the fire barrier blazed around them, the Sylvans all huddled under their cloaks with their backs to each other and searched the murky swamp beyond their knoll of refuge for signs and sounds of enemies.

Twice Katja swore she heard a distant chittering. But each time she raised her earplugs to her ears, it stopped and then the only sound was Glashtin's labored breathing. After the second occurrence, Lauraisha went to check the kelpie.

"How is he?"

"Bad and getting worse." The human laid a sleeping fur over the kelpie's quivering form and sighed in frustration. "I don't know what else to do for him."

"Contact Damya. See if she has any advice or aid for our current predicament."

"I have—again and again—and still she remains silent. Ever since our meeting with the naiads, the only sign I have seen from this useless rock is an occasional glimmer."

"Try again."

Lauraisha sighed and closed her eyes in concentration as she held the Sapphire Keystone between her fingers. "Damya?" After a moment, she opened her eyes and shook her head. "Nothing."

Katja growled and gouged heavy marks into a nearby tree with her claws to vent her frustration. "Where is she?"

Lauraisha's brow was creased in concern as she watched Glashtin's chest rise and fall. The sound of his breathing had taken on the wet tones of a gurgling wheeze.

"I don't know."

Finally, Katja's ears perked to the waking calls of birds and insects and then her nose noted a subtle change in humidity. She looked up to witness blessed light invading sky's eastern edge.

"Dawn is approaching," she said.

A thin smile creased Daya'lyn's lips. "So it is."

In that moment, Glashtin's rattling breath ceased, and Calder wailed.

* * *

Battered, bruised, and broken, the survivors of the allied Inquisition and Clan Shamgar warriors staggered into the safety of Fort Barak just as the sun set. The injuries sustained during the first irkling attack meant that a trek that should have taken two hours instead ate up the rest of the day. Thanks to the darkness caused by a midmorning rainstorm, the group had endured even more casualties. The whole situation enraged Katja.

"We have to destroy her!" she said as the fort's harmhealer stitched up her injured packmates.

"With what, Katja?" Daya'lyn retorted. The Inquisitor muffled a cry as the healer yanked on the broken bones of his left wing to straighten and splint them. "We have seven beings and two beasts to burn and bury. Of those of us left alive, Borgar cannot walk, Tyron cannot run, I cannot fly, and Calder is inconsolable. The only whole-bodied beings in this group are five ogres plus Lauraisha and yourself, and the two of you tried to kill each other mere hours ago!"

The werecat's eyes narrowed. "Inquisitor, Alqama is responsible for the death and enslavement of countless Sylvans including seven of our own company. She must be held accountable for her evil!"

"I agree, but we no longer have the advantages of strength in numbers or surprise against her. If we confront her and lose, we will jeopardize our main mission to Tyglesea and could very well jeopardize all Sylvans in the process."

"Then what would you have us do? Leave an enemy on our flank to continue threatening our lives and those of our allies? She will only grow stronger as time passes. If we do not destroy her now, she may well grow powerful enough to threaten all Sylvans in these marshlands and in Vihous."

Daya'lyn groaned and slid a gloved hand down his sweaty face. "Borgar, you know this territory and its occupants best. What are your views?"

The Clan Shamgar Brute shook his head. "I feel as if we are caught between the cliff's edge and a forest fire. Alqama has the advantage and now she knows we are vulnerable. There will be no safe passage along the Merrow Road while she controls the island and its surrounding territory. Clan Shamgar cannot hope to destroy her or her allies without aid. Everything now depends on what the Clan Barak ogres decide."

XII
THE HAG'S NEST

Katja crouched under a dead tree with the nauseating stench of death assaulting her nostrils and a slimy scapula digging into her scarred right paw. She stayed still despite the discomfort—watching, sniffing, and listening to every part of the decrepit environment around her. Across the sluggish river from her position, the Hag's Nest lay quiet in the afternoon light. Few things stirred in the cool sunshine, but Katja gripped her bone staff tighter nonetheless.

It had been quite an ordeal for Borgar to convince Gornash, the Barak Fort Brute, to lead his ogre warriors against the Hag's Nest. In the end, only Borgar's challenge of a traditional Hornbutt had decided the argument. The two ogres had stood horn to horn, both snorting and pawing at the dirt like the angriest of rams. Despite Gornash's best efforts, Borgar managed to push him across the center rope line. It still amazed Katja that Borgar had been up to the task in the first place. While she had done what she could to help Borgar and Daya'lyn recover from their injuries, the Barak harmhealer deserved most of the credit. He had used all of his considerable skill to ensure that Borgar had indeed been healthy enough to endure the Hornbutt challenge. The Barak leader conceded the match after only a fourth of an hour, and then spent the rest of that evening planning strategy with Daya'lyn and Borgar. Two days later, three-fifths of the fort's warriors moved out to join those remaining Shamgar warriors and gnomes in surrounding the island with the intent to

202 • ALYCIA CHRISTINE

destroy everything on it.

Katja looked up at the sky's blue expanse to see Gornash's prized raven wheeling lazily overhead. When the big black bird gave a single, cacophonous cry, Katja cautiously moved forward. Her keen ears noted her allies' quiet advance around her before her eyes did. Altogether, the island raiders emerged from their hiding places and descended down the shoreline.

Calder, Borgar, and two gnomes used their waterweaving skills to congeal paths atop the murky river for the others to run across. As they neared the isle, the waters on either side of their temporary paths began to churn. Basals and sawtooths began launching themselves from the dark waves and dragging any being they could bite into the muddy depths.

"Sproutsingers!" Borgar roared.

A hail of spelled crossbow bolts arched from the riverbanks on both sides. As they struck their intended targets, the sproutsingers sang in high, clear voices and nets of vines coiled around the beasts. The Sylvan allies then kicked their ensnared foes back into the river to drown or be eaten by other river predators before pressing on to the island.

Once there, Katja gasped. The isle was even worse than even Curqak's memories had shown. The ground was little more than a pile of crumbled bone and excrement. Any vegetation that grew was thorny, gnarled, and vindictive toward anything foolish enough to stray near it.

"Oh, perfect, more asp's thorn," Lauraisha said as she launched an orange fireball into the nearest spiny branches lunging toward Katja. The werecat hacked off the smoldering heap at its base with her spear and kicked the offending plant's twitching tendrils away even as Lauraisha seared a second writhing plant.

Katja hissed as she swung her bone staff at a third plant—piercing its creeping tendrils with her staff's attached sunsilver spearheads. "Jierira! These things are even worse than the ones that Perefaris cultivated!"

"Lauraisha, more fire!" Daya'lyn called.

More of the human's fireballs lit up the afternoon and turned the isle's plants into ash. Since there were no fireforgers besides Daya'lyn and Lauraisha, the process of clearing the vile brambles was slow and arduous. As the first twenty raiders hacked and slashed their way toward the island's center, their allies joined them. An outer ring of ogre warriors secured the isle banks against the tenacious basals and sawtooths, while the inner ring of allied warriors advanced on the central tower.

They had cut through half of the nightmarish undergrowth when Katja's ears perked to the sounds of muffled movement. She heard the muted scuffling under her own back paws and looked down in alarm. She saw nothing, but followed the sounds as they continued to one of the recently hewn asp's thorn stumps.

"Katja, what is it?" Borgar asked.

She shook her head. "I'm not sure—"

A small humanoid head popped up from a hole wedged under the base of the scorched plant. Its wicked yellow eyes peered at her around a bulbous black nose. The irkling's wee gray lips parted in a sharp little grin and then its split tongue began to vibrate rapidly in its mouth. Suddenly the tiny monster's fellows began to pop up from shaded holes all over the island between the two lines of ogres—chittering a chilling welcome to their guests.

Lauraisha stared in horror. "Creator, keep us! They'll break the lines!"

"Irklings! Sylvans, plug your ears!" Katja shouted even as she and Lauraisha reached for their own.

The reverberations grew louder until the ground itself shook beneath Katja's paws. As the Sylvan warriors tumbled off of their paws and feet, Katja looked toward the tower and realized that the vibrations weren't coming from the irklings. Instead they were coming from the tower itself. She watched in dawning horror as a massive bundle of branches grew out of the top of the quaking keep. The thorny branches spread out above the stone fortress like the crown of an enormous tree—splitting off and branching until they covered the entire island in deep shadow. The irklings, who had evidently been waiting for the darkness, jumped from their holes to stab the downed ogres with their tiny Tainted spears—their chittering increasing to a deafening cacophony with each new attack.

Those fortunate enough to have donned their earplugs before the ground quake were now fighting to stand amidst the onslaught. Those left without such protection were huddled on the ground whimpering as their attackers' blades brought blood.

They're slaughtering us! Lauraisha screamed through their minds' link even as Katja decapitated an irkling. *What do we do?*

Tell Daya'lyn to scorch the tree! Katja replied.

Moments later a huge blue fireball grew between the hybrid's ungloved talons. With a bellow of rage, Daya'lyn launched the blaze toward the tree. It streaked like a comet and exploded three thick boughs on contact. A sticky rain of sap began to pelt those fighting underneath even as the flaming debris began to catch other parts of the tree on fire. Patches of sunlight began to appear, eliciting shrieks of pain from the irklings. A few retreated, but most pressed their attack.

Thanks to the protection of their mage allies, those ogres and gnomes who were nearest to the fireforgers and sproutsingers managed to regain their stances. These now began the gruesome task of chopping the irklings off of their Fallen brethren. Sunsilver blades flashed and irkling heads rolled. The few ogres still alive on the ground had cloth earplugs jammed into their ears by their clan members and were soon able to regain their sanity enough to join in the fray.

Katja and Lauraisha trudged through the deluge of sap and scorched debris, decapitating enemies as they went. The tree's billows of black smoke began to overshadow the hard-won patches of sunlight.

We're running out of time! Katja thought as she avoided a basal's strike in time to stab it neatly in the back of the head. She rolled the twitching corpse over several irkling holes to block them, while Borgar and Lauraisha made quick work of a second basal behind her. *Lauraisha, do we have a shadowshaper with us who is powerful enough to push the smoke clear?*

Lauraisha looked at Borgar, who shook his head.

No, Katja, he says that we had one, but he is dead…as are six of our eight sproutsingers.

"Rippezahnen!" the werecat cursed aloud.

Now what?

Before she could reply, Katja once again felt a tremor

beneath her paws. It was not as powerful as the quake when the shade tree had grown, but it was violent enough for the werecat to check her stance before lunging after an irkling. The irkling and the few left of its fellows were running through the chaos toward the tower. Katja frowned and looked behind her. The deadwalkers' tunnels must have collapsed when the shade tree grew. With their places of ambush caved in and the sproutsingers' stout vine nets keeping most of their allies off the island, the irklings were being overrun. *Thank the Creator! They are retreating!*

Katja grinned as she saw her allies pulling their earplugs out. The outer ring of warriors was largely unbroken as they decapitated the fallen, and then stabbed irkling holes with burning torches just to be certain that they left no enemies behind them. Eventually the outer ring joined the fragmented inner circle and together they swept toward the keep from every side.

Katja felt the tremor again and frowned.

"Murderers!" screamed a shrill voice.

Katja looked up at the top of the cracked tower. A female stood on the keep to one side of the smoldering tree, wrapped in a deep purple robe and wearing her former master's crimson bloodstone on a gold chain. Her curly hair was as brilliant red as Zahra's, but the hag's skin was more ash-gray than vibrant green and was pulled taut on her bones like that of a starved being.

"You murdered my children!" she screamed. Katja stared in horror as she realized that the hag was holding a headless irkling in her arms—sobbing as she rocked the body back and forth in her cradled arms. "You will answer for your evil!"

"No, Alqama, you will answer for the countless murders of Sylvan males, females, and children," Daya'lyn's deep voice rang out. "As Inquisitor, I call you to task for your crimes."

"You? Inquisitor? Hah! You look like my scorched Víchí master!"

Daya'lyn launched a fireball at the hag. She ducked in time to avoid it.

"So the rumors are true! The true-blood grandsons of Luther do exist."

Daya'lyn's scarlet eyes narrowed. "You have one of two

choices, Asheken. Either you surrender yourself for a proper Witch Trial and I make your demise quick, or you continue to fight us and I make your demise very slow."

"You shall gain neither form of satisfaction from me, quisling!"

The wooden door of the tower exploded into myriad splinters and mud flowed from its depths. The sap coating everything began to flow of its own accord back toward the tower. Then it congealed together within the mound of clay. The greenish mud then split into two masses—each of which formed into what Katja could only describe as a sculpture of a giant. The two mud-and-sap creatures towered over even the ogres by more than a body-length. They stood upright on two massive feet with arms that reached well past their barrel chests to their knee joints. While they were slow to walk, the mud-giants could swing and elongate their arms like a massive pair of vines.

"Golems," Gornash shouted.

"Creator, keep us!" Borgar said.

"How in the blue blazes did she make those?" Lauraisha asked.

Katja stared in awe as Borgar said. "She restructured the tree. Those mud giants are neither beings or beasts, but reconstituted plants wrapped in a mud-clay body to make them mobile. They are loyal only to their rebuilder."

"How do you destroy them? Fire?"

Borgar shook his head. "I'm not sure. Golems are troublesome. The sap running through their plant-root veins helps hydrate their clay-based bodies, so fire does very little harm to them unless you manage to hit the top of their heads, where the leaves grow."

"The only one who can get high enough to reach above their heads is Daya'lyn and he has a broken wing!"

"We'll have to cut them off of their feet first," Daya'lyn said as he ran to the two females' position. "Borgar, we have other problems. The sawtooths have begun to bite through the sproutsingers' vine nets. We'll have enemies in front and behind us!"

"Gornash and I will do what we can to reinforce the barriers, Inquisitor."

"Thank you."

As Borgar and several other ogres ran toward the island's perimeter, Daya'lyn took a long draft from his blood-filled wineskin, grimaced, and then swung it back behind his shoulder as he gripped his sunsilver staff.

Lauraisha starred at his eyes, which were now almost as deep red as the blood he had just drunk. "Daya'lyn, are you well?"

The male looked at her suddenly fearful face. "I'm becoming weary and my supply of nourishment has begun to coagulate."

"Are you…?"

Daya'lyn shifted his stance and grimaced. "We need to finish this battle quickly."

Lauraisha swallowed and nodded.

"Run!" Katja screeched as a golem shambled closer and swung a huge arm toward them.

The three dove in different directions just in time to avoid the slap of the whip-like appendage. As she leaped out of the way, Lauraisha's sunsilver sword swept across the limb's end and sliced off a piece. The severed golem limb flopped and writhed against the ground like a snake before remolding itself into a small sphere and rolling back toward the attacking golem. As the mud ball touched the golem's foot, it was absorbed back into the golem's body.

"This is a cruel jest," Lauraisha yelled. "Those things can reform themselves!"

"Don't get too close," Calder yelled as he kicked a basal with his back hooves. "If one of them catches hold of you, it can suck you into its own body and suffocate you."

"Thanks for the warning," the human replied acidly as the two of them avoided another attack.

Katja risked a glance behind her. Most of the remaining ogres were busy dealing with the invading sawtooths and basals at five separate choke points around the island. Although they had routed the irklings once, nightfall was coming quickly and the survivors would soon be able to attack the Sylvan allies without the need for their collapsed tunnels. Of the original eighty ogres and thirty gnomes who had assaulted the Hag's Nest, barely half were left and a precious half of those living remained free of serious injury. If the members of the Inquisition could not bring down the golems soon, they would all be slaughtered.

"Katja! Help Lauraisha!" Daya'lyn yelled.

The werecat turned to see Lauraisha desperately trying to parry a golem's swing with her sword while Daya'lyn fought its twin with his sunsilver staff also ablaze with fireforger's flame. While Daya'lyn still had enough energy left to fight with scarlet flames, Lauraisha did not and her deepening desperation was evident to all.

Without realizing it, Katja began to skinshift. Her need to protect Lauraisha and Daya'lyn drove her instinct and she felt herself take the form of a full lioness at will for the first time in her life.

"Katja, what are you doing!" Daya'lyn yelled.

"I have no idea. Just keep them busy!" the lioness roared back. Somehow the skinshift gave Katja a renewed amount of energy and she leapt into the air. Her claws were fully extended as she sailed over the whip-like arms and plunged against the thing's slimy throat. Sap and clay flew in every direction as she clawed her way through the fiend's neck to the other side.

The golem's decapitated head went sailing toward the tower while the rest of its body collapsed into a puddle. Katja heard a wet smack as her paws hit the ground and the golem's head struck the tower stones and slide down their surfaces.

"You destroyed it!" Lauraisha said breathlessly even as she ran to help Daya'lyn fight the second.

Katja's answering grin vanished as she looked toward the tower. She heard Alqama's triumphant laughter above her as the golem's head began to roll toward its reforming body.

"Daya'lyn! Fire the head!" she screeched.

Daya'lyn's answering orange fireball struck the top of the golem's head—singing its leaves and crusty outer skin— but still it kept rolling. Katja raced toward the rolling head in panic. She grabbed hold of a leafy tendril with her fangs and dragged it away from the lunging body. She couldn't let the two rejoin! Daya'lyn's fire hadn't caused enough damage to be truly effective against the mud monster. If fire couldn't destroy it, what could?

Creator, guide me! she prayed silently as she ran. She dodged past the second golem toward the opposite edge of the island. There was a small rip in the vine net ahead of her in which a basal was trying to struggle through. No ogres were close enough to defend against it, so Katja charged the beast herself. With a swing of her head, she launched the golem head at the basal. Her aim was true and the head knocked the basal back across the narrow beach of bleached bones into the water. The golem head began to fizzle and steam when it touched the River Ehud's water. Then it dissolved and dissipated completely. Katja frowned and looked back at the golem body behind her. It was now bumbling toward her as if blind. She dodged its clumsy swipe and looked back at the river. The river still steamed where the head had been, but the head did not reform. Comprehension dawned.

"Gornash! Calder! We need your waterweaving skills!" she yelled.

The huge ogre brute swung his war hammer to crush the skull of a sawtooth and then looked at her. His eyes widened in surprise as he saw the lioness.

"Drown these golem fiends!" Daya'lyn yelled at him and the kelpie.

As Calder raced to their aid, the ogre frowned from Daya'lyn to the headless golem. When understanding finally took hold, he too raced to a safer position amid the fighting. Together Gornash and Calder raised their right paw and hoof in a beseeching gesture. As one they yelled a single incomprehensible word of Kwaërm. The river water behind them rose of its own accord into a waterspout that swirled past the beach and moved onto land. It caught the headless golem and then swallowed its twin inside its rotating vortex before churning across the island and out over the river once more. With a shout and the lowering of fist and hoof, Gornash and Calder collapsed the spinning waterspout—dumping its contents into the rippling waters. The river frothed and churned with its strange new acquisition. A single muddy hand reached up through the steaming waters pawing vainly at the air. Then it too melted into a stump which then dissipated below the hissing eddies.

"No!" the hag cried, wringing her black-clawed hands.

"Surrender, Alqama!" Daya'lyn yelled. "Your power is broken and there is none left who will defend you!"

Katja looked around and saw that the Inquisitor's statement was indeed true. Any basals, sawtooths, and irklings that were left were fleeing the island in all directions. The sawtooths sank into the depths of the River Ehud while the basals and irklings retreated into the moss-choked woods beyond its shores.

"I will never surrender to the likes of you!"

"Enough of this!" Calder bellowed. At his one-word command, a boulder-sized ball of water gathered itself over the river and then drifted to pour out its contents over the top of the tower. With a screech of panic, Alqama found herself carried along with the sudden deluge down the tower's inner stair steps and out of the broken front door. She stood up, shivering among the sunsilver blades of twenty-nine enraged ogres and gnomes. Meanwhile the kelpie collapsed trembling to the ground—the last of his energy gone.

"For Glashtin," he whispered.

"Inquisitor, when you are ready," Gornash said and bowed.

"Katja, I'm in need of your wraithwalking strength if you can spare it. My own is about spent," Daya'lyn murmured.

The lioness nodded. "Gladly, Inquisitor." Katja reached to touch the male's uncovered hand with her right paw. Her crescent moon-shaped scar and his dragon-shaped mark glowed incandescently as they touched and strength passed between them. At once the lioness felt bone-weary while her companion stood a little straighter.

"I wish to help, too, Inquisitor," said Sorbash, the only surviving ogre harmhealer.

"As do I," Lauraisha agreed.

Daya'lyn nodded. "Very well. Lock hands with me."

The four mages stood hand in hand and hand in paw with one other.

"Katja?" Daya'lyn looked expectantly at the lioness.

The wraithwalker closed her eyes a moment and opened them again, seeing the deadwalker before her through the vision of truth. She saw the dark crimson shapes clinging to the hag's decrepit soul and felt the eyes of dead and undead alike peer back to her. Darkness buffeted her mind as she cut through the Drosskin to see the soul of a once kind and caring dryad. Memories assaulted her of the dryad's Turning by the fangs of her vampire master and then of her murder of hundreds of other Sylvans at his command. The vampire Lothian had been destroyed during the Second War of Ages by none other than Katja's own father Kevros, and the memory of his valiant fight caused a low moan of grief to escape the lioness's maw.

"Katja, what is it?" Lauraisha asked.

The lioness shook her head and kept sifting through the hag's soul. Much of Lord Lothian's bloodstone's power had been drained through the hag's soul this day, but there was a little left untapped. Katja quickly blocked the hag's access to it and sequestered the stone with her will before giving Daya'lyn the approximate count of those slain by the hag's actions.

"Alqama, dryad Turned to hag, sproutsinger Turned to shaman, you are hereby judged and found guilty of the murder and enslavement of 437 Sylvan beings including the fifty-one ogres and one hundred seventy-eight Turned and Unturned gnomes who perished here today. This is by your own reckoning," she said solemnly.

Daya'lyn took a breath to steady his rage. "As Sylvan Inquisitor appointed by the Ring of Sorcerers for the protection of all Sylvans, I therefore sentence you to destruction by fireforger's tongue."

"Do your worst, Inquisitor, but know that I will take great pride when you Fall and join me in the Wraith Realm lands beyond the boundary of Edgewater."

Daya'lyn watched her a moment, his red eyes boring into her black ones. Only when she flinched did he say, "Mages, begin."

The wraithwalker, harmhealer, and two fireforgers linked paws and hands that then glowed with the transfer of magic. Daya'lyn stared at Alqama almost mournfully, and then opened his mouth. A horizontal pillar of pale blue fire burst between his fangs and consumed the hag before him. As Katja held the hag's soul in place, the fireforgers' combined magic incinerated her body and purified her entire being.

With one last scream, Alqama was reduced to ash. Then her bloodstone cracked and a crimson haze wafted from its fractured core. The four collapsed against the bone and ash ground when the deed was finished and in their midst, a single white tendril of mist floated into the sky and vanished in the last rays of the setting sun.

* * *

The cleanup of the Hag's Nest took seven days and nights, during most of which the Sylvan survivors recuperated from their injuries and burned the dead. Once Katja and Lauraisha had managed to purge the island of its remaining deadwalker and Sylvan corpses and their corresponding wraiths, the island itself proved a fairly peaceful refuge. No deadwalker or evil beast dared set paw on the place after the cleansings were finished, and so the Barak and Shamgar ogres began construction on a memorial to honor the dead using the stone from Alqama's tower. From the rubble, they built an altar to the Creator and sacrificed the best of their meat to Him as thanks for their victory. Katja watched the altar's kindled flames with bitter-sweet tears running down her face as she stood apart from the others. Her skinshift during combat had unnerved many of her newest allies. Although Borgar had still welcomed her as family, Gornash and his allies had kept their distance from her and from the rest of the Inquisition members in the days following the Hag's Nest Battle.

During much of the reconstruction, Daya'lyn sequestered himself within an undemolished room of the original tower and would only allow Lauraisha or Katja to attend him. Lauraisha had quietly told Calder that Daya'lyn desperately needed Tyron's nourishment, but the kelpie doubted Tyron's ability to travel from the Barak Fort to the island since the horse was still recovering from the leg injury he had gained during the irklings' first attack.

"What do we do?" Lauraisha asked Daya'lyn the third night after the fight.

The hybrid male lay trembling upon a bed of straw. He looked far more like a vampire than a half-elf now and Katja's hackles rose at the resemblance.

"Katja and you will have to hunt for me since I dare not

do it myself and risk exposing my state to the ogres. Will you do this for me?"

The females nodded.

"Would you even be able to hunt now, as famished as you are?" the human asked.

Daya'lyn groaned as the werecat mopped his fevered brow with a damp cloth. "You forget, Lauraisha, that I become stronger when I thirst rather than weaker. That was why I was able to escape my tower prison to aid you during the fight with the dullahan Perefaris on the Isle of Summons."

"The bloodlust adds strength to my limbs and keenness to my senses in preparation for the hunt. But all magic comes with a price, and blood magic is no exception. To give my body its added strength, the Thirst robs my mind of its sanity."

He shook his head and cursed. "I should not have waited. I should have crept out of camp the night of our victory to hunt, but I feared that my absence would seem too suspicious. We already had issues with the ogres' ill will set against Katja. None here know that I am a blood drinker, although a few may have guessed. My rankings as a fireforger master and as the Inquisitor have kept the questions at bay, but I have no notion how long that can last. My wits dull as we speak and the danger grows."

Katja frowned. "How long until your sanity fails?"

"Two or three days at most."

Katja nodded and stood. "We had better get moving then."

"Katja, wait."

"What?"

When she turned back to him, the male held up to a pair of iron chains to her. "Bind me please, before you leave—to ensure all of our protection."

* * *

I don't feel right about all this subterfuge, Lauraisha mentally whispered as the two females stalked through the marshes in search of prey.

Nor do I, but I don't see any alternative at this moment. Do you? Katja replied even as she sniffed the scratch marks on a cypress.

Not at the moment, no... Katja?

What?

What is that movement over there?

Katja looked in the direction that Lauraisha was pointing and saw a shaggy, brown beast shambling along near a thicket. It stopped to sniff the air and then began to paw at the rotting bark of a fallen tree.

That is a bear.

I thought they preferred more forested terrain.

They usually do.

Then what is it doing out here?

I have no idea. Katja watched the beast closely. For a bear, it was fairly small—something she and Lauraisha might be able to carry between them. While still thin from its winter hibernation, it did not appear sick or injured. Still the werecat could not understand why a healthy bear would wander this deep into a swamp. The male wasn't fully grown yet, so perhaps it had yet to establish a territory and was simply foraging for whatever food it could find wherever it could find it. Whatever the reason, she was grateful for the warm-blooded creature's presence since it would surely prove a better meal for Daya'lyn than a sawtooth...if she could figure out a way to capture it without it managing to mangle either her or Lauraisha. Katja climbed the stout trunk of a twisted tree and scanned the area for any other large beasts. When she found none, she groaned. This hunt would not be as dangerous as what they faced at the Hag's Nest. Even so, it would prove anything but easy.

Lauraisha, we need to capture that bear.

Are you daft?

Probably, but it is the only warm-blooded beast anywhere close to us and a warm-blood will sit far better in Daya'lyn's stomach than a cold-blood. Not to mention that a predator will nourish him better than a prey beast.

Lauraisha pursed her lips. *Agreed. Oh, how I wish Zahra was with us. She could lodge an arrow in between that beast's eyes before it could even flinch.*

That she could, but that would do us little good in this case since we need it alive and unharmed.

Lauraisha inwardly sighed. *I was right. You are insane.*

Katja nodded in fervent agreement before she slid down the trunk.

What is your plan?

Give me the net. When I give the word, I want you to light your sword with flame. Keep the fire weak, enough to singe the fur but not enough to scorch his skin. I want him afraid, but not harmed.

What about me? How do I stay afraid, but unharmed?

Katja's smile was rueful. *Keep your sword between the two of you at all times and stay on your toes. Try to push the bear toward that tree up that hill so that I can get behind it and have some room to drop my net on top of it. Don't ever turn your back or run from it. Just be prepared with a fireball in case it tries to charge or escape. Hopefully, we'll be able to entangle it within the net without it biting or clawing either of us.*

Lauraisha nodded. *You lead, werecat. I'll follow.*

Katja set off at a brisk but silent pace and felt more than heard the human trail behind her. Katja felt sudden pride as the princess slunk into ambush position. The human's hunting skills had improved so much since their first meeting nine moon-cycles ago. Too bad the werecat could not say the same about her own fishing skills. Perhaps Lauraisha could teach Katja once they were closer to the coast. First, though, the werecat had to net a bear.

The bear's low growl greeted them as they moved close the bright green thicket. Fire flowed in curling ribbons along the princess's sword as she wedged herself between the bear and its main means of escape. Katja unfurled the fishing-net just as the beast charged at the human's blade. The fireforger flicked the sword tip near the bear's nose—opening a wide gash in the sensitive skin. The bear roared in pain and swiped at the burning blade with its paws. Lauraisha gritted her teeth and swept the flaming sword back and forth in front of the growling beast, forcing it to retreat up the hill.

The fire glowed in Lauraisha's determined eyes as she repelled the bear's second roaring charge. It snapped at her sword and once more backed away from the flames singeing its nose. The princess flicked small fireballs at the beast's paws whenever it tried to turn and run. While its full attention was on the human, Katja crept up the tree behind the bear with the leading edge of her net pulled wide between both front paws.

A moment before she tossed it on top of the bear, the angry beast swiveled its head, saw her, and rushed between the two of them. The net fell on empty ground.

"Catch him!" Katja hissed as she slid down the tree and bolted after the bear. She scooped up the net in mid-stride and launched it once again after the beast as it ran toward the safety of the thicket.

The net caught the creature just before it clawed its way over a lichen-encrusted log and gained its freedom. The bear thrashed against the binding cords in panic and tangled itself up even worse within the weave. Katja jerked two of the net's ends out of the beast's reach. When the beast rolled and tried to push itself toward the werecat, Lauraisha struck her extinguished sword just before the bear's face. It roared and retreated long enough for Katja to grab the last two ends. She yanked all four net corners upward, jerking the bear onto its back in the process. As it jerked and writhed in the confines of its sturdy fiber restraints, Lauraisha cut a pair of paw-width-thick limbs from a nearby tree and helped Katja slide the net's end loops onto the poles. Once their snarling load was secured, the two hunters laboriously picked their way through the marsh back toward the island camp with the poles settled between their shoulders.

They walked in silence for a time and then Lauraisha sighed. "Katja...may I ask you something?"

"You know that you may ask me anything."

The human nodded and blew out a heaving breath. "I...I did see you and Daya'lyn together that night after the Shamgar Clan's ceremony."

Katja stopped their advance around a bog and looked over the pole at the human. Confusion and anger wove conflicting shadows across Lauraisha's face. The werecat sighed. "Yes, he comforted me that night. Why does that trouble you?"

"Because you love him."

She nodded and gestured to the bear. "If I didn't love him, I would never have agreed to track down such dangerous prey for him. But, as I told you before, Daya'lyn is more my match as a brother rather than a potential lifemate."

The human stared at her, tears trailing down her sweaty, dirt-smeared cheeks.

"We never meant to harm you, Lauraisha—either of us. Surely you know that."

"If you don't love him, then why did you curl up with him in the dead of night?"

Katja shook her head. "I had a nightmare and then became ill from too much mead. Daya'lyn found me and took pity on me. I accepted his offer of warmth and comfort. That was all."

Lauraisha frowned in confusion. "I don't remember sharing a nightmare with you that night."

"You didn't. You slept soundly even though I screamed myself awake beside you."

"Show it to me."

Katja opened her memory of the nightmare and the following conversation with Daya'lyn. She shared all that she could with the dreamdrifter without breaking her promise to Daya'lyn not to share his family's secrets. Lauraisha's eyes were wide with shock once the memory finished. "Zahra nearly killed herself and Vraelth and you didn't tell me! Why did you keep this from me?"

The werecat scratched one of the scabs left on her arm from where an irkling had stabbed her. As exhausted as she'd been, she had barely been able to skinshift back to her normal form after the battle. She hadn't had enough energy to completely skinshift her own wounds closed during the transformation and so now she had to let them heal naturally. "If you'll recall, we've been a bit busy over the past fortnight. Either way, though, I am sorry for causing you such pain."

Finally Lauraisha nodded. "I am too. I shouldn't have made assumptions without discussing my fears with you. Please forgive me."

Katja smiled. "Done."

"Done."

The two friends clasped each other's hand and paw in reconciliation since hugging around the biting bear was out of the question. Then the pair slogged on through the green marshes toward the dead island and to the male who needed both of their care.

XIII
LOVE'S PERILS

"How did you capture it?" Daya'lyn asked, his deep voice tinged with wonder. Katja and Lauraisha cautiously set the net and its ferocious occupant on the stone floor.

"A heap of courage and even more luck," Katja replied as Lauraisha closed and barred the door behind her.

"I hope you are satisfied with this beast because I will *not* be hunting one of his kind ever again," Lauraisha said.

Daya'lyn watched her. His voice may have said, "Thank you," but his scarlet eyes seemed to express something else. Lauraisha watched him for a long moment and then Katja felt a barrier once again rise within their mental bond even as Lauraisha's mind drifted toward the male's.

"Careful, Lauraisha," Katja and Daya'lyn spoke in unison. The werecat's eyes snapped from Lauraisha back to Daya'lyn when he spoke. Daya'lyn's low voice lacked his usual calmness and was instead infused with the single-minded strength of a predator.

"Are you truly willing to steady my mind while I feed?"

Her eyes never left his. "I am."

Katja's hackles rose and she licked her lips in her nervousness. This felt wrong. She suddenly felt as if she were listening to Daya'lyn's and Lauraisha's conversation in the Citadel dungeon on the Isle of Summons when she had been completely invisible to both of them.

The muscular male fought against his bonds and managed to push himself to a stand—the rusted links whining as he strained against them.

"Daya'lyn, what are you doing?" the werecat asked.

No answer. His scarlet eyes never left the human's even as the wraithwalker lowered herself into a defensive crouch and used her magic to see the hybrid through the lens of full truth. A war played out in Katja's scarlet-tinged vision. Daya'lyn's soul still radiated a golden fire that was almost blinding within his refined features, but he also bore fangs and clawed talons that rivaled those even of his physical form. His eyes shifted back and forth between a burning blue and a sullen red. In them, she saw his fervent wish to protect life battle with his dark desire to conquer it.

"If you value your life and hers, werecat, do not interfere."

"I value yours, Daya'lyn…as does Lauraisha. You are not your brother."

"No," he whispered as he considered her. "I am stronger."

He turned back to Lauraisha and watched her. "Do you have the courage to contend with me, dreamdrifter?"

It was at once a question and a challenge to the human. Katja turned back to Lauraisha, whose eyes were locked with the male's. Although she trembled, the princess did not break her gaze. "What do you want, Daya'lyn?"

His voice lowered to the barest whisper. "You know my mind; you know my need and my desire."

"An equal."

"Yes…"

Lauraisha sighed. She looked so much older now than sixteen winters. "The time is premature, Dayalan."

"I know."

"Will you wait?" Lauraisha asked.

"Will you?" Daya'lyn's voice was strained with longing, pain, and terrible hunger.

"I will wait for you," she said simply.

"Then I will wait, Lauraisha."

She lifted her chin then. "Then I can steady you; now, break your bonds and gain your nourishment."

The scarlet-eyed hybrid's muscles flexed then and Katja watched the links of ancient iron snap free from around the male's chest as if they were made of twigs. Katja's eyes went wide and before she could even blink, the male leaped across the room to stand before Lauraisha and the cowering bear. He stopped with his elongated white fangs less than a claw-length from her lips, his breath coming in ragged gasps. She reached up gently to cup the hybrid's scruffy jaw with her hand and he slid his own clawed fingers over hers, pressing her palm hard against his hollowed cheek.

"Please," he pleaded.

"No."

With a roar of frustration, Daya'lyn turned from her to the bear. He ripped the net apart with a single swipe of his black claws, grabbed the bear by the scruff of its neck, and slammed it against the stone wall.

Daya'lyn sank his full fangs into the creature's pulsing neck and drained the beast dry. When the deed was done, Daya'lyn gently laid the bear's carcass on the ruined net and then fell to his knees. Without a word, Lauraisha wrapped her arms around Daya'lyn's quaking shoulders as the now blue-eyed male wept.

* * *

When the warriors of Clan Barak's main city were finally able to send supplies to their brethren and allies at the Hag's Nest, Calder brought Tyron and the surviving nacken Runnel to the packmates. The steeds' arrival could scarcely have come at a better time since Daya'lyn had gone more than a fortnight without Tyron's blood. The bear's blood had slaked the hybrid's thirst well enough for him to hunt with some sanity, but the marsh itself had offered few choices in the way of other large warm-blooded beasts suited to Daya'lyn's unique needs. In the end, Borgar realized the packmates' dilemma and quietly arranged for the hybrid to find and feed from a flock of goats while they waited for Tyron to heal. Katja and Lauraisha kept Daya'lyn sequestered in the tower's storage room during most of those interim days so that Sorbash could continue to help heal the male's broken wing while Lauraisha worked to calm his troubled mind. As Daya'lyn regained his sanity, Sorbash switched his talents to Tyron's leg—rebuilding the muscle that had been torn during the irkling attack.

Ten days after the Hag's Nest Battle, the members of the

Inquisition once more traveled westward along the Merrow Road under the protection of the Clan Shamgar ogres. They traveled three days through the bright blooms of spring-touched marshlands until they spied the blessed safety of the Vihous border. Katja, Lauraisha, and Daya'lyn bid their ogre protectors farewell and passed through the Ring Spells' threshold into Vihous's lands. The Hamos Watchtower guards welcomed them as they crossed the guarded river border and then escorted them to the nearest wayfarers' inn inside the city.

For the packmates who were now accustomed to sleeping near each other on the hard ground, the idea of separate rooms and beds was both welcome and daunting. With nightfall, Katja found herself lying alone upon the relative softness of a straw mattress with her thoughts centered on Felan. Was he well? Had they found safe passage through the forests yet? Had he met many deadwalkers in battle? She longed to see him and wished more than anything to hear his gentle voice and feel his warm touch upon her fur…maybe even have him caress her lips with his own once more. She remembered their first kiss and an ache of sadness crept over her soul.

To ease her sense of loneliness, Katja pulled the pair of books that the werewolf had given her out of her rucksack and began to read. She studied the skinshifting techniques and then examined Felan's notes that he had scribbled in the margins. Most were additional instructions or tips that he had found useful during his own skinshifts. A few were gentle encouragements to trust herself and trust her skills. Then Katja found "I love you" scribbled in the corner of a particularly worn page. Hot tears streamed through the fur of her cheeks as she read his words over and over again. She was still reading them when she fell asleep.

The nightmares that assaulted Katja after she had cried herself to sleep seemed as if they were half memory and half prophetic. She kept seeing Curqak's memories of Naraka and of Luther flash through her mind. Then she experienced a variation of a dream she had dreamed during her first night in Crown Canyon, just after the ghoul and his allies had massacred the Feliconas Clan…

*

Katja felt bright blades of green grass whipping wet past her furry flanks as she sprinted through their midst. The bright sun overhead emanated joyous warmth as she sniffed the rich air. It was alive with scents of sea, sand, grass, birds, fresh fruits, and seedling sap. She looked over the escarpment toward the sea. There was a storm closing fast over its boiling waters. The wind howled and shrieked as it bore bulging black clouds weeping angrily within its clutches. She ran for shelter near a tree and flinched back as a bolt of white fire singed a barrier at her feet. The tree was struck to pieces by the lightning's blow and her only other choice was to dive for cover in an abandoned badger burrow.

She lunged toward its safely just as the sky's white wrath attacked again, and she found herself in a small cave with intricate runes carved in a circle around its walls. As she watched, the symbols began to glow with the same fire that she had stepped through upon her entrance to Crown Canyon. The symbols lifted themselves off of the stone walls and began to spin in midair around her, growing brighter and moving faster until they formed a solid ring with her as their center.

Suddenly the ground beneath her shook, an altar sprouted before her feet, and a smooth green stone—Verdagon's emerald—blossomed in its center. She picked up the gem, and held it close as the altar melted into the floor and King Canuche's voice called from the shadows before her.

"This is your future," the griffin's voice intoned.

She saw herself reflected in the stone's silky surface, not as she was, but with a human's head attached to her werecat body, a segmented black tail curving up away from her body, and a terrible fury haunting her golden-ringed, green eyes. The image faded away to be replaced with a likeness of Felan. The powerfully built werewolf was standing upright on his back paws with his father's huge double-bladed war axe held ready in his furry forepaws. The male partially skinshifted so that his head was that of his human form while the rest of his dark-furred body remained the same. As she watched, the mighty wings of an eagle sprouted from his broad shoulders to shadow his muscular form in a canopy of black-and-gray feathers. A red sun rose behind the pair, illuminating them as they embraced each other in the midst of a corpse-strewn battlefield.

The image within the stone faded again and the forbidden corridor in Caerwyn Castle appeared in its visage. Once again Katja followed the hall's length to the closed door of the mirror room. The door creaked open to reveal the red carpeted room holding the full-length mirror of Ott vre Caerwyn standing almost whole in its ancient iron frame save the shard now split and imbedded in the packmates' own spearheads.

Daya'lyn stood inside the room looking at the mirror, but the door blocked most of the male from Katja's view. She pushed it wider and stepped inside. Daya'lyn kept his focus on the mirror and ignored her. She moved to stand beside him as he stared at its visage.

"This is her past," called Canuche's voice.

Katja watched the mirror reflect only blackness and then flicker white with a bolt of lightning. On its surface she spied a midnight storm break over a castle by the sea. She felt herself being sucked into the scene as a bolt of lightning struck a section of the castle's battlements just as two horses bearing riders wildly galloped through the castle's war-torn gates toward the sanctuary of the forest far beyond.

Arrows arced from the unscathed section of battlements and rained down upon the fugitives racing across the open ground. Both horses but only one rider escaped into the sheltering edge of trees. Three arrows found the other rider — a valet wearing the old royal Tyglesean coat of arms — and sent him tumbling to his death amid wails of anguish from the other rider.

"Arlis!" the survivor screamed as her hood snapped back in a gust of wind. Katja stared at the young human female who closely resembled Lauraisha in all features save the shape of her nose, her hair color, and her height.

Amid the jostling of the galloping steeds, the human's eyes locked with Katja's through the mirror's surface and spoke. "Time grows short and the dead are at the door! Come to me quickly, wraithwalker, before all is lost!"

*

Katja bolted upright from her bed in a cold sweat. She searched the dark room around her for enemies and, after finding none, wrapped the scratchy blanket tighter around herself and fought to slow her panting breath. Instead, a knock on the door nearly jolted her out of her fur. She opened the door hoping to see Lauraisha and discovered Daya'lyn standing outside her room as well.

"Good morning, Katja," Daya'lyn greeted her.

"If it is a good morning, which, in this case, I highly doubt," she replied as she pulled the door wide to admit them. "What time is it?"

"I heard four bells peel some time ago," Lauraisha said quietly as she and the male stepped over the threshold. Katja gestured for them to sit. Lauraisha and Katja both sat on the bed while Daya'lyn sought the floor.

"Did you both share my dream?" Katja asked pointedly.

They nodded. Katja sighed in relief. If Lauraisha was sharing dreams with her again, then at least one thing was back to normal.

"What do you make of it?"

"Nothing good," Daya'lyn said at last.

"Who was the woman at the end, Lauraisha?" Katja asked.

"I'm unsure. She looked so much like me." The dreamdrifter frowned. "But I don't understand the context."

"You don't know why she fled the castle?"

The princess shook her head.

"Do you recognize the castle?" Daya'lyn asked.

She nodded. "I think it was Summersted as it appeared before the Great Fire during my father's revolution. He burned the original keep and half of the neighboring forest after he killed King Aedus and his family, then usurped the throne. The current keep is much taller than the original was said to be."

"Are there any female dreamdrifters in your family besides you?"

Lauraisha shook her head. "If there are, they are dead. By my father's royal decree, the only mages in the kingdom serve in the priesthood and all of those are harmhealers. All others undergo a Witch Trial and, if confirmed as mages, are put to death."

Katja scratched her head. "Then who sent the warning? Canuche?"

Lauraisha spread her hands.

Daya'lyn grimaced at Lauraisha. "None of this makes sense. We all shared a dream in which two of our noblest packmates turn into ancestral beings who then begin a murderous rampage, and then your probable ancestor flees her own home, but asks Katja to come at once. Every single scene in the dream is a contradiction."

"Contradiction or not, it does not bode well," Lauraisha said. "You know, there are nights that I absolutely despise being a mage."

"Agreed." Katja nodded.

Daya'lyn looked at the two of them and frowned. "Was this nightmare fairly typical of those that you share?"

Katja sighed. "They are not always that detailed, but yes."

Daya'lyn's jaw tightened. "Now I know a portion of the terror that the two of you endure each night. I'm sorry."

"So am I. I've a suspicion that we are just about to kick open a huge hornet's nest," the human muttered.

They heard the cry of a cock then, signaling the coming morning.

Daya'lyn stood and stretched. "We had best not worry more about it now. Come, sleep is of no more use to us. Let us pack, eat, and journey on. We still have a few days' travel before we reach Jorn and we'll endure a full moon's night between now and then."

The females each adjourned to their own rooms to dress and pack while Daya'lyn went in search of the innkeeper. Once he had seen to their steeds and packed his own gear, Daya'lyn led the females to the bar of the main meeting room.

Lauraisha seized hunks of bread and hard cheese from the platter before them even as Katja tore into the innkeeper's proffered meat. The subdued trio finished the morning eat, paid their host, and led their steeds onto the road once again. Once on the main road toward Vihous's capital city, the group relaxed a little—grateful to be trotting through the brisk open air once more. The spring days seemed fresher now that they had abandoned the cloying humidity of the marshlands in favor of the somewhat dry coastal plains.

The sunlight lent such a keen edge to all of their brilliant surroundings. The werecat smelled the heady aroma of mid-spring flowers and opened her mind to see beyond the depth of her eyes, as Joce'lynn had taught her to do. Now, among the sharp lines of the stunted trees and short shrubs, she glimpsed pale gossamer-winged shapes floating with the breeze.

"Pixies," she murmured.

Lauraisha and Daya'lyn followed her gaze.

"Are you sure, Katja?" the princess asked.

"I'm sure." She smiled and pointed. "Look there."

One of the pixies, a being whose body was no longer than Katja's forearm, flitted out to the roadway and greeted the werecat with a kiss on the nose. "Well met, Inquisition." She turned to bow to Daya'lyn, Lauraisha, and Calder. "I am Eiriana and I am at your service."

Katja reined in her mount in surprise, but managed to keep her courtesy. "Well met, Eiriana."

The pixie bounced energetically. "Holis, the emissary, requested my kin's assistance to watch the roadways for your party's arrival. He received word from the naiads that the Inquisition had passed through their borders over four weeks ago. You are much delayed."

"We met some deadwalker resistance," Daya'lyn supplied. "Fortunately the Shamgar and Barak ogre clans proved excellent allies in our fight to destroy them."

Eiriana's iridescent lips pulled away from her sharp little teeth in a snarl. "More of the contemptible Asheken brush our northwest border every day. None of us knew that they had migrated so far south, though!"

Katja bowed her head. "It is a grave concern of ours as well."

The little sprite scratched her head. "Holis will certainly need to know of your discoveries, and soon. He awaits you in the capital city. I will guide you to him in the Chamber of Echoes, if I may."

Do you trust her, Katja? Daya'lyn asked her through Lauraisha's mental bond. The female watched the diminutive being with her wraithwalker's sight and nodded ever so slightly.

"By all means, lead on, Eiriana," Daya'lyn said.

Eiriana bobbed her thanks to him and flitted ahead along the road in front of the party.

You sense no malice at all from her, Katja? Lauraisha asked within her mind.

No, but my hackles are raised nonetheless. I feel someone else watching us from the trees, but I cannot discern the source.

Shadowshaper cloaking spells? Daya'lyn's unspoken question passed from Lauraisha's thoughts to Katja's mind.

She nodded again.

Daeryn?

I'm unsure.

We'll take a loose defensive riding formation, then. Appear relaxed, but stay alert, Daya'lyn conveyed through Lauraisha.

Katja nodded as she and her new mount dropped behind the other party members on the pretense of checking the supplies on one of the packhorses. The group rode on in relative silence and, despite the werecat's warning, met no resistance. Noon found them between towns, and they set their campsite far away from the road in a secluded but defensible grove of plum trees. Even with the ogre harmhealer's best efforts, Tyron's injury was still serious, and so the group had opted for a rare noontime camp to rest their steeds.

"Is it true that you've conversed with a Pyrekin?" Eiriana asked Lauraisha as the group settled around a small campfire for the mid-day eat.

The human swallowed her bite of dried meat before carefully replying. "Occasionally. Why do you ask?"

"Oh, forgive me. I do not mean to pry. It's just that there are rumors of your deeds that have reached us and I would know for myself if such things were true."

Katja's ears perked. "Rumors of what?"

"Of your consorting with and riding a dragon."

Katja sniffed at the skinned deer leg Daya'lyn offered her before commenting, "The dragon Verdagon was hatched on the warming sands of the Isle of Summons roughly four moon-cycles ago. I have had the privilege to speak with him many times and to ride with him once."

"How fortunate for you!" the pixie trilled in delight.

"Holis said that you were named the green dragon's steward and an elf was named his herald. You must find flying even more wonderful than I since you can soar so high among the clouds and all."

When Katja did not reply, Daya'lyn changed the subject. "Eiriana, how many days will we travel before we reach Jorn?"

"It should take no more than three days by Kings' Highway. But, I warn you that this path strays into the Seaward Leas. It's a place more suited for satyr and centaur, but brownies and toadstool folk are its main tenants. Stubborn farmers, you know. They are the main crop-growers for our whole country. I suppose they're a fair enough folk, but they're fiercely protective of their plants. Set one wrong foot or hoof on their vineyards and gardens and their sproutsingers might just permit the crops to strangle you. If you're a thief, the trek will prove troubling even if you hold the stoutest of hearts."

"Not to worry, Eiriana." Daya'lyn's tone might have been mild, but his azure eyes smoldered at the pixie's challenge. "Everyone in this group is honorable."

The pixie's answering whistle sounded more like a servile tweet. "Oh, glad to hear it! We should make haste for Kings' Highway early on the morrow then."

"Very good, then." Daya'lyn nodded and then took a small sip of the bloody contents of his wineskin.

The afternoon saw their brisk northwestern ride along the dusty, worn stones of the Merrow Road soon give way to the bricked ribbon of Kings' Highway, which wound its way just west of the bridge at Hamos. The steeds' trot soon brought tilled fields into view. Katja found the ordered rows and uniform plant growth an odd contrast to the wide variety of grasses and low shrubs normally found in this grassy region. Here and there, small brown-bodied beings scurried beneath the shady sprouts of wheat or bounced between rows of burgeoning cabbages. Katja looked for the brownies' pale-skinned, mushroom-hatted cousins, but saw none of the gnomes.

"Where are the toadstool folk?" Lauraisha asked their pixie guide.

"Sleeping the day away in their burrows, of course! Did you actually expect them to risk exposing their sensitive skin to full sunlight? They'll be along soon after sunset."

The Tyglesean's flush was almost as dark as the skins of the harvested beets in a nearby wagon. The group's laughter was short-lived. A brownie grumbled at them to keep their attention on the road so that he could keep to his business in the fields and then added his share of fresh-picked beets to the cart. With a flick of his dirty-encrusted fingers, bloated green vines slithered their way through the dust toward the packmates. They stopped just short of the fence near the road and rose off the ground as if ready to strike. They seemed so serpent-like that Katja could almost swear she heard hissing as the vegetation writhed back and forth.

Katja's eye widened. "Per myn ehre! They really are serious about trespassing punishments."

"I did warn you," Eiriana replied.

"That you did. My thanks for that," Daya'lyn said and then urged Tyron onward. "Come; let us pick up the pace. I would rather not tarry and exhaust what little hospitality is left for us."

* * *

Sunset found the packmates huddled together on a widened section of the road watching Eiriana barter for their supper with a pair of gnomes. One silver and three brass coins finally earned the group three cabbages, a sack of barley, a sack of oats, two haunches of lamb, a wheel of cheese, and a skin of wine.

While Katja and Calder attacked the lamb with gusto, Lauraisha consumed some of the lamb and cheese, and shared the wine and cabbages with Eiriana as the other steeds sated themselves with the grain. They stored the evening's remainders in their saddlebags for the following morning's eat and curled up in their sleeping furs for some much needed rest.

* * *

A whisper of a sound stirred Katja from a dreamless sleep. She sat up, glanced at Lauraisha's and Daya'lyn's empty sleeping furs, and perked her ears. The soft wind carried Lauraisha's voice with it, but the sound was too faint for the werecat to discern the human's words. Katja looked over at Eiriana. The tiny pixie was snuggled between two feed sacks—her iridescent body perfectly hidden beneath the folds of burlap. Katja frowned. Lauraisha's words had not stirred Eiriana from her sleep as they had roused Katja, and the werecat wondered if she heard the words with her mind as well as her ears.

She slipped out from under her blanket and shivered. Even though the night sky was thick with clouds, she still felt the full moon's call tugging at her suddenly chilled bones. She chose to ignore the urge to skinshift in favor of searching out the human's voice. She soon discovered Lauraisha, Tyron, and Daya'lyn hidden in a grove of pecan trees between the road and the brownies' overgrown fence line.

From the scent of fresh blood and the look of the skin on Tyron's lower neck, Daya'lyn had evidently just imbibed his fill from the horse and the towering beast now rested his considerable bulk against a stout trunk while the two beings quietly conversed. Katja kept herself hidden from mental and physical view so that she would not interfere. She felt a twinge of guilt in not revealing herself, but that was overridden by her need to test the purity of Daya'lyn's motives toward Lauraisha.

Daya'lyn's arms were crossed tight upon his chest as he glowered at Lauraisha. "...That is a poor excuse, Lauraisha. We both know full well that examining Tyron's health after my feeding tonight was not your only reason for this visit. Why have you really come?"

The human stared at him. "I...I just wanted to make sure you were well."

Daya'lyn answered her with a derisive snort.

"You're always so solitary when you feed and I thought—"

"What? That I needed supervision?"

"—you might prefer some company." Lauraisha looked close to tears.

Daya'lyn regarded her—surprise and confusion showing in his roughish face. Finally he spoke—his voice a mere murmur. "You know what happens to me when I feed. Why would you ever want to be near me when that happens?"

"I do not fear you—"

"You should! It is far safer for you if you do!"

"Daya'lyn, you are not your brother and you strive always to do what is honorable."

"So Katja has told me, but she has not seen the darkness rise in my soul and in my mind the way you have."

"That is true," she murmured. "I saw you in your most dangerous state when we were forced to share a prison chamber on the Isle of Summons, and then again in that tower room after the Hag's Nest Battle. Twice your bloodlust caused you to act more feral than rational toward me, and yet you still had the presence of mind to shackle yourself rather than risk harm to me."

For a few moments Daya'lyn said nothing and simply watched the female before him with eyes now tinged violet from a strange mingling of scarlet and blue hues. Katja gaped at him. Only twice before had she ever seen his eyes take that hue—once when he and Lauraisha were imprisoned together in the Mage Citadel tower, and then again when the male had fought the dullahan Perefaris. What did it mean?

The hybrid cleared his throat. "I might remind you that my bonds only held for our first encounter, Lauraisha. You witnessed me snap the restraints during our second."

"And yet you did not bite me."

"I wanted to…" His voice was a sharp whisper of shame. "Fangs, Lauraisha, I even asked to…"

"And when I told you no, you restrained yourself because you love me." Tears now stood in the princess's azure eyes as the male turned away from her. "Don't try to deny it, Daya'lyn. I felt it in your mind; I saw it even in your reddened eyes…I see it now."

He turned back toward her, his jaw clenched in determination. "It is because of my love that I thirst after you! How can you not understand? My love feeds my bloodlust; it is that which poses such a danger to you!"

Lauraisha crossed her arms in stubbornness. "I know that, Daya'lyn. Despite what others seem to think, I'm not naïve. I know the cruelty and evil hatched by the lusts of males."

"If you know that evil, then you know why I warn you to keep away from me!"

The human laughed humorlessly. "The evil I speak of

came from my father, not from you."

He frowned at her. "From his attempts to kill you?"

Lauraisha watched him a moment and Katja knew that memories were passing between them. Daya'lyn gaped at her in wide-eyed horror and then his nostrils flared and his lips curled back, exposing his white fangs. "Merciful Creator, keep you! He did *this* to you?"

"Now do you see the difference between your deeds and his?" Lauraisha asked even as she shivered. "Daya'lyn, it is your love for me that helps you fight your thirst. It is my father's hatred of me that fuels his depravity."

"You didn't have to do this," the male whispered as anger and sorrow clouded his violet eyes. "I would never have asked you to show me such a memory."

"What else could I do, Dayalan?" The human shut her eyes as tears spilled down her flushed cheeks. "The male I love tells me to flee, but how could I run from the only one who has ever shown me any semblance of real love?"

Daya'lyn reached out and placed a tentative glove on her shoulder, drawing her to him. She leaned against him, buried her tear-streaked face in his barrel chest, and sobbed.

"I'm so sorry…" he whispered, tears flowing from his violet eyes. "For everything."

He held her close and let her cry against his barrel chest for a long time before asking, "Why would you ever volunteer to go back, knowing the danger that he poses to you?"

"It is my duty, Daya'lyn."

"How so?"

The Tyglesean pulled back to stare to him and a mixture of dismay and longing filled Daya'lyn's features as she did. "My decision to return to Tyglesea was not made lightly. I chose to do so with the conviction that I must do something to help those members of my family and my country who have risked so much to save me from Father's wrath.

"My mother and brothers are trapped by the tyrant that we call king and they have no way to protect themselves should Kaylor turn against them. My mother is doomed to dwell in a violent marriage to protect her children. My siblings are doomed to remain as part of a tormented court to protect all other Tygleseans from Kaylor's rage.

"Whether Naraka has gained Father's allegiance through political promises or through Turning him, I would see him destroyed rather than watch my fellow Tygleseans' endure any more hardship."

Daya'lyn whistled softly. "You hope to start a coup?"

The weight of Lauraisha's gaze could have cracked granite. "Why not? It's a family tradition, after all. Father murdered the rightful king and stole the crown from his head even before King Aedus had wheezed his last breath. Clergywoman Ist'lynn prophesied that such an act would happen again through an act of defiance by the dead king's daughter and Kaylor's own daughter. That leaves me, my sister Kyla, and an unknown woman to accomplish the task. Kyla is far too fond of Father to do him any harm, so that leaves me as one of the two murderers."

Daya'lyn's shock and dismay was almost palpable. "Prophesies have been known to fail."

She shook her head. "Not this one, not from this seer. Ist'lynn is descended directly from Aaron—the only mage prophet to ever correctly predict that Aribem's fiery death would destroy a third of the deadwalker hordes and split the continents."

The male heaved a sigh. "But this burden is too heavy for so young a female to shoulder."

"I was forced to mature well past my own age long ago, Daya'lyn. I don't need your pity; I need your help to make certain that my father never harms another being again."

"You have it—"

A distant rumble of thunder interrupted his reply and all three packmates looked to the southwest. The moonlight had brightened the sky enough for Katja to see angry clouds commence their hailing assault on the grassy hillock just beyond the vineyards.

Tyron's neighs were sharp with panic.

Daya'lyn cursed and looked back at Lauraisha. "That hail will pummel us to death if we remain here in the open. Back to the camp! Quickly!"

XIV
TEMPEST'S WRATH

Katja sprinted just ahead of the others and found their pixie guide flitting about in terror. "Eiriana, we need shelter!"

"Where have you all been! Never mind, I know a place not far from here. Come, let's be off!"

Katja felt the temperature drop even as she kicked dirt on the campfire coals and Lauraisha threw on saddles. Lightning erupted from the green-tinged thunderheads with a vengeful force even as the storm's paw-sized hail pounded the land beneath it. While spring thunderstorms were commonplace, Katja had only known one other of such violence. The werecat's ears flattened at the memory of its aftermath.

"That's a twister in the brewing, make no mistake!" the pixie shouted over the whipping wind. "There's no time for odds and ends! Leave the saddles and ride bareback. Follow me! Hurry!"

"Daya'lyn!" Calder neighed. "Tyron is too weak to bear your weight now. Ride with me instead and let Lauraisha take him."

The fireforger bounded onto the kelpie's back. "Go!"

Katja slung two knapsacks over her shoulders, bounded onto the nearest bridled beast, and kicked it into a gallop behind Daya'lyn and Calder. She could feel Tyron's hot snorts just behind her as Lauraisha guided her mount with one hand and led the finicky packhorses with a rope in the other. Eiriana led them down a semi-overgrown path just north of Kings' Highway beyond the pecan grove. Another turn led them out of the path's safety and onto a grassy creek bank. The werecat felt the wet grass whip past her back paws as her nacken sprinted through their midst. Then she began to feel a slithering sensation as the stalks rose to curl around her back limbs.

Katja shouted over the deafening thunder and wind. "Daya'lyn, Lauraisha, you'll have to keep a fire barrier between us and the plants if we're going to survive this race without being dragged off our mounts!"

The fast-moving storm choked out the moonlight and they galloped blindly for several moments until Daya'lyn managed to spread a flaming ring around the party. Plants shrank back and shriveled in the wake of the fire even as the steeds pitched and screamed at the sudden conflagration. On and on, they rode as thunder roared and lightning snapped at their heels. They raced through the creek bank and up the dale toward the ruin of a limestone watchtower just as hailstones the size of goose eggs began to pelt them. Katja ducked one only to be bruised by a second.

"Quickly, quickly," Eiriana yelled as they urged the steeds up the rubble that was once a hillside staircase.

As they reached the relative safety of a limestone outcropping, a bolt of lightning struck the stone above their heads. The steeds pitched their riders and bolted as its thunderous impact cracked the corner of the giant slab.

A chunk of stone fell, knocking Calder senseless. The kelpie toppled to the ground with Daya'lyn still on top of him—pitching the fireforger out into the angry storm.

"No!" the females screamed in unison as a second bolt struck the pair. White fire engulfed Daya'lyn and then surged out of the fireforger's feet into the flame ring surrounding him. For one terrifying moment, the flames reached the height of the tallest tower ruin and then extinguished themselves. The smell of scorched flesh and hair filled the moist air as the terrified steeds bolted through the dying embers of the fireforger's flame ring and onto the wet meadow. Katja stared at Daya'lyn's and Calder's still bodies. The kelpie looked and smelled as charred as a cinder.

As the three females lay dazed against the hard-packed dirt, deadly vines wrapped themselves around their limbs.

Lauraisha screamed. "Daya'lyn! Calder!"

"It's no good, Lauraisha!" Katja said as she clawed and snapped at the vines. "They are either stunned or dead. You'll have to free us now!"

"I can't!"

"You can and you must!" Katja shouted before a creeper wound itself around her neck. Daya'lyn's motionless body was already buried beneath green tendrils as the deadly ice stones continued to fall.

"Creator, keep us!" Lauraisha shouted.

A third lightning bolt suddenly struck the knoll they were trapped upon and sent smoldering plants shooting in all directions. Lauraisha's reactionary blaze was the only thing that shielded the group from the blast. Light from the explosion revealed the entrance to a half-hidden cellar roughly three body-lengths down the slope under the ruin. If Lauraisha could burn them loose, they would be able to take refuge there until the storm passed. Katja prayed to the Creator that the hovel was free of enemies even as she bit the nearest of her imprisoning tendrils in two.

"Lauraisha, Eiriana, try to reach the cellar!"

"I see it!" the human shouted back and then scorched the last of her bindings off. She feverishly worked to free Eiriana and then Daya'lyn and Calder even as Katja gnawed and twisted her way out of her own bonds. Once the last tendril was severed, Katja sprinted to where Lauraisha knelt. The female was weeping.

"We have to get out of the storm!" the werecat roared.

"Calder," the human mouthed.

Katja's eyes watered from the stench of the kelpie's burned corpse. She checked his pulse even though she knew the act was useless.

Thunder bellowed and the werecat glanced fearfully at the boiling green sky before grabbing the human by both shoulders and shaking her. "Lauraisha, we must seek shelter...help me move Daya'lyn!"

The Tyglesean helped Katja drag Daya'lyn down the slope while Eiriana flew ahead to investigate the cellar. Katja and Lauraisha pulled the fireforger to the far corner of the underground chamber just as sky's white wrath struck again.

"Daya'lyn? Dayalan! Katja, I can't find his pulse!" Lauraisha's voice screeched in panic.

"Move!" Katja pushed Lauraisha aside and knelt over the big mage. She pressed one paw over his nose and mouth and the other against his throat, simultaneously checking for breath and heartbeat. She found neither.

"Merciful Creator, help us!" she prayed and delved deep into her skinshifting magic. "Lauraisha, bond with me! I'll need your strength!"

"Is he...?"

"Just do it!" Katja felt the mental link between her mind and the dreamdrifter's open. Lauraisha's panic lapped against the wraithwalker's fortitude in nauseating waves. "Per myn ehre, lytzsibba! I cannot help him when you are like this! Keep a tight mental grip on your fear!"

"Sorry!"

Lauraisha's mental yank on her own emotions nearly knocked the werecat off of her knees. The skinshifter caught herself and pushed her senses into Daya'lyn's body through the touch of her scarred right paw on his forehead. Katja frowned as the crescent-shaped scar tingled. Her soul felt through the layers of Daya'lyn's body.

The lightning had left no lasting burns anywhere on his body, but the fall had cracked his skull and the lightning jolt had stilled his heart. He would die if Katja couldn't restart it. Katja drew in a sharp breath and wished Neha'lyn and Felan were here.

Dear Creator, what do I do? I'm no harmhealer! she prayed. At once, the mental image of an ethereal hand squeezing Daya'lyn's heart came to her mind and Katja understood.

"Is he dead?" Lauraisha said, her voice stricken with panic.

She shook her head, not trusting herself to answer immediately. "Eiriana, I need light. Lauraisha, lend me more of your strength."

The skinshifter closed her eyes and pushed her magic once more into Daya'lyn's body through the touch of her scarred paw even as Eiriana began to light the ceiling's moldy braziers with flint and steel. She delved back into the layers of his heart and massaged the muscle with her magic. She took a few deep breaths to calm herself and then urged the fireforger's heart and lungs to move in time with her own.

After several tense moments, Daya'lyn's heart began to beat of its own accord, and then he took his own breath. With the immediate danger averted, Katja turned her attention to the mage's head injury. The fall had jostled his brain against a hairline crack at the back of his skull. While Lauraisha worked to make the unconscious male as comfortable as possible, Katja tried to encourage the bone of his skull to knit itself back together along the thin break. She was dimly aware of the storm raging above them, but pushed that knowledge to the back of her mind as she worked. At last, the exhausted skinshifter pulled her magic back into herself and shakily sat back—beyond grateful that Daya'lyn had suffered no other injuries.

"The fall cracked his skull and concussed him. I repaired what I could, but I won't know if there is any lasting damage until he wakes," Katja said as Lauraisha helped her cushion the fireforger's head against a blanket bundle from the werecat's rucksack.

Lauraisha nodded and let out a heavy sigh. "What now?"

"Help me secure the entrance!" Eiriana yelled over the rising din of the storm.

Katja and Lauraisha sprinted across the dank cellar and together they pushed a thin stone slab across the narrow stairwell that served as the cellar's entrance. They left a thin slit of space open so that air could pass through and keep them from suffocating. However, with the stone covering the entrance and Eiriana's lit braziers already guttering with what little oil they still held, the cellar was as dark as a tomb.

"Lauraisha, would you add more light please?"

The human reached to retrieve Damya's Keystone amulet from underneath her robes and blew across its surface. The gem began to glow pale blue, lighting the gloom with cold fire and casting eerie shadows on the companions' faces.

"What is this place?" Lauraisha asked.

"This is the little of what remains of the Tower of Bards," Eiriana replied.

Katja looked around the room, squinting hard at the broken pot shards littering the structure's floor. "I know this place…I remember its name from the lessons in my kit years. This was once the southernmost watchtower in Vihous, when the country was much smaller. "

Eiriana nodded.

Katja perked her ears as the storm outside grew worse. The wind howled like some unleashed monster and the rain struck the roof of the cellar in pounding waves. The werecat grimly stared at the world outside through the entrance slit. Every few seconds a lightning strike would unveil diagonal sheets of rain smiting the hail-pecked ground. "It has been a long time since I have seen a storm violent enough to birth a cyclone."

"I have known some intense squalls, but none like this," Lauraisha said.

Katja growled. "Count yourself fortunate. The last cyclone I remember from my catling years ravaged a sister village of werecats twice the size of my own. The only thing recognizable when that storm was finished was the lower half of the amphitheater. Only eight werecats were left alive out of the original four hundred."

Lauraisha covered her lips with her hand, clearly reliving Katja's memories of the event.

"What happened to the survivors?" Eiriana asked.

"Our village adopted them among our ranks," Katja replied while staring at the rain outside with unseeing eyes. "Those eight and their kits were some of the first to die during the deadwalkers' massacre of my village."

Lauraisha frowned at her. "Why?"

The werecat shook her head. "I have no idea."

The roar of the wind and lashing rain suddenly ceased and then began all the harder a moment later. Katja grabbed the other two females and hauled them away from the entrance. "Get down!" she shouted, but the roar of the wind overpowered her voice. She pushed the others to the ground over Daya'lyn's prone form and then lay on top of them.

"Creator, protect us!" she prayed as the churning winds tore at the ruins. Above them, Katja could hear boulders being lifted by the tornado. Lightning revealed rain being pushed sideways by the swirling winds. The whirlwind roared and whistled at its prey, ripping at the stone and mortar of the roof protecting them with mindless vengeance.

The night of her village's massacre, Katja had known the terror of helplessness. Now she felt that terror again and mewed like a newborn kit. Lauraisha's hand somehow found her paw in the darkness and clasped it tightly.

It will be over soon, Katja, Lauraisha's thought whispered through their bond.

Katja clenched her fangs and flattened her ears. *Perhaps or perhaps not. We have no notion of how long this storm will last, Lauraisha.*

Agreed, but what else can we do except hope?

Pray, Katja thought and then did so as the southwest section of the cellar roof gave way.

* * *

The full moon peppered the ruined landscape with its pale light as it finally won the war against the dissipating clouds. A single shaft wormed its way between stone and found its mark in Katja's bleary green eyes even as she heard the last growls of thunder in the distance.

"I'm alive," she whispered in disbelief as she sat up. "Is everyone well?"

"I think so," Lauraisha answered from her huddled position nearby. The four Sylvans had pressed themselves into an alcove as far away from the cellar's caved-in southwest corner as possible.

"Eiriana?" Katja looked around for the little pixie.

"I'm here," she twittered even as she extricated herself from a crevice in the wall behind Lauraisha.

Katja let out a breath in relief and leaned over to check Daya'lyn's pulse. His heartbeat was strong, but he had yet to wake.

When he wakes, Lauraisha's thought entered the werecat's mind. *we need to be ready with proper nourishment.*

Katja nodded slightly and then looked at the pixie as the little being checked her delicate wings for damage. "Can you fly?"

She nodded.

"Daya'lyn seems well, but I hesitate to move him until I know for certain his condition. We need the horses."

Eiriana furrowed her minute eyebrows while she thought. "He'll need a cart. That much is certain. I could ask the local farmers, but my guess is that they're in the same dismal shape that we are after that storm. I might as well fly to Jorn and tell the situation to Holis. He can offer relief for the locals and safe passage for you."

"Do you think that you are well enough to make the journey now?"

The pixie nodded again. "I'm awake, alert, and angry. That will get me to Jorn and back again in no time at all."

Katja bowed deeply to the little female with both paws lifted pad-side up to show her deep gratitude and trust. "Thank you."

She and Lauraisha followed Eiriana to the original entrance, heaved the slab away from the partially collapsed door frame, and crawled up the stone stairs. At the top step, Katja stood and surveyed the devastation. The white tower had been reduced to its base by the cyclone—its once spotless stones scattered like gravestones across the grassy knoll.

The werecat watched the pixie's flight over myriad rows of broken and uprooted plants as she waved farewell. She tried to find a single grapevine that had been spared by either hail or wind and failed.

Lauraisha stood beside her and pursed her lips at the devastation. "Well, on a positive note, we won't have to worry about any more plants trying to strangle us on our journey."

Katja heaved a chuckle. "That is true, thank the Creator."

"Katja?"

The werecat cocked her head at the human's troubled expression. "What?"

"Did you manage to keep Daya'lyn's personal 'wineskin' safe through the storm?"

Katja nodded. "It and my own rucksack were the only bags I managed to grab in the panic of the storm. You?"

"My personal sack, Daya'lyn's, and one small food bag."

"At least we'll all have something to eat and drink. I doubt I'll find anything to hunt after this much devastation."

Lauraisha bowed her head, her gaze still troubled.

"What is it?" the werecat asked gently.

"It's just...what if he succumbs to the bloodlust like he

242 • ALYCIA CHRISTINE

did after the Hag's Nest Battle?"

Katja put a paw on the younger female's shoulder. "Then we deal with it, just as we did before and just as we will again. As my mother often said, 'believe in the best, but train for the worst.'"

"You miss them terribly, don't you?"

Katja nodded. "I—"

"Lauraisha?"

At the sound of Daya'lyn's weak voice, the females turned to peer down the steps into the cellar's darkness. Lauraisha sprinted to Daya'lyn's side with Katja on her heels. The werecat grabbed the bloody wineskin and turned to see Daya'lyn opening his red eyes and then shut them again as he groaned. "What happened?"

Lauraisha knelt beside him. "How do you feel?"

"I hunger, my head feels like it's about to split in two, and the whole of my body is sore. What happened?"

"You and Calder were struck by lightning," Katja said as she passed the blood skin to Lauraisha.

"And Calder?"

Slowly Katja shook her head.

Daya'lyn shut his eyes. "What of Tyron and the other mounts?"

"We don't know." Lauraisha said as she unstoppered the skin and held it to the hybrid's lips so that he could drink without sitting up. "They bolted in the storm when you were struck."

"Where are we?" Daya'lyn asked before taking a deep draft of blood from the skin.

"Careful now. Drinking too much or too fast could make you retch," Lauraisha said as she tried to pull the wineskin from his lips.

He glared at her. "I might do that anyway. Now, where are we?"

"Under the ruins of the Tower of Bards in Vihous," Katja answered. "It was the only shelter we could find in which to escape the cyclone responsible for this area's destruction. I'm thankful that you are so powerful a mage. I doubt that a lesser fireforger could survive a direct lightning strike, and yet—with a little skinshifting help—you have. Even so, you cracked your skull when you tumbled off of Calder."

The big male groaned and took another swig of blood. "My head certainly hurts like it…I need sleep."

Lauraisha gently touched his shoulder. "Then, lay still, Daya'lyn, and take some rest."

The male groaned again and then sank into a deep sleep. Lauraisha watched his barrel chest rise and fall with his even breath. "I've never seen him so weak."

"Nor have I," Katja replied.

"Why didn't he become physically stronger and feral this time, like he did after the Hag's Nest Battle?"

Katja shook her head. "I don't know. Since this is a physical injury instead of simple hunger or exhaustion, perhaps his body reacts differently. It also could be that his recent meal from Tyron is sustaining him well enough that he doesn't have to sacrifice his mind to save his body. In truth, I hadn't expected him to survive the lightning strike at all. For him to come through it with even this little damage done is a rare miracle. If Calder hadn't thrown him and had landed on top of him instead, the kelpie could have crushed him."

"He wouldn't have survived at all if you hadn't interfered. Katja, I'm eternally grateful."

The werecat shook her head once more. "I'm no healer, Lauraisha. I was able to knit some bone and squeeze a couple of muscles. That is all. If it had been anything else…if it had been some sort of sickness, there would have been nothing that I could have done."

Lauraisha laid a hand on her shoulder while tears streamed down the human's face. "Nevertheless you did what you could, and he is alive because of you."

Tears stood in Katja's eyes. Her skinshifting skills had now saved two lives, but how many more had been lost or Turned? She had been on the run from her clan's murderers for nine moon-cycles now—the catalyst for a war between two continents, all because her enemies prized her mage abilities for more than her allies did.

Don't you dare think that way, Lauraisha's words echoed in her mind. *Your claws were not the ones laid across your loved-ones' throats—Curqak's were. He and his fellow monsters hold sole responsibility for the atrocities committed against the Feliconas*

Clan.

"Yes, and I helped destroy him for his crimes," Katja replied through clenched fangs.

"Yes, you did. And did his annihilation satisfy your need for vengeance?"

The werecat closed her eyes as the tears roll down her cheeks. "No," she whispered. "Because Daeryn and Luther still survive and still threaten those I love."

"And will Daeryn and Luther's destruction dispel your anguish and your misery?"

Katja watched Daya'lyn's rhythmic breathing as she reached to feel Daeryn's bite scars on her neck. Finally, she shook her head. "I don't know. Destroying them would help ensure that they can never again harm others and that will help ease my dreams. Even so, those that I've loved and lost will still be dead."

Lauraisha slid an arm around the female's shoulders. "So what are you going to do?"

"I don't know."

The weary werecat leaned against the human and, for the first time in many months, allowed herself a long cry. Finally, when her eyes were finally devoid of tears, Katja fell asleep. Katja and Lauraisha had only one dream during their slumber of exhaustion—one of Felan...

*

Sparkling specks of dust drifted through the full moon's rays illuminating the grass cloaking the forest floor. Felan sat half in and half out of the speckled light, breathing deeply and staring off into the distance.

Why is the skinshift not occurring? he wondered.

He moved further into the moonlight and waited.

Still nothing.

The massive werewolf held his clawed paws out before him and frowned. Something was definitely wrong. As the wan light bathed him, Felan sensed the urge to skinshift, but did not feel his body intuitively change forms the way it usually did. His paws remained a werewolf's paws; they did not lose their black fur and claws to take on full human shape, nor did they meld into the smaller, thumbless paws of a full wolf.

Felan stared at his paws and then at the rest of his body. He felt the skinshift take hold, but saw no changes of any kind. Then he felt an itching tingle along his spine, shoulders, and head. At the snap of a twig, the skinshifter tried to turn his ears toward the sound and froze. He stared at Verdagon as the dragon approached and then Felan slowly reached a paw to touch his own suddenly human head.

"Verdagon, what is happening to me?" he whispered with mixed awe and fear.

"The same thing that has begun in Katja," the Pyrekin replied. "Prophesy..."

*

Lauraisha's scream woke Katja and she sat up bleary-eyed as the human darted away from her with eyes wide and fireballs ready. The reaction shocked Katja until she looked down at her body and discovered that she had skinshifted in her sleep.

"What happened to you?" Lauraisha asked, her back against the cellar wall opposite the skinshifter.

Katja stared at herself. She had taken the form of a lioness, or at least mostly a lioness, but her forepaws and back paws had skinshifted into human hands and feet. She reached up to touch her face and felt the bulging nose, bare cheeks, and full lips of a human.

Katja's ears were flat even as she frowned. "I have no idea, but I think Felan just encountered the same problem that I have."

"I really want him here right now."

"So do I." Katja pushed the skinshifter magic out from her soul throughout her body, concentrating on making her bones feel like liquid and her muscles like mud. She felt the change overtake her and welcomed its progression. Her body skinshifted back into the form of a werecat seamlessly, without any of the usual pain that she had so long associated with the process. She grinned at the satisfaction that it brought her, and looked at her body in wonder. She had more energy now than she had had before the skinshift!

Lauraisha watched her in alarm. "Is Daeryn...?"

246 • ALYCIA CHRISTINE

She shook her head. "I don't feel his presence. Do you?"

After a moment of sifting through the skinshifter's thoughts, Lauraisha frowned and slowly shook her head.

Katja sighed in relief. "Good. At least I managed to evade his evil...for now."

* * *

Once the moon set and the sun rose high, Katja and Lauraisha set to work gathering what scattered supplies and food that they could. They nursed Daya'lyn back to health with the blood supply they had available, but all three knew that it would not be enough. With few prospects for hunting in sight and no sign of Tyron, the male decided to sleep as much as possible to conserve his strength and curb his appetite.

On the morning of the second day, the two females decided to try to dig a proper grave for Calder using some flat stones they had recovered from the tower's rubble. They were in their second hour of digging when Katja's ears perked at the sound of a horse's neigh coming from somewhere off to their right. She and Lauraisha turned toward the sounds of trotting hooves and wooden wheels, and soon spied a small caravan of four wagons drawn by kelpies and centaurs coming over the hills toward them. At least a dozen brownies and pixies rode in each wagon, their high, thin voices raised in song:

> Wounded, he traveled alone.
> Bleeding, he scorched Luther's throne.
> Dying, he gave up his own
> Life for us.

> Singing, we walk hand in paw.
> Knowing, he gave us his all.
> Hoping, that he will impart
> Fire to us.

> Weeping, we watch and we wait,
> Dreaming of love's greatest blaze,
> Fearing to know Aribem's Fate,
> Sire to us.

Seeing, we now from afar,
Viewing the fireforger's star,
Trembling, the lands now divide.
Rise for us.

Feeling the fire all around,
Forging the sparks that abound,
Hearing hope in the sound,
Life in us!

The remnants of the brutalized plants parted peacefully for the party as it progressed down the hill and then up the draw toward the Inquisition's place of refuge. Katja smiled as she saw Eiriana flitting before them, warbling "The Rift and Gift of Aribem" at the top of her little lungs along with the others.

"I came as quick as I could," the pixie said.

"We are very grateful," Lauraisha said.

"How fares the Inquisitor?"

The princess shook her head. "We're not sure. He needs the help of a healer as soon as possible."

"We brought one with us," Holis said as he jumped from the nearest wagon and bowed to the females. "I'm sorry to be seeing the both of you under such dire circumstances."

Katja and Lauraisha returned the bow.

"It's worse than you know, My Sir," Katja said.

"How so?"

"Lauraisha, we do not have a lot of time or privacy. Will you quickly show him the details?"

The human nodded and closed her eyes. Holis's own eyes widened as she quickly shared several memories with him. "Two of your party are dead, Your Highness?"

She nodded. "The kelpies Glashtin and Calder, My Sir."

Holis's eyes narrowed. "I see. I will see to it that our local Mage Council members are informed."

"Have our packmates arrived in Vihous yet?" Katja asked.

Holis frowned at her. "Packmates?"

"The werewolf Felan Bardrick, the elf Vraelth Verd, and the dryad Princess Zahra Zahlathrazel Etheal," she said.

"Ah, yes. They entered our fair country a few days ago

and should be joining us in Jorn by river ferry shortly. As I understand it, they too were waylaid by deadwalkers."

"Kind Sir," Lauraisha interrupted. "Did you happen to see my horse Tyron on your journey to us? His absence greatly distresses me."

Katja's ears perked again and she touched the princess's shoulder. "Lauraisha."

The human looked in the direction Katja pointed. An eighteen-hands-tall sorrel stallion was trotting up from the back of the last wagon. Holis turned to see the object of the females' attention and half-smiled as the horse came closer. "You have a very loyal steed, Princess Lauraisha. He would not allow himself to be tethered to a wagon, but he has nonetheless followed us for two days."

"Two?"

Holis nodded. "I set out with a local caravan three days ago in the hope that I could intercept you before you made it to Jorn. Eiriana found me en route yesterday."

Katja frowned. "Why?"

Holis turned to Lauraisha. "I do apologize, Your Highness, but there is an emissary at our court from Tyglesea. King Kaylor knows you have traveled to our fair country."

"How?"

Holis shook his head. "I have no notion."

Katja growled. "This doesn't bode well."

Lauraisha nodded in agreement and turned back to the Vihouset human. "Holis, we need a litter of some sort and two strong males to carry Daya'lyn out from the cellar."

"I'll see what I can arrange, Your Highness," Holis said before he turned back to the wagons.

As he strode down the hill, Tyron trotted past him to stand before Lauraisha with his head bowed and his nostrils flaring in agitation. She caressed the side of his neck, tracing the faint scars where Daya'lyn had repeatedly bit the beast.

"Why did you run off, Tyron?" she whispered gently. "You know how much I need you…and how much Daya'lyn needs you."

The horse returned her gaze as he nuzzled her, and then looked toward the cellar. The females led the stallion down the cellar steps. The Vihous entourage had already cleared the entryway of rubble, which made Tyron's journey underground far less treacherous.

As they neared Daya'lyn's prone form, Katja watched the male a moment. Daya'lyn seemed the perfect image of health, but the werecat noticed that his breath came in shallow rasps as he slumbered.

Lauraisha looked at the lone being kneeling beside him—a brown-feathered harpy harmhealer. "How does he fare, My Madam?"

Sora'lynn shook her human-like head in frustration. "I'm not certain. He seems well enough. I cannot detect any lasting sign of heart or brain damage. All of his other organs seem fine as well. However, his skull fracture is troublesome and he is malnourished. Despite my best efforts, I cannot get him to eat anything. Usually my patients are far less reticent about food, but this one has gone so far as to spit out anything I've managed to push between his lips with the exception of water."

Lauraisha looked at Katja. "He's always been a fussy eater. Would you mind giving us a few moments alone with him?"

The harpy stood. "I would be pleased to…perhaps, then, you can coax some nourishment into him."

The Tyglesean princess nodded. When she and Katja heard the female swoop up the cellar steps, she whispered to the male, "It is just Katja, Tyron, and me with you now, Daya'lyn, so you are free to be yourself."

The prone male opened his scarlet eyes and stared from the females to the horse. "Tyron, you came back."

The horse walked forward and nuzzled the fireforger's outstretched glove—as if in apology.

Daya'lyn watched the horse a moment, his eyes narrowing in speculation. The ashen male's white fangs lengthened until they extended past his lower lip even as he shut his scarlet eyes and groaned. "The injuries have taxed my strength, Tyron. I need more nourishment. Are you still willing?"

With some difficulty, Tyron lay down beside the hybrid and bent his neck toward him. With Lauraisha's and Katja's aid, Daya'lyn crawled the short distance to the horse. He reached out with both hands to steady himself over the horse's neck and then bit into the stallion's scared flesh, lapping the ruby stream into his mouth with his tongue.

"Easy, Daya'lyn," Katja cautioned. "He has not had the time to fully recover from his leg wound, your last feeding three days ago, or the bruises he gained during the hailstorm."

The male's red eyes watched her in hungry incomprehension and, for a moment, Katja saw Daeryn. She shuddered, and then the blue finally won its rightful place. Daya'lyn raised his fangs away from the trembling horse's hide. "True enough."

He turned back to Tyron, closed the beast's wound with a swirling flick of his tongue, and sucked up the excess blood from amid the steed's fur. He studied the horse a moment before asking, "Are you well?"

To Lauraisha's and Katja's utter shock, the horse slowly nodded before pushing himself slowly to a stand. Lauraisha and Katja helped support the huge steed as he sluggishly walked to the nearest cellar drainage cache and buried his quivering muzzle into its cool waters.

As the horse drank, Lauraisha looked at Katja with worry furrowing her brow. *Daya'lyn is imbibing more often and consuming more at each sitting to sustain himself than he ever has before,* she whispered through their mental bond.

Katja watched the beast a moment before she nodded in agreement. *The more he fights, the more he drinks. He'll kill the horse if he continues in this way.*

Lauraisha's eyes darted back and forth between the male and the steed. *And if Tyron follows Daya'lyn's first bloodmate Bren to the grave, then the hybrid will have to find a new beast bloodmate even stronger than the previous two to withstand his feedings.*

And, if there isn't, he'll become feral and hunt a being.

Lauraisha's face grew pale with her fear. *He'll hunt me.*

XV
JORN

Within an hour of their arrival, the Vihous citizens had packed the Inquisition members and their remaining supplies onto the wagons and were transporting the packmates toward the capital city of Jorn. Katja and Lauraisha sat in one wagon while Daya'lyn lay in the second and Calder's remains rode in the third under a tarp. The supply wagon brought up the rear. The caravan moved steadily across the countryside roads, their handlers taking care not to jostle their precious cargo. The horse Tyron walked beside his master's cart. Since he was the only steed to return to the packmates, Katja doubted that the other horses had survived the storm.

It took three days for the caravan to finally reach its strange yet magnificent destination. Jorn itself was a city crafted half underground and half aboveground. While Katja knew the city had been constructed on top of the ruins of the ancient dwarven city of Delvendeur, she had never imagined that Jorn's current residents would be quite so efficient with their new constructions. The city's aboveground buildings crowned the height of a bloated hill overlooking the rolling sea. A massive stone wall bordered the hill's base far beyond the city's outskirts—stretching from one corner of the peninsula to the other. The wall held three entrances in the cardinal directions of north, south, and west. The iron entrance gates themselves were quite small, only allowing enough space for two horses to pass through at a time. Stone steps led from the heights of the walls down into wide tunnel shafts burrowed out beneath the ground, where much of the city's residential housing lay. More shafts of stairs punctured the landscape in alleyways nestled between administrative buildings and workshops. Katja saw workers scurrying up and down those stairways as the party passed along the main road toward the capital's basilica. The whole place reminded the werecat of an oversized ant hill.

The basilica itself was a lofty affair constructed of iron, copper, and sandstone all mined from the bowels of the city. Enormous external buttresses loomed above the main building to eventually join into a massive support system for the structure's central dome. Katja stared at it in awe.

"Incredible, isn't it?" Lauraisha said.

"I have never seen its like," the werecat replied. "Have you?"

"I accompanied my father here once before as a child...it was a trip full of many new experiences," she replied, staring at the greenish patina of the basilica's copper dome with tears standing in her eyes.

A memory of Kaylor dragging the sobbing Lauraisha from the deck of his ship into his private quarters surfaced in Katja's mind. The female suppressed a wave of nausea as she witnessed the first time the king's touch had turned cruel. She had shared the memory before when it had been dredged up in Lauraisha's mind during Mori'lyn's interrogation, but that did nothing to staunch the fear now rolling in her stomach.

"Lauraisha..." Katja groaned.

"Sorry," the dreamdrifter said and pushed the memory from their minds.

Holis watched them with concern. "Are you both well?"

The Tyglesean princess took a breath to steady herself before answering. "Yes, Master Holis. This place apparently elicits ill memories for me."

"I'm sorry for that."

She shook her head. "Don't be; I'm quite fond of your country. It's just that my childhood otherwise was less amiable."

While Daya'lyn was transported to the Halls of Healing, Katja and Lauraisha were given special accommodations beneath the main basilica. The females' chambers rivaled those of the Mage Citadel's in grandeur and opulence. Cut crystal chandeliers festooned the rooms' vaulted ceilings while mosaics of marble and granite tiles adorned the floors. The females' bedchambers shared a washroom with a heated bathtub the size of a small pond, which was a far cry from the chamber pots and wash basins usually used on the Isle of Summons.

Despite the grandeur of their new surroundings, Katja and Lauraisha spent little time in their chambers during those first few days. If they were not sleeping, eating, or conversing with dignitaries, the females stayed near Daya'lyn's bedside in the city's Halls of Healing. With so many foreign dignitaries about, including those from Tyglesea, the Inquisition members all decided it would be safer if Katja became accustomed to the habit of appearing as a human anytime she was in public. Rather than tire herself needlessly by constant skinshifting between forms, Katja resolved to simply stay human in appearance while in Jorn and only transform her ears and forepaws when she was alone in her chambers. Besides her packmates, only Holis and Sora'lynn would know who and what she truly was. In the meantime, Lauraisha renewed her lessons on human mannerisms and insisted that Katja practice the princess's "table manners" at every opportunity, including the state dinner held a week after the companions' arrival.

"Madam Escari, would you please pass the plate of salmon?" Sora'lynn asked the skinshifter halfway through the third course of their evening meal.

She nodded toward her. "Of course, My Madam."

Katja picked up the cold tray nearest her and gently thrust it toward the harmhealer mage.

"Well done," the harpy murmured before spearing some of the meat with a fork.

Katja smiled at the compliment and absently reached up to tug on one of her ears.

Stop that! Lauraisha said through their bond and kicked Katja's shin with her slippered foot before the skinshifter's hand could reach its destination. *You'll draw attention to yourself!*

I can't help it! the new human whispered back. *My ears*

should be on the top of my head, not the side of my face.

Quiet, or someone might hear you! Lauraisha whispered through their link. *We aren't the only mages here and we can't afford for my kin to be tipped off that you are not what you seem.*

Katja nodded glumly and then spent the next hour trying not to touch her head. She easily remembered to assume the correct walking and sitting postures that Lauraisha had taught her, but was constantly frustrated by her wandering hands. She was miserable without her feline ears, especially since she liked to swivel them to listen in all different directions. These immobile human ears were so restricting!

Halfway through the evening, Katja finally uncovered a blessed secret that kept her hands properly stowed upon her lap. She discovered that with some practice she was actually able to flex her human ears slightly up or down to focus on the hall conversations. However, after a series of alternately appalled and antagonistic expressions from Lauraisha, Katja prudently decided to save her bodily experiments for a more private setting than the dining hall.

* * *

The sun was a most unwelcome guest the following morning as Katja dressed in formal robes and donned her best jewelry. She adjusted her manticore-adorned broadcollar over her robes to hide her three spearheads and clan signet amulet, which were tucked beneath her garments. Then she covered her bite scars with a choker-style necklace of naiad palm ivory beads and pearls that Daya'lyn had created for her during his recovery at the Jorn Halls of Healing. As she walked out of her room in search of food, she tried and failed to flick her ears in annoyance at the shrill squeaks that her new leather riding boots made against the polished floor with every awkward flat-footed step that she took. After that, she stamped down the rest of the corridor muttering darkly.

The door to Lauraisha's room opened as the pseudo-human passed it. The Tyglesean Princess emerged and mumbled a "good morning" to the skinshifter as she too adjusted her own formal attire.

Katja considered her. "After your annoyance yesterday, I'm amazed that you're still actually speaking to me."

Lauraisha stopped fiddling with her sash and looked up to stare at Katja. "Oh...I am sorry, but I did not recognize... Why are you in human form today? We aren't scheduled to meet any foreign dignitaries, are we?"

Katja shrugged. "Not that I've been told, but I might as well practice being human while we are in friendly territory, so that I am prepared for the test of my skills that is fast approaching."

Lauraisha nodded before turning to stride down the hallway. Katja followed her, wincing at the sounds of their twin footsteps echoing behind them. They followed the carved corridor to one of the main stairwells leading up into the basilica. As they rounded a corner just above the stairs, Katja stopped dead in her tracks. The female's mouth hung open in astonishment even as Lauraisha turned to see why she had halted.

"That pot has holes in it!" Katja said as she stood staring at the vase on the pedestal before her in singular dismay.

Lauraisha smiled. "Oh, yes, I noticed that particular vase earlier. Isn't it beautiful?"

Katja said nothing.

"Of course those are technically carvings, not just holes. I think they add a nice amount of interest to the piece, don't you?"

"What interest? The sculptor ruined the jar by adding all of those *carvings*. What good is a hole-filled pot? It cannot hold water or food or store much of anything, really. Perhaps you could put oil and a wick in the bottom of it and turn it into a lamp, but then again, the base is too shallow to hold much oil so you would constantly have to refill it..."

Lauraisha rolled her eyes in exasperation at the skinshifter. "Honestly, Katja! Not everything in this world has to have a practical purpose! Sometimes looking attractive is enough."

"Now you sound like Durhrigg!"

"Says the female whose neck currently carries a link of pearls that serve no other purpose besides decoration."

"Not true! This necklace is costly and could be traded for supplies if needed, unlike the pointless pot."

The princess rolled her eyes again. "Only because others currently attribute value to the pearls. If pearls became worthless to others, would you still wear the necklace?"

Katja frowned for a moment. "Yes."

"Why?"

"Because the naiads gave the pearls to me and Daya'lyn made them into a necklace as a gift. Wearing the pearl necklace is my way of honoring others for their kindness and generosity."

Lauraisha nodded and smiled. "Then how is displaying the carved pot any different?"

"Because a holey pot isn't useful, so it holds no value."

"To some beings, value isn't solely determined by usefulness."

"Well, they're wrong," Katja said stubbornly.

With a half-strangled scream, the human threw up her hands in exasperation and trudged down toward the kitchen, her booted heels slapping the marble with each annoyed step. Katja followed her, still muttering about the idiocy of impractical decorations.

* * *

The morning eat consisted of uncooked fish, stewed lamb, various cheeses, grapes, dark breads, and mulled wines all served in the grand dining hall. Holis and Sora'lynn found the females when they were only half-finished with their meal.

"We must speak with both of you," Holis said as he gestured them away from the table.

"What's happened? Is Daya'lyn well?" Lauraisha asked when the four of them were sequestered in a corner of the corridor outside the kitchens.

He cleared his throat uncomfortably. "Yes, Your Highness, he is. This is about your mage allies from the Isle of Summons. It has been over a week since Vraelth, Felan, Princess Zahra, and the dragon Verdagon have been sighted in Vihous. In the meantime, my informants tell me that there are rumors swarming the Tyglesean Royal Court that King Kaylor has your allies in his custody."

"What!"

"King Kaylor has also officially demanded that we turn you over to him for trial," Sora'lynn said.

Holis nodded. "He has sent a special envoy to escort you

back to Kaylere by ship."

Lauraisha crossed her arms. "And if I refuse?"

"Tyglesea is prepared to declare war on Vihous unless we are prepared to deliver the fugitive princess," Sora'lynn answered.

Lauraisha's expression could have stalled an ogre. "Really? Tyglesea just invaded Vihous in order to capture our allies and now Kaylor has the gall to threaten war against you? By all rights, Vihous should declare war on him for invading your lands."

"I don't disagree, Your Highness," Holis said. "Unfortunately though, the Vihous leadership does not believe that we have the resources or the strength to fight a war on two fronts. We are vulnerable and King Kaylor knows it. In any event, he will likely argue that your allies invaded his country. We have no way to disprove that right now."

"Father has always been a good thief and liar. Even so, I have full diplomatic protection as a member of the Inquisition. Consequently, I don't have to comply with any of his demands, and as a member of the Inquisition, I might even be able to make a few demands of my own."

"King Kaylor will not recognize your claim to such rights without a signed and sealed letter from the Inquisitor himself stating that you are part of his personal entourage."

Lauraisha pursed her lips in thought and looked at Katja. "Did the Ring of Sorcerers even give Daya'lyn a signet ring?"

The skinshifter shook her head. "No, but they gave him the Inquisitor's Crest. A wax impression of that on a formal document should work well enough."

Lauraisha frowned. "The Inquisition is under orders from the Ring of Sorcerers to investigate the Tyglesean Royal Court, so we must journey there regardless of the circumstances. I knew Kaylor would deny my rights of diplomatic immunity; however, I did not expect such a loophole in the terms of my surrender nor did I anticipate Father using our packmates as bait. I should have known better." She shook her head.

Katja looked at Holis. "How long do we have?"

The male scratched his close-cropped, black beard. "The envoy has given us three days to produce Her Royal Highness before Tyglesean ships begin their blockade."

"Time is of the essence, then," Lauraisha said, turned to Katja.

"Is Daya'lyn even well enough to travel?" Katja asked.

"He has made significant progress over the past several days. Thanks to Katja's aid and to the harmhealers here, he should be healthy in another week or two." Sora'lynn frowned. "Yet he is in no fit state to forge a flame and that will greatly limit his Inquisitorial duties in Tyglesea. I fear for all of your safety with Daya'lyn's abilities so limited."

"His abilities may be diminished, but mine aren't and neither are Katja's. With luck, Father won't yet know of our added mage skills," Lauraisha said.

Katja nodded. "We need to talk to Daya'lyn immediately. The longer we wait, the less our and our packmates' chances of overall survival will be."

The princess turned back to Holis. "What does your king say regarding all of this?"

Holis shook his head. "We've kept the information secret until now, but you may as well know that His Majesty is gravely ill."

"What!" Katja and Lauraisha said simultaneously.

Sora'lynn sighed and rubbed her forehead with the back of her talon. "King Daan was found two weeks ago sprawled semiconscious on the floor of his bedchamber. The harmhealers have worked day and night to try to cure his illness, but so far we've been unable to break his high fever. Even if we do, His Majesty is so elderly that I doubt he will survive."

"So this is why he was absent last night during the state dinner," Lauraisha surmised.

Sora'lynn and Holis nodded, their expressions grim.

"So we can expect no royal aid in this matter," Katja said.

"I'm so sorry, My Madams," Holis said. "I feel utterly useless to you right now."

"Can you stall for us?" Lauraisha asked.

"How long?" Holis asked.

"Give us four days if you can before I am required to parlay with the envoy. That will give us at least a little time to prepare for the meeting."

He nodded. "I'll do what I can. In the meantime, we only

hope Master Daya'lyn has a better plan to resolve the present situation."

* * *

No matter how many times Katja entered Daya'lyn's room at the Halls of Healing, she never could feel comfortable with the sight of the muscular male laying on his sickbed. Daya'lyn wasn't supposed to become weak. She had seen him tired, enraged, and feral with bloodlust, but never weak. It unnerved her in a way that not even Daya'lyn's blood-thirstiest moments had.

At the sound of his door opening, the fireforger opened his blue eyes and greeted the two of them with a slight nod. "Good day," he murmured.

"Good day, Daya'lyn, how do you feel?" Lauraisha asked as she and Katja dragged stools alongside his bed.

He shifted his head to look at her. "Roughly the same."

"No improvement at all?" Katja asked.

"The pain is gone and the healers say that I'm doing well considering the circumstances, but if I have to lie here in this infernal bed for one more day I'm going to go stark raving mad," he said through clenched fangs.

"Well, you may get your wish sooner than you expect," the skinshifter said.

"How so?"

Lauraisha cleared her throat. "King Kaylor is threatening a blockade against Vihous if I am not turned over to Tyglesea within the next three days."

"He can't have you," Daya'lyn snarled. "You have diplomatic immunity. More importantly, you are a member of my entourage and therefore under my protection."

Katja shifted uncomfortably. "That is what we told Holis and what Holis will tell the envoy, but Lauraisha already warned you and me that Kaylor will not be moved on this issue."

The hybrid's eyes flashed scarlet with his sudden ire. "We will see."

Lauraisha lifted a hand in appeasement. "The Tygleseans want a signed and sealed document written in your own hand dissuading their rash action."

He frowned. "That is something at least, but it may pose a problem."

"How so?"

"I cannot write Tygeré. I can speak it well enough, but I rarely have had the need to read or write in the language, so my spelling and grammar is appalling."

She nodded. "I can help with that. Regardless, though, even the seal of the Ring of Sorcerers' chosen Inquisitor may not be enough to discourage them."

"Then what will?"

Lauraisha pursed her lips as she watched him. "In my country, the oath of a Champion protector carries a weight more valuable than gold. If I appeared in the Tyglesean court with the Mage Inquisitor himself as my personal Champion, the odds of my acquittal would be well-stacked in my favor."

Daya'lyn's eyes narrowed. "If I declared myself your Champion, you would be protected from your father's wrath?"

Lauraisha swallowed in sudden nervous. "Not completely, but it's the best idea I have at the moment."

Daya'lyn cocked a black eyebrow at her. "What happened to your plan of being put on trial as a way to build diplomatic bridges between myself and your father?"

"We have additional problems," Katja said.

Daya'lyn hissed a string of curses when the skinshifter explained the ailing king's situation and the rumors of their packmates' imprisonment in Tyglesea. "So all of this is a trap that we will trigger no matter what we choose. Perfect."

"Holis and Sora'lynn are stalling for time, but they really hope we can find a way out of this predicament," Katja said.

The Inquisitor folded his arms across his massive chest and stared at Lauraisha. "If my memory of Tyglesean law serves me correctly, I would have to be betrothed to you in order to claim the title of your Champion."

Lauraisha smoothed the wrinkles of her robe and said nothing.

"Lauraisha?"

The princess hunched her shoulders and nodded.

"Your Highness, I am not comfortable with this," Daya'lyn told her. "If someone discovers our ruse, we could be in even more danger than we are already."

"Does it have to be a ruse?" she asked quietly.

Instead of looking angry, Daya'lyn actually appeared anguished. "Did you hear nothing of my warnings to you the night of the cyclone?"

Lauraisha lifted her chin and, for a moment, appeared every bit as regal as she was. "The Creator's design has brought us together, Daya'lyn, whether you will it or not."

"The Creator or you?"

"Perhaps both."

Daya'lyn's rebuke was almost gentle. "As noble as your blood may be, it still courses through the body of a being holding only sixteen winters of age. You yourself said that our timing was premature. Your love warms my heart, but it is still the adoration of a child. One as dear and precious to me as any friend could be, but a child nonetheless. I cannot yoke myself to a female half of my own age. To do so would be beyond cruelty to you."

"My father would see me married to a man a score older even than you without a second thought."

Daya'lyn half-rose from the bed. "I am not your father!"

Tears broke the borders of her eyes and made their escape down Lauraisha's pale cheeks. She fled the room.

Daya'lyn sat back against the pillows and cursed in frustration and weariness. "Why? Why, no matter what I say or do, no matter how I try to protect her, why do I always seem to hurt her instead?"

Katja shook her head. "We often hurt the ones we love, Daya'lyn, even when doing so is what we fear the most."

* * *

Katja, Lauraisha, and Daya'lyn sat in overstuffed chairs alongside Holis and Sora'lynn. Katja clasped her hands firmly in her lap to keep herself from fidgeting with her human ears or blunt fingernails while the Inquisition members and their hosts awaited the arrival of the Tyglesean emissary.

It will be fine, Katja. Do not worry yourself, Lauraisha said through the bond linking their minds.

Katja cocked an eyebrow at her, a habit she was becoming more accustomed to doing whenever she needed to show sarcasm while in human form. *Are you saying that to calm my mind or your own?* she asked.

Both, came the reply.

She nodded slightly and then glanced at Daya'lyn. The handsome male looked strong and healthy as he sat erect against the chair back in all of his fine robes, but Katja knew better. While the male had been released from the Halls of Healing, Sora'lynn had still forbade him from forging fire of any intensity for two more weeks lest he rob his body of the strength necessary to finish healing his fractured skull.

The massive wooden doors opened and all five stood to greet the Tyglesean emissary as he entered the meeting hall.

"Welcome, Your Excellency," Holis said and quickly ushered the new arrival to his seat. "Emissary Federicos, may I present Inquisitor Daya'lyn Calebson, the honorable Katja Escari, the healer Sora'lynn, and, of course, Her Royal Highness, Princess Lauraisha of the House of Astraht'a."

Katja felt confusion flicker through Lauraisha's mind as they exchanged pleasantries. While all the others regained their seats, Lauraisha and Federicos continued to stand and watch each other.

"It has been a long time since we have spoken, Your Royal Highness," Federicos said.

"Federicos? Is that truly you?" Lauraisha asked in Tygeré. "The last time I saw you, you were resolved to follow in your father's footsteps."

"Plans change, Princess," he said coolly.

She cocked a brown eyebrow at him. "So I see."

After a silence seething with tension, Lauraisha asked, "How fares your father?"

"Dead."

"I am so sorry," she said quietly.

"You should be, Your Highness, especially since it was your wilderness escapade that cost Commander Escos his life, along with some thirty of Tyglesea's finest warriors."

"I did not mean to—"

"Shuck the apology." Federicos sneered and then added, "My Princess," when Daya'lyn quietly walked over to stand behind Lauraisha.

"If you are quite finished showing your insolence

toward a member of your own royalty," Daya'lyn began in Tygeré, "and insulting a member of my Inquisitorial party, let us commence negotiations, Emissary Federicos," he said, finishing in Shrŷde through clenched fangs.

Federicos took an involuntarily step back from the hybrid and then seemed to bolster his courage. "What negotiations, Your Eminence? My orders from His Majesty, King Kaylor, are to take Princess Lauraisha back to Tyglesea to stand trial as a witch and a political dissident."

"A witch!" Lauraisha yelled in protest.

"How dare you!" Daya'lyn thundered. "The princess is a member of my party. You have no right to try a mage under the protection and instruction of the Ring of Sorcerers."

"I have every right!" Federicos shouted back. "That ragged band of warlocks and witches cannot dictate law of any kind to my king and if they try, my countrymen and I will be more than happy to prove the superiority of our strategies and weaponry in battle."

"I welcome you to attempt it," Daya'lyn said in a deadly whisper as he drew himself to his full height.

"My Sirs, My Madam," Holis said. "Let us sit and discuss this rationally...please?"

Lauraisha, Daya'lyn, and Federicos all grudgingly took their seats. Katja was grateful for the action, if nothing else, because it would give Daya'lyn a chance to rest without showing any apparent weakness toward their adversary.

"Now then, My Sirs and My Madams," Holis began. "As the officiating delegate, I wish to hear each of your grievances and concerns one at a time, beginning with Emissary Federicos."

The Tyglesean male inclined his head in recognition before retrieving a scroll from his satchel. "Thank you, Your Excellency. I have here a signed and sealed declaration from His Majesty, King Kaylor, stating grievances against the political dissident Her Royal Highness, Princess Lauraisha, originally of the House of Astraht'a. They are as follows: 'abdication of royal duties without due process of law, co-conspiring against the royal crown, co-conspiring to murder the Captain of the Guard, stealing and harboring a known mage weapon with intent to use it against the crown, practicing witchcraft, and general sedition.'"

With each charge, Lauraisha's face became more and more flushed with anger.

"As you can see, Master Holis, such charges and grievances cannot merely be ignored or forgotten. She must accompany me back to Tyglesea to stand trial before her own people in keeping with the law," Federicos said.

Holis bowed to Federicos and then turned to Lauraisha. "What is your response, Your Highness?"

Lauraisha pursed her lips and stared down Federicos with eyes like daggers. "Commander Escos died defending the Lady Katja and me from Asheken deadwalkers, and from the treachery of his own soldiers. I count such a sacrifice as the highest of all acts of love and fealty toward another, and yet such a waste of life could have been prevented if my father, His Majesty, King Kaylor, had acted with half of the honor that his Captain of the Guard achieved!"

Lauraisha stood, her hands curled into white-knuckled fists. "I am deemed a witch by my own family and my countrymen despite the fact that my dreamdrifting talents are mage abilities recognized and lauded by the chief governing body of all Sylvan Orders, the Ring of Sorcerers, in accordance with the Sylvan Code, the highest and oldest set of governing laws in existence. My father claims that I abandoned my royal duties and conspired against him despite the fact that I fled Tyglesea before my sixteenth birthday to protect my life against the actions of assassins, who were hired by my own father to destroy me lest I fulfill some absurd prophecy predicting the downfall of his rule.

"If I am guilty of any of those bombastic charges, it is sedition. And if I am guilty of sedition, it is only because our king is paranoid and has thus set his will against the righteous."

Federicos was unmoved. "If such are your claims, Your Highness, then I suggest you issue them in a proper Tyglesean court of law with full burden of proof."

Lauraisha scoffed. "Emissary Federicos, you know as well as I that any trial in Tyglesea consists not of the accused properly defending herself before the judges, but the judges heckling and jeering a defendant while she is gagged. The same will occur at my own trial because I will appear before a corrupt court."

"That remains to be seen."

"No, that is to be expected."

"Not if the accused, such as yourself, is Championed by either her betrothed or her husband." He looked at her expectantly. "But, as you have neither…"

"According to whom?" Daya'lyn interjected.

Federicos gawked at him. "You Champion her?"

"I do."

"But, Lord Daer—" Federicos coughed and cleared his throat. "Excuse me, Master Daya'lyn, you must be betrothed to the one you wish to Champion, and I see no ring on her right middle finger indicating intent."

Daya'lyn frowned. "I was not aware of the custom of giving a ring to symbolize our betrothal. Lauraisha, why did not you tell me?"

Lauraisha looked at him, startled, but quickly recovered. "Considering our present situation, I did not think it relevant."

Daya'lyn gave her a disapproving look and did it so well that Katja wondered for a moment if the two had indeed become secretly betrothed overnight.

"Let me make sure that I understand this correctly…the Tyglesea Princess is not only a member of your company, but is your betrothed as well, Master Daya'lyn?"

The hybrid nodded. "Indeed."

"And by whose authority was this betrothal granted, since His Majesty was never asked his consent to your union as is his right as a daughter's father under Tyglesea law?"

Daya'lyn crossed his arms and stared Federicos down. "King Kaylor gave up his right to patriarchal power when he ceased acting in his daughter's best interests by mistreating her and then ordering her murder. Therefore by the Sylvan Code—which trumps Tyglesean law—King Kaylor has lost his right to claim Lauraisha as heir and ward once she began her studies at the Mage Citadel on the Isle of Summons. As a student of the Ring of Sorcerers, she is now a ward of the self-same governing body. Consequently, His Majesty has no right or jurisdiction to say how his former heir can conduct her affairs."

"And the members of the Ring of Sorcerers have approved this match?"

Daya'lyn slowly shook his head. "Not at this time. At this time the Ring members would prefer a minimum five-year hiatus between our betrothal and our subsequent marriage. Such a period of reflection would ensure that Lauraisha's full training as a mage and her lawful maturity as a female have been completed. I happen to agree with such an arrangement."

"I see," Federicos said. "And, as her Champion, do you wish to defend her in the Tyglesean Court of Law?"

"No." Daya'lyn leaned forward in his chair. "As Inquisitor, I intend to go to Tyglesea to discover why the Tyglesean Royal Court is willfully undermining the Code set forth and adhered to by the rest of the Sylvan Orders."

XVI
BEFORE THE GOLDEN THRONE

The journey to Kaylere aboard the ship *Nedaleta Benefta* was one of the oddest Katja had ever experienced. Never before had she traveled by ship on the open sea, nor had she ever been treated as a political prisoner until now. The combination of new experiences proved altogether unnerving. While Daya'lyn was treated with a deference bordering on obsequiousness by the ship's diplomats, captain, and crew, Katja and Lauraisha were shown polite aloofness by their guards, who never let either of the females out of sight unless necessity dictated a trip to the ship's head or the females' own tiny cabins.

Katja had expected to ride out the weeks-long voyage in the ship's brig, and instead she and Lauraisha were treated almost as well as Emissary Federicos himself in terms of personal comforts. Far from feeling reassured, Katja found the dual experience of civility and custody disconcerting. The combination of her periodic seasickness, persistent supervision, and constant human form wore on the skinshifter's already frayed nerves. As disgruntled as she was, however, Katja's discomfort paled in comparison to Daya'lyn's. Never had she known a being to become so seasick so easily. The fireforger spent most of his time either in his cabin with a pail at his bedside or up on deck with his head hung over the side railing.

"He really should see a healer once we set foot on dry land again, Your Highness. I mean it's just not natural for a male to be so sick at sea," the ship's captain had remarked to Lauraisha on the seventeenth day of the voyage between Jorn and Kaylere. Lauraisha had unsurprisingly proved herself as the only one of the three companions who seemed fully at ease on the sea.

"Yes, well, fireforger mages are not known for their high tolerance to travel across large bodies of water, and Master Daya'lyn has lived his whole life on dry land," she replied as she and Katja grimaced at the sound of Daya'lyn's dry heaves.

Katja frowned as she shifted her gaze between the two Tygleseans. How was she understanding Tygeré with such ease? She was not that familiar with the language, just Lauraisha's occasional mutterings in it.

My mental bond with Lauraisha must have strengthened my language skills, she thought.

"It's probably none of my business, but if it was me picking an Inquisitor, I'd be sure the male knew his way about a ship." The captain shook his head. "Ah, well. I expect we'll be at the wharfs by seventeen bells this eve, Highness, and that'll provide him all the relief he needs. In the meantime, ye should continue seeing to it that he drink lots of water and a good draft of wine every now and then to help settle his stomach."

Lauraisha nodded, her eyes gazing gloomily across the distance sea. "I am indebted to you, Captain Tylner. Thank you."

He bowed to the two females before leaving them to resume his other duties.

Come, Katja. Come, Daya'lyn, Lauraisha mentally whispered as she stared after the limping captain. *If he expects our arrival in Kaylere tonight, we should wear our best clothing and finish with the last of my teachings about Tyglesean etiquette.*

* * *

True to the captain's prediction, the wharf bell began tolling seventeen times that evening just after the *Nedaleta Benefta* was docked. What the captain had not foreseen was the upheaval that his passengers would cause upon their arrival. Two warships escorted the ship into the harbor and twenty mounted cavalry along with thirty archers greeted the ship with weapons ready once it was docked.

The members of the Inquisition were met by the new Captain of the Guard, Sir Onofré, as they descended the gangplank.

"I apologize for the inconvenience, My Lord Daya'lyn, but I cannot allow a mage or any of his companions to go before His Majesty, King Kaylor, armed. Please relinquish your weapons and totems."

Daya'lyn surveyed the archers and cavalry surrounding them with rage smoldering in his blue eyes before turning on Onofré. "Am I to assume that I and my staff are prisoners, Captain?"

The shorter male cleared his throat; his discomfort evident. "As I understand it, Lord Daya'lyn, His Majesty would prefer to meet you and your fellows with as little magical interference as possible clouding the issues of state."

"I will not agree to go before the king chained," Daya'lyn growled.

Onofre's gaze turned dangerous as he took a step away from the Inquisitor. With a twitch of his fingers, archers on all sides took aim. "Nevertheless, you must comply. Think carefully, Lord Daya'lyn. Your reputation is that of a powerful fireforger mage, but even you cannot hope to deflect thirty arrows launched at once away from yourself or those under your protection."

Daya'lyn glowered at the Tyglesean as the archers pointed their barbed arrows at his and the females' hearts. Grudgingly the Inquisition members complied with the captain's orders. The packmates were searched and stripped of all weapons, and then fitted with thin shackles made of a curious bright-blue metal around their wrists. Katja growled when the guards confiscated her clan's signet crest, the females' jewelry, and all of their spearheads.

Careful, Katja, be true to the mannerisms of the skin you now hold, Lauraisha whispered in the skinshifter's mind.

The three members of the Inquisition then made their way via chariot toward the palace of Summersted in the company of their forced entourage. They wound their way through the paved streets of Kaylere ever watchful of their surroundings. Horse-drawn chariots and wagons clattered past them, their red-painted wheels flashing in the flickering glow of the great city's light fires. Despite the danger of their situation, the packmates' journey from Kaylere's harbor and wharf district onto the avenues housing the city's upper echelon proved quite interesting to Katja, who was far from familiar with such spectacles.

Kaylere's harbor was the jewel of the city—indeed, the jewel of all Sylvan harbors. It boasted a rectangular commercial harbor with wharfs running parallel to each other along two built-up arms of land, so that they provided easy unloading of ship goods. Then the interior bay had been converted into a circular port to house military ships along the port's inside circumference and along a central dock.

The housing along the wharf district was filled with goods, slaves, and merchants all housed in square, gray stone buildings a spruce-length or more tall. Katja had never seen such free-standing construction. She was far more familiar with dens or full cave dwellings being carved into existing mountains and hills. Even Jorn and the Isle of Summons were built up from the foundations of the ancient dwarf cavern systems. In contrast, these Tyglesean "apartment" systems were set on no such preexisting construction and looked young in comparison with the Mage Citadel's far more weathered towers.

The poorer districts adjacent to the warehouse district had narrow streets cutting between plain-faced buildings boasting mere arrow slits for windows while the richer houses closer to the castle boasted facades with detailed carvings and wide, fitted stained-glass windows.

Looming over all else stood Castle Summersted with its expansive double-bailey and central keep. Summersted was the oldest structure in the city, having been built up from the original wooden fort in the ancient kingdom's infancy. The massive stone walls were blackened and battle-scarred, but otherwise showed none of the destruction that had leveled the rest of the old city during Kaylor's ruthless rise to power in the Warlock Wars forty winters ago. Katja suppressed a shudder as she surveyed the great rectangular keep. She could almost smell the rank stench of evil emanating from within its walls.

What is it? Lauraisha asked within her mind.

Katja stared at the keep and swore that she saw glimmers of crimson etched in some of its stones as they drew closer to the castle's outer walls. *I'm not sure. Perhaps I've heard and experienced too many of your memories of your father and it is affecting my judgment toward this place, but I swear that I just smelled the charnel reek of deadwalkers.*

Lauraisha and Daya'lyn's jaws tightened at her response.

Lauraisha, is our treatment now a normal reaction to foreign dignitaries? Daya'lyn asked through the bond that Lauraisha had opened between the three of them.

She gave a slight shake of her head. *No, this is far above my father's usual paranoia.*

I thought as much. Whatever happens to us, stay close to me. I will do all I can to protect us.

"Who goes there?" one of the Summersted guards called from the parapet above them as the party crossed the main bridge and stood before the castle's main entrance.

"Captain Onofré with Envoy Federicos, Inquisitor Daya'lyn Calebson, the Lady Katja Escari, the Princess Lauraisha, and personal entourage," Onofré called. "They wish to enter Summersted Castle at the request of His Majesty, King Kaylor."

"Your request is granted, My Sir. Please proceed."

Katja heard the creaking of massive wooden wheels as a wood-and-metal ramp was lowered onto the bridge from the elevated gateway. As their steeds trekked up the ramp and passed under the teeth of the raised portcullis, Katja felt as if they were being swallowed by some enormous monster.

"This way, My Sirs and Madams," a young page said to Federicos and Daya'lyn even as the stable hands saw to Tyron and the cavalry horses. "His Majesty is expecting you."

Under heavy guard, they followed the page from the inner gatehouse past the central fountain of the inner ward and on into the castle keep. As they walked, Katja took the chance to survey her surroundings. Summersted's gilded gut was festooned with pennant flags resplendent in hues of maroon and purple and bearing the royal house's coat of arms—a diamond-shaped shield sectioned into quarters with a fish, a sword, an anchor, and a spear emblazoned in gold and silver threads against fields of gray and blue. The drooping pennants reminded Katja more of streams of blood cascading down the gray walls than of fine fabric.

She shivered as they entered the keep's throne room. Then, as she spied the raised dais and the corpulent human seated on its gilt throne, Katja suddenly felt nauseated. King Kaylor leered at them from his place of power as the page announced their names in turn. She felt Lauraisha trembling beside her.

"And who speaks for this assembled band of ruffians?" King Kaylor asked as the newcomers all bowed.

Daya'lyn's jaw tightened, but he kept his deep voice level. "I am Master Daya'lyn Calebson. As Inquisitor, I speak by the authority vested in me by the Ring of Sorcerers and I have sought this audience with Your Majesty at their behest."

"I see, Inquisitor Daya'lyn," Kaylor replied. "And what token can you produce to prove that you indeed hold the authority of the Ring?"

Daya'lyn glowered at him. "Unfortunately, your captain relieved me of my crest and several other accessories when he and his fellows chained me under your orders. Such treatment of a diplomat is highly irregular."

A memory not her own vied for Katja's attention as the males verbally sparred...

*

"My Lord Daeryn, I am sorry to keep you waiting," King Kaylor's personal envoy said, in what he hoped was an even tone of voice as they greeted each other with a bow. He was struck by how much of Marga's visage was reflected in this handsome male's appearance.

"With all due respect, Your Excellency, I had expected to meet with His Majesty this evening, not you," Daeryn said.

The ghoul Curqak suppressed the tremor of fear that coursed through him at hearing something so close to Caleb's voice after all these years. Instead the envoy affected an urbane smile—tight-lipped to hide his pointed, yellow teeth—and gestured for his guest to take a seat in a nearby chair. "Of course, my apologies, Good Sir, but I am afraid no one sees King Kaylor without speaking with me first, as is the age-old custom of the Tyglesean Royal Court. Now, you did state that the matter in question was urgent, so shall we come to it at last?"

Daeryn narrowed his eyes, but sat nonetheless. As Curqak sat down opposite his guest, he felt sudden sweat bead up through the heavy makeup cloaking his ashen face and black-tipped ears. Would Daeryn be able to sense the decrepit state of his body underneath all the finery, just as Daeryn's mother had? If Daeryn discerned him to be a deadwalker...but no, the male was now busying himself with repositioning a chair cushion and surely couldn't smell the charnel scent masked by Curqak's heavy perfume...

"Where is my mother?" Daeryn asked.

"I beg your pardon?"

"My mother Marga disappeared over a year ago. She was last seen in this kingdom, so where...precisely...is she?"

*

Someone nudged Katja.

"Katja, are you well?" Lauraisha asked.

The wraithwalker blinked and the present-day throne room swam back into view. She realized now that everyone was staring at her in silence. She tried to stand more erect, but crimson shapes collided in her vision and she fell to her knees.

"Katja!" Lauraisha and Daya'lyn cried simultaneously.

She gasped as the memory of Daeryn's interrogation of the ghoul continued to play out in her mind's eye. "Curqak and Daeryn were here in this very room!" she gasped.

She felt Daya'lyn's protective grip shake her shoulder. "Katja, are you sure?"

She bobbed her head emphatically.

"I think, given the circumstances," King Kaylor said as he hoisted his pudgy, pale form off of the golden throne, "that perhaps I should dispense with further pleasantries and instead introduce my royal suasor to all of you. Inquisitor Daya'lyn, please allow me to introduce the Lady Evita, whom I believe you already know by another name."

Crimson exploded in Katja's vision anew as a breathtakingly beautiful female walked gracefully around the back of the throne curtain to stand beside the king. The

274 • ALYCIA CHRISTINE

skinshifter snarled.

Daya'lyn's blue eyes darted from Katja to Evita in confusion and then transformed to scarlet in his sudden recognition. "Naraka!"

"Grandson!" She curtseyed toward him mockingly, her pouty pink lips revealing sharp fangs as she smiled. "It's so nice that you recognize your true kin after all."

The hybrid glowered at her. "You are no kin of mine, falíchí!"

"Really, Dayalan, you wound me," the female vampire jeered. "Our first meeting and already you seek to disown me? Your brother, at least, was wise enough to offer me the proper amount of respect."

Katja smiled as she felt the energy of Lauraisha's fire building within the human's body beside her. Without warning, then, the magic extinguished without giving off even a single spark. She and Lauraisha gasped in surprise and then the human fireforger sagged against Daya'lyn's bulk— overwhelmed with exhaustion.

Daya'lyn looked at Lauraisha in alarm and then frowned down at his own manacles. A moment of concentration was quickly followed by horrified comprehension. "You bound us with water chains," he snarled.

"Indeed," Kaylor said and then looked toward Federicos. "You have done well, Envoy. Leave us now."

Katja watched with gathering panic as the emissary led his entourage and the rest of the guards out of the chamber. They barred the doors after them.

"Father," Lauraisha cried. "What have you done?"

"I have done nothing, Lauraisha, except what I must to protect myself and my kingdom from those who would oppose our quest for immortality." He turned to Naraka. "Destroy them. I'll not risk any more interference this close to victory."

"What of the ones I requested, Your Majesty?" The eagerness in Naraka's voice sickened Katja.

Kaylor looked at his daughter for a long moment. "As I have told you before, I keep my promises. By my authority, they are yours. You may do with them what you wish so long as you make certain that Lauraisha cannot fulfill the prophesy set against me."

Lauraisha screamed as Kaylor left and Naraka approached.

"You cannot have them," Daya'lyn growled as he stepped in front of Lauraisha and Katja.

"And who will stop me? You?"

"Yes." His voice was something between a growl and a whisper.

Naraka searched his eyes for a long moment. "Your affections toward her are doomed, Dayalan. Lauraisha is far too weak to be a match for one such as you. Now step aside."

"Never," Daya'lyn snarled.

A slow, cold smile parted Naraka's lips to once again reveal her yellow fangs. She lunged and pushed Daya'lyn to the ground — her black claws reaching for the soft flesh of the hybrid's neck and collarbone. Daya'lyn brought a leg up between them as they fell and kicked his attacker off just as Naraka leaned in to stab him with her talons.

Naraka rolled to her feet and lunged again as Daya'lyn righted himself. The two crashed to the floor again. Katja couldn't believe that anyone besides Felan was a match for Daya'lyn's strength, but in his weakened state, Luther's bloodmate kept easy pace with him. She lunged again, but this time Daya'lyn was ready for her. He struck Naraka hard in the throat with the heels of his bound hands and then landed a kick to her ribs. Naraka fell to the ground sputtering and coughing.

Tendrils of fog crept along the floor as the two fought. Katja pulled Lauraisha further away from the struggling pair and pushed her mind against the mist, praying that her wraithwalking abilities could somehow fight Naraka's shade magic even with the manacles on her wrists. She struck the vampire's deception with her knowledge of truth and the fog of confusion retreated. It was then that she understood. The water chains were not designed to hinder her wraithwalking abilities; they just suppressed the magic of fireforging.

Naraka suddenly cried out as a bright yellow ball of fire — Daya'lyn's fire — erupted through the chamber's gloom to hit her full in the chest. The vampire was launched backwards into a small table and it splintered under her weight. She crumpled to the floor and, as the females watched in horror, so did Daya'lyn. They rushed to the fireforger's side.

"Creator, keep us!" Katja whispered as they drew near.

The fireforger groaned in pain as Katja pulled off the smoldering gloves clinging to his raw, bloody fingers. The skinshifter looked around for Naraka's body and saw only gathering gloom as the mist snuffed out the hall's candle flames one by one. The hackles on her neck rose as she heard Naraka's laughter echo in the vaulted chamber. In the sudden darkness, she could smell little and see even less. She felt her magic pushing against the boundaries of Naraka's power and keeping it at bay—barely.

"We have to escape this place now!" she hissed to Lauraisha.

"Go! Run!" Daya'lyn said through clenched fangs.

"We will not leave you!" the human cried.

"Where will you go, changeling?" Naraka whispered in the darkness. "No matter how far you run, you can never escape us."

The wraithwalker's answering roar shook the throne room, but it could not pierce the vampire shade's darkness.

The attack came as the wall of blackness finally overwhelmed Katja's senses. Ghouls, imps, and zombies converged on the three packmates from all sides—gagging them and dragging them at knife-point away from each other. Then the darkness lifted and Katja and Lauraisha saw Naraka as she stood over Daya'lyn—a splintered table leg held high in her clawed hand.

"You will watch," she snarled.

The females' screams strained against their muffles as the scorched deadwalker stabbed Daya'lyn over and over again with the impromptu stake. When the laughing vampire had had her fill of vengeance, she kicked the fireforger's mutilated body back toward his sobbing packmates.

"Should we kill them, too, Mistress?" one of the ghouls asked.

"Not unless you want to be bled dry yourself." Naraka hissed. "The High Elder wants to bleed them himself. Confine them. We'll deal with the lot of them when he arrives."

"The castle cells, then?"

"Those cells aren't strong enough to hold them. Throw

the three of them into a drowning dungeon."

"Those are already occupied, Mistress."

"Then add them with the others and triple the guard! I'll not be responsible for destroying the High Elder's prize before he has had the chance to taste it!"

The undead guards hefted Daya'lyn, Lauraisha, and Katja through a dank hallway and down a spiraling stone staircase.

Katja heard the high-pitched squeal of old iron hinges as two guards unlocked and opened a large grate securing the entrance of a dungeon pit carved out of the solid stone beneath the castle.

"Let us see how defiant you feel after a few days of communion with the dead," Naraka sneered as she shoved Katja headlong into the yawning darkness beneath them.

Instinctively the current human flipped upright and stretched out so that her back feet found the hard stone floor first. As her toes found solid purchase, she leaned backward and rolled her right hip over the opposite shoulder across the ground to reduce the impact of the fall. She came to a stand on her back feet and winced. She had garnered several bruises from the four-body-lengths-long fall, but at least nothing seemed broken.

Lauraisha was less fortunate. She was tossed into the dungeon mere moments after the skinshifter. Even before Katja had fully comprehended the sickening sounds of the human's cracking bones, Daya'lyn was falling. The unconscious fireforger crashed into the prone princess just as the iron door slammed shut above them.

Lauraisha groaned as Katja tried to pull Daya'lyn's bloody body off of hers.

"How badly are you hurt?" the werecat asked.

Lauraisha winced as she clutched a mangled hand and arm to her chest. "Don't worry about me, help him!"

The sound of claws scuffing against stone stilled the human's words. Both females turned to peer into the darkness. Katja growled a warning and sank into a defensive crouch with her fists ready as a huge, furry figure stalked slowly toward them.

"Katja?"

The new human stood perfectly still. She knew that

voice—that strong, gentle tenor voice.

"Felan?" she whispered.

The huge black-and-gray werewolf moved into the dim circle of light beneath the pit's locked grate. "Thank the Creator, it is you!" Felan bent and gave her a fierce hug.

"You're here!" she asked breathlessly while still cradled against his furry chest. "But where are the others?"

"We're here, Katja," Zahra said as she and Vraelth slowly approached. They both bore deep purple bruises along their wrists and bare ankles, and there were dark shadows circling their eyes.

"How did you—"

"Katja!" Lauraisha screamed.

Terror filled the skinshifter's eyes and she turned back to Daya'lyn. "Help me, Felan!" the skinshifter cried as she delved back between the layers of the fireforger's body—knitting the skin of his gashes back together.

"Merciful Creator!" Felan prayed. Daya'lyn's breaths were coming shallow rasps and red splotches now riddled his pale skin. Blood gushed from the fireforger's multiple wounds. "Zahra, Vraelth, tourniquets!"

Within moments, Katja felt Felan's reassuring skinshifter magic flow alongside hers within the torn muscles of Daya'lyn's body. As they worked together tying tourniquets around gaping wounds, Felan asked, "What happened to him?"

"Naraka ambushed us in Kaylor's throne room. Daya'lyn tried to fight her with fire despite wearing water chains. He managed to launch a single fireball before the manacles turned his magic against him—burning him. While we watched, Naraka then stabbed him with a wooden stake."

"Mahogany?"

She nodded. "It must be."

"And mahogany wood makes him and his brother deathly ill," the werewolf said grimly.

"Yes."

"Where is the Pyrekin Panacea, Zahra?" Lauraisha asked. "We can use it to help heal Dayalan! Where have you hidden it?"

Zahra's face was a mask of true sorrow. "I am truly sorry,

Lauraisha, but I already tried to use it to restore Qenethala. There are a precious few drops left and those were confiscated when we were imprisoned here."

Lauraisha stared at Zahra and then at Felan with tears coursing down her face. With a cry of anguish she punched at Vraelth's chest with her good hand. He caught it and brushed it aside as he pulled her into a protective embrace. Katja bit back a sob as she watched the human weep into the elf's tattered robes.

"Katja, his heart falters. If you can keep it beating and his lungs breathing, I will try to repair as much of the damage as I can," Felan said. "Zahra, I need you to extract as many splinters from his wounds as possible, so that we can hopefully stop this adverse reaction. Vraelth, I need you to destroy the water chains. If you have any pixie dust left, I need you to sprinkle it in each wound after Zahra is done, so that we can stave off infection. Quickly now, or he will die."

Despite her growing fatigue, Katja gritted her teeth in determination.

"Creator, aid us!" Lauraisha tearfully whispered as she watched her packmates work.

"Calm down, Lauraisha," Katja murmured. "You still have the Sapphire Keystone. Try to contact Damya; we'll need her help."

Lauraisha nodded and began pulling out the stitching of the inner hem of her robe where she had hidden the Keystone necklace.

Katja gave the dreamdrifter a half-smile of encouragement and then turned back to the prone male. She felt Daya'lyn's heartbeat and breaths strengthen, but only while under her magic's influence.

Katja turned to the werewolf. "Where is Verdagon?"

Felan shook his head. "He fell behind. I have not the time or energy to explain the story now."

"Felan," Zahra said. "How bad is it?"

"She stabbed him twenty-four times. Most of them are fairly shallow, but a few… He has lost a lot of blood. He has hairline cracks in the three lowest of his left ribs and he has a head injury."

"Old or new?"

"Old—almost mended, with no new injury that I can feel."

"Well, that is something at least," Katja said through clenched teeth.

Zahra shook her head. "Felan, even if we had a harmhealer like Neha'lyn here, this would not be easily cured."

"I know."

"Are you sure you both can risk the energy healing him?" she whispered.

Felan nodded. "We have to try."

Vraelth blew out a breath as he too nodded. He took hold the Tyglesean princess's manacles. "I am sorry, Lauraisha, but this may hurt a little."

"I know," she whispered through clenched teeth as the charmchanter jerked on the water chains and muttered a breaking spell in Kwaërm. A few moments later the right shackle unlatched itself from Lauraisha's raw wrist with a sullen click and Vraelth went to work on the next. When he finished freeing the human's chains, the elf did the same for Katja and for Daya'lyn. As Vraelth slumped to the floor in exhaustion, Lauraisha's yellow flames grazed the floor— sanitizing it. Her four packmates then moved Daya'lyn to the cleaned workspace.

"Lauraisha, gather all of the blankets and rags we have and sanitize them as well as you can. We'll need to burn some of them for added light, so find the best place in the dungeon to do that," the werewolf instructed as they gently laid the Inquisitor's body upon the warmed stone.

Katja felt Felan delve deep between the fibers of Daya'lyn's muscles as he worked behind Zahra and Vraelth to shift the hybrid's wounds closed. Lauraisha and Katja could not feel Daya'lyn's thoughts at all. Even if Felan managed to drain all of the toxins and patch every wound, Katja had no way of knowing if the male's soul could actually cling to his damaged body, or if it must permanently pass into the Creator's care. Naraka's underlings had thought that Daya'lyn was already dead. Looking at him now, she could scarcely dispute that assumption.

Katja wanted to weep like Lauraisha, but there was no time or energy for such an emotional purge when she had to keep reminding Daya'lyn's organs to function. She closed her eyes and fought for calm even as she continued to will Daya'lyn's heart's rhythm to match her own.

The work was long and exhausting, and Katja felt little encouragement that its eventual outcome would even be worth the hardship. Daya'lyn was all but dead; he could not even sustain his own heartbeat and his body had already begun to swell. Katja's ears drooped in defeat even as Felan repaired the last of the fireforger's wounds. Throughout the process, Lauraisha stayed silent and cradled Damya's Keystone in her injured hands even as she continued to feed her small flames lighting their work with the rags.

Katja watched her tear-streaked face a moment more and then looked past it as a glimmer in the gray wall caught her eye. Half-hidden in the dungeon's darkness, just beyond their meager circle of light, was a small stone altar with gilded carvings around its foundation. She stared slack-jawed at the circle of intricate letters. In the presence of Lauraisha's fire, they glittered in hues like those of the iridescent Ring Spells protecting Crown Canyon, Caerwyn Castle, and the Bridge of Sky. Katja gaped at the familiar markings. She felt Daya'lyn's pulse quicken to match her own as she recognized the language of her homeland in the middle of a Tyglesean dungeon.

"Dei Dyvesé it unmygn ort ol restel. Nur dei reinen ol sere finden Me frieden," she read aloud.

"Katja? What is it?" Zahra asked as she and Lauraisha followed the skinshifter's gaze.

"It's Felis," Katja whispered.

The Feliconian werecat language was carved here?" Lauraisha shook her head. "That's impossible."

"Clearly not," Zahra said as she gazed between the iridescent markings and a stunned Katja.

"What do the carvings mean, Katja?" Vraelth asked.

"The Creator is our refuge. Only the pure of soul will find His freedom," the Feliconian translated.

"What a statement to carve in the middle of a dungeon," Zahra said.

"How could it have possibly gotten here?" Lauraisha asked, her eyes reading the letters over and over again.

Katja said nothing, but turned back to watch Felan as he quietly finished his mending work. With a last boost of Lauraisha's and Zahra's added strength, Felan stitched the last lesion closed. Katja continued to will the fireforger's organs to operate, but transferred as much of her extra strength to Felan as she could so that he would have enough energy left to mend Lauraisha's injuries.

"It's done," Felan said as he set the bones of Lauraisha's hand and arm back in place.

"But could you remove the toxins that his body built up in response to the wood?" Zahra asked as she splinted Lauraisha's arm and hand.

Felan shook his head. "He needs a harmhealer to draw it from his blood."

"There is none."

"I know."

"So he'll still die?"

Felan rubbed his face with a paw. "Since Katja is the one willing him to breathe, he may be dead already."

Daya'lyn's heart fluttered then, and the little wraithwalker felt the barest whisper of a presence brush against her awareness.

Daya'lyn? she called silently, opening her mind with her wraithwalking ability just as Joce'lynn had taught her.

"Katja…" a familiar voice called.

The Felis symbols carved into the stone around the altar flashed with mage fire. The altar shook and a beam of light shot upward from its center through the darkness. The silvery light flared and then vanished, leaving two ethereal figures to float above the metal offering basin atop the altar. Although Katja knew both of the beings, it took a few moments for her mind to comprehend their sudden presence. She stared open-mouthed at the pair of translucent beings before finally finding her voice. "Kumos?"

"Moarns ljocht en ehre, myn liebte un sibbe," he greeted her in Felis before switching to Shrŷde. "I never expected to see you as a human. I must say that you do make a pretty one." The werecat wraith grinned mischievously.

"How? How?" she stammered.

"I brought him here, Katja," Damya said as the firesprite flew up to hover beside Katja's eldest brother.

"Damya, what is happening?" Lauraisha asked.

"We have come to help you," the firesprite calmly replied.

"Can you heal Dayalan?" the true human asked.

"No; Verdagon is the healer, not me, and he will not arrive in time to tend to this," the firesprite said. "Felan has done most of the physical work required. However, there is more that must be done. I can help purge his blood with my fire, but we need you, Katja, to go to the Wraith Realm and petition for the return of Daya'lyn's soul. Kumos is here to guide you there."

Katja's gaze slid from the firesprite to the wraith of her dead eldest brother in confusion. "I don't understand."

Kumos chuckled, his voice somehow reminding her of the swaying of tree limbs in a breeze. "Sister, the Creator has

Daya'lyn's soul currently in His keeping…"

"You mean that Daya'lyn is dead, but his wraith has not been banished from the Dyvesé Realm?"

Damya regarded her in confusion. "Banished? Why would he be banished? He pledged his faith to the Creator long ago, so when I told you he was pure of the deadwalker Taint, I meant it!"

Kumos resumed. "There is a sickness in the Wraith Realm, Katja, and it will not be easily cured. The Creator has sent us here to guide your soul beyond the First Veil between realms so that you can, in turn, help return Daya'lyn's soul to his body—if he is willing."

"Why me?"

Katja's eldest brother raised a quizzical eyebrow. "Would you rather I try to find another wraithwalker to go in your stead?"

"Oh. No, certainly not. Very well, then. What do I do?"

The flickering blue firesprite put a tiny hand on the prone fireforger male's temple. "First of all, let me take over Daya'lyn's body's functions."

"Gladly." Katja heaved a sigh of relief as she pulled her paw from the fireforger's chest and felt the ebb of power from her own mind cease. She then realized how much of her strength she had used to keep the male alive and the depth of her exhaustion unnerved her.

She stared from Damya to Kumos to Daya'lyn dubiously. "With as much skinshifting magic as I have used to keep Daya'lyn's body alive and functioning, I don't know that I have the strength to successfully wraithwalk now. The strain of doing so might kill me."

Damya shook her head. "Not to worry. Kumos will add to your strength and keep you from straying too far in the Wraith Realm."

Kumos nodded. "It will all be well, Katja. You'll see. Now, come, lie back next to Daya'lyn and hold his ungloved hand with your paw."

Katja did as Kumos instructed. She pulled off the ragged remains of the male's left glove and slipped her right paw gingerly around his still raw and swollen fingers.

"Katja?"

The prone female turned to look at Lauraisha as fresh tears rolled down the human's pale cheeks. "Please come back. I can't bear to lose you both!"

Katja smiled. "Courage, lytzsibba."

The little human looked from Katja to Kumos. "Please watch over her!"

He gave her a gentle smile. "I always have, Lauraisha. Do not worry yourself."

Katja watched her wraith of a brother glide close and hover over her. It was odd that she could see straight through his body into the gloom of the dungeon beyond, and yet easily trace the delicate silvery outlines of his ethereal form's features with her eyes. Strangely, he was more handsome now than she had even remembered.

"Close your eyes, Katja, open your mind, and expect some discomfort," he said as he reached out to touch her paw. As soon as their paws touched, she gasped. The eerie contact gave her the sensation of being dunked in the eddies of a half-frozen river. Her eyes snapped open and she found herself floating paw-in-paw with her brother over her own body. What a strange creature she saw: a bruised and bedraggled human with dark circles of exhaustion under her closed eyes. Katja looked from her Erde body to her own ethereal form and noted for the first time in weeks that she was in her natural werecat form once again.

"Oh, that's uncanny," the werecat wraith murmured.

"Don't trouble yourself," Kumos replied. "Damya will keep your body properly functioning while your soul is separated from it."

"Am I a wraith, then?"

Kumos grimaced. "Strictly speaking, no. A being has to have his or her soul permanently separated from the body by death to be considered a true wraith."

"Then what am I?"

"We have no name for your current state of being, as you are only the second being in history to be able to do this."

"Who was the first?"

"Luther." Kumos's tone was matter-of-fact.

"Oh, that's comforting!"

Kumos shrugged. "It is simply fact and nothing else.

Luther was deceived and drawn across the First Veil between the Erde Realm and the Wraith Realm by the Abomination. The Darkkyn drake then corrupted the wraithwalker— Turning Luther into the world's first necromancer vampire— and then sent his tarnished soul back to his body so that he could Turn others."

Katja shivered despite no longer having the ability to feel cold. They were floating over the metal dais of the altar now.

"What is this place?"

"'Tis a portal room where our father would sometimes come to commune with the Creator and his Pyrekin."

"Father came here?"

Kumos nodded as he guided her floating form toward the altar. "A long time ago. You can ask him about it if we see him on our journey. I have no doubt Kevros would love to explain the way the portal works to a fellow wraithwalker. He's so proud that you gained both his and Mother's mage abilities."

"He wouldn't be so pleased if he knew the trouble I've caused with them so far," Katja replied dejectedly.

Kumos chuckled. "Oh, he knows. Mother was mortified when she found out about Lauraisha."

If Katja's ears could droop in this ethereal state, they would have. Kumos squeezed her shoulder. "Cheer up, lytzsibba, your own adopted little sister is perfectly healthy and she cares for you greatly."

"Can Lauraisha see us?"

Kumos shook his head. "We became imperceptible to her the moment our paws touched. The dreamdrifter cannot sense us with either mind or body."

"Sibbe, do you mind that I call her lytzsibba?"

Kumos shook his head. "You assume that familial ties matter to wraiths, which is, in point-of-fact, very true. You call Lauraisha your younger sister even though she is not blood-kin, but I will also refer to her as lytzsibba after her Erde life is finished, just as I do all females of every race who die after me. Now, I am called lytzsibba by all those who died before me— at least I am if they speak Feliconas. Among the wraiths, all are united as family because we are all the Creator's children, no matter our race. Now, come! Your time is short!"

As they hovered over the altar, a pillar of silver light

enveloped them. Once its radiance faded, Katja looked around and realized that stone walls no longer surrounded them. Instead they were standing among grass and trees so green that Katja's eyes wanted to water from the overpowering color. The sky overhead was not blocked by solid stone as she had remembered it, but was an endless expanse of ever-changing arrays of color in every hue imaginable—like an eternal sunrise without sight of the sun.

Katja felt overwhelming awe and joy. Her senses—now so much sharper than even her own keen wraithwalker perception—reveled in the unparalleled beauty of this place. She hugged Kumos and then ran for the sheer delight of feeling the bright stalks of dewed grass whipping past her furry flanks as she sprinted through their midst. She sniffed the rich air. It was alive with scents of salty sea, sand, grass, birds, fresh fruits, and seedling sap—just like that of her dream.

Kumos leisurely strolled behind her, grinning at her antics. After a moment more, he sauntered up to her and put a gentle paw on her shoulder. "The challenge of this place is that those who come here never wish to leave. I was loath to do so for a few moments even to bring you."

Katja stopped skipping, the smile vanishing from her face as realization struck. "Daya'lyn won't want to leave."

"Do you?"

Katja slowly shook her head.

"And Daya'lyn has travelled to the Creator's very gates, which is why we'd best be in search of him now, or your packmates will certainly lose both of you."

Katja forlornly nodded her consent. The two travelled on in silence for a time while Katja took in every color, shape, smell, and sound. The pair of white-robed werecat wraiths crossed streams holding water as clear as fine crystal cradled between banks of sparkling sand. The beauty of this realm was beyond any effective description. Every flower petal was seamlessly shaped and every sound perfectly pitched. The sweet air enticed Katja to inhale it even though she no longer needed to breathe to survive.

While they could easily walk or run, Kumos preferred to keep to the faster travel found in flight. It was a new perspective for Katja, who had only experienced flight either while in Daeryn's clutches or while strapped into a harness on Verdagon's back. Freely floating without being buffeted by wind or bounced by powerful wings was quite a pleasant sensation and Katja actually found herself enjoying the view from beneath her dangling paws.

"Stay close to me now," Kumos said, and then, drawing a glowing sword from the scabbard strapped to his back with one paw, he took hold of her right paw with his left. "We'll have to traverse near Edgewater before we can come to the Dyvesé Realm's Gateway and find Daya'lyn."

All at once, the scene of magnificent grassy meadows changed. Parched, bare dirt led to a foul-smelling river roughly a spruce-score across. Black liquid bubbled and boiled within its turbulent depths. Surface bubbles burst, causing droplets of ooze to spray the surrounding shore. If any plants sprouted near the river's bank, they would surely wither under the sizzling fluid.

Beyond the black river, the land smelled of ash, rot, and soot. Jagged brown peaks and the white corpses of trees stood in stark contrast to the vibrant green of the rolling plains. The multi-hued sky faded into a crimson nightmare.

Katja shivered. "What is that awful place?"

Kumos growled. "The Abomination was shunned to that part of the Wraith Realm. You can see how his decrepit presence has Tainted the land—making it barren of growth. His evil is ever-present, leaching out and destroying any good it can find."

Katja was incredulous. "This horrible sickness is what Luther was drawn to?"

Kumos shook his head even as he steered her away from Edgewater. "The Creator had barely cast the Abomination out of the Dyvesé Realm when Luther discovered the veil between realms and wraithwalked through it. The land was still green then, and the Abomination had barely gained control of his captive dragon's body. Luther, therefore, would have only sensed the monster's great power and coveted it for himself. Thus the first Turning occurred before Luther fully understood the evil that was done to him."

"But, if he hadn't been obsessed with power in the first

place, we wouldn't have the current deadwalker disaster!"

Kumos inclined his head. "True. Ignorant or not, Luther still chose evil and then persisted in choosing it rather than begging the Creator's forgiveness. This is why he will be condemned to eternal company with the Abomination in the horrific lands beyond the boundary that is Edgewater once his Asheken form is destroyed. Likewise those deadwalkers who allowed themselves to be Turned into the monsters that they are rather than die as they were being bitten by their would-be sires, are also sequestered in the Tainted Lands."

Katja frowned at Kumos. "Deadwalkers have a choice to be Turned?"

He smiled knowingly at her. "When Daeryn bit you, did you?"

"I begged the Creator to save me."

"Yes, and He did. That was your choice and I'm so proud of you for making it. All Sylvans can choose death instead of Turning. The fireforgers may even choose to destroy their enemy as they choose death. However, some beings like you and like Marga may choose something more."

Katja shivered again and tightened her grip on Kumos's paw. "What keeps the Abomination and his slaves on the other side of that river?"

Kumos squinted into the distance and then pointed. "That."

Katja looked in the direction of his extended claw. A dirt-encrusted being had crawled on all four of its blackened limbs close to the boundary, just out of reach of the burning spray. With a defiant screech, it launched itself on tattered wings toward them only to be hurled back by a sudden wall of blue-white flame erupting skyward from the black river's middle. The wretched fiend screamed and flailed as fire engulfed it. Katja heard a sick thud when the charred corpse fell to the bare dirt.

"There are Ring Spells even here?"

Kumos nodded. "The difference is that ethereal fire cannot destroy its victims. Instead, wraiths who chose evil in life are tortured eternally in death."

Katja watched as the pitiful ash-cloaked creature slowly dragged itself away from the burning bank toward the shelter

290 · ALYCIA CHRISTINE

of a nearby rock fissure, groaning low with each excruciating movement of its smoldering muscles. "That is horrible!"

Kumos nodded. "Yes, but it's necessary. The Taint persists even here and it is as eternal as the Abomination who sired it. If left unsequestered, the Taint will corrupt and destroy anything it contacts. We must keep it contained or life in any realm will be cursed."

Katja bit her lip and said nothing more for a while as they flew along the outskirts of Edgewater. Finally she spoke again. "Brother, a question?"

"Yes?"

"Why was the being that flew at us from beyond Edgewater so misshapen? Even the most hideous deadwalkers I've seen couldn't compare to that monster's deformities."

"That was once a griffin, if you can believe it."

Katja saw the twisted, blackened creature again in her memory and cringed. "That?"

Kumos nodded.

"Was that thing a gargoyle—a griffin Turned into a deadwalker?"

"Not as you know them, but, yes, that was what remained of a deadwalker gargoyle's soul. Be glad that you saw only the ruin of an Erdeken and not one of the Darkkyn." The werecat shuddered. "They are truly hideous to behold."

"But why?"

Kumos looked thoughtful. "You know the difference between a being and a beast, yes?"

She nodded. "A being has a soul while a beast does not."

"Correct. Many beings in our world so closely resemble beasts that it is often difficult to distinguish which is which. As a skinshifter, you yourself have seen the line between Erdeken and erdeling blur almost completely. Yet in all cases, even yours, beings remain separated from beasts specifically because of the existence of souls within beings and the complete lack of souls within beasts.

"Our souls are our connection to the Wraith Realm and, ultimately, to the Dyvesé Realm and our Creator. Our souls don't just allow us to think and feel; they allow us to understand our choices. A beast relies on its limited thinking, instincts, and emotions for guidance. Yet we beings rely on our souls to guide us. Our souls grant us access to the Creator. Mages find that connection more powerful because of their special abilities, but ordinary Sylvans have it too."

"What about our minds?" she asked.

"What is the mind except a physical extension of the ethereal soul?"

"So, what is your point, sibbe?"

"My point is that beings have a responsibility to act wisely and thoughtfully because we, unlike beasts, have the ability and therefore the choice to do so."

"And if we don't?"

The werecat wraith's expression was grave. "There are serious consequences—chief among them being soul wounds. Every time a being chooses to act against the perfect laws set in the Sylvan Codes, that being will tear his or her soul. Adultery and murder are two that cause deep soul wounds, but lying, stealing, coveting, and other forms of spiritual rebellion will all rip the soul. Of course, the Creator can heal soul wounds, but He will not do so unless the afflicted being truly wishes to be restored. Healing, after all, is a choice we must make just like any other."

"And so every time we choose against the natural order of things, we wound our own souls?"

He nodded. "And often the souls of others, as well. Some beings' souls become so scarred that they're barely recognizable as wraiths at all. They look and act more like twisted, gnarled beasts than anything resembling a being."

The sound of refined voices raised in song tickled Katja's ears as the pair soared closer to the Dyvesé Realm's Gateway. They flew up and up over the now-forested hills until they reached the bottom step of a staircase made of gold so pure that it looked almost as clear as the crystalline rivers winding below it. With all of her being, she longed to ascend those steps and join the voices raised in joy beyond its veil.

As they approached, Katja stared at the great winged lion which stood guard at the foot of the steps. The lion's fur was as white as fresh snow and lightning blazed in his eyes and maw. Six enormous wings sprouted from his back and shoulders, concealing his powerful body with cascading fans of feathers.

"A Hayoth lion," she whispered in awe.

Kumos smiled as he greeted the Pyrekin being with a bow. "Greetings, Kapriel."

"Greetings, Kumos. I see that you bring your sister to us at last. I am honored to finally meet you, Katja." The Pyrekin bowed to her.

She returned the bow and stammered her thanks.

"It is urgent that we find Daya'lyn. Do you know his whereabouts?" Kumos asked.

The Pyrekin nodded. "He is helping the fire factions secure the Second Breach as we speak."

Kumos bowed his thanks and tugged Katja behind him away from the base of the golden stairs. "Come quickly!"

"Are we not going to the Dyvesé Realm's Gateway?" she asked.

Kumos shook his head. "No, if you ascend past the veil and beyond that Gateway now, nothing I could say or do would make you wish to leave." Her brother's expression grew grim as he tightened his grip on his radiant sword and then led her forward beneath the stairs and over the tall trees once more. "If events continue as they are, I fear that you may never have the chance to see it."

"What do you mean?"

The werecat wraith shook his head, his eyes ever watchful of the distant shores of Edgewater as they flew parallel to the jagged river's edge. "Evil has gained new strength in this realm. The Tainted Lands have begun expanding in certain places and there have been breaches in Edgewater where the Abomination's influence has begun to spread past its shores."

Katja stared at him in sudden fear. "How?"

"The balance of power in your realm effects our own," Kumos said. "The breaches here began two summers ago by Sylvan time measurements. The last time that breaches of this magnitude occurred was during the Sylvans' Second War of Ages when the Asheken were close to victory."

"There is a connection?"

He nodded. "The recent breaches coincide with Daeryn's Turning and the Asheken deadwalker invasion of Sylvan lands. The Darkkyn and Drosskin have always gained power through the strength and number of the Asheken in the Erde

Realm. With more Asheken added to the ranks daily, their counterparts here gain supremacy and set their will against us. For now, we are winning the war, but if the situation in your realm worsens, so will our own."

They travelled on, flying over the forested foothills toward an open patch of sand dunes just beyond an outward bend in the course of Edgewater. The rainbow-hued sky gave way to crimson clouds and it was there under that turbulent darkness that Katja saw trailing fireballs light the gloom.

"Fireforgers?" she asked as Kumos began to descend toward the barren land, pulling her by the paw after him.

"Yes. They are using wraith fire to destroy the Taint seeping past the breach into the sands," Kumos pointed a claw as their paws touched the grit of the sand. "And there is the fireforger whom we seek."

Katja followed her brother's paw to focus on a male currently casting a light blue fireball across the sand. He was garbed in the same glistening white robe that she and Kumos wore, and yet his chest was draped with a pale yellow sash. His hair was snowy white instead of its usual black and his skin carried a pale lavender hue instead of being white. Yet all of these details paled in comparison to the changes to his hands, eyes, ears, and mouth.

"Dayalan!" Katja sprinted toward him and nearly toppled the male off of his feet when she sprang to hug him. He stumbled backward a few steps while trying to balance her presence against his own even as they embraced.

When they finally separated, Katja stared at him in astonishment. "Daya'lyn, what happened to you?"

His smile showed no sign of fang and his ears held no black spikes at the end of their graceful, pointed tips. Even the black claws of his fingers and toes were gone! "Do you like the changes?"

"Per myn ehre, you look like a summer-born elf!"

He laughed. "I feel like one, as well."

She hugged him again and found him quick to embrace her in return.

"So what happened that you should travel to the land of the wraiths?"

"She is here for you, Daya'lyn."

Katja looked past Daya'lyn to see a male unicorn walking toward them.

Daya'lyn's pale blue eyes swiveled from hers to the white Pyrekin's. "What do you mean, Azmar?"

Before he could answer, a startled shout came from one of the other fireforgers. "Drosskin!"

Daya'lyn snarled as he shoved Katja behind him and added extra fire to Kumos's sword blade. Above where the wraiths all stood, Katja saw a wave of twisted, black shapes rise from the ruined land just beyond Edgewater and dive through the air toward them. There was a place in the great burning river awash with Tainted sand. The river's blue-white flames rose up on either side of the sandy sludge, but could not penetrate the muck. The Drosskin monsters flew toward that breach in protection with singular purpose.

"Fire them all!" Azmar called. A crackling streak of white fire erupted from the spiraled horn on the horse-like being's forehead. The fire arced in midair and charred the first of the Drosskin to reach the breach squarely in the chest. With an anguished scream, the ruined being fell out of the marred sky and crashed into the boiling, black waves of the river.

In a wave of blinding light, dozens of fireforger mages and Pyrekin cast fireball after fireball at the Drosskin attackers—causing them to share their leader's fate. Without thinking, Katja added her wraithwalker's roar to the assault even as she watched hundreds of Drosskin drop from the sky. Her roar shook the ground where the defending wraiths stood and caused Edgewater's fires to spread closer to the breach. The gap shrank a little but not enough and one of the Drosskin broke through. He dove sideways toward Daya'lyn and Kumos.

"Nach, help us!" Daya'lyn cried as he launched a flaming stream toward the winged fiend. The Drosskin gargoyle folded his blackened wings, twisted in midair to avoid the fire, and barreled toward Kumos and Katja. The two werecats hit the sand as he rushed past. Kumos's flaming sword was the only thing that kept either of them from being sliced by the monster's black fore claws. Nach was there, then—a torrent of fire pouring from his open beak.

"Hold the line!" The great griffin fireforger cried as he

caught the charred monster by the wing and hurled him headlong into the black river. With one last screech, the gargoyle disappeared beyond the blue flames of Edgewater's Ring Spells. With his defeat, the other Drosskin retreated away from the river.

When the immediate threat passed, Daya'lyn breathed a shaky sigh of relief and turned back toward Katja.

She stared first at him and then at the river in disbelief. "Has that happened often?"

He nodded. "I have aided the other mages battle the Drosskin and Darkkyn ever since I arrived among the wraiths." He studied her then. "Katja, are you a wraith? You look different from any that I've yet seen."

Azmar spoke then. "She looks different because she still lives, Daya'lyn. She has wraithwalked here in search of you."

His awed gaze moved from Katja to the unicorn. "She can do that?" When the unicorn nodded, Daya'lyn frowned back at her in confusion. "Why would you risk such a dangerous undertaking, Katja?"

"The Creator still needs you—both of you—in the Erde Realm, Daya'lyn," Azmar said.

The color drained from the male's face. "What?"

"We cannot hope to win either the conflict here or the war in your realm if you do not return."

"I cannot go back!"

The unicorn's blue eyes grew soft. "I know that this is difficult for you—"

"Difficult! Azmar, going back means regaining the bloodlust and living under its enslavement. You know what it could cost me—"

"Not as much as it will cost us, Daya'lyn—no matter what you choose. You, Katja, and your companions are the only ones who can stop the Taint now. If you do not, Luther, Daeryn, and the Abomination will win. There are no others willing or powerful enough to complete the task. It will take all of you working together to accomplish this. If the two of you do not return to your allies, they will not be strong enough to stop the Taint in your realm from spreading fully to ours. The Dyvesé Realm alone can remain pure of the Taint, but it and its inhabitants would be cut off from all other beings in the Wraith Realm and in the Erde Realm."

Daya'lyn stared at Azmar. Twice the male opened his mouth to speak and twice he closed it before finally shutting his eyes and sighing. "I'm sorry."

"Daya'lyn, you know that all of us delight in having you with us. The Creator would never force you or Katja to go back because He believes that giving beings the freedom of choice is the purest form of love. As with everything, you must choose for yourselves what path you will take. However, know that the timing of your arrival among the dead is wrong, and I must warn you that the consequences will be dire if either of you fail to return to your rightful roles within the Erde Realm. If you stay, all connection to the Creator's good could be severed. If that happens, everything in the Wraith Realm and Erde Realm will be forever cast in evil's darkness."

Though he tried to hide it, Daya'lyn visibly trembled. "But if I fail once I return...I could not live with myself if I drank—"

"Peace, Daya'lyn. The Creator will always give you strength when you ask for it. He does not promise an easy road for either of you, only that He will be with you to guide your steps and lift you up when you fall. Always."

Azmar raised his head to sniff the wind. "Creator, keep us!" He prayed. "More Drosskin are coming and I sense Damya is weakening. You must return now. You cannot afford to leave her or the rest of your packmates alone any longer now that evil is set so firmly against all of us. Kumos will guide you both back to your Erdeken bodies. Go now before we are forced to battle again!"

"But I should stay and fight!"

"You can do even more good there than you can here. Go!"

Kumos bowed to the Pyrekin before he turned to pull Katja back through the parched sands. Daya'lyn took a step after them and turned back to face Azmar. "What will happen if I awake weakened and cannot consume Tyron's blood quickly enough after I reach consciousness?"

"All Erde beings fail from time to time, Daya'lyn. It is part of the Taint's curse." Azmar tapped his spiraled horn first on one of the fireforger's shoulders, then on the other.

"When such times occur, love can always lead you out of the darkness—if you are willing to let it guide you."

Daya'lyn swallowed and then bowed deeply.

"Come!" Kumos said as he launched himself into the air. Daya'lyn ripped his dragon-like wings through the back of his gleaming white robes and, holding Katja firmly around the middle, soared into the sky after Kumos.

Kumos flew fast through the multihued sky, heedless of his robes buffeting his tail and limbs. Daya'lyn's own wings pumped fast to catch up. Katja did her best to hover within his grasp so that the male's burden was lightened, but they were hard-pressed to keep pace with her brother.

"Kumos, slow yourself! We cannot match your speed!" she yelled.

"I cannot slow, Katja, for I fear Damya may not be able to protect your bodies much longer. I must bring aid to her soon for your and Daya'lyn's sakes. Do your best to follow me!"

"Dear Creator, lend us speed!" Katja cried and at that moment Daya'lyn lurched and shot forward at twice the pace he had flown before.

Katja roared in appreciation of the answered prayer even as they began to shorten the distance behind Kumos. They passed around the bend in Edgewater without incident and then flew over the green forests and grassy fields until Kumos, at last, guided them to an ancient-looking stone altar rising out of the undulating waves of grass. The altar itself was carved from what looked like flecked basalt and held an obsidian basin in its center.

Once Kumos's paws touched the ground, he took a single sprig from one of the many silphium plants growing around the altar's dais and laid it in the center basin. The moment the plant touched the bottom, it was consumed by the molten silver puddled therein. The silver then began to bubble up, filling the basin and then stretching itself upward into the shape of a small tree. Katja watched as the shape shimmered and then seemed to partially evaporate so that one moment she saw her soul's reflection while the next showed her the grassy knoll beyond the altar.

"Ah, Kumos, you come to me twice in one Sylvan day?" The silvery being's voice reminded Katja of drops of water echoing off of a cavern pool.

"Yes, Sylph Cyrena. I must return these two souls to their rightful bodies."

"Very good, then. Please hurry; Damya has been harassing me for the past hour regarding your return." The sylph sighed and then seemed to unwind her trunk into two separate stems so that her entire midsection formed a semi-transparent oval. "Through you go, then."

Kumos leaped toward the oval and vanished from their sight in a twinkling of light.

"Daya'lyn, take this with you," Cyrena said as one of her branches plucked a silphium plant out by its roots and placed it in his outstretched hand. "Hold onto it as you realign your soul with your body and it will help expel the toxins from your flesh."

After a moment's hesitation, Daya'lyn bowed his thanks and then jumped into the sylph's portal with Katja following him.

XVIII
A LITTLE PIECE OF HOME

With a rainbow-hued flash, the three wraiths were floating once again inside the dank dungeon under Summersted Castle. After the brilliance of the Wraith Realm, Katja felt blind. She saw nothing but darkness. When her sight finally adjusted to the gloom, she saw all of her packmates sitting or lying against the cold sandstone floor. Lauraisha sat cross-legged next to the werecat's own body. She was hunched over Katja's body with both of her hands covering the intertwined paw and talon of Katja and Daya'lyn. The human female was weeping and praying while Zahra and Vraelth gently gripped her quaking shoulders—their heads bowed in reverence. Felan lay sleeping just a body-length away—his wolfish face etched with deep exhaustion. Daya'lyn's body resembled something closer to a swollen corpse than anything living and Katja's fared little better.

Daya'lyn's wraith gasped beside Katja. "Is that what I look like? Fangs, I can't even recognize my own body!"

The Feliconian symbols twinkled and Lauraisha looked toward the altar. "Katja? Dayalan?"

"We're here, Lauraisha!" Daya'lyn answered even as he drifted close to her.

Her blood-shot eyes swiveled past his imploring gaze to the firesprite kneeling on Daya'lyn's body's forehead.

"Are they here, Damya?"

She sighed with obvious relief. "Yes, dear one, they are here."

"Why can't I see them?"

"Yes, why?" Daya'lyn asked with a hint of panic edging his voice.

"Only a wraithwalker can see souls," Damya answered.

"But, Damya, that makes no sense," Katja said. "Lauraisha could see Kumos before, why can't she see him or any of us now?"

The firesprite gave the werecat's soul a weary smile. "When your soul pulled away from your body, your mind broke its ties to Lauraisha's. She could see Kumos before because the mental bond between the two of you was so strong that she could sense many of the same things you did. Now she cannot."

Katja instinctively reached toward Lauraisha's mind and discovered the horrible truth in Damya's statement. The bond between her and the human was gone! She gulped down her sudden fear. "Is the separation permanent?"

The firesprite shook her head. "I do not know."

"Damya, how do we repair this catastrophe?" Daya'lyn asked.

The minute Pyrekin heaved a labored breath and then stood atop the fireforger's swollen forehead before answering. "I'm not quite sure what to expect once Katja's and Daya'lyn's souls rejoin their bodies. Vraelth, Zahra, keep ready just as I told you to do. Felan, I'm sorry to ask since you have already done so much and are so exhausted, but I need your skills as a skinshifter one last time. You must keep Daya'lyn's body functioning while I work to rejoin the ties that were severed."

Felan groaned as he pushed himself off the floor, but nonetheless complied with her request.

"I will need your talents as well, Lauraisha. Build me a small fire within which I can renew my energy once the deed is done."

Lauraisha gently squeezed Katja's and Daya'lyn's intertwined fingers before bowing to Damya and amassing the last of the packmates' available rags. She kindled a small flame and watched as it flared bright along the mound.

"Daya'lyn, Katja, come, float over your own bodies and do not touch anything unless I tell you to. Kumos, lend me your strength please."

Zahra and Vraelth stood ready while Kumos glided over to take hold of Damya's right hand. It was an odd sight since Damya was so small that she could barely wrap her fiery fingers around the tip of the wraith's thumb claw. Once Katja and Daya'lyn did as directed, Damya began to weave a complicated web of fire between each of the wraiths and their respective bodies with her free hand. When she was finished, she touched one end of each web to the forehead of each wraith and then touched the other end of the fiery web to their bodies' foreheads. Katja felt a strange tingling throughout her soul and saw Daya'lyn shiver beside her.

"Katja, Daya'lyn, I want both of you to move your souls so that they are positioned the exact same way as your bodies are right now."

Katja and Daya'lyn did so.

"Now, when I give the word, I want you to lower yourselves down and merge into your bodies." Katja heard the rustling of cloth and fur as Felan moved his paws away from the bodies. "All right, merge!"

Katja felt the constraining flesh of her body encompass her soul. The feeling was one of swift imprisonment. Panic overwhelmed her as her soul adjusted itself to the walls of her mind and the limitations of her body. Hormones now governed her thoughts, dull pain now governed her movement, and every breath was once again born of necessity. The werecat tried to move her heavy limbs and could not. She tried to voice words that simply died on her tongue. She was paralyzed.

"All right, Lauraisha, try to connect with their minds now and we shall see what happens."

Katja heard the words with her soul, but not her ears. A violet shaft of consciousness shot into her dull mind. "Katja, Dayalan, are you here?"

Katja sensed Lauraisha's and Daya'lyn's minds precariously connected to her own. "Yes, Lauraisha, we're here," she tried to answer. Then she lost what little sensation she had.

* * *

Smell was the first sense to finally overcome Katja's

unconsciousness. Her nose wrinkled at the scents of wet stone, moss, charred linen, and rotten meat.

"Katja?"

The werecat slowly opened her heavy eyelids to see Lauraisha sitting next to her prone body.

"Oh, thank the Creator!"

Katja tried to move her lips...to form words, but her tongue felt like lead.

"Would you like me to try to contact you through your mind?" Lauraisha asked.

"No, Lauraisha, it is better for her to try to use her body to communicate than her mind right now," Damya replied from her position among the rag fire's dying flames.

Katja felt her brows try to knit themselves together as she tried to form the word: "Ku...mos."

"He's gone, Katja," Damya replied. "He asked me to tell you that he loves you. He said he remembered that neither of you had the chance to say that to each other before he died."

"Love 'im...too." Katja felt hot tears stain her cheeks even as blackness once again overwhelmed her.

* * *

The second time she awoke, Katja found herself resting on a heap of blankets with her aching head propped against the gray stone wall by a roll of robes. She lay there for a long time, watching Daya'lyn's slow, steady breathing. The mage had been moved to a pallet of blankets and furs similar to the one on which she lay. She took her eyes off him and smiled slowly as Lauraisha sat down next to her with a large, shallow saucepan and a steaming cup of water.

Before Katja could say anything, she felt her gut spasm and she wrenched her body to one side to retch into Lauraisha's proffered pot. The human grimaced as she waited for Katja to finish emptying what little was left in her stomach into the container before offering her the cup. The skinshifter gratefully accepted it and used its contents to wash the bile from her mouth.

"Sorry, I wish I could make you some mint tea to help settle your stomach, but water and moss are all we have in the way of sustenance right now."

Katja propped herself up a bit and passed the cup back to the true human. "Thanks, lytzsibba. How did you know?" she said weakly.

"Damya warned me that you'd likely be queasy when you awoke. It's a side effect of your soul, mind, and body trying to reconnect with each other."

"So you...still can't read my thoughts then?"

Lauraisha shook her head. She stared down at the metal cup. Her hands emitted a soft glow as she warmed its contents. "Perhaps now that you're awake we can try to reestablish the bond—if you're feeling strong enough to try."

Katja nodded and then winced. The chamber immediately started spinning before her eyes and she sank back against her makeshift pillow with a groan.

"Not yet, then."

"No...sorry."

"How do you feel, apart from the stomach sickness?"

"Not so much sick as dizzy now, but I guess I am still healthier than him," Katja said, and gestured toward the fireforger male's still form. Some of his body's swelling had gone down, but he still reminded her of an overstuffed sausage. Lauraisha passed her the reheated cup without a word. Katja swirled the metal cup and brought it to her mouth. Such a description might have been humorous if it had not referred to one of her closest friends. She sipped the water and then, not noticing when it burned the roof of her mouth, she sipped it again. "Has he tried to communicate with you?"

Lauraisha shook her head. "At one point, his body jerked to the side and emptied the contents of his stomach just as you did. What came out was..." She grimaced. "Damya said that he'd managed to expel most of the toxins that his body had amassed when he did that. She thought that he might wake then, but he didn't."

"Is he at least breathing on his own?"

Lauraisha shook her head.

Seeing the pain in her packmate's eyes, the wraithwalker switched subjects. "Have we had any contact from those above us yet?"

"The deadwalkers threw down meat and extra blankets earlier." Lauraisha's face skewed in disgust. "The meat was decent, but the blankets smelled like grave clothes. Vraelth had to sterilize them using the last of the pixie dust he had smuggled in the hem of his cloak."

Katja frowned. "Why was the elf carrying pixie dust at all?"

Lauraisha peeked around the chamber and then whispered, "I don't know. It was certainly useful, but he's an odd being to be secreting such things in the first place." She leaned in closer and lowered her voice even further. "I think he's in love with Zahra."

"What makes you so certain?"

The human shook her head. "His mannerisms around her. He frets more about her wellbeing than anyone else's, including his own."

"Well, that would confirm the dream I had while we were guests at the Clan Shamgar edhuklo."

Lauraisha nodded.

Katja gazed over at Felan, who was lying just beyond Daya'lyn's still form. The hulking werewolf slept without so much as an ear-twitch. "I wonder if the other part of our dream proved accurate."

Lauraisha frowned. "Which part?"

Katja sighed. "The part of the dream showing that Felan is just as much in love with Zahra as Vraelth is."

"Katja, I'm sure that was nothing." Lauraisha did not sound particularly convincing.

Katja kept her gaze locked forlornly on the werewolf until tears stung the corners of her green eyes. She shut them against the pain of seeing him just lying there.

"Maybe…" she whispered and blinked.

She was still gazing at him when Zahra joined them. "He went to sleep shortly after you awakened the first time. After all of his recent exertion, he needs lots of rest or he could be just as sick as Daya'lyn," the dryad said. "I doubt even a dragon's roar would wake him now."

Katja realized, then, that the dryad's face was just as haggard from both fatigue and crying as Lauraisha's. She looked beyond her to where Damya lay on Daya'lyn's chest. The little blue firesprite was so dim that Katja barely noticed her in the dungeon's faint green light. The quasi-human blinked and looked around the room. The quick movements of her head worsened her dizziness, but she no longer cared. With Damya so dim and the rag fire long extinguished, the dungeon should be shrouded in complete darkness, but it wasn't.

Katja frowned at Zahra. "Why can we see? With that heavy grate covering the entrance and no fires kindled, it should be as black as the dwarven mines down here."

"That is my doing, Katja," Zahra said and smiled. "Do you remember that curious moss that I was cultivating in my cell when we were imprisoned on the Isle of Summons?"

Katja thought a moment and then gingerly nodded.

"That is what is lighting this place."

Katja stared around at the dungeon again. She smiled at the now-glowing moss weaving its way along the cracks in the walls above them. Their fires had overpowered its wan light before, but now it lit the chamber fairly well. "I once found this kind of plant growing inside a small cave in the forest outside my clan's village. It was what gave me light to see by on the night of the Feliconas Massacre when the moon rays were cloaked by the deadwalker revenant. Do you know the name of it?"

Zahra shook her head. "Actually, I have a confession to make: I discovered it because of you."

"Me? How?"

The dryad smiled sheepishly. "When you and Lauraisha first came to the Glen and you skinshifted back into a werecat, I had all of your belongings searched while you were unconscious. I found a piece of the luminous moss in your rucksack and it captured my curiosity, so I confiscated it. When we were incarcerated on the isle, I had nothing else to do, so I began experimenting with it. The end result is what you see before you."

Katja smiled wistfully. "A little piece of home."

Zahra nodded. "And a much needed supply of food for Vraelth and me. We have had little to eat during our imprisonment because the mongrels above us keep throwing down half-rotted meat as nourishment. Felan at least has stayed strong until now, but it has not been easy for Vraelth and me to wait for the plants to grow large enough to sate our hunger. Without nourishment, we haven't been strong enough to do much of anything—including try to escape."

"How long have you three been down here?" Katja asked.

Zahra grimaced as Vraelth sat down beside her. "We were ambushed on the road," she said.

The skinshifter female gave her a questioning look.

The elf answered her silent query. "Our journey thus far has been a difficult one. We were able to retrieve the Ursa Agate from Qenethala's Sacrificial Pine near Denth Crater, but Zahra and I inadvertently Merged with her sister's tree in the process and Verdagon had to destroy the pine to save us."

"So Qenethala is dead?"

"She and my Great Aunt Eliza both died in the dragon's flames."

Katja saw the tears pooling in Zahra's eyes and squeezed the dryad's shaking hand in sympathy.

"Deadwalkers found our temporary place of refuge in the aftermath of that fire," Vraelth continued. "We fought our way out onto open ground where Verdagon had enough room to launch himself into the sky and fly once Felan, Zahra, and I had mounted his back. However, Felan was injured and we had lost most of our supplies during the skirmish.

"With few options, we sought help from the Glen. The closer we flew toward Mount Sol'ece, however, the more resistance we met. There was a massive deadwalker troop buildup besieging the dryad stronghold and several flocks of gargoyles and sirens patrolling the skies just beyond the reach of the mountain's Ring Spells."

"Ring Spells? Since when does Mount Sol'ece use defensive Ring Spells?"

"Katja, they do now," said Zahra. "My mother has used the skills of every mage holed up at the Glen to defend all those besieged. To tell you the truth, the sudden racial cooperation between different Sylvan Order races and clans is remarkable."

The skinshifter female nodded, her mouth was a grim line. "It is a sign of the times: stand together to fight for survival or be hunted down one by one and destroyed."

"True," Vraelth replied, before explaining that once he, Zahra, and Verdagon had managed to maneuver through the enemy and delivered the injured Felan in the safety of the Glen, the three flew out to destroy as many of the deadwalkers as they could. While Verdagon flew and sprayed fire at the enemy on the ground and in the air, Zahra used vine-arrows to ensnare gargoyles and other winged deadwalkers in midflight.

"The netted monsters dropped like stones upon their own allies!" Vraelth said, grinning. "It was amazing!"

"As I was doing that," Zahra continued, "Vraelth charmchanted a small earthquake around the battlefield below us. It scared Mother almost as much as it did the enemy, but the result was nothing short of spectacular!"

Vraelth blushed a deeper purple. "I can't really take credit for it, since it was Verdagon who told me where to focus."

Zahra crossed her arms. "Oh, yes, you can. It was brilliant! He caused an up-thrust of land just above were a shallow lava seam ran. The superheated spray from that fissure destroyed an entire deadwalker battalion!"

"And half of the forest around them, too," the charmchanter replied glumly.

Zahra touched his shoulder in comfort. "It will grow back and, besides, all of Mount Sol'ece and her occupants were spared. That is the important thing."

"So how many deadwalkers were left at the end of the battle?" Lauraisha asked.

"Several hundred," Vraelth answered. "Our contributions were enough to make the enemy fall back. That gave our Sol'ece allies enough of an advantage that they were able to send out attacking ground troops for the first time in three months. Felan's clan proved especially adept at driving the deadwalkers toward my steaming, fiery trench."

Katja frowned. "What happened to the Isle of Summons troops that were supposed to bring relief to Zahlathra's besieged allies?"

Zahra shook her head. "Most of them were waylaid by the storms at Reithrgar Pass and Reith Valley. They should have arrived at the Glen by now, but they certainly weren't there when we were. In any event, we were able to give Mother and her allies extra aid before the main troops were due to arrive. We stayed at the Glen a few days while Felan healed—several harmhealers and his skinshifter father helped with that—and then we flew on toward Vihous."

Katja cocked her head to one side. "How did you end up trapped down here?"

Vraelth shook his head. "That was my fault—"

"It was not!" Zahra protested.

He silenced her with a rueful look. "We were camped along a road in Vihous one night. We thought we were safe enough since we were well within Vihous borders, so Verdagon flew off to hunt while I took first watch and the other two slept." He grimaced. "I don't know how, but I fell asleep while on watch. I awoke to discover that we three had been kidnapped by Tyglesean soldiers.

"Their deadwalker allies smuggled us into Kaylere and took us before King Kaylor. He is in their pocket, Lauraisha; thoroughly bought and paid for by Naraka. She took one look at Zahra and me and realized that we matched the description of the dryad and elf seen decimating deadwalker troops during the Battle of Mount Sol'ece. Naraka had me cuffed in shifters' manacles to neutralize my charmchanting abilities and then beat Zahra almost to death so that she couldn't remove them from me. Naraka tossed the three of us down here, not realizing that Felan was a skinshifter. He is the reason that Zahra survived and that I am unshackled."

The dryad rubbed the elf's shoulder as he suddenly shuddered.

"It sounds like your journey has been as much trouble as ours," Lauraisha replied.

The dreamdrifter told the others about their meeting with the naiads, Curqak's destruction, their packmates' allied attack of the Hag's Nest with the ogres, the deaths of Glashtin and Calder, the cyclone, and Daya'lyn's current convalescence. Even with her simplified version of what happened to Daya'lyn after he defeated Alqama, Zahra still commented, "If and when he awakens, Daya'lyn will be extremely weak and his bloodlust is something that we must guard against."

Katja sighed and nodded. "Unfortunately, but there is little we can do about it while we are imprisoned here... although perhaps Damya might be able to help solve that problem."

Damya's faint voice drifted to the skinshifter female's ears. "I am too weak, Katja. I am sorry."

"What about Verdagon?"

Lauraisha shook her head. "Father is the most paranoid male that you will ever meet. He has spent his entire reign bulwarking Summersted Castle against outside attacks because he fears even his own citizens. There is no way that any one being can successfully storm this castle—not even a dragon. Besides, Verdagon does not even know where we are."

So we are trapped on our own here, Katja thought. She swallowed hard as she watched the hybrid a moment and then changed the subject. "Lauraisha, when was the last time you slept?"

She sighed. "A day, maybe. I don't remember."

Katja's paw on the human's cheek was gentle. "Lauraisha, go lie down."

"But you're hurt—"

"I can manage myself now and you'll do us all only harm if you add yourself to the number of the infirm. Go sleep."

When Zahra and Vraelth vehemently agreed, the human finally stumbled toward her sleeping furs. As she curled up inside the covers' warmth, Katja crawled to where Damya lay. "How is he?"

"He's alive, but his body is still too traumatized to work properly, so most of my attention has been spent simply keeping him breathing. I'm worried, Katja. If his soul is properly merged with his body and all of the toxins have been purged from his system, then his mind should at least be able to take over the function of his lungs."

Katja frowned at her then at Daya'lyn. "Azmar said that he needed both of us fully healed in the Erde Realm if those in the Wraith Realm are to have any chance fending off the Darkkyn and Drosskin."

Damya nodded slowly, waves of weariness rolling across her dark blue face. "I know what my Creator requires of me and I am doing my best, yet I doubt my finest efforts alone will be enough to save Daya'lyn, let alone restore him to complete health. I need the help of the other Pyrekin and yet I can reach none. It's odd." She shook her head. "I had expected that

Azmar would wake at this point since his Keystone is now so close to my own and since he has already dealt with you and Daya'lyn in the Wraith Realm, but all I hear when I call to him is silence. It's as if something is blocking my communication."

Katja frowned. "Something or someone?"

Damya shook her head. "I don't know."

A whisper of a word caused Katja to perk her ears then. Beside her, Daya'lyn's body suddenly flinched. Katja opened her mind with her wraithwalking skills and quieted her thoughts so that she could listen with her soul as well as her mind.

Daya'lyn! she sent the thought out.

The male's mental voice answered her with an unnerving chuckle.

Dayalan?

No, my dear changeling.

XIX
DAERYN

Katja felt fear rise in the back of her mind and slither its way through the rest of her being.

She could almost see Daeryn's pale lips pull away from his long, yellow fangs as the vampire's laughter echoed throughout her awareness. *Nacht macht en bloed, Katja. Myn lytzahn en liebte.*

How do you know that language, fiend!

Your brother Kayten was kind enough to teach me a few phrases after I Turned him. However, most of what I know, I have learned from your own thoughts.

Katja snarled in hatred. *Bis dich, hunza!*

"Katja, what's wrong?" Zahra's spoken question blessedly broke through Katja's concentration.

"It's Daeryn! He's here!" she screeched.

"Lauraisha!" The dryad's frightened bellow brought the princess out of slumber and into an unsteady fighting stance faster than Katja thought possible. "Daeryn is attacking Katja's mind! Help her!"

Another moment found the human holding Katja's head in both of her hands and desperately trying to bond with the skinshifter's mind. Katja's awareness resisted the dreamdrifter's sudden presence, but Daeryn's seemed to welcome it. She felt Lauraisha's mind link not with her own, but with his. The uncanny connection unnerved her even more than Daeryn's sudden presence.

Princess, so good of you to join us.

What do you want, Daeryn? Katja could hear fear and determination in the dreamdrifter's echoing mental voice as she fought to establish the females' bond.

The male's cool voice was tinged with pleasure. *To offer my gratitude for your destruction of Curqak and his allies. He was, after all, the one who abducted my mother and set all of us on this wretched, twisted course of fate. Thank you for saving me the effort.*

Katja growled. *Fine. You've given your appreciation. Now leave us be.*

Cold laughter answered her. *And what good would that do, Katja? Dayalan is barely alive and the rest of you are scarcely better off. Trapped as you are by Naraka's allies, you could use some help, and I am the perfect being to offer you that.*

At that moment, Damya gave a shrill scream as her tiny body hurtled backward toward Lauraisha's amulet. The firesprite's blue flaming hair touched the Sapphire Keystone's surface and she disappeared in a swirl of silver smoke.

"Damya!" the three females cried as one.

Daeryn's silky voice cut through their shock. *You had better tend to Dayalan, Katja. He will not last long without your efforts.*

The skinshifter swore even as she laid both hands on Daya'lyn's chest and willed his lungs to continue their efforts. They revived with a wheeze and Katja blew out a breath of relief before railing against the male's malignant awareness on the edge of her mind. *You bent-fanged hunza!*

Daeryn's answering laughter raised chill bumps on her skin.

When I get my hands on you, Daeryn—

Why wait, Lauraisha? Why don't we have that little wrestling match now? Drakes know how long I've wanted your delicious body all to myself. I'm sure my brother will be overjoyed to know I am finally taking an interest in the things he cares for…of course, that is if he wakes up at all.

An unnatural fog rolled into the dungeon, blanketing the females' sight with waves of dull gray. They heard a creaking noise overhead near the entrance of the dungeon and then turned to glimpse a tall muscular figure standing atop the altar in front of them with his drake-like wings half-opened for balance. The mist then coiled around their faces and Daya'lyn's brother addressed them from beyond the shielding haze. "Good evening, my dears."

The females gasped in unison and began to frantically drag Daya'lyn's and Felan's prone forms behind the remains of a row of stalagmites for added protection. Vraelth stepped in front of his allies with his fists raised for a fight. As Katja watched, the charmchanter began to utter a guttural recitation and the ground beneath their feet began to shudder.

"Show yourself, coward!" the elf bellowed.

Silence greeted his challenge for a long moment and then Daeryn's deep voice echoed over the pit's tremors. "So you are the charmchanter mage. Interesting. You and I both know that you will win any underground bout between us, but there are others besides ourselves to consider, Vraelth. Just think what would happen to your two injured companions or to the females if you in your exhaustion accidentally caused half the castle to topple upon their heads during our skirmish. Katja is an orphan and Lauraisha's father would not care, but explaining Zahra's and Felan's deaths to their own mothers might prove a bit daunting."

For the first time since Katja had known him, she saw true fear flicker across the elf's face. Vraelth ceased his chanting and the stone around them grew eerily quiet.

"You can't give in to him!" Zahra shouted from behind the charmchanter.

"Zahra, he's right," Vraelth responded even as he tried to balance himself on unsteady feet. "There is no way to destroy him here without risking the rest of your lives in the process."

"Fine! It is up to me, then." The dryad looked mutinous. She gazed at the greenish light coming from the moss just above Daeryn's unnatural haze and raised her voice in song. At once the moss's glow brightened as Zahra tried to lengthen and twist its tendrils into a net.

Zahra suddenly screamed in anguish as Daeryn's sunsilver swords sliced through the wall's growing vegetation. The chamber's light dimmed. "Let's have none of that, sproutsinger."

Katja heard twin thumps as Zahra and Vraelth both fell backward on the stone floor. She screeched in anguish as she felt Daeryn's shade magic overwhelm their minds.

"Sorry, but I intend to enjoy our time together without

distractions," Daeryn said.

"Oh, no you will not!" Lauraisha shouted and launched an orange fireball toward the vampire's voice. The flames cut a path through the mists toward the Felis-inscribed altar and struck the wall on the far side of the chamber. The altar was empty.

"Your best is an orange-level flame?" Daeryn's derisive voice called from somewhere off to their left. The Tyglesean princess scowled and sprayed flame in the fiend's general direction. "Pathetic."

"Lauraisha?" Katja murmured.

The fireforger let lose another small fireball.

"Lauraisha!"

"What!"

"He's goading each of us into using the last of our energy in futile attacks and you're letting him do it. Cut off your anger for a moment and help me protect Daya'lyn and the others!"

Daeryn's laughter simultaneously echoed within the dungeon and within their minds. *"And how do you presume to protect the falichi when he can't even breathe on his own, changeling?"*

Katja frowned when Daya'lyn's heart fluttered in his chest. Was Daeryn somehow doing that? The skinshifter probed deep within his body. She sensed a change, but could not discern its nature. She studied the male's face in the glow of Zahra's last few undamaged plants. Her eyes could be playing pranks on her, but she swore Daya'lyn's face looked almost normal in the inky darkness. His heart fluttered more violently this time and Katja lost control over his lungs in her surprise. The lungs kept breathing of their own accord. Katja was slack-mawed.

"What's wrong, is he—?" Lauraisha asked.

"Is he dead?" Daeryn's phantom voice was right behind her left ear.

This time Katja was the one to strike out in rage. Freed of Daya'lyn's basic functions, she lashed out with her mind, using her wraithwalking sight to see the truth beyond the deceptive darkness that Daeryn was using to confuse her senses.

Lauraisha! There! Katja called through their faint bond and lent the human her discerning sight.

The werecat felt a blinding pain as Lauraisha's fireball struck Daeryn's shoulder. Daeryn's scream reverberated from Katja's own maw. She felt the fire scorching the flesh around the spearhead shard imbedded in his chest is if it were burning her own.

"Katja!" Lauraisha cried.

The werecat looked down and saw that her own flesh was charred. The smell of singed skin was nauseating. *What just happened?*

Daeryn's smile was full of fang as he caused the dark mist to dissipate around him.

"You can see your dilemma now, don't you, Lauraisha?" he whispered, his red eyes glinting. "If you try to harm me, you will burn her instead."

Lauraisha stared at Katja in terror as Daeryn chuckled.

"This bloodstone shard of yours is truly useful, Katja. By the way, I have seen the moon tonight and it is quite full and bright," he mocked her. "I feel the beast within you stirring; let us unshackle it together."

At his words, Katja felt her skinshifting magic unlock deep within her soul without her command. She gaped at him in horror as the change took hold and forced her down onto all four paws.

"Katja, what the—"

But the werecat could no longer speak. She felt Daeryn within her body and within her mind, governing her every movement. The change in form happened far faster than any she had previously experienced. She tried to fight back, to use her wraithwalking abilities to puncture the shade's hold over her mind, but she was too exhausted. Her body began to shift and to meld from her mostly-human form into the body of a tawny-haired lioness. She felt feral instinct overtake her logic even as her ears migrated back to the top of her head and her sleek form sunk low to the ground. A change which should have taken minutes happened in a matter of moments. The lioness felt strength return to her body even as her last tenuous mental link with Lauraisha was severed. Power flowed through her veins and she roared in pleasure.

"Good," Daeryn breathed. "Now come to me."

The lioness turned and considered the male. She sniffed in his scent; it was sweet with blood and musk. He was a predator like her: strong and efficient. He was dangerous, and that excited her. She sniffed him again and found his physique pleasing to her senses. He would be a good ally during her hunts, perhaps even a good mate.

"*Come to me...*" Daeryn whispered aloud and in her mind, his voice as enticing as a spring's cool waters on a hot summer's day.

"Katja, no!" Lauraisha screamed even as the skinshifter began to stalk toward the shade. A fireball landed just before the lioness's paws. The orange flames should have singed her fur, but it was Daeryn who screamed in pain instead of Katja. The fire rekindled some dim part of her awareness amid the overriding instincts. Katja's mind awoke to find her body moving within a nightmare. She fought to gain control of herself as her limbs carried her closer to the vampire. Daeryn reached for her, the black claws of one hand outstretched toward her neck while the other talon conjured a wall of mist between her and Lauraisha. The mist obscured Lauraisha completely now, but the lioness could still vaguely hear the human's screams.

"Lie down for me, Katja."

She did so.

"You will be my convert at last..." Daeryn purred. His crimson eyes held her spellbound as he knelt in front of her. As Katja felt Daeryn's claws close around her neck and saw the Víchí's yellow fangs lengthen in anticipation, she felt her mind finally gain control over her wayward body. "One of the most powerful wraithwalkers in history... Oh, how I've desired you ever since the night I first tasted you..."

"Creator, keep me!" she whispered as Daeryn leaned toward her.

The vampire stopped and stared at her—fear ruling his eyes.

In that moment, Katja struck. The lioness turned her head and bit down on the male's left hand, mangling it with all the strength held in her powerful jaws. Pain nearly blinded the skinshifter even as Daeryn jerked away from her. His hand was damaged, but so too was her left paw. They each stared at their own injuries a moment and then looked at each other. Katja's eyes shifted to the tip of the imbedded sunsilver-and-bloodstone shard protruding from Daeryn's burned chest near his right shoulder. It was the cause of their continued Blood Bond and so it also likely governed their ability to share pain and injury. She growled at it.

Daeryn watched her with his eyes and his mind. "Do you have the courage, little changeling?" he whispered aloud. Through their mental bond, he asked, *Do you have the strength?*

A wave of nausea suddenly swept through Katja and she felt the miraculous strength given by her recent skinshift ebb away—flowing through their bond into Daeryn's being. She stared in horror as the male straightened and drew one of his two sunsilver short swords with his good hand.

"I control your strength, changeling, and I will decide if and when you challenge me!" he hissed. *Who do you think gave you the strength to destroy Curqak in Edelsteen Uitgraven or helped you battle Alqama's golems inside the Hag's Nest? I have aided you through every skinshift and every battle since our bond first awakened, and yet you still spurn me!*

The male's sword flashed and Katja screamed. Deadwalkers could not withstand the burns from sunsilver weapons nor could they wield them without burning themselves. Yet Daeryn now used his own sunsilver blade to slice Katja across her burned shoulder. A ruby trail of blood seeped from the wound and onto the mist-covered, stone floor. In shock, Katja looked for the laceration along Daeryn's own skin and found none.

"How are you not—?" she whispered.

"Bleeding? How indeed, Katja?"

"Deadwalkers cannot use sunsilver—"

The male's sword flashed again, but this time the lioness avoided his strike. They circled each other in the mist. Daeryn struck and Katja sprang. Feinting and lunging, they each waltzed with death. Daeryn's blade bit Katja three more times before she managed a strike to his injured shoulder. They both screamed at the contact as the werecat plunged her fangs deep into Daeryn's pale chest. Her teeth ground against bone and metal and, although the pain was excruciating, Katja's maw managed to close around the spear shard. She yanked it out of the vampire's bloody flesh as they toppled over backward and then sprang out of his reach. The lioness landed on all four paws and then sank to the ground upon her own ravaged chest. The dislodged shard ricocheted somewhere into the mists. Daeryn dropped to his knees wheezing and clutched his own wound, trying to staunch the bleeding. His eyes glowed crimson as he watched her. With one hand clutching his sword and the other holding his chest wound closed, Daeryn began to crawl toward the lioness. Try as she might, Katja could not muster the strength to rise again. Her chest wound was bleeding profusely and the lacerations on her limbs and back caused her searing pain with every movement. She clenched her fangs and scooted backward away from him.

"I will have you, Katja. One way or another," Daeryn said as he crawled after her.

Katja's haunches touched cold stone. She was now trapped in the corner of the dungeon farthest from her packmates and from the altar. Daeryn edged toward her and, although some of the shade's mist had dissipated with his injury, she still could not see Lauraisha.

The lioness roared in anguish as Daeryn's claws closed around her head and pushed her against the sandstone wall. The Víchí's breath came in low rasps as he gripped her flank with his bloody hand. He pinned her down with far more strength then she expected of one so injured and bent his mouth to her wounded chest. Katja struggled futilely against his hold as she felt the icy touch of Daeryn's tongue flick against her torn muscle and lung tissue. He did not bother to bite her, but simply lapped the blood already flowing from the gash. She shuddered in horror as the strength of her life's flow began to rebuild the tissue of the vampire's chest. Her own skinshifting ability was healing him!

Daeryn leaned back and gazed into her eyes when he felt her shudder. "You fear me, Katja, because you mistrust the power I wield, but when you have that strength and dominance for yourself, you will understand the full worth of my gifts."

"Never," she whispered as the last of his injuries knit themselves together. The strength of his grip intensified and his eyes glowed deep crimson with thirst. He reached up to caress her maw with a thumb—leaving traces of moisture from his black claw across her lips. The taste of his touch made her want to retch.

"I want you, Katja, and I will Turn you regardless of what you wish, but it will be easier for you if you are willing to undergo the change," he whispered in her ear. "What strength I took from you, I give back to you now so that you may bond with me as an equal."

The mist swirled around them and then Katja felt magic flow back into her body through their bond. Once again the transformation of her body came unbidden. With a ruffling of her fur, the skinshifter's wounds closed and she took the form of a full werecat once more. He pinned her changing form to the wall and smiled as he watched her transform.

The werecat squirmed in the vice of his grip. While the skinshift had made her body once again whole and uninjured, she had lost a lot of blood, and that coupled with the two rapid transformations had drained what strength he had given her.

"I know you remember how it felt to bond with me, Katja, before Verdagon ruined our communion together," Daeryn said in a husky voice as he lowered his lips to her neck. He brushed the flat of his fangs against her fur and whispered. "I want you to feel that power again."

"*Lauraisha!*" she cried with both voice and mind before Daeryn's healed hand clamped tight over her maw.

"*Bond with me!*" Daeryn commanded with both voice and mind. Katja whimpered as the sharp tips of the vampire's fangs pushed against the scars from his first bite.

A blinding white ball of flame suddenly sliced through the mist and collided with Daeryn's body. Although Katja felt its heat, she did not share Daeryn's scream of pain as the fireball knocked him sideways. The shade's mist abruptly evaporated as he tumbled into the sandstone wall. Katja glimpsed two glowing white figures standing near the altar before she had to shut her eyes against the intense light. A vision of a tall, winged elf and a horned white horse glowed against the blank backs of her eyelids.

"It can't be!" Daeryn screamed.

Katja squinted at him as he scrambled back against the wall. His face was filled with absolute terror.

"You have plagued us for the last time," Daya'lyn said, his voice echoing strangely in Katja's mind.

A second flaming white ball lit in Daya'lyn's left hand even as he gripped the mane of the white unicorn Azmar with his right. The fireforger cast it at his brother with an almost negligent flick of his wrist.

Daeryn dove aside as the conflagration struck the stone and exploded in a shower of sparks and smoke. The half-burned vampire screamed as he scrambled back, and then flew out of the den's entrance just as a third fireball hit the wall a mere claw's length from his feet.

"We must hunt after him!" Daya'lyn told Azmar.

The Pyrekin shook his head, tossing his fiery mane. "No, you are still far too weak for that. Neither he nor his allies will soon return after your show of strength tonight, and I fear you have damaged your own recovery as it is. There is much for you yet to do, but for now, take your rest, Daya'lyn."

The fireforger nodded and then slumped against the Pyrekin's shoulder.

"Lauraisha, help him!" Azmar called.

The princess came running from the far corner of the chamber. Together she and Katja did their best to catch the big male as he slid down the unicorn's flank. Daya'lyn was unconscious again even before his body was prone.

Katja sat down with a thump beside him.

Lauraisha knelt by her side, cradling Daya'lyn's head in her hands. "Dayalan!"

"All will be well, Lauraisha," Azmar said.

"Is he...?"

"Daya'lyn will need much care, but he will recover." the unicorn replied. "The others, too, will recover. Just give them time."

"Thank the Creator." Lauraisha closed her eyes as tears drenched her flushed cheeks and then turned to the werecat. "Are you well? Did Daeryn harm you?"

The werecat shook her head and then hid her face in her shaking paws. "He drank from my blood, but failed to bite me... He—he healed himself with my own magic and then healed me... He shifted me back into a werecat so that I could bond with him as an equal..." she shuddered. "What happened to you, Lauraisha? Where were you?"

"I tried to rekindle Damya, but she was too weak. She awakened Azmar instead."

Katja looked up at the Pyrekin and deeply bowed. "Thank you for saving me."

The unicorn returned her bow. "Not at all, Katja, I am always willing to help."

"Is Damya hurt?" Lauraisha suddenly asked.

Azmar bobbed his head. "She will recover, but this is greatly troubling. Never before has a deadwalker other than Luther been given such direct aid by the Darkkyn until now. The Abomination and his commanders must feel that the balance of power is changing in favor of the young vampire rather than the Víchí High Elder."

Katja frowned. "Luther is losing his Wraith Realm allies?"

"That is my guess, but I cannot be certain without additional investigation. I must return to the Wraith Realm to help Damya, but I will leave the six of you with a guardian sphere." Azmar aimed his spiraled horn at the oubliette's entrance and shot a glowing ball of white fire out of the opening. The fireball hovered just over the closed grate above, giving off light and heat. "Its light will help heal you and its fire will protect you from your foes until your own strength can return. Be well."

"Thank you," the females said in unison and both bowed to the unicorn as he shifted into a glowing white conflagration and flowed through the Opal Keystone and into the realm beyond.

Katja leaned back against the altar, suddenly beyond weary. Tears began to trace through her golden fur as all of the memories of Daeryn's attempts to claim and Turn her as his own suddenly overwhelmed her. She felt Lauraisha's hand on her shoulder and leaned against the human for support. Lauraisha slid both pale arms around the female's quaking shoulders.

"I am so sorry, Katja," she whispered as she pulled the tearful werecat close. "I'm so sorry."

The sudden comfort of Lauraisha's gentle embrace was so different from Daeryn's lustful grip. Suddenly the werecat felt the protective arms of her older brother Kayten the day he held her after the Feliconas Clan Massacre. Sweet Kayten, who had been Turned by the same monster that had nearly succeeded in Turning her. Her brother had been destroyed in mercy by the broken male who now lay in her dearest friend's lap. Lauraisha held her the same way as Kayten. Did she know? Did she know from Katja's memories that this was the way that he had once held her? Their bond was fragmented now, yet Katja could feel her dead sibbe's firm reassurance resonating in her adopted lytzsibba's touch.

The tears came faster. For the second time in ten full moons, Katja finally surrendered to the walled-up agony she had carried so deep within her soul for so long. Katja bent her head back and released all of her sorrow and anger into a roar that shook the stone around them.

Lauraisha took her hands from her ears and pulled the sobbing werecat into an embrace. "I'm so sorry. Never would I wish this for you, Katja…that you would understand such an evil violation."

Katja looked up and wiped the fresh tears from the princess's cheeks. "Nor I for you, Lauraisha," Katja said as she hugged Lauraisha tight.

* * *

"Still no change?" Katja asked as Lauraisha tried to mentally contact Daya'lyn.

"Nothing." The human sighed. The two of them had awoken some hours after their encounter with Daeryn to find Azmar's fiery orb still lighting the dungeon from its position above the grate and the others still trapped in the hazy sleep of Daeryn's illusions. Katja's wraithwalking skills had broken through most of that, but all of the packmates were still very groggy. The dreamdrifter now tried to revive Daya'lyn, but that was proving impossible. "I wish we knew more. All I can do is change Daya'lyn's bandages and feel useless."

"How do his wounds look?"

"All of the swelling is gone, even around his wounds. Many of those are scabs now."

"He's healing that quickly?"

Lauraisha nodded.

"Azmar said nothing about his reawakening?" Katja

asked.

The Tyglesean shook her head. "No. When you screamed my name the last time, the unicorn just flowed out of the Opal amulet, shot white fire into Daya'lyn's mouth, and helped the mage stand. Together they drove Daeryn off before Daya'lyn sank to the ground unconscious again. So now we must once again wait with no idea how long it will be before he awakens again or what to do for him in the meantime."

Katja nodded, her growl matching Lauraisha's sigh in frustration and loneliness.

"You miss your family and clan deeply today, don't you?" Lauraisha asked, laying a hand on the werecat's shoulder.

The werecat nodded, grateful that Lauraisha was so astute even without their mental link. "Why does it hurt so much when those we love die?"

"I don't know, Katja. I've never known. You came from a family that loved you fiercely. I come from a family divided in their love and in their hatred of me. I can't even be fortunate enough to have an uncomplicated romantic relationship, because the male I love treats me like a leper half of the time." She grimaced.

Katja gently squeezed the human's hand resting on her shoulder. "You already know he loves you. He proved as much while you were incarcerated together and then again during my skinshifting madness."

Lauraisha shook her head. "He refused to bite me at the Mage Citadel because he didn't want to Turn and become a deadwalker monster like his brother. That proves nothing."

Katja crossed her arms over her chest and stared unblinking at the other female. "You've shared his dreams and memories. Will you also claim such doubt when he tried to protect you from me while I was a lioness?"

"His natural instinct is to protect others just like Felan."

"And what of the Hag's Nest?"

"The Hag's Nest?" Lauraisha bowed her head in thought. "He failed to bite me then because I told him no. He is the only male I've ever known besides my brothers who would put my wishes before his own, and yet..."

"And yet?"

"And yet what will happen when he wakes again, Katja?

He had not fully recovered from the lightning strike or his sea sickness before he tried to use fire against his own water chains and Naraka stabbed him for it. He nearly died—"

"He did die."

Lauraisha nodded as tears coursed down her cheeks. "It's been days since his last draft of nourishment. He is so much weaker now than he was even after the fight with Alqama and there is no chance for him to feed from Tyron or any other beast like there was then."

Katja watched her a moment. "And so you fear that he can't fight the thirst this time."

"Worse than that," Lauraisha whispered. "I'm afraid that I will let him drink from me."

Katja stared at her alarm. "Why? Why would you do such a thing?"

"To save his life."

"But you'll destroy him instead! Lauraisha, he does not want to become like Daeryn!" Katja shook her head and growled. "If the Inquisitor Turns, then all hope for our freedom from the deadwalkers is lost."

"I know, but what else can I do with Tyron gone and no adequate bestial blood source available? I love him, Katja. I can't watch him die... Not again."

XX
AWAKENING

Katja sat in silence as she and Lauraisha watched Felan pace the dungeon floor, snarling and kicking over anything in his path. Never had she seen the gentle male this angry and it scared her. No amount of reasoning given by any of the other packmates seemed to appease the werewolf's rage once he discovered that he had slept through Daeryn's attack and had left his packmates so vulnerable to the vampire.

"Felan, it wasn't your fault nor was it—" Lauraisha began.

One withering glance from the hulking male silenced her midsentence while he continued his pacing. Vraelth watched the werewolf a moment more and then looked at the human as they all sat huddled near the stone altar. "It doesn't matter what you say, Lauraisha," he said quietly. "You'll never convince any of us that we're blameless in this situation."

"Daeryn has always been a powerful shadowshaper, Vraelth. Now he is an even more powerful shade as well as being a full vampire. Even Katja could barely resist his influence and, according to Joce'lynn, she is one of the most talented wraithwalkers to be born this century!"

Katja's furry ears twitched at the compliment.

Vraelth sighed. "While I'll admit that the logic of your argument is sound, it still does little good to try to ease his mind or mine."

"At least Daya'lyn and Azmar managed to drive him away even while the rest of us were incapacitated. That, at least, assured your safety, and that is all that matters," Zahra said.

Katja stared at her. Ever since the packmates had reunited in the dungeon, the dryad's conduct had softened toward the werecat. Now that both females had lost siblings in the war, they seemed far more kindred in spirit than they had ever been.

The packmates all flinched as a crack of stone and bone resounded in the gloom of their underground prison. Felan howled in pain as he cradled his bloody paw and glowered at the thin, spidery fissure he had made in the stone when he had punched it.

Katja stood with a growl of frustration and walked past the others to where Felan stood cursing at the wall. "Let me see your paw."

Felan snarled. "Leave me be, Katja!"

She stood her ground. "You are still not strong enough to be skinshifting yourself."

"What makes you think that I don't welcome the wound?" he barked at her.

Katja did not drop her gaze nor did she retreat. Instead her ears went flat. "Felan, cease your stubbornness and let me help!"

He glowered at her a moment more and then finally relented. Katja gently took his paw in both of hers. She felt the skinshifting ability unlock inside her soul at her command and spread through the center of her body to her outstretched paws. She pushed her awareness into Felan's flesh, feeling the bruised tissue surrounding his now fractured bones. A soft orange glow emanated from beneath her paws as she knitted the werewolf's bones back together and then mended his muscles and skin. The simple act exhausted her, but it was worth the trouble to see Felan's face relax with relief from his pain.

Vraelth walked over just as Katja was wiping the blood away from Felan's newly whole knuckles. "Nice work, Felan," he said as he stared at the cracks in the wall, "About twenty thousand more of your punches ought to be enough to break a tunnel out of here."

"Quiet, you," Felan snapped, but Katja saw the corners of his maw working to suppress a smile.

Vraelth smirked back at him and then the elf's face grew

serious again. "Now what, Pack Leader?"

Felan shook his head. "I have no idea. None of us will last much longer down here without a decent supply of food. With Azmar's fireball blocking the entrance, we'll not be able to get any more from the deadwalkers."

Vraelth nodded and squinted at the entrance above them. "If they have any brains left in their heads at all, they won't go anywhere near that thing. And clearly they do, because it looks like no one has bothered to relock the grate since Daeryn's grand exit." He frowned. "They'll likely still have reinforcements bulwarking the exit door in case we figure out a way to climb the walls in here and get through that grate."

"All the more reason for us to find another way out of this place," Katja said.

Felan groaned, suddenly looking very weary. "There is no other way out, Katja!"

"I am not so certain," Vraelth said as he bent to examine the damaged wall once more. He began tracing his long, dark purple fingers over the cracks.

The werecat frowned as she watched him probe a particular spot. "What are you hunting?"

The elf frowned and cocked his head to one side. "Zahra, would you come over here please?"

When she and Lauraisha joined the group, Vraelth had the dryad poke her green fingers in the same places that he had touched moments before. "Do you feel that?" he asked her.

She nodded and frowned. "What is it?"

He shook his head, sending lavender locks flying. "I'm not certain, but it definitely feels like an anomaly of some kind."

"Its texture is almost like talc." She then bent to stare at the flaky powder coating the fissure where Felan's paw had impacted the stone. "But it's black, not white."

Vraelth nodded.

"Let me see," Lauraisha said.

Zahra and Vraelth moved aside for her. The princess rubbed a pair of fingers across the surface and sniffed them. Frowning, she held them up to Katja. The werecat curiously sniffed the black smudges and frowned at the familiarity of the scent. A memory of the dwarven room where Verdagon's egg had been hidden under Crown Canyon sprang to her mind. "It can't be!"

"It is."

"Is what?" Felan asked them.

"Black powder."

"Why would black powder be here?" Zahra asked. "This was never part of the dwarves' ancient territory."

Lauraisha shook her head frowning. "Vraelth, can you sense how far back the vein of powder runs?"

The elf shut his eyes and began chanting in a low murmur as he brushed the stone wall's surface with the tips of his slender fingers. When he finally looked back at her, his eyes widened in surprise. "As exhausted as I am, it's hard to know precise measurements, but I can tell you that there is a significant cache of powder less than a body-length behind the wall's surface. Oh, there is something else odd as well."

"What?"

"Firesalt."

"Firesalt?"

Vraelth nodded. "There is a strip of the substance running just below the powder cache. And there are firesalt flakes interspersed with the black powder. Neither deposit is natural."

"Someone put it there for a purpose? How? Why?" Zahra asked.

"There's a tunnel," Katja said. She peered at the wall, the altar, and back again. "There has to be."

"Katja?" Zahra looked at her quizzically.

"When I was in the Wraith Realm, Kumos told me that our father had used the altar in this very room to communicate across the Veils with inhabitants in the other realms. I'm unsure of his reason for doing so, but the fact that he did tells me that there was once another easier entrance into this room. From the rock formations, we know that this room was likely part of a cave system, so the entrance must have been walled up when the room was turned into a dungeon."

"But why keep the altar?" Zahra asked.

Lauraisha spoke. "The Tygleseans probably didn't know its true purpose, so they left it intact for use as a prayer altar for the prisoners incarcerated down here."

"Either that or they couldn't tear the altar down because of the magic bound within the stone," Vraelth added.

Lauraisha considered that, and then nodded. "More likely."

"So how does this information help us?" Zahra asked.

"Firesalt is the only substance I know which can burn without air around it," Vraelth replied. "We may have just found our escape route if we can find the end of that strip and set it ablaze. If done right, it should set off a chain reaction that will cause an explosion to clear the tunnel."

"What kind of a flame will you need to do that?" Felan asked.

Vraelth gazed at Lauraisha and then at Daya'lyn. "A very hot one."

Lauraisha frowned. "I think I might be able to muster enough of a spark for what you need. Should we try to blow open the tunnel then?"

"Not without Daya'lyn awake," Felan said. "We have no idea what is on the other side of that powder reserve and none of us can hope to battle our way out of this place if we have to drag Daya'lyn's unconscious body through the fight."

"And there's another problem," the charmchanter said. "As weak as I am, I doubt I could protect us from the blast of rock that will result from the explosion. Our attempt at freedom might bury us in an early grave instead." He grimaced. "And waking Daya'lyn may prove a far worse problem than even that."

"How so?"

The elf cleared his throat and suddenly looked like he would rather be discussing anything else. "First, let me just say that Daya'lyn has proven himself very honorable in the past, but..."

"You're worried that when he wakes that he will go feral and attack us in his bloodlust," Felan supplied. "Believe me, Vraelth, we all fear that."

Vraelth shook his head. "It's not just that. My grim suspicion is that the deadwalkers want Daya'lyn to lose control and Turn, and that they have planned for it to happen using us as the bait."

When the werewolf gestured for him to continue, Vraelth scratched his matted hair and said, "Follow my logic here. You, Zahra, and I are all known associates of Inquisitor Daya'lyn Calebson. We were all captured on our way to meet him and the rest of the members of the Inquisition so that we might help them infiltrate Tyglesea and discover if King Kaylor has indeed formed an alliance with the Asheken deadwalkers." The elf began marking off his points using his fingers. "When we were caught, we were not killed as enemy combatants. Instead, we were incarcerated in a dungeon at Castle Summersted in Tyglesea—the very place where the Inquisitor had to travel to meet with the king. While we were imprisoned, we were kept together, we were never tortured for information, and we were fairly well fed and treated."

Felan quelled Zahra's sudden protests with a scowl before turning back to the charmchanter. "Go on."

Vraelth nodded. "We waited weeks without word from above and then, all of a sudden, Naraka's underlings toss Katja, Lauraisha, and Daya'lyn into our dungeon. Like us, the females are relatively unharmed, but Daya'lyn has been brutally stabbed."

He glanced at Felan. "Did it trouble you at all that Naraka—a vampire with a millennium's worth of experience killing other beings—never managed to perforate Daya'lyn's major organs despite stabbing him in the chest and stomach multiple times?"

The werewolf nodded. "One minor kidney lesion and a tiny lung puncture was far too small a price to pay for the violence enacted against him."

"Exactly."

Felan wiped a paw down his sweaty snout. "When I felt the damage, I wondered then... But by that point, it did not matter. We were too involved our work to save him for me to concern myself with the motives of our enemies."

There was no warmth or humor in Vraelth's answered smile as he regarded Daya'lyn's sleeping form. "I must admit, it is an inspired plan. Make a show of violence against your enemy in front of his allies to manipulate their emotions. Hurt him just enough so that there is significant blood loss, but not enough to kill him outright. Then incarcerate him with two skinshifters who can and will help heal him for you. They and their allies can then feed his Thirst when he awakens weak and wild."

"Wait, this makes no sense to me," Lauraisha said. "If Naraka wanted to hurt him but not kill him, why would she use a mahogany stake? His reaction to such a dangerous substance could hardly be controlled."

Katja thumped her tail in sudden realization. "She must have no knowledge that the wood poses such a danger to the brothers! How could she know, if Daeryn never told her?"

Lauraisha stared at her. "You doubt he told her?"

Katja grimaced. "Daeryn would never willingly divulge a weakness to anyone, especially not to Luther or his mate. He hates Luther even more than Caleb because of what Luther did to his and Daya'lyn's mother."

"But why would Naraka want to Turn Daya'lyn?" Zahra asked. "As powerful as he is, Daya'lyn would always be a danger to Luther whether or not he was Turned because of Luther's treatment of Marga."

"We are assuming at this point that Naraka was acting as Luther's ally when she arranged all of this, but no one truly knows where her loyalties lie." Vraelth reminded her.

"As a vampire and his mate, isn't she instinctively beholden in mind and soul to Luther?" Lauraisha asked.

"Naraka is not a soul servant like Curqak was," Katja said. "She is a vampire, equal to Luther in mind and soul if not power. If she wished, she most certainly could start a coop against him."

"Yes, but regardless of whether Turning Daya'lyn is her plan or someone else's, I think there is little doubt that all of this was done to us with strict intent."

"I agree, Vraelth," the werewolf growled.

"So what do we do?" Lauraisha asked.

"We trust the Creator and we trust Daya'lyn," Felan said.

"After all that we've discussed, you still want to wake him?" Vraelth asked.

He nodded. "I do. The Creator wouldn't have sent Katja through all of the trouble of wraithwalking and returning Daya'lyn's soul to his body, if He didn't trust the male to make the right decision."

"I agree with Felan," Zahra said.

Vraelth groaned and bowed his head in thought. "And yet the deadwalkers are confident that he will Turn."

Katja frowned. "When I remember what Azmar said in the Wraith Realm, it makes me believe the Creator sent Daya'lyn back to make his final choice. More to the point though, the last battle with his brother stole most of the remaining energy he had. Even with all of our healing efforts, Daya'lyn's body has expended every remaining resource fighting to keep him. Without further nourishment, he'll die…again. Even with the added energy from Azmar's guardian sphere, I lack the strength to lead his soul back a second time."

"Daya'lyn has done all he can to protect and keep us alive," Zahra said. "Now, it is our turn to help him."

"So we must wake him and wake him soon," Vraelth said.

Felan sighed. "While I have done all I can to heal him, it would be best if you and Lauraisha awoke him together, Katja, so that you could use your skinshifting abilities to heal whatever injury still needs it."

"I have no idea if that is even possible, Felan. Ever since I walked in the Wraith Realm, our minds' bond has been tenuous at best."

Felan rubbed his furry, white muzzle and stared at the floor. "Lauraisha, you know him best, so I will leave the decision to you. Do you believe that you can rouse him without causing harm to him or to us?"

Lauraisha shut her eyes and took a deep breath before she answered him. "Felan, I honestly don't know what to expect. Dayalan could awake sane, but most likely he will be feral because of his lack of blood nourishment. I hate the thought of rousing him without an alternate source of bestial blood available, but the longer we wait, the more dangerous our situation becomes."

"I'm not certain how much good it will do, but I think I have an alternate plan," Vraelth said as he stared at the grate-covered entrance high above them. He studied Katja in speculation. "How high can you jump right now?"

She frowned as she peered at the dungeon ceiling. "I can usually scale a single spruce-length tall tree in six or seven leaps, but I need solid branches to jump off in order to do that.

If you're suggesting that I try to jump for the entrance above us that will prove impossible since the walls are too smooth for proper paw holds. I would likely make it three-fourths of the way up and then fall straight down again."

"And what if Felan tossed you?" the elf asked.

Katja blinked and cocked her head as she considered the werewolf. "Do you think that you're strong enough at the moment to launch me all the way to the top?"

Felan scratched his muzzle in thought. "I certainly feel far stronger than I was. If I started off in a crouch while you stood on my shoulders, I think it's possible. But what good would it do? You would only be protected from deadwalkers by Azmar's fiery sphere while you stayed in the same room with it. Trying to escape that way is beyond dangerous."

"I know, but it's likely a better solution than exploding part of the dungeon while we are still inside of it. At the very least, we might be able to trap Daya'lyn down in the dungeon if he proves feral while the rest of us stay relatively safe in the guardroom." Katja glanced again at the orb and then looked away as its white light blinded her. A memory of another Pyrekin's orb was tugging incessantly at her mind now—the one of Lauraisha's miraculous healing from a basal's venomous bite in the midst of King Canuche's chamber. If such an orb could heal Lauraisha and help awaken her fireforging abilities, why could it not heal and sustain a more advanced fireforger mage like Daya'lyn? She turned to Lauraisha. "Do you agree or disagree with my thoughts?"

"What thoughts?"

Katja growled in frustration at their broken bond and then explained her memory of Lauraisha's miraculous healing to the group. "If I can make it out of the dungeon and find some rope to lower down to all of you, we could conceivably hoist Daya'lyn up by it. We could then prop him up so that he touches the orb," she concluded.

Felan frowned at her. "And you really think this is a good idea?"

She shrugged. "It's better than trying to wake him down here with absolutely no means of nourishment."

"I agree," Lauraisha said. "The orb in Canuche's cavern is the only reason I survived the basal, so it stands to reason that this orb will ensure Daya'lyn's survival as well."

"But are you certain that the orb will heal and strengthen him completely?" Zahra asked.

"No," said the human, "but what it's a better plan than any others we have."

"It is still a huge risk for you to take, Katja," Felan said, turning back to her. "I could probably catch you if you fall, but none of us can help you once you make it past the grate into the guard room."

"It is a risk I'm willing to take, Felan. If I fail, we can still try to blow open the black powder, but any explosion is sure to cause enough noise to draw half the castle guard down here, so we must leave that course of action as the very last resort."

Felan looked at Lauraisha, Vraelth, and Zahra in turn as they each slowly nodded. The werewolf's worried face suddenly looked as if it had aged ten winters as he finally nodded his consent. "Please be careful."

"Always," Katja said. "Now then, let's try this."

The werewolf walked directly below the dungeon pit's entrance and bent down so that Katja could scramble onto his back. "Agh! Mind your claws!"

"Jierira, sorry!"

"Ready?" Felan said as Katja perched precariously on his massive shoulders.

"Just remember to launch me straight," she growled as he gripped her shins with his large paws.

She stiffened her prehensile tail for added balance as he straightened his posture. "Don't worry, I will."

"On your count of three?" he said.

Katja took a deep breath and crouched on his shoulders. "One… Two… Three…"

The werecat felt the surge of Felan's muscles as he straightened his body to a full stand and then leapt toward the ceiling in one fluid motion. Werewolves were not as naturally agile as werecats, but Felan's back paws still managed to clear his own body-length by the time Felan's paws pushed Katja off of his shoulders. She vaulted into the air above him and shot toward the closed grate above her. She had pushed off of Felan at a slight angle, but their shared momentum was still enough to get her within touching distance of the entrance. She scrambled madly as she came close to the grate. She bruised her right paw as she reached for the rounded side, but she managed to grab hold with her prehensile tail and her left paw before gravity managed to reassert its dominance over her body. She heard her packmates muffled cheers as she desperately clung to the rusting iron. The flat metal encircling the entrance bit into her palms as she maneuvered for a better grip. To make matters worse, the infernal blazing ball floating a body-length above her head had warmed the iron enough that she would not be able to hold on for long without burning herself.

Grimacing, the werecat scanned the guard room. There was no one in sight and the opposite door looked to be barred shut against her. On the floor close to where she was hanging was a single pile of ash—a sign of Azmar's orb's fiery destruction of the nearest deadwalker guard. Katja wrinkled her nose at the acrid smell and then gasped as she saw a ring of keys lying on the ground between the ash pile and the door. Those door keys could just be the means of freedom for herself and her companions—if she could push open the grate that was covering the dungeon entrance first.

She propped her back paws on opposite sides of the stone wall where it tapered into the dungeon's entrance hole to help support her weight while she adjusted her paw and tail holds on the burning metal. Then she pushed up against the grate. The heavy iron would not budge. She felt her grip slipping on the hot iron, but she refused to give up just yet.

"Katja, how are you faring?" Felan asked.

She looked down at him and silently shook her head. His quiet growl of frustration matched her own. She repositioned her tail against the hot bars and then her eyes went wide with a new idea. She looked down at Felan again. "I want to try something else. Be ready to catch me if this fails," she said.

He nodded as he stood under her.

Dear Creator, let this succeed, she prayed silently.

Katja once again used her back paws to brace herself against the stone hole while she pushed against the iron hatch with her back. This time, the grate moved—if only a little. She shimmied closer to the grate and tried again. The old iron hinges creaked in protest as she swung it up and open with her shoulders, back, and tail. With the encouragement of her packmates urging her on, she hauled herself out of the pit on sore paws and crawled to the far side of the guard room away from the dungeon entrance and pyre orb. There, beside a large coil of rope, she collapsed panting against the cool stone floor.

Katja lay on her back, gulping down moist air. She half-expected that someone would hear the sound of the grate being moved and come to investigate, but no one did. Instead of reassuring her, the conspicuous absence of enemies made Katja all the more nervous. She kept a suspicious eye on the door as she waited for her hammering heart to slow its pace. When she was rested enough, she uncoiled the rope that was attached to the wall beside her and began tying knots into it once every arm-length so that it would be easier for her packmates to climb.

As she waited for the others to ascend, Katja searched the guardroom for provisions. The ill-fated guards had left a few treasures behind when they were incinerated. She found several hunks of raw meat, two folded-steel swords, a few gold coins, and an ornate dagger among the ashes as well as a strange gold necklace with a large red stone pendant.

While Katja gnawed ravenously on a leg of lamb, she studied the necklace without touching it. The pendant's smooth, round stone looked like the bloodstone that Alqama had used to try to destroy her and her allies when they attacked the Hag's Nest. Katja shivered and looked away. A crimson glimmer near the guardroom's only entry door caught her eye. As Vraelth pulled himself up into the room and then helped Zahra out of the dungeon, the wraithwalker cautiously moved to the door. The door was made of stout wood and was clad with metal, but neither material was responsible for making Katja's hackles rise.

"Katja, what is it?" Zahra asked as Lauraisha and finally Felan climbed out of the hole. Vraelth walked over to the panting werewolf and together they began to haul up the rope they had just climbed.

The werecat touched the door with her scarred right paw and jerked backward in surprise at its dampness. "This door is wet."

Zahra stared at its sweating, bulging surface. "And there is water beyond it."

The sound of sloshing liquid registered in Katja's perked ears then. "What have they done?"

Lauraisha bent and rubbed a finger in the water seeping around their feet. She held it to her mouth and tasted it experimentally. "The one thing that they could do to try to extinguish the orb and destroy us. They're flooding the passageway with sea water. They mean to drown us."

"Creator, keep us!" Katja prayed fervently as water trickled under the door.

Felan looked over from where he and Vraelth worked to haul up the rope, which was wrapped around Daya'lyn's limp body. "So much for their plan to Turn Daya'lyn. They must have abandoned the notion whenever his fireballs drove Daeryn out of the dungeon.

Zahra grimaced. "Felan, we can't escape from here."

The werewolf cursed.

Lauraisha looked at the females who were edging away from the waterlogged door, and then to the dungeon entryway where she held the rope in check while Felan helped Vraelth pull Daya'lyn through the hole. "That leaves blowing up the powder cache and hoping it's a dry means of escape."

"I don't know how long that door will hold back the flood," the dryad said. "Whatever we can do, we need to do it now."

Katja nodded. "We have to wake Daya'lyn."

"Agreed," said Lauraisha.

"Creator, keep us if we're wrong," Felan prayed as he gently laid the hybrid down on the stone floor. "Do it, Lauraisha."

"Wait, let me chain him first," Vraelth said, indicating the thick manacles attached to the wall on the other side of Azmar's sphere. "If he is feral, then he'll have to fight the irons before he can get to us. It will give us at least some time to find a way of escape."

"I'll not leave him to drown," Lauraisha said.

"With all due respect, Your Highness, you may not have a choice."

"Felan, wait!" Zahra said.

"Zahra?" Felan looking over at the dryad as she stared down at the prone male in their midst.

She pursed her lips and looked at Lauraisha. "As dangerous as waking Daya'lyn is, you should not have to do it alone—particularly after Daeryn has meddled with all of our minds. There is a technique that sproutsingers sometimes use to weave roots together so that trees can more easily carry our message songs to each other. Are you willing to let me try a variant of it on your and Katja's minds to help you regain some of the connection that King Canuche first granted you? It might be dangerous to attempt on two beings instead of plants, but it is the best idea I have at the moment."

Katja and Lauraisha both nodded vehemently.

"Do it quickly," Felan said and Vraelth nodded.

Zahra took a deep breath. "Katja, Lauraisha, hold hands with me please."

The females did so. The sproutsinger told the human and werecat to stare into each other's eyes while she closed her own eyes. "Try to ignore everything else around you and only sense each other's thoughts," she instructed.

A soft green glow illuminated the veins beneath the dryad's skin as she began to sing. Katja watched out of the corner of her eye as the light crept through the veins in the dryad's face to her neck, shoulders, and arms with the rise and fall of the sproutsinger's voice. The green light flowed into her fingers and then beyond into Katja's and Lauraisha's own bodies. As the light crept into Katja's paws, it turned from green to scarlet and the werecat felt Zahra's song calling forth her wraithwalking ability. She stared at Lauraisha's eyes as Zahra's green light changed to a deep violet within the veins of the human's hands and then flowed upward toward her head. The three stood together, their veins alight with green and red and violet hues. Katja opened her mind with her wraithwalker's sight just as she felt Lauraisha do the same with her dreamdrifting abilities. She felt Zahra's song weave green tendrils of light between her red-tinged awareness and the human's violet-hued thoughts and then watched in amazement as the dryad tightened the cords between them—pulling them close and creating a connection between them. The bond was not the same as the one Canuche had created, but it was powerful nonetheless. Katja could hear the whisper of the human's thoughts and, if she concentrated hard enough, could even discern the emotions woven around her mind's words. And she felt something else, too—another presence besides Lauraisha's.

Katja blinked and looked at the dryad as she stopped singing. *Zahra?* she called with her mind.

I'm here, the sproutsinger replied. Katja could barely feel the dryad's jumbled emotions, but she could clearly hear the dryad's voice. Her sudden presence in the werecat's mind was like a cool autumn breeze. She and Lauraisha both stared at the female in confused wonder.

Zahra looked at the floor and blushed even as the connection between her and the two females began to fade. *I'm sorry,* she whispered within their minds, *but I wanted to feel what it was like to know the two of you as well as you know each other, if only for a moment.*

Katja frowned. *You're lonely when the three of us are together.*
Yes...

Oh, Zahra, I'm ever so sorry. We never meant to make you feel excluded! Lauraisha thought, and she threw her arms around their tearful friend.

A loud creak from the door snapped them all back to the peril of the moment. "We can explore the connection later," Katja hissed.

"Agreed," her packmates said together.

Vraelth and Felan laid Daya'lyn under the floating orb and raised the fireforger male to a sitting position against the stone wall so that they could lock the shackles around Daya'lyn's wrists and ankles.

"You're sure that you can unlock these if needed?" Lauraisha asked Katja. The werecat flicked her ears as she jingled the cuff key on the guard's key ring that she'd snatched from off of the floor. The human blushed and said nothing else.

Katja felt a little better about the task that she and Lauraisha were about to undertake once the irons were secured. Unlike the rusted irons at the Hag's Nest tower, these shackles were new and well-maintained. Still she gritted her fangs in apprehension. "I hope you know what you are doing,

Lauraisha," she said.

"So do I," the human responded as she waited for Felan to finish his ministrations and join their packmates by the door. Lauraisha gazed at Katja. "Are you sure you want to do this with me?"

Katja sighed. "I will not leave my dearest friend and adopted sister to do this alone."

Lauraisha inclined her head. "Thank you," she breathed. "Let us begin."

Lauraisha and Katja closed their eyes and fully opened the mental link between them. The contact was still somewhat tenuous, but it was at least tangible.

Ready? Katja asked.

Lauraisha nodded. Katja propped Daya'lyn's head and torso away from the wall while Lauraisha moved his left hand up toward Azmar's pyre sphere. As the male's pale hand touched the fiery orb, a jolt knocked the females away from him. The male lifted off the ground and floated in midair as the orb broke into a myriad of small flames, which then penetrated every exposed part of his pale skin. As each small light disappeared into the hybrid's body, the bandages around his body burned away. The wounds from the water chains and Naraka's stake now looked more like old scars than fresh scabs. The room went utterly black as the last of the small blazes were consumed.

"Is anyone hurt?" Felan called in the darkness.

"No," Katja groaned as she and Lauraisha pushed themselves off the hard floor. "I despise that part of the process."

"Agreed," Lauraisha said as she lit a flame upon her finger and used it to set one of the wall's torches ablaze.

"Are you suggesting that that was supposed to happen!" Zahra's voice was shrill as she looked between them and Daya'lyn's floating body.

Katja nodded as she rubbed her now-bruised shoulder. She turned her attention back to the still-unconscious fireforger. Daya'lyn's ankles and wrists were still bound by chains to the wall, but the rest of his body floated freely as if he were a corpse drifting in the waves of an invisible sea. Katja growled at the sight. If they failed to wake him in time, they all would be joining him in that position soon. "Let's be done with this," she said.

She and Lauraisha stood on either side of the male as his body settled to the floor once more and each gripped one of his scarred, black-clawed hands. Together they delved between the layers of Daya'lyn's mind, gently brushing his awareness with their own.

Dayalan, hear us! They thought in unison.

Silence met their plea.

Dayalan!

Lauraisha…Katja? The male's mental voice sounded groggy as his awareness touched their minds.

Yes, Dayalan, we are here, the dreamdrifter asked.

No, you should not…wake me.

I know it's dangerous, Lauraisha responded. *But we have little choice. My skut of a father has sealed us all in a place about to be flooded with water. If we do not find a way out soon, all of us will die. We may have found a path of escape, but we cannot hope to fight our way free while carrying you.*

That seemed to get the male's attention. Katja felt his heart rate increase as his mind strained against the confines of his sleep.

Please, Dayalan, you must wake! Lauraisha pleaded. *There is little time left. We cannot leave you here to die… I cannot leave you…*

The hybrid's mind let out a low chuckle and Katja felt his body twitch against its restraints. *Do you love me?* he murmured.

Of course! Lauraisha replied in surprise.

Good… the male mentally whispered.

Terror traced its signature along the length of Katja's spine. Daya'lyn's deep voice had just purred in the same way Daeryn's had when he was about to bite her mere hours ago.

Daya'lyn, are you certain you are well? the werecat asked.

I am… His stream of shared thoughts suddenly ceased as Daya'lyn's body's own voice spoke in the faintest of whispers. "Thirsty."

XXI
KINDLING A CHOICE

Katja jerked Lauraisha away from Daya'lyn as the hybrid opened his blood-red eyes. He smirked at the packmates at the far side of the room as he shifted his weight and used the metal bound around his wrists to help him sit upright against the wall. His gaze toward Lauraisha was that of a predator's as he experimentally jerked on his manacles. "You were wise to restrain me."

Lauraisha cleared her throat. "We thought it best considering previous situations."

His smile was full of fang as he looked at the water tickling under the guardroom's single door. His scarlet eyes met Lauraisha's. "A question, Princess. How do you expect to escape from here when you say that you will not leave me behind, and yet you have chained me to a wall?"

She swallowed hard and said nothing, nor did she shift her gaze from his. They watched each other even as Katja once more delved into her wraithwalking abilities. She observed Daya'lyn with a discerner's vision—looking for malice, hatred, and other forms of corruption. The war that she sensed within him overwhelmed her.

He turned his gaze upon her, his expression dangerous as he opened his soul to her. A tide of dark desires flooded her vision. "I sense you, wraithwalker. Tell me what you see in me."

She watched him in silence—suddenly afraid.

"Tell me," he whispered.

What can we possibly lose from the truth? she thought.

She took a breath and spoke aloud. "Your honor and your lust for power battle for dominance within you, Daya'lyn. You love and you fear Lauraisha for the power she holds over your affections. You, in your power lust, would see her Turned to prove your dominion over her, but you in your honor would see her revered for the kind and loyal being that she is toward you and toward others."

"And what of my attitude toward you?" he asked.

"You admire and hate me for my purity, which you see as far better than your own. Your power lust would see me corrupted so that I would seek to hide in the darkness as you often wish to do, but your honor would see my grief over the loss of my clan washed forever from my thoughts and my joy restored.

"For you who has never known a sister, I have become one to you. My grief over the loss of my family has become your own just as your sorrow over the brokenness of your family has become mine."

Katja blinked hard as tears suddenly rolled through her fur and she could not continue. Felan was beside her then. He, Zahra, and Vraelth all stood in a semi-circle in front of the hybrid. The werewolf spoke, "Daya'lyn, I know and respect you because you fought against your own brother to save my life and Katja's life even when we had not yet trusted you to know our skinshifting secrets. You would rather sacrifice yourself than hurt the ones you love."

The others all nodded as the hybrid's scarlet gaze settled on each of them.

"Daya'lyn," Vraelth said, "you were chosen as Inquisitor not because you were the strongest of all of us, but because you alone understood the evil that threatens to destroy us all. You understand it intimately and yet you continually spurn its temptation. When one such as you can fight the Víchís' temptation, it gives the rest of us hope."

The packmates nodded in unison again and then Zahra spoke haltingly. "Daya'lyn, I have doubted and feared you since our first meeting…"

His smile toward her was full of fang.

"But I was wrong to do so. Even when you were weak

and alone, you came to my aid against the dullahan spy. You kept Perefaris's fangs from my neck even when I held you in such contempt. You saved my life then and you have saved our lives against Daeryn twice now. Let us now return the favor. Let us save you."

"In the Citadel and at the Hag's Nest you chose honor over personal power and gained all of our loyalty and friendship because of it," Katja said through her drying tears. "We love you, Daya'lyn. All of us love you—each in our own way—and your behavior now cannot change that. Even so, you have a choice now, Daya'lyn, between love and life, or dominance and death, just as all of us have had the choice before you. Vraelth and Zahra chose to tend your wounds despite knowing you likely wouldn't survive. Felan and Damya chose to risk their very lives to heal you. I chose to go to the Wraith Realm to retrieve your soul despite not knowing if I could return. Azmar and the others chose to protect you. Lauraisha chose to wake you despite the danger you pose to us. We all chose to save you because we love you. So what will you choose now, Daya'lyn?"

The hybrid's lips pulled away from his white fangs in a snarl. He watched them all as he slowly stood—wrenching against the thick metal bands encircling his wrists and ankles. With a resounding crack, the wall behind him began to crumble as he pulled the chains free of it. Katja and her packmates looked at each other. A grim understanding passed between them as they stood before the hybrid, holding each other's paws and hands. If they were to die, then they would do so together.

The hybrid finally wrenched his bonds away from the stone. "I choose to never be bound or imprisoned again!" he hissed.

He let his mended, dragon-like wings unfurl from his back and stepped toward them. Hand in paw, Katja and Lauraisha and the others watched as the male approached— the chains still dangling from his wrists. He stopped before Lauraisha and slowly raised a clawed hand to her face. She did not flinch when he touched her.

"Such courage," he whispered as he caressed her cheek with a black-clawed thumb.

"Please, let us help you," the human whispered, her voice sounding almost calm as she stared into those haunting red eyes.

His virgin fangs flashed in the flickering torch light as he laughed without mirth. "There is only one here besides the Creator himself who can help me and, as young as you are, the task should never have fallen to you. Even so, what will you choose, Lauraisha? I can feel the love and lust battle within you even as it does in me." His hand slid down to the pulsing artery in her neck and the cold smile faded from his lips. Fear, longing, love, and lust warred with each other in his eyes as he watched her.

"I have heard from the others," he whispered. "But what do you say?"

"I love you, Dayalan. I have loved you ever since I first touched your mind. It isn't the love of a child as you have long assumed. My love for you is real and true. In the depths of your darkness and your shame, I have stood and I stand there again now. I made a promise that I would wait for you and it is a promise I will keep."

Sadness crept into his gaze then even as his fangs grew to their full length. "I cannot wait any longer. Time and again, I have tried to distance myself from you to protect you from my desire and it has all been for not. The Thirst calls and I need you now. Please…" He snarled then. "Prove to me that you love me, Lauraisha. Now."

Lauraisha's hand slipped from Katja's grasp and slid on top of Daya'lyn's.

"Lauraisha…" Katja murmured in warning, but the human was already moving, pushing the others away and standing on her tiptoes so that her lips could reach Daya'lyn's.

"I cannot give you my blood as nourishment," she said, "But I can give you my fire and I give it to you freely. Take all that you need."

Before any of her packmates could react, the human pressed her lips against the flats of the hybrid's full fangs. A spark of light and heat burst forth as she kissed him, knocking the others back. Flame seemed to erupt between Lauraisha's lips—lighting the pair's faces and casting bizarre shadows on the walls around them. Daya'lyn's arms encircled Lauraisha's waist and pulled her against his chest even as she held onto his shoulders. When he pulled back from her for a moment, Katja saw his fangs shrink and his eyes transform from scarlet to violet.

"Lauraisha…" he breathed and kissed her hungrily. With one powerful sweep, his wings launched the pair backward to hover a moment over the open dungeon pit a moment before the hybrid folded his wings and the two dropped out of sight.

"Lauraisha!" Katja screeched.

Katja lunged toward the entrance after them, but Felan caught her before she fell into the gloom below the hole. From where she crouched, Katja could see Daya'lyn and Lauraisha as they settled to the stone floor below her. Even when their feet found the ground, neither of them let go of one another. Fire arced in strange symbols and patterns around them as they held each other, still kissing. Lauraisha's mouth was open against Daya'lyn's—feeding him her fireforging flame—as she cupped the back of his neck and head with both hands. His firm grip on her back and neck matched her desperation as he inhaled her fire.

Finally, he pulled away and gazed at her. "You're shaking."

She nodded. "I'm very weak now."

"Let me do for you what you have done for me." He leaned toward her again. As he kissed her, Daya'lyn's own fire leaped from his mouth to hers. For a moment both of their faces lit with a shared blue glow and then Katja watched as the fire seemed to light every part of the pair inside and out. She gasped as Daya'lyn's waist-length hair turned from black to the palest silver, just as it had done when he had first shown his fireforging abilities to the assembled Council of Mages so many moons ago. She watched as his claws and the pointed tips of his ears changed to match the flesh of his hands and ears. Lauraisha's hair also paled, transforming from its customary auburn-hued waves to the likeness of flax.

When they separated again, Daya'lyn and Lauraisha stared in wonder at each other's new appearances.

"Now I'm yours, Lauraisha. Just as you are mine." Daya'lyn murmured. "Always."

Katja could not hold back her own tears as she saw the joy

in Daya'lyn's and Lauraisha's matched expressions.

"What in the fires of Edgewater just happened?" Felan growled beside the werecat.

Before Katja could reply, the door behind them gave a loud crack and water began flooding into the chamber from underneath it.

The werewolf shouted at the pair below them, "The guard's door is giving way! Lauraisha, fire the tunnel!"

"Vraelth, are we safe enough at this distance?" Lauraisha asked, looking past the werewolf to the wide-eyed elf.

Vraelth tossed part of the rope down the hole. "If you fly up to the rope, you'll be as safe as you can be. Tell Daya'lyn to keep his wings at the ready, though. Light it, Lauraisha!"

The human fireforger nodded. As the water from the guardroom swirled around the companions' feet and paws and plummeting into the pit below, Daya'lyn gripped Lauraisha, flew up to the drenched entrance and gripped the wet rope leading out of the dungeon. They dangled there a moment so that Daya'lyn could steady his hold on both the rope and Lauraisha while she took aim at the stone fissure and its cache of powder. With a wave of her left hand, the now-flaxen-haired fireforger coaxed a fist-sized scarlet fireball into existence and shot it across the cavern. It slammed against the wall with a shower of sparks, one of which caught and ignited the vein of firesalt. The burning white substance lit the entire dungeon with a brightness that rivalled daylight.

Just as the packmates finished hauling Lauraisha and Daya'lyn back up through the dungeon's entrance, the stone beneath their feet and paws violently shook from the black powder's explosion. Katja and the others clung to the guardroom walls as a sound like rolling thunder echoed in the deep. The water flowing under the door ebbed to a mere trickle while the sudden sound of rushing waves filled the dark pit below them.

"Are you both all right?" Katja asked Daya'lyn and Lauraisha.

Lauraisha nodded, but Daya'lyn just stood frowning at the werecat and the human in amazement.

"Daya'lyn, what is it?" Katja asked.

The male put a white-clawed hand to his mouth and

rubbed the tips of his now-stunted fangs. "The Thirst...it's gone."

She shared his stunned stare. "Are you certain?"

He nodded. "I feel the need for nourishment, but my thirst no longer overwhelms my thoughts as it always has. I'm free of it..." Tears welled up in the male's violet eyes. "Oh, good Creator, I'm free!"

Suddenly Katja knew what had happened. She knew that Lauraisha's vow of commitment and her loving kiss of fire had freed Daya'lyn from the slavery of his bloodlust just as Marga's love had Redeemed his father from the slavery of full vampirism. Lauraisha could not have known what she was doing because Daya'lyn had forbidden Katja from sharing the knowledge of how Marga had Redeemed Caleb with the human. Nevertheless Lauraisha had performed the same sort of miracle and had likely just saved all their lives because of it.

"How?" Lauraisha asked.

"You, Lauraisha. Your love and courage freed me." Daya'lyn frowned then and looked at all of his packmates in turn. "And all of you helped her do this. If you had not made your stand of courage..."

"We thought we had lost you," Katja whispered.

"You did. For a moment..." The male fireforger pulled her into a tearful embrace and then the other packmates surrounded him. "Thank you, all of you. I'm overwhelmed..."

They embraced each other and wept together, but their moment of joy was short-lived. Shouts and screams of panic echoed up from the swirling waters of the dungeon below them.

"I will go," Daya'lyn said quietly. He gripped the rope as Felan and Vraelth lowered him past the narrow opening and into the yawning darkness once more. The companions all tensed. Katja bent over the edge of the hole, but could see nothing besides the faint spark of fire in Daya'lyn's pale hand as he flew up to catch the partially lowered rope once more.

"Someone, help me!" he yelled as he pushed a drenched body toward them.

"It can't be!" Lauraisha whispered as she, Katja, and Zahra helped haul the sputtering human out of the darkness. They laid the portly male on his side and moved back to let him cough the rest of the water out of his lungs. "It is!"

Zahra stared at Lauraisha quizzically. "Is what?"

"Lauraisha," Daya'lyn called from his perch below the hole, "I need your help."

She frowned at him, and then slipped down the rope and into the male's arms. Together they swooped back into the darkness. Katja heard Lauraisha yell the word "Trynt" followed by a conversation in Tygeré which was too muffled for her to understand.

Katja frowned into the darkness as the rope twitched and swayed, and then realized that someone was climbing up to them. While Vraelth held the rope steady, Zahra and Felan reached down to help pull a second human male onto solid ground. The sight of the packmates made the human shriek and try to shiny back down the rope.

"Tryntin, stop that! You cannot climb back down on top of me or we'll both fall!" Lauraisha shouted in her native tongue from below the terrified male.

Zahra grabbed the human male's hand with one hand while Katja held onto her other. Together the females and Felan pulled the trembling male out of the dungeon into the guardroom and, in turn, did the same for Lauraisha and Daya'lyn.

At Felan's questioning glance, the winged male shrugged. "He took one glance at me and refused to fly up with me."

"I'm sorry," Lauraisha murmured.

"I am not. In fact, I welcome the reprieve. I doubt I can support anyone else's weight at present." He stretched his pale membrane wings with a grimace.

The younger of the two human males coughed again and finally cleared his lungs. Both he and the thinner male were curled in the corner furthest from the packmates, eyeing all of them, including Lauraisha, with terror.

"Who in the bloody fangs are they, Lauraisha?" the youngest Tyglesean finally exclaimed.

"Please, Saldis, you needn't be crass," Lauraisha replied in Shrŷde, before turning to Katja and the others. "Everyone, may I introduce two of my four brothers. This is His Royal Highness, Prince Tryntin, Duke of Tyglere, the second in line for the Tyglesean throne." She indicated the older, thinner male. "And this is His Royal Highness, Prince Saldis. Third in line for the Tyglesean throne. Your Highnesses, may I present, Katja Kevrosa Escari—"

"Jierira, Lauraisha, now is not the time for formal introductions! We need to find another way out—"

"How dare you address Her Royal Highness by so familiar a title!" Tryntin sputtered.

"I have given her permission to do so, brother. In any event, most of those in our present company are either equal to our station or actually outrank us."

"I find it difficult to believe that anything with more fur than hair on it could ever hold a rank—"

Felan's roar shook the room. "Enough! We have no time for this. The water is once again rising. The explosive opening of the tunnel between the adjoining dungeons has somewhat slowed its progress, but we are all still in grave danger of drowning unless we get to higher ground. You two, how do we escape from here?" The packmates and Tygleseans all stared at him in shock. "Well?"

Saldis slowly nodded. "If we can get the door open, there is a servant's stairwell not far from here that will lead us to some of the castle's higher levels."

The werewolf nodded. "Good. Daya'lyn, please help me open the door."

"With pleasure," growled the Inquisitor.

Katja tossed Daya'lyn the keys so that he could finally open the metal manacles still dangling from around his wrists. Once those were off and the door was unlocked, he handed the key ring back to Katja and both males set about pulling open the warped door. While Felan wrenched at the handle, Daya'lyn used one of the guard's swords to help pry the door open. On the third great tug, the handle pulled free of the door and Felan found himself suddenly seated on the hard stone floor. With a snarled curse, the werewolf was back at the door—clawing at its edge. Finally, it opened enough that Katja could see through the crack to the castle beyond. With no one in sight, the allies quickly gathered what supplies they could and prepared to leave the guardroom.

"Daya'lyn, what about this?" Katja held the odd necklace up for his inspection by the tip of the ornate dagger's blade.

"How did a bloodstone find its way here?" The fireforger glared at the necklace. "Katja, I'll trust you as our wraithwalker to keep that dangerous trinket safe. Wrap it in a strip of leather, but do not touch it. Keep it secret until we see my father again. He will know how to properly destroy it."

Katja did as he instructed.

"Your father? Are you one of Caleb's sons, then?" Tryntin asked.

Daya'lyn glanced at Lauraisha's elder brother. "I am Inquisitor Daya'lyn Calebson, the leader of this group and a fireforger mage. Daeryn is, unfortunately, my brother. I am here to put an end to his schemes if at all possible."

Tryntin bowed awkwardly. "I apologize for my previous behavior, My Sir; had I known... I am honored by your presence, Inquisitor Daya'lyn."

Saldis joined his brother and also bowed. "As am I."

Daya'lyn bowed to them in return. "Thank you, My Sirs. Now, then, would the two of you be so kind as to lead us out of this wretched place?"

"Certainly, Inquisitor," Saldis said as he and Tryntin edged toward the door.

"Keep silent on the stairs," Saldis cautioned them. "I have no way of knowing who or what may be listening."

Lauraisha and the others nodded. "By your leave, brother."

Equipped with the guardroom torch and the swords, the three Tygleseans led the packmates out into the darkened corridor. The allies kept their senses alert and their weapons and claws ready, but encountered no one as they trudged through the cold, salty waters behind Saldis. Despite seeing and sensing no one in this part of the castle, Katja felt horribly defenseless without a single piece of sunsilver weaponry among the group. How she longed for the familiar feel of Durhrigg's bone staff with its sunsilver spearheads in her paws. Lauraisha and Daya'lyn would be well-protected against any deadwalker they encountered, but no one else in the group could claim such a thing—not even a wraithwalker.

"Be mindful of your feet," Tryntin whispered. "We have no way of knowing what the water destroyed once they let it in. There may be broken glass or pot shards beneath the waves."

"Or a revenant lurking about," Katja told them. "Be on your guard."

Those allies now holding weapons gripped them tighter as Saldis led them around a corner and into a narrow corridor through a broken door. The stone of this passageway was more roughly cut than that of the main hallway, which likely meant that it was used mainly by servants and slaves.

"Here we are," Saldis said as he stopped in front of a rough wooden door and began pushing on the handle. The latch would not budge. "It's stuck."

Vraelth put his plum-hued hand on the handle and hummed idly to himself. "No, it's locked."

Saldis looked at him in bewilderment. "How can you tell?"

The elf regarded him. "Well, I am a charmchanter after all. Metal, stone, and I have a natural affinity."

Saldis and Tryntin backed away from him as he began to examine the lock. "You are a mage?" Saldis asked.

Vraelth frowned at the Tyglesean. "Well, of course. We all are. Surely you knew that your sister was a dreamdrifter, at least."

Tryntin turned to Lauraisha. "Is this true?"

She nodded. "That was one reason Father wanted me dead. I am sorry not to have told both of you, but I was trying to protect you. The less you knew about the circumstances of my escape, the better."

Saldis squinted at her speculatively. "Does Mother know?"

Lauraisha nodded. "And Ashomocos and Sandor. Ash knew because Mother told him. Sandrie found out by accident. He was the first one whose dreams I shared. The three of them knew that I would never be safe from my own abilities or from the Witch Hunters unless I traveled to the Mage Citadel to receive proper training. Consequently, I've been on the Isle of Summons for the past several months."

Tryntin's eyes darted from his sister to Katja and then on to each member of the group. "And you met the rest of these mages there on the island, did you?"

Lauraisha shook her head. "Only Vraelth. I met the others

along my journey there. It proved to be a good thing, too. We have all saved each other's lives countless times on the journey there and back again."

"Does Kyla know of your abilities?" Tryntin asked as Saldis watched Vraelth's murmurings at the door handle in fascination. The portly male looked at his older brother and suddenly shuddered.

Lauraisha frowned. "No, but why is that bad? What is wrong with Kyla?"

Tryntin began to speak and then shook his head. "It would be better if Ash explained."

"Where is he?"

"The last we knew, he, Mother, and Sandrie were all being held as prisoners in Mother's private chambers. Father has lost his mind and has fully allied himself with the Asheken — or did you know that?"

She nodded. "We saw him and Naraka before we were incarcerated. He turned us over to her for execution and Turning. Her hold over him is sick."

Tryntin shuddered. "You have no idea."

"If we're to free our mother and brothers, we'll need our own weapons," Lauraisha said. "Saldis, you know every servant and spy passage in this fortress. Can you get us to the armory?"

Daya'lyn laid a hand on her shoulder. "Lauraisha, we need to go to the stables first."

She and Katja looked sharply at him. There were dark circles under the male's eyes and he had begun to visibly tremble from the cold water that was now pooling around their hips. "The fire wasn't enough?" the human princess asked.

The fireforger slowly shook his head. "It helped more than you can ever know, but I still need blood to replenish myself."

Katja peered at him. "Are you — ?"

"My thirst isn't overpowering, but my body is weak. I won't last long without nourishment."

Tryntin stared at him. "How can a vampire be a fireforger?"

Daya'lyn looked at the male. "Traditionally speaking, they can't. Such a curse and a gift cannot inhabit the same being. But I am not a vampire. Thanks mainly to Lauraisha, I am now what my father would correctly term a dhampir—a living being who drinks the blood of beasts as his nourishment, but is not a slave to his bloodlust like the vampires are. I have most of their strengths and none of their weaknesses."

Tryntin watched the male with hard eyes. "We will see."

The latch clicked and Vraelth and Felan heaved the door open against the current. The water swirled into the semi-dry room and up four of the first stone stairs rising from the far side of the small supply room.

The companions reached the stairwell and trudged out of the dampness as Vraelth and Felan pulled the door closed behind them and locked it shut. Saldis grabbed a few apples from the barrel floating next to the stairs and tossed them to the others. He took a bite of his own and then began ascending the stairs two at a time. The others followed him into the darkness of the spiraled stairway—eating as they climbed.

For a time, the only noise on the stairwell was that of soft footfalls and the occasional crunch of an apple. Katja watched Lauraisha as the human climbed beside her. Even in the dim light of Tryntin's flickering torch, she could clearly see the tension between the Tyglesean princess's brothers and her packmates played out in the deep lines of worry etched across the female's face. To help Lauraisha think on something besides the tumultuous state of her family, Katja quietly asked, "How could Summersted Castle ever become flooded in the first place? The entire city is built well above sea level."

"This castle was built so that its lowest floors are below sea level," Lauraisha replied. "It is one of the castle's many defenses. In the case of a breach by their enemies, the residents of Summersted will evacuate the lower levels and then the palace guards will unseal the lower dike. When open, it will flood everything and kill all those within the water's path. When they need the levels cleared, the soldiers simply reseal the dike and have the slaves turn huge wheels attached to pumps to draw the water out again. All but the lowest dungeons can be cleared in a matter of days."

They stopped long enough for Tryntin to swap out his dying torch on a landing halfway up the stairs, and then they all trudged on along the stairs.

The werecat hissed. "Lauraisha, when I get my paws on your father…"

"Katja, you also will have to wait your turn," Daya'lyn growled.

"First we have to find him and that will likely mean a full assault on any deadwalkers guarding him," Felan growled. "We can't hope to succeed in that task without our weapons and more allies."

"You needn't worry about that, werewolf," Tryntin said. "As soon as they discover just who Father has as his secret consort, half of our country will gladly rise up against him."

"Yes, and a lot of good that will do, Trynt," Lauraisha retorted. "Most of our countrymen don't own weapons."

Saldis nodded as he stopped and turned to face them. "From this point on, we'll need to be absolutely silent," he said in hushed tones as he gestured to a door ahead. "We're almost to the stables."

The Tyglesean slowly opened the door to expose a small passageway bathed in shadow. A low growl greeted them from the darkness beyond the torch's glare. Felan cursed and yanked Saldis back around the doorframe as a bolt flew out of the black and lodged itself into the wood near where his head had just been. The werewolf slammed the door shut as more arrows flew.

"So much for secrecy!" He growled at Saldis as he held the door shut against the sudden rain of whistling destruction.

"This passage is never used!" The portly male gulped as an arrowhead tip wedged its way halfway through the door.

Felan swore as another bolt pushed partially through the stout wood near his paw. "You're welcome to explain that to the fiends now shooting crossbows at us!"

XXII
LAURA'S TALE

T hat corridor is the only way to get to the stables without being seen!" Saldis said.

"Of course it is," the werewolf snarled. "Daya'lyn, Lauraisha, any ideas?"

The fireforger male turned to Saldis. "How much wood makes up that passage?"

Saldis shook his head in bewilderment. "I don't understand—"

"If I launch a fireball down that hallway, can it cause any serious damage to the structure of the castle or will it simply burn our assailants?"

Saldis frowned. "The hallway is made of mortared stone and there is nothing flammable in it besides the trap doors that lead to various places on the castle grounds."

"Good enough," the male said as he gestured for Felan to be ready to open the door on his command.

"No, Daya'lyn, you are not strong enough yet to do this on your own!" Lauraisha pleaded. "Let me help!"

He looked at her a moment and reluctantly nodded. "Very well, we'll do this together. Stay behind me as you feed me your flames."

She nodded. Saldis and Tryntin both jumped back as scarlet fire erupted from Lauraisha's hands and then arced into Daya'lyn's palms.

"On my third count, Felan, open the door," Daya'lyn said as he built the flames in his hands into full blue fireballs.

"One...two...three!"

Felan wrenched the door open and the fireforger attacked. The sudden light from the Inquisitor's twin fireballs illuminated the low-ceilinged corridor and revealed the terrified faces of three ghouls at its end. They screamed in unison as the flames engulfed them.

Vraelth rolled his eyes. "So much for this being a stealthy operation."

A final fireball from Daya'lyn silenced the deadwalkers' agony.

"Let us hope there were none in the stable to hear that," Tryntin grumbled as Saldis led them past the smoldering corpses and to the hatch they had been protecting.

Katja wrinkled her nose at the sudden stench and sneezed.

"Or that," Saldis observed.

The werecat's ears flicked with her guilt and annoyance and then perked as Saldis opened the hatch above their heads. She could hear humans' shouts upon the distant battlements, but nothing closer to them. She snuck past the others to peek into the stall in which the trap door lay hidden beneath a thin layer of straw. No horses were kept here, only spare tack. She pushed past the hay and crouched beside the stall door, listening with her ears and sensing for any evil with her mind and soul. The combination of hay, horse hair, dust, and urine caused her to sneeze again. Katja froze in fear, waiting for the sound of paws or feet to come running in her direction. Nothing beside the horses stirred.

Katja, anything amiss? Lauraisha asked through their bond.

The werecat looked back toward the hatch entrance and shook her head. *Come quietly, though.*

While Katja stood guard, her packmates and allies slipped up the ladder and into the room beyond the hatch. Daya'lyn unlatched the stall door and slipped past her into the dim stable. With a nod at Felan, Katja followed the male to the stall across the way where Tyron waited. The horse pawed the ground impatiently as Daya'lyn removed the lock on his stall.

"Tyron, I'm sorry, but I am in desperate need of your nourishment," he told the stallion. "Are you willing?"

The horse watched at the stable's main door with flicking

ears. He pawed at the ground and tossed his main before offering his neck to Daya'lyn. A tingle of apprehension crept up the length of Katja's spine. Whether it was from the stallion's seeming ability to understand Daya'lyn's words or his seeming warning, she was unsure.

"Katja, can you sense any deadwalkers?" Daya'lyn asked.

She shook her head. "Even so, I'll keep watch while you feed."

He nodded in relief. "Thank you."

Daya'lyn's white fangs lengthened as he turned back to Tyron. With a trembling hand, he gripped the stallion's mane and lowered his ashen face to the horse's neck. Katja heard the telltale sucking and lapping sounds as Daya'lyn drank even as she scanned the stable for signs of trouble. Their companions were busy searching through the chest in the back of the tack stall for weapons and supplies. Katja's eyes widened in surprise when she saw that the sunsilver blades, her own bone short staff, and Daya'lyn's sunsilver quarterstaff were all there. Even though they were still missing the Agate Keystone, Katja's Feliconian signet amulet, and the rest of the packmates' jewelry, sunsilver weapons were certainly a step forward in progress.

Daya'lyn finished much faster than the werecat expected and licked Tyron's wound closed.

The horse nickered at him in surprise.

He smiled and patted the huge horse in affection. "That was more than enough. Thank you."

"I cannot believe that they left these here," Katja murmured after the human female retrieved the staffs and spearheads from the chest and passed out the weapons.

Lauraisha shook her head. "I agree. It makes little sense, unless…"

The sudden creak of the stable's main door caused all of the packmates to lunge behind concealment of the stall doors. Katja peered in between the stall's wooden slats and snarled silently as she saw the traitor Federicos moving cautiously toward the back of the building along the center aisle between the stalls. He was alone and unarmed. The werecat's smile was full of fang and her muscles tensed in anticipation of attack as the human stopped just beyond the last stall where

Katja's packmates crouched.

Federicos frowned as he stood utterly still and whispered, "Who is Laura?"

"About bloody time," Saldis said, suddenly standing. He turned to Federicos. "Laura is the true queen."

"All hail to Queen Laura!" Federicos quietly intoned.

"Saldis, what are you doing!" Lauraisha glared at her brother.

"Relax, sister. We have this well in hand," Tryntin said as he also stood and turned to the newcomer. "Report!"

"You're both alive! Thank the Creator!" Federicos replied with a bow. "When they released the lower dike, Prince Ashomocos and I feared the worst."

"You've been in contact with our brother?"

"Yes, Your Highness."

Tryntin nodded. "Good. That will make things simpler."

"Princess Lauraisha, is everyone in your party well?" Federicos asked. "We had heard that the Inquisitor was gravely injured and…"

"I am quite well." Daya'lyn stood up, crossed his arms, and glowered at the Tyglesean emissary, his face still flushed from feeding. "Thank you for your concern."

Federicos took an involuntary step back from Daya'lyn and stared at the dhampir's changed appearance in consternation.

"You betrayed us, Federicos!" Lauraisha exclaimed.

"I am sorry for the insults and the deception, Your Highness," Federicos said, not taking his eyes from the male, "Please forgive me. I had to play my part to protect your brothers and mother. I can assure you, though, that I am loyal to the crown—the true crown."

Saldis shook his head and sighed. "Enough of that, Federicos. Her Highness does not yet know the story and I would appreciate it if Her Majesty could have the opportunity to explain it in her own time."

"My deepest apologies, Your Highness," the emissary said. "Of course."

Lauraisha turned to Saldis. "Tell me what?"

He shook his head. "Not now. Our escape from this place and our rescue of Ashomocos, Sandor, and Mother is more important."

Tryntin turned to Federicos. "What has happened since we were all imprisoned?"

"Much, My Prince. As you know, the Allied Sylvan Orders broke through the Tyglesean border wall at Portarbre ten days ago. Their troops are advancing across the country much faster than anyone anticipated. The Tyglesean battle lines have broken twice now—once at Bosc Road and once at Pautat. In the meantime, Vihous warships have blockaded the Kaylere harbor. It seems that the good citizens of Vihous really didn't appreciate King Kaylor's allies poisoning King Daan. I'd say it'll take little time at all before they lay siege to Castle Summersted." Federicos smirked. "It's almost as if our soldiers are tired of fighting for a despot."

Tryntin returned the other's grin. "What of the Royal Guard?"

The emissary shook his head. "They are still loyal to the king. Although I suspect that is largely because so many of them have been Turned by the royal suasor and her ilk."

Lauraisha looked at Daya'lyn. "Would you tell us what we face in regard to Naraka?"

He nodded. "Yes, but not here. We are too exposed in this place. I have what I need and, if the rest of you have your necessary supplies, I suggest we continue this conversation elsewhere."

Everyone nodded in agreement.

Tryntin turned to Federicos. "Do you have a plan?"

The emissary nodded. "Your mother and brothers are still being held under heavy guard in the queen's private chambers. My suggestion is to free them so that they can bolster the resistance movement while your father is preoccupied with the defense of his precious capital city."

"If we can rally our allies, we may be able to stage a full coup inside Castle Summersted," Tryntin said. "Such an event would mean the defeat of Kaylor and his deadwalker allies with far fewer casualties and much less damage to the city than the Sylvans could expect from a full-scale siege."

Federicos nodded. "That is my thought as well, Your Highness. I believe Prince Saldis knows of a passage that will lead us to the rest of your family with minimal resistance; although, judging from the current array of your weapons, I doubt we'll have too many problems in any case." Felan grinned as the human eyed the werewolf's double-bladed sunsilver battle axe with its bejeweled end-spike in appreciation.

Saldis retrieved two small stilettos from the wooden chest and pushed them into his boots. "Yes, thank you for these."

The emissary smiled. "Did you find everything you needed?"

Lauraisha shook her head. "I did not find the Agate pendant or Katja's clan crest."

Federicos cleared his throat uncomfortably. "The pendant and crest were deemed to be of great value and were taken to the treasury before I could lay hands on either of them. I'm sorry. The best that I could do was to make certain that your weapons were smuggled here out of the armory." He frowned. "Truth be told, I think most of the Royal Guard were glad to be rid of the weapons. They thought them cursed."

Felan laughed. "Most of our arms are imbued with sunsilver and if what you say about most of the Royal Guard being deadwalkers is true, they would quickly learn to fear and detest the weapons, since a mere touch would cause them severe burns."

"We have to retrieve the amulets soon," Daya'lyn said. "They cannot stay in the clutches of the enemy!"

Tryntin nodded. "First, though, we need to free our mother and brothers. I'd wager that if anyone could find a way into the treasury, it's Ash."

Saldis nodded and looked around at the group. "Ready?"

When the new allies all nodded, he led the way back down the supply stall's floor hatch into the corridor from whence they had come.

* * *

Katja peered past the tapestry concealing the entrance to their hiding place to watch the eight guards pacing just outside the queen's chambers.

How do we get past them? she asked Lauraisha through their bond.

I have no idea, came the human's answer. All eight of the companions were crammed into a narrow corridor that was little more than a tunnel leading up from the main passageway running underneath the stables, garrison, kitchens, and practice yard of Castle Summersted. When he had taken power, King Kaylor had ordered all such servant passages filled in or barred to prevent spying. Saldis and Tryntin, of course, had worked tirelessly ever since their wayward youth to clear as many of these passageways as they could for their own personal amusement.

"How many maidens have you brought back here, Sal?" Lauraisha had asked as they crawled through the tunnel toward its covered entrance.

"Quite a few. I've lost count actually," he replied urbanely. That earned him a half-hearted kick from his sister.

"You two, quiet!" Tryntin whispered and the group quieted as he surveyed the scene ahead of them and then motioned for Katja—the smallest of all of them—to do the same.

Now the werecat knelt beside him and together they waited not so patiently for the changing of the guard.

"When they are finished, I'll give the signal and we will rush the four remaining guards," Tryntin whispered.

Saldis tapped him on the shoulder. "I have a better idea. Try using these when the time is right." Saldis gave his older brother a sack that Federicos had just passed to him. Tryntin gingerly opened the bag. Inside it were several oblong metal spheres which had short metal needles poking out from their ends.

Tryntin looked at Saldis. "Sandrie's dart-spines?"

Saldis nodded and handed him a pair of thick leather gloves, a short flute-like tube, and a glass vial of clear liquid. Tryntin removed the cork stopper and sniffed experimentally. "Sleep syrup. How strong is this mix?"

"A single dose should easily knock out these for an hour or two."

"Yes, assuming they're human and not zombies," the male replied sourly. He pulled on the gloves and then set about carefully dipping the spiked ends of a dart-spine into the phial's thick liquid. Once it was properly coated, Tryntin slipped the dart-spine into the tube and resealed the end. He gave Katja the gloves and motioned for her to prepare a second dart-spine as he took aim.

Slowly, he raised the sealed end of the blowgun to his mouth and pushed the other end of the device just past the concealing tapestry. He took aim and blew hard into the mouth slit as a guard walked into range. Tryntin was already loading Katja's prepped dart-spine into his blowgun as the first guard put a hand to his suddenly pierced neck and crumpled to the stone floor. He fired again as a second guard rushed to help the first. Although the human's aim was accurate, the second guard didn't even sway as he pulled the dart-spine free of his pale skin. A low guttural growl emanated from the guard's mouth as he stalked close to the tapestry.

"Sklaaf!" Katja hissed and pulled Tryntin away from the entrance as the deadwalker tore the heavy cloth from the wall.

She pushed Tryntin flat beneath her as Lauraisha took aim and threw an orange fireball at the zombie's leering face. It moaned as the flames scorched its skin.

"Go! Go! Before they can call for aid!" Katja hissed. She pushed past Tryntin and threw a kick into the burning zombie's chest as she exited the hole. She thrust her bone staff into the head of the writhing body as it hit the floor to further incapacitate it and then summersaulted away before its twitching fingers could successfully grab her leg. She held her bone staff ready as the other two guards sprinted toward her. Zahra's vine arrow hit one full in the chest, but he kept coming.

"More deadwalkers!" the dryad warned.

"Katja, Zahra, drop!" Daya'lyn yelled and lobbed a fireball over their heads as they lunged to the floor. Fire exploded against the guard's mail-clad chest—knocking him into the stone wall—even as Felan's battle axe collided with the other guard's shield. Vraelth was by Katja's and Zahra's side then, his sunsilver sword cleaving the zombie's head from its smoldering shoulders.

Shouts came from the stairs leading into their corridor and Katja knew that reinforcements had just arrived. With a roar of rage, she grabbed the lifeless zombie's head in her gloved paws and threw it at the guards running up the steps. Screams and the crash of metal greeted the blazing skull as it hit one male in the chest and sent him tumbling backwards down the stone steps while his allies dove out of the way.

"Daya'lyn, the reinforcements are human!" Katja shouted just as Felan's battle axe found its way past the guard's dented shield and into his flesh. The werewolf snarled as he pulled his weapon clean of the twitching deadwalker's stomach and then beheaded the monster.

The Inquisitor nodded as he stepped between the new arrivals and his allies. All twelve of the guards came to an abrupt halt as the fireforger kindled blue flames within his white-clawed hands.

"Those who support Kaylor and his deadwalker allies will share this fate," Tryntin said in Tygeré, and then he kicked the burned, beheaded corpse of the zombie in front of him with the heel of his boot to emphasis his point. "All of those who support Queen Manasa will fight under the protection of her Sylvan and mage allies." Daya'lyn, Saldis, Lauraisha, and Federicos stepped to stand behind him with their weapons drawn as he spoke.

"Choose your alliances carefully, fellow Tygleseans," Saldis said.

One by one, the Tyglesean soldiers dropped their weapons and knelt before the royals and their allies—all but one. A lone guard stood in defiance and spit toward Daya'lyn. "Lord Luther and Lord Daeryn will pick their fangs clean with the shards of your broken bones, *Inquisitor*."

The dhampir shook his head once and sighed. "Then Edgewater is your choice, traitor," he said, and flicked the fire in his right hand toward the human. The guard didn't even have the time to scream before fire consumed him from head to toe. In moments, the charred corpse fell to the floor behind the line of kneeling Tygleseans.

Tryntin stepped forward. "Arise, my countrymen, and guard well my mother's door. We have private business to discuss with the queen and you are to stand in protection against all comers until we take our leave. Is that understood?"

The soldiers bowed and spoke in unison, "Yes, My Prince."

Tryntin nodded. "Good."

"Prince Tryntin, what should we do with the unconscious guard?" The Tyglesean sergeant asked.

Tryntin looked at Daya'lyn. "Inquisitor, your thoughts?"

Daya'lyn regarded the guard lying near the door to the queen's chambers with Saldis's dart-spine still protruding from his neck for a long moment before he replied. "He made his stand with the deadwalkers even though he was not yet one of them. Can anyone here vouch for the character of this soldier?"

No one spoke.

"My Sir," the sergeant said, "I have reprimanded him multiple times for misconduct. This male is well-known among the taverns and the brothels. His family has long supported the king, so I cannot dismiss him or bring charges against him."

Daya'lyn looked over at Katja, who nodded. "He speaks the truth."

"So be it," the Inquisitor said. "Behead him. Give his body to his family for a proper burning and burial. However, burn his head and fix his skull atop the castle battlements as a warning to all who would willingly side with Luther's ilk. Do this for every traitor in your midst."

Tryntin nodded and grimly turned to the Tyglesean sergeant. "You will see it done once we retake this castle."

The male nodded. "Yes, Your Highness."

As Federicos and the nine soldiers stood watch, Katja's allies stepped over the dead guards and beyond the lacquered double doors into the center of an ornate room.

A tall female wearing a pale blue satin gown stood near an overstuffed chair on the far side of the room. One of her small hands held an old leather-bound book while the other gripped an ornate letter-opener. A pearl-encrusted circlet adorned her dark auburn curls.

"Mother!" Lauraisha sprinted toward the Tyglesean and wrapped her arms around the older female's frame.

Queen Manasa dropped the items she held and stared wide-eyed at her daughter. "Lauraisha, can that really be you?"

"I'm here!" she said as they embraced.

"You've grown taller and stronger, and what has happened to your hair?"

The Tyglesean princess frowned and examined her own pale locks for a moment before looking at her mother in consternation. "I'm not exactly certain. I'm still becoming accustomed to the change myself."

"I'm afraid it is partially my fault, Your Majesty," Daya'lyn said quietly.

The Queen of Tyglesea stared at him in sudden fear and hatred. "Daeryn, what have you done to my daughter!"

Daya'lyn cleared his throat uncomfortably. Manasa glared at him as she clutched Lauraisha to her.

"Mother, that is not Daeryn. That is his brother—"

"Dayalan," Manasa breathed. "You've come to us at last."

Daya'lyn's violet eyes narrowed as he watched her. "How do you know of me, Your Majesty?"

Sorrow filled Manasa's eyes then. "Your mother spoke highly of you. I had always hoped that we would meet some day."

They stared at each other a moment until two human males walked into the room through the open door just behind Manasa. Lauraisha squirmed out of her mother's grip and sprinted to embrace the two males even as Saldis and Tryntin followed suit.

"You're alive...all of you!" said the eldest. Tears formed in his eyes as he embraced Lauraisha. "How I've missed you!" he whispered to her.

"We are alive, in large part thanks to them," Saldis said, indicating the packmates.

The youngest male frowned between Saldis and Lauraisha. "Who are they?" he asked and Katja noted a mixture of fear and awe color his gentle voice.

Lauraisha smiled. "I believe proper introductions are finally appropriate. Mother, brothers, these are my friends and allies, some of who have been with me since just after my escape beyond the borders of Tyglesea. I'm not quite certain of the proper order of introductions given the wide variety of the titles each of my companions holds, so please bear with me.

"May I introduce Her Highness, Princess Zahra Zahlathrazel, daughter of Queen Mother Zahlathra Ellazel Etheal of the Zolaramie Tribe of dryads. She is a sproutsinger mage and archer of great skill." Zahra stepped forward and gracefully curtsied.

"This gentle male is Felan Bardrick, the son of Chief Fenris and Vilda Bardrick of the Geirgerd Clan of werewolves." The huge werewolf stepped forward and bowed. "Felan is a fierce warrior in his clan and a powerful skinshifter mage."

"Next we have the Honorable Katja Kevrosa Escari, daughter of Kevros and Devra Escari of the Feliconas Clan of werecats"—Katja winced in sudden grief at the name of her clan even as she stepped forward and awkwardly copied Zahra's curtsy—"and she is a ranking skinshifter and wraithwalker mage who is beholden as steward to the Pyrekin dragon Verdagon."

"May I also introduce Vraelth Verd, of the Avery clan of elves, journeyman charmchanter mage and herald to the dragon Verdagon." Katja felt a surge of jealousy at the elf's graceful bow.

"Finally, may I introduce Master Daya'lyn Calebson, son of Caleb Luthrial, the Redeemed, and Marga Amerielle. Daya'lyn is a master fireforger mage of the Isle of Summons and holds the rank of Inquisitor given him by the Ring of Sorcerers. He has also acted as my Knight Champion along the journey to Tyglesea." Daya'lyn grimaced as he bowed, although Katja doubted his doing so had anything to do with the act of bowing itself.

The eldest male, who looked just over thirty winters old, stared hard at the Inquisitor as Lauraisha finished formal introductions. "Zahra, Katja, Felan, Vraelth, and Daya'lyn, may I present my mother Queen Manasa, my eldest brother Prince Ashomocos, Duke of Westylere, heir apparent to the Tyglesean throne, and my youngest brother Prince Sandor, Earl of Protegir and Blindar. And, of course, you have already met my brothers Prince Tryntin, Duke of Tyglere and Prince Saldis, Marque of Bonasal."

They all bowed to one another.

Ashomocos cleared his throat. "Master Daya'lyn, would you kindly explain how you became Her Highness's Knight Champion?"

Daya'lyn took in a slow breath as he watched the other male. "Of course, Your Highness. Given the delicate and dangerous situation into which Her Highness was pushed thanks to King Kaylor's royal summons, I could not in good conscience allow her to return for trial without an added layer of political protection. We therefore announced to Emissary Federicos that I acted as her Knight Champion."

"But you are not betrothed," Ashomocos noted.

Daya'lyn shook his head. "Not formally, no. You must know, however, that the terms of our arrangement were made in no way to insult you or other ranking members of your family. I would not, in good conscience, seek such an arrangement before I asked your blessings to marry Her Royal Highness."

Queen Manasa watched him closely. "Do you love my daughter, Master Daya'lyn?"

He gazed into her dark blue eyes. "Yes, Your Majesty, I do. With all my being, I love her."

"Surely he is too old for her, Mother," Ashomocos said. "The sons of Master Caleb are barely three winters older than me, after all—"

Her upheld hand silenced him.

"Mother," Lauraisha said quietly. "He has already proven himself willing to die to protect me."

The Tyglesean Queen stared from Lauraisha to Daya'lyn and back. "As is the honor and duty of any Champion. But he has done more than that...he has changed you. How?"

Lauraisha took a breath and held up her right hand. A single golden flame guttered to life just above her upheld palm. As they watched, the fire changed from gold to bright yellow, then from bright yellow to orange, and from orange to scarlet. Katja and the others gasped as Lauraisha's scarlet flame then changed to a deep violet tinged with the barest blue. Never before had she managed to kindle that intense of a flame. Lauraisha held the fire a moment longer and then extinguished it as her packmates and family looked on with varying displays of pride and awe playing across their faces. "I am a fireforger mage as well as a dreamdrifter mage. Daya'lyn has tutored me on the uses of my soul's fire ever since I first discovered my gift several months ago. His patient training has helped me gain control over my abilities, but it is his love for me and my love for him that has added new intensity to my flame. And a level of healing that I could scarcely have imagined before...it has transformed us both."

Manasa's hand covered her lips as she stared at the two of them. "Marga's Redeeming kiss to Caleb…is this what has happened to you?"

Lauraisha nodded.

Manasa closed her eyes against sudden tears. After a moment, she said. "How long Marga had hoped…" She shook her head and sighed. "We will discuss this more later, but, for now, we have other things that beg our attention. Chiefly among them, my true identity."

Lauraisha frowned. "Your identity?"

Manasa nodded and then looked at Katja. "You must know by now that I was the one who begged your aid while you traveled the roads toward Jorn."

Katja frowned and then nodded. "I had wondered… And being in your presence now confirms it. You are a dreamdrifter mage like your daughter…Queen Laura." She bowed.

Manasa turned back to her daughter. "You need to know, Lauraisha, that you were named after Princess Laura, the last surviving and rightful heir to King Aedus's throne. In other words, you were named after me."

Lauraisha stared at her mother in confusion. "How is that possible?"

Manasa sighed and rubbed her forehead. "At the height of the revolution, when Kaylor slew the king and usurped his throne, King Aedus had one loyal servant whom he trusted implicitly. That servant's name was Arlis. On the night of his death, Aedus charged Arlis with the protection and care of his youngest daughter Princess Laura. Arlis was to smuggle her from the castle and out of the country, so that the royal family line could endure…"

*

The queen's words evoked a memory that Katja and Lauraisha knew from long ago. In their minds, the werecat and human saw a midnight storm break over a castle by the sea. A bolt of lightning struck a section of the castle's battlements just as two horses bearing riders wildly galloped through the castle's war-torn gates toward the sanctuary of the forest far beyond.

Arrows arced from the unscathed section of battlements

and rained down upon the fugitives racing across the open ground. Both horses but only one rider escaped into the sheltering edge of trees. Three arrows found the other rider—a valet wearing the old royal Tyglesean coat of arms—and sent him tumbling to his death amid wails of anguish from the other rider.

"Arlis!" the survivor screamed as her mount sped on into the sheltering trees…

*

Katja blinked at the vision and looked at Lauraisha. The dreamdrifter gazed at her in confusion. "Why did we just share that memory, Katja?"

The werecat smiled sadly. "Lauraisha, the first dream that we ever shared together while in Crown Canyon was Canuche's way of preparing us for the truth of your mother's story—for the truth of this moment. Canuche showed us a part of your mother's past—of your past—to help us now."

Lauraisha studied the werecat and then her own mother incredulously. "Why? Why would you run away and then return, knowing the danger that Father posed to you?"

Tears suddenly flooded the Tyglesean Queen's eyes. "I was to seek refuge with my father's half-kin in Vihous and take my place as a noble in Jorn. But it was not to be."

"Not knowing where to go without Arlis's guidance, I blindly fled Tyglesea and found refuge for a time with the dryads. Eventually Queen Zahlathra helped me make my way to Jorn. There at the capital, I studied court politics for five grueling winters.

"My education under Queen Zahlathra in the Glen and under King Daan in Vihous prepared me well for my return to Kaylere. I planned to use my training to overthrow Kaylor and take my place as rightful queen of the country. I arrived at Castle Summersted as a visiting courtier with a new false name and land entitlement. However, instead of finding a way to befriend the king's enemies and stage a coup, I caught the interest of none other than Kaylor's own brother Tristin. At first I was beyond repulsed. This was the brother of the man who had killed my father, after all! But, slowly, I began to pay attention to the praises the people sang to him and to Kaylor. Tyglesea was prosperous in those days—more prosperous than it had ever been under my own father. In a span of seven winters, Kaylor and Tristin had secured the country's borders and helped merchants gain a new level of wealth through strengthening internal trade and purging crime from the capital.

"I had begun to believe the propaganda spread to my own people of the new regime's goodness. Tristin lived up to the accolades. Kaylor did not. Even so, in those days, Kaylor was charming...so very charming." She shuddered.

"I never planned to fall in love with Tristin—truly I didn't—but it happened anyway. I had hoped to use him to get close to and kill Kaylor, but once I saw the affinity that Tristin had for his brother..."

She sighed. "Tristin began to court me soon after I arrived and married within a year. Within a month of our wedding, Tristin was killed in a horse-riding accident. With his death, the last vestige of my joy was destroyed. In desperation and foolishness, I turned to Kaylor for comfort.

"Kaylor was in love with me and he would buy me whatever I wanted just to see a smile on my face. And while I soon discovered that Kaylor was a monster to others, he was always loving and generous toward me. I lost my purpose. If I had known then, what he would become..." she shook her head. "Tristin's death was no accident. I soon discovered that Kaylor had orchestrated his own brother's murder so that he could have me for his own."

"Within a month of Tristin's death, I realized that I was pregnant with his child. I knew that Kaylor would kill the baby if he discovered that Ashomocos wasn't his own, and so Kaylor saw his wish fulfilled. I feigned love for Tristin's own murderer and married him to protect my lover's child."

She sank into the chair and wept for a few moments while Ashomocos held her hand and Lauraisha and the other packmates looked on in stunned silence.

"By the time Kyla was born, Kaylor had begun his descent into madness. He was still protective of me and of our family, but his actions toward others were growing more and more mistrustful. By the time you arrived, Lauraisha, Kaylor had descended into full lunacy. He began leading the first campaigns of the Warlock Wars just after your third winter. By the time you had manifested your dreamdrifter gift at the age of twelve, the Guard Wall along Tyglesea's eastern border was complete and Tyglesean mages had been slaughtered by the hundreds."

"Why ever did you stay here, Mother?" Lauraisha asked.

The queen smiled sadly. "With six children, where could I go, Lauraisha? I could not take you all with me—the borders were too well-guarded for that. Instead I chose to stay and fight for my home. No matter the circumstances, Tyglesea has always been my country, my home, and my responsibility. I chose to stay to protect each of you and all of our people as well as I could. If I left, who else would be able to stand as a buffer against Kaylor's rage?

"Throughout the years, I've kept my secrets well. Kaylor has never discovered that his firstborn son isn't his or that his own wife is a dreamdrifter mage and the rightful heir to the throne he stole." Her smile turned cold. "Until this past summer, Kaylor still believed that his betrayal of his own brother had remained hidden and that the woman that he loved for so long truly loved him in return. Only when the royal suasor Evita uncovered some of my secrets did Kaylor realize how much I loathe him. I have done everything in my power to undermine his edicts and that includes saving the lives of countless mage—including his own daughter—by helping to smuggle them out of the country."

"I have held back the tide for as long as I was able, but, now, the deadwalkers have come and not even I am safe." As she spoke, the queen turned her head to the side and brushed her hair away from her face. Katja spied a dark line of bruises following the line of her jaw down to her neck, which were partially concealed by cosmetic powder.

"Mother!" Lauraisha said with tears in her eyes.

As the males saw the bruises, Daya'lyn's and Vraelth's jaws tightened while Felan gave a low snarl.

"Coward!" Tryntin spat.

"I'm sorry, Lauraisha, but the whole of the country now lies in ruins. I have failed to stop him..." Manasa whispered.

"With all due respect, Your Majesty, King Kaylor had a great deal of help destroying Tyglesea," Daya'lyn said.

Queen Manasa glanced at him questioningly.

"Evita is not what she seems, Your Majesty," Daya'lyn said. "Her real name is Naraka. She is a vampire shade and Luther's own mate. We believe that Naraka was sent to Tyglesea as a deadwalker spy specifically by Luther."

Vraelth stepped forward. "Your Majesty, I believe she was sent here to gain a foothold here in the kingdom for her undead allies and, possibly, to steal a new Tyglesean knowledge. Do you know what that might be?"

The queen's eyes went wide. "Black powder!"

The elf frowned in confusion. "The dwarven invention? But the original formula was lost centuries ago during the Dwarven Plague. The recipes that Sylvans have now are far less effective."

The queen shook her head and turned to Saldis. The portly male squinted at the elf. "True, but I have been working to improve the substance and find new uses for it. We were attempting to use black powder to launch large flaming projectiles over long distances using an iron tube to help aim the bombards. The 'cannon', as Sandrie calls it, is similar to the blowgun I was using against the guards earlier, but it's much larger and its ammunition causes far more damage at longer ranges."

Lauraisha frowned as she looked at him. "We?"

"Tryntin, Kyla, and I..." Saldis stopped and stared at his mother in sudden horror. "Fangs, the spy really *is* Kyla!" Saldis whispered.

XXIII
BLOOD BARGAINS

The queen suddenly covered her mouth with her hands. "No! Kyla can't be the traitor!"

Ashomocos's lips flattened into a grim line. "She must be."

"And just who is Kyla?" Vraelth asked.

"Kyla is my sister," Lauraisha answered him.

"And a traitor," Ashomocos said.

"She can't be," Manasa repeated.

"Mother, she must be. We all knew that she was far too loyal to Father, despite his violence toward her. And, from what I have seen, she is far too friendly to Evita—I mean Naraka."

"She must have been coerced," Manasa insisted.

"Perhaps, but that matters little now," Ashomocos replied. "What is important is that we find her before she can explain the full process of making and using black powder to the enemy. If the deadwalkers discover a way either to use or counteract cannons, any and all military advantage that we have over them is lost."

Katja stared at Ashomocos. "How would they even be able to use black powder? It requires ignition by a spark of fire to burn or explode and deadwalkers absolutely hate being around fire of any sort."

Ashomocos shook his head. "I'm more concerned of how they will learn to counteract it rather than to use it. Regardless, we must find Kyla."

Sandor frowned. "I think I might know where she is; or, at least, where she would go while the castle is under siege."

They all looked at the youngest of Lauraisha's brothers. Ashomocos spoke, "Where?"

"There is a particular room that Kyla prefers to visit whenever she is upset. It's little more than a storage room, really, with a large mirror inside it. I've caught her sitting in front of that mirror and just staring at it—sometimes for hours. I can't understand what she finds fascinating about it; I despise being around the thing." He shuddered and shook his head. "There is something disturbing about it."

Daya'lyn's expression was guarded when he spoke. "Would you please describe the mirror?"

"It's massive," Sandor replied. "Large enough for Master Felan to view his full reflection without stooping, and the mirror seems ancient. Its frame is ornate—with images of drakes and bones worked into the black metal. Its surface has a red cast to it and I swear that I saw it ripple once when Kyla touched it—as if it was a pool of blood instead of a mirror."

"It cannot be…" The tremor in his deep voice frightened Katja.

Lauraisha turned to him. "Daya'lyn?"

Fear flashed in the dhampir's violet eyes as he looked at her. "If what your brother says is correct, then it means that your sister has discovered the Ott vre Cael—the first of the bloodstone mirrors."

Katja stared down at the Ott vre Caerwyn's scarlet shard embedded in the broken spearhead that she wore around her neck. She remembered how she had accidentally discovered and repaired the shattered mirror in Caleb's castle. Even as an unstudied wraithwalker, she had demonstrated her incredible gift and had unnerved Daya'lyn and Caleb in the process. And, yet, despite all of her talents, she had not been able to locate the missing shard tip after she had clawed it from Daeryn's chest hours ago. She growled and then looked up to find Daya'lyn intently watching her.

"Daya'lyn, I thought there were only two mirrors: the one in your father's possession at Caerwyn Castle and the one in Luther's possession at his fortress in Blaecthull."

The dhampir slowly shook his head. "There were

originally three: the Ott vre Caerwyn, the Ott vre Blaec, and the Ott vre Cael. They were built by the first five coven lords at Luther's and the Abomination's command as a means of instantaneous travel from one point in our world to another. The Ott vre Cael was the first threshold mirror to be built and so it was the crudest of the three mirrors—nearly twice the size of the other two, and made from the hammered bloodstones of the oldest vampires as well as the transmuted corpse of a sylph."

"A sylph?"

Daya'lyn mouth was a grim line as he nodded. "Cyrena's sister."

Tears suddenly stung Katja's eyes as she remembered the gentle guardian of the altar gateway. Without the sylph, Katja and Daya'lyn might never have returned from the Wraith Realm to the Erde Realm in time to save themselves and their packmates.

"The Ott vre Cael was lost when the most of the Caelum Archipelago was sunk during the First War of Ages. If the mirror is here and intact, we are all in the gravest danger."

"Why?" asked Lauraisha.

"If the threshold gateway between mirrors is active, then the two mirrors can transport small numbers of deadwalkers from Blaecthull to Summersted every time both mirrors are fed with a blood sacrifice. Depending on how long the Ott vre Cael has been active, there could be a large number of deadwalkers now standing between us and Naraka. Even worse, though, is the prospect of what will happen if Naraka succeeds in permanently mating the two mirrors."

"Invasion?" Felan asked.

Daya'lyn nodded. "Luther would be able to send countless numbers of Asheken to this castle from Blaecthull and overrun the whole of Tyglesea with deadwalkers."

"And then the rest of the Sylvan Continent," Felan surmised.

Katja scratched her maw in thought. "They would be able to assault the Southern Continent from two fronts: the Sphinx's Gape in the north and Tyglesea in the northwest."

"And no one would be able to stop them." Daya'lyn said. "We have to find that mirror and destroy it now!"

"Wait, if we destroy that mirror, what will stop Luther from simply sending deadwalker troops through the other mirror you mentioned instead?" Ashomocos asked.

Daya'lyn pointed at Katja. "Her."

Ashomocos stared at the werecat in disbelief. "Her? Why her?"

Daya'lyn shook his head. "I'm not sure. What I do know is that Katja is a powerful enough wraithwalker that she managed to gain full control over the Ott vre Caerwyn even before she had undergone proper training from Ring Sorceress Joce'lynn on the Isle of Summons. If anyone could have a hope of destroying or controlling the Ott vre Cael, it is Katja."

The werecat stared wide-eyed at Daya'lyn as Lauraisha asked, "Sandrie, how do we get to the chamber housing this mirror?"

Sandor scratched the faint stubble clothing his chin. "We need to use the main corridor leading to the treasury to avoid the flooding. If we can fight our way to that point, I think I can lead us to the mirror room."

"We have to rescue the Agate Keystone from the Summersted Treasury anyway," Vraelth said.

"Agreed," Daya'lyn said, before taking Azmar's Opal pendant from around his own neck and giving it to Lauraisha. "I want you to keep both Keystones safe together. The mirror will cause all sorts of magical interference, so, hopefully having the two stones next to one another will help lend Damya and Azmar some added strength against its evil."

When she nodded and tucked both Keystones necklaces beneath her robes, he turned to her youngest brother. "Well then, lead on, Prince Sandor."

The Tyglesean royal family set off for the treasury at a brisk pace, surrounded by their guards and the packmates. With weapons drawn, the twenty-one-member party raced along the maze of corridors toward their destination. They met little resistance along the way, which Ashomocos assumed meant that every spare warrior had been called to defend Kaylere against its besiegers. By the time they had wrenched open the heavy iron doors of the treasury, Katja was disoriented and, truthfully, somewhat bored. She quickly remedied that by helping the others search high and low for Mainmangi's Keystone among the rows and rows of stone shelves lined with boxes of coins, jewels, and tarnished trinkets. Even with twenty beings, searching the huge chamber was a colossal task.

After a time, Katja thumped her tail in frustration. "It has to be here!"

Zahra shook her head. "It's not."

"That makes no sense." Her tail thumped again and came dangerously close to knocking over a gold urn.

"Katja, try using your wraithwalking ability to search it out," Felan said. "Since the Keystones are not quite of this world, you might be able to at least sense the Agate Amulet if it's here."

Katja shut her eyes and took a slow breath to calm herself. As she felt her wraithwalking ability well up within her, she pushed her mind toward the intended target of her search. In her mind's eye, Katja clearly saw the earthy brown of Mainmangi's Agate and the great Pyrekin bear associated with the sacred stone. Once she had the Keystone's true nature firmly fixed in her mind, the wraithwalker pushed her mental senses outward—searching for the merest trace of her quarry from among the less important items in the room.

Katja was shocked when her search revealed not one Keystone, but four.

Katja opened her eyes and looked at Felan. "I can feel the Emerald Keystone flying high above us. I think Verdagon is about to attack the castle—"

A thunderous roar shook the stone fortress as she spoke and Katja and the other packmates grinned.

"A dragon? Here?" Wonder and terror tinged Ashomocos's voice.

"Don't worry, brother," Lauraisha replied, "Verdagon is our ally."

Katja's smile slid from her face, then. "We have a problem. There are three other Keystones located down the corridor from us in the same room that holds the mirror, and I can feel deadwalkers near the stones as well."

"Wait, three Keystones?"

She nodded.

"How many deadwalkers?" Vraelth asked.

She shook her head. "I do not know. There are three at least, but there may be more...it feels like far more, but I cannot be certain."

"Can you tell if the mirror is active?" Daya'lyn asked.

Katja shook her head.

"I would wager that the mirror is interfering with your discernment then. If it is active, they will be in the process of transporting the Keystones to Blaecthull. We must act quickly."

"Follow me," Sandor said, and strode out of the treasury without another word.

The passage beyond the treasury was as dark as pitch and the stench emanating from the corridor was one of the foulest Katja had ever smelled. With weapons at the ready, the group advanced—the light from their torches and fireforged flames glinting off a thick yellowish slime that coated the walls of the hallway.

"Lauraisha," Daya'lyn murmured, "no matter what you see or hear, do not hold back your flame. Understood?"

She nodded in the dimness and sent a jet of violet flame arcing along the blade of her sunsilver saber. Low cackles echoed from beyond the shadowy veil then, and the first attack came. A hail of arrows burst through the cloud toward the allies. Daya'lyn's kindled flame broadened and flattened ahead of the group to form a huge shield of fire—destroying the barbed bolts as they touched it. As soon as the arrows disintegrated, however, a sudden gust of wind blasted against Daya'lyn's fiery wall. The fireforger had to extinguish his flames almost as quickly as he had kindled them to keep the fire from scorching his own allies. With the fireforgers' flames and the companions' torches suddenly snuffed out, the horror of total darkness engulfed the Sylvans.

Katja growled in the unnatural gloom and muttered a prayer that her father had taught her when she was a kit. "Creator, you do not give me a soul full of fear. Only your love, power, and discipline guide me forever."

Once again she unleashed her wraithwalker's sight to perceive the truth beyond the shade-shaped illusions. She opened her mind's link to Lauraisha and Zahra as scaly monsters slunk into her view. She could see the serpentine forms of glycons slithering fast toward them—venom-laced weapons held ready in their clawed hands and full ring mail shirts covering their humanoid upper bodies as they glided on their snake-like tails toward the attack. Beyond the advancing deadwalkers, a squadron of goblins watched them from their post outside of a large wooden door at the far end of the corridor. She could not sense the shade who was wreaking havoc with their eyesight among any of the deadwalkers in the hallway, which meant that he must be waging war against them from inside the mirror room itself.

Katja snarled as she focused on the immediate threat. "We have Turned lamia coming fast toward us," she said.

"Katja?" came Daya'lyn's voice. "Can you neutralize the shade?"

"I will try."

Katja felt panic rise within her as the scraping sounds of the glycons' snake-like lower bodies came closer. Her allies would be utterly helpless if she could not find a way to penetrate the black fog clouding their senses. The wraithwalker forced herself to take deep breaths and relax despite the imminent danger. She mentally pushed past the Turned lamia's minds and focused on the squadron of Turned trolls. As she searched around the goblins' dark thoughts and brushed against the three beings' Tainted minds in the mirror room beyond, she caught a faint echo of cold laughter drifting along the edge of her awareness.

Daeryn's low chuckle then rolled fully through her mind. *Not now, Katja, wait your turn. I am not ready to play with you yet.*

Katja hissed at the darkness and quickly opened her mind wide to Lauraisha. *Daeryn is the shade! I need your and Daya'lyn's fire now!*

Lauraisha, however, didn't answer her.

Lauraisha? Lauraisha!

Daeryn's laughter overwhelmed her panicked thoughts. *I told you to be patient, Katja. When the glycons are finished with your allies, then you and I can spend some time together.*

Katja's answering roar of rage rattled the stones and momentarily halted the glycons' advance. She lashed out with her mind against the lie of Daeryn's conjured darkness and felt the male's presence retreat a step as she fractured his shadowed creation with the truth of her wraithwalker's voice. She roared again and mentally struck him a second time, then a third. With each new attack, Daeryn's darkness withdrew a little further down the corridor and his thoughts retreated away from hers.

"Daya'lyn! Lauraisha! Can you use your fire now?" she asked aloud as the first glycons charged out of the thinning mists.

The male spoke slowly as he came out of his daze. "Yes."

Fire erupted from Daya'lyn's outstretched palms and consumed the first two Turned lamia. More glycons slithered out of the black cloudbank even as Katja pressed her mental attack against the fireforger's Fallen brother. As she kept Daeryn at bay, Daya'lyn cast flames onto his allies' sunsilver weapons and charged into battle against the hissing onslaught—his blazing sunsilver staff whirling.

In the next moment, Daeryn's cloud vanished completely and Katja frowned in confusion. Resisting Daeryn had always been much more difficult and yet now she had forced him to retreat completely without even the help of her allies' fire. Something was wrong. Had he been severely weakened from her and Daya'lyn's attacks in the dungeon or was something far more ominous at work? Katja glanced at Lauraisha and realized in horror that the female was still standing as cold and stiff as a statue in the middle of the chaos surrounding her. Daeryn's main focus was to dominate the dreamdrifter's mind rather than her own. But why?

Katja shook her head to clear her thoughts and pressed her advantage. As she pushed Daeryn's influence completely from her mind, the werecat yelled for Tryntin and Sandor to pull their immobile sister away from the battle's front lines to safety alongside Queen Manasa and her guards. Meanwhile Katja covered their escape with her twirling bone staff—blocking two glycons' attempts to push past her with a furious flurry of fiery stabs and swings. She destroyed one of the hissing monsters with a backward swing of her staff, which knocked it stunned and smoking into the nearest wall. Before it could recover, she stabbed it at the base of its skull with a flaming spear point—severing its brainstem from its spinal cord in a gush of fluid. As the smoldering glycon slid limp down the wall, its partner hissed and pressed its attack—slicing Katja's arm with its venom-laced sword. Katja roared in agony at the shallow cut, but continued fighting with her staff and mind. She pushed the glycon into Felan's path and the werewolf sent the monster's head rolling with an overhead swing of his massive sunsilver battle axe.

Tryntin and Ashomocos were right behind the huge werewolf, wielding cutlasses laced with one of Saldis's paralysis poisons. Without the interference of Daeryn's illusions, Zahra was able use another of Saldis's concoctions to deadly effect on the tips of her arrows as she and several guardsmen defended Queen Manasa and Princess Lauraisha. Vraelth led a second party of guardsmen against the glycons while Daya'lyn's fireballs kept the glycon archers too busy to shoot his allies.

At the height of the battle, Katja had managed to slaughter five glycons and assist in destroying two others. The werecat's and her allies' pressed their advantage. They had pushed their foes closer to the mirror room door and littered the stone corridor with smoldering bodies in their wake, but still more of the snake-like monsters came. To make matters worse, the four Turned trolls had abandoned their post at the door of the mirror room to fight alongside their hissing allies—adding brute strength enough to rival Felan's to the fray.

"We cannot endure much more of this!" Felan roared as he dodged the swift swing of a goblin's massive battle hammer. With the added strength of arms, their enemies had begun to push the packmates back, causing Katja's allies to slowly retreat down the slimy hallway—tripping over bodies as they gave ground. Katja was weakening; her swings were becoming increasingly sluggish as the deadwalker venom coursed through her right arm. A Tyglesean guardsman was cut down beside her. Then his goblin attacker turned its attention on her.

Verdagon, where are you! We need you! Katja sent the thought out as a scream. *We are being overrun!*

Verdagon's response was faint. *The stone is too thick and the mirror's presence saps my strength. I cannot get to you in time!*

Creator, keep us! Katja prayed desperately as she rolled

to avoid a hammer-strike to the face. Vraelth was beside her then—his weapons flashing. She starred at the elf in sudden comprehension.

"Vraelth, charmchant!"

"What?"

"Charmchant the stone roof open!"

"Have you gone mad? That could bury the mirror room entrance!"

"Please! It's the only way for Verdagon to come to our aid! We'll die without him!"

"What of the other Pyrekin?"

"There is too much interference from the mirror for them to help right now. Verdagon is the only help we have left!"

The elf nodded even as he dodged another swing. Katja gritted her fangs and charged the goblin—her staff raised. The surprised monster stepped back in consternation as Katja pressed her attack. The distraction gave Vraelth enough time to focus on the layered gray stone above him and chant. A clear, bright note issued from the tenor's lips and the walls began to tremble.

"Vraelth, what in fangs' name are you doing!" Daya'lyn cried as dust fell from the ceiling.

"Bringing the dragon!" Katja answered for him. "Fall back! Everyone, fall back now!"

The allies did so as the stones above began to crumble. Rays of sunlight suddenly shot between them and their attackers. The glycons and goblins to cowered and screeched as the daylight burned them.

A mighty roar shook the castle as Verdagon circled overhead—his massive green wings blotted out the sun above them. A great thump heralded his landing.

"Sylvans, retreat and cover yourselves!" the dragon roared as he lowered his angular head into the large rift that Vraelth had made. Katja and her allies scrambled back as the Pyrekin inhaled and then blew a pillar of swirling blue flame into the hallway. The fire enveloped and destroyed anything in its path. Katja barely heard the screams of her foes before their very existence became little more than a smoldering memory.

Verdagon turned his head to regard her with unblinking

eyes. "Hurry, my Keystone brethren are in grave peril as is one of your packmates. I cannot stay near the miasma of that mirror any longer. You must destroy it before more deadwalkers find their way here. I will continue to keep the rest of the castle's defenders too occupied to interfere with you. Go!"

With a massive thrust of his membrane wings, the dragon launched himself from the roof and into the sky.

"Quickly, then," Daya'lyn said as he kindled a violet flame. Katja and Felan moved quickly behind Daya'lyn—skinshifting the wounds of the living closed even as the fireforger charred the bodies of the dead.

"Are all accounted for?" Daya'lyn asked.

Katja looked around the scene of destruction. She cringed as the mutilated bodies of beings and monsters brought forth similar memories of her dead clansmen. She shut her eyes and took a slow breath to calm herself before continuing her count. Of the nine guards who had accompanied the royal family and the packmates, only three were still alive and two of those were mortally wounded. Her packmates were relatively uninjured as were all of Lauraisha's family except Saldis, who had received a deep gash on his head. With the help of one of Saldis's medicines, Katja was able to draw the venom out of her arm and his head before Felan skinshifted their wounds closed.

As Felan attended him, Katja looked around again in sudden panic. "Where is Lauraisha?"

Ashomocos spoke. "I thought she was fighting alongside you."

Katja shook her head. "Daeryn had ensnared her mind, so I asked Tryntin and Sandor to pull her out of harm's way."

"We did," Tryntin replied. "We left her within the protective circle of Mother's guards before returning to fight. Mother, where is she?"

"I have no idea!" Manasa said in panic. "One moment she was right beside me. Then the goblins attacked and killed so many guards, and now she is gone."

Katja turned toward the door at the end of the corridor. "That means that—"

"—Daeryn has her and the rest of our Keystones, then,"

Daya'lyn said, finishing the werecat's sentence. "Felan, do you think you have enough strength left to open that door?"

"For Lauraisha, I had better," the hulking werewolf said.

Gripping his heirloom war axe, Felan sprinted to the massive wooden doors—the other battle survivors close at his heels. He lifted the sunsilver axe overhead with a roar of rage, and brought it down against the thick wood surrounding the iron lock. The blood-slicked blade split the wood like kindling. Felan snarled and brought the axe against the barred doors again—sending splinters in all directions. The doors groaned under the force of Felan's second strike, but did not give way until his third blow. Then the doors swung partially open on sagging hinges.

With weapons at the ready, Katja and her allies entered the chamber through the splintered entrance that Felan had just crafted. The spare room still felt small compared to the enormous artifact that it housed. The Ott vre Cael stood against the chamber's back wall, partially hidden behind stacks of clothes chests and other furniture. The mirror's large, crimson reflection roiled and shimmered like the surface of a pond under a storm—lighting everything else in the room in the eerie hue of blood.

The hair rose along her spine as the werecat spied Daeryn standing in the center of the room watching them. Daya'lyn's recent burn marks were clearly visible along the male's right arm, shoulder, and neck. He stared at the companions with hatred simmering in his crimson eyes while Lauraisha stood stiff and silent in front of him. A heavy chain holding Mainmangi's Agate, Damya's Sapphire, Azmar's Opal, and, of all things, the Feliconian Clan crest amulet was hanging from the human's neck. Of more importance to Katja, however, was the ornate dagger that the vampire held under the princess's clenched jaw. Lauraisha was gagged and bound with water chains and her eyes stared straight at Katja without focusing on the werecat or blinking. The dreamdrifter breathed slowly as if in slumber, but Katja could not communicate with her fogged mind.

"You will not interfere," Daeryn hissed as he watched them. "If you do, she dies."

Katja peered past him to see a bed with two females

laying upon it a mere paw-width span in front of the mirror's roiling surface. A human female lay submissively against the bed's black, silken sheets while the vampire Naraka drank deeply from a fang wound on her neck. A desiccated corpse lay curled on the cold stone beneath the bed. The sight of its shriveled skin nearly caused Katja to retch.

"Kyla, no!" Ashomocos, Tryntin, Saldis, and Sandor screamed in unison.

Lauraisha's older sister lifted her head from the bed for a moment to sneer at them with crimson eyes before laying her head once more on the black pillow. Naraka never paused her feeding to even acknowledge them.

"She is already Turned," Daeryn said. "Soon Kyla and Naraka will finish her tasks and the mirror will open forever to us. And not even you, Katja, will be able to close it then."

"You traitor!" the werecat hissed.

Daeryn's answering hiss was low. Katja felt his voice echo in her mind. *I am not a traitor to you! I fight against Luther the same as you, Katja. Join me. You know you cannot defeat Luther alone. Bond with me and together we will wield power beyond our darkest dreams. My power is the key to Luther's destruction. Let me help you end Luther's reign.*

She felt his thoughts slip into her mind and immediately used her wraithwalking skills as a shield against his whispered suggestions and attacked him with truth. *With a blade to Lauraisha's neck, you would ask me to ally myself with you? Never!*

To her surprise, Daeryn's mind did not try to attack hers. Instead he opened his mind to her—laying bare every thought and emotion to her scrutiny. *Katja, I have never wished you harm.*

Grim tales, liar! She snarled. *You've bled me twice on Luther's orders and have tried to possess me, mind and soul, at every opportunity!*

Daeryn's crimson eyes bore into hers even as his mind recalled their encounters from his perspective. The werecat was stunned to feel the male's fear, admiration, and deepest yearning for her mixed in with the lust and overwhelming thirst that she already knew so well. *Katja, I have tried and failed to Turn you into my equal at great personal risk. Luther wants you brought to him alive and unspoiled so that he can Turn you himself and I have dared to defy him—not once, but twice. You are my greatest hope of freeing my mother and myself from Luther's domination. I need you as an ally. Help me!*

Katja's ears were flat as she snarled at him. *If you wanted my aid, you shouldn't have attacked the beings I love. You shouldn't have Turned Kayten, or nearly killed Felan, or harmed Lauraisha, or tried to Turn me in the first place!*

A crimson haze blotted out the werecat's vision as Daeryn's memories of Blaecthull and of Luther flooded her mind. Katja saw his first visit to the deadwalker fortress after Daeryn had crossed the Thornblood Sands bearing the arm wound from his father Caleb. She witnessed the massive fortress of Blaecthull rising like a great black crown of spines out of the surrounding thicket of asp's thorn and felt fear caress the length of her spine as the fortress's spiked gate opened wide and admitted Daeryn into the grim abyss beyond. She saw the Víchí High Elder seated on his obsidian throne atop its towering dais—a half-ruined figure wrapped in resplendent, black robes. Crimson eyes bored into her from a face half-melted like candlewax over angular bones. Was it Daeryn that had approached Luther while wounded or was it herself? Katja could no longer tell…

*

"You have your father's bearing, Daeryn," Luther said as he studied the newcomer.

Daeryn saw legions of deadwalkers from every Fallen Asheken race watching him from the shadowed edges of the throne room and swallowed hard before answering. "It is true, High Elder, that I have his likeness," Daeryn said raising his injured left arm, "But I hold none of my father's disingenuous sense of loyalty."

"Caleb did that to you, did he?"

"He did."

Luther regarded him in silence and Katja had the distinct impression that the vampire was weighing Daeryn's potential as an enemy or an ally. "Why are you here?"

"I have come to free my mother."

Luther's eyes narrowed. "Have you now? And what makes you believe that Marga is here?"

Daeryn matched Luther's cold stare. "Your servant Curqak informed me that she was your captive."

Annoyance flashed across the Víchí's face. "Did he now? I find it intriguing that you would trust a ghoul's word — particularly Curqak's word, given your family's adverse history with him."

Daeryn's answering smile was full of fang. "Fair to say, but, in this case, I do. I can be very persuasive when I need information."

"And where is Curqak now?"

Daeryn smirked. "I left the little fiend tied up to a tree a few paces south of the Sphinx's Gape. On a windy day, she will be able to smell him, and that should provide good sport for her if she feels inclined for such a game."

Luther's yellow fangs flashed with his answering smile and he slowly leaned forward. "A very good game indeed. I myself rather enjoy such games. And you, Daeryn, do you play them often?"

The smirk slid from Daeryn's face as he realized that Luther felt no concern about Curqak's safety. The hybrid had thought to use the ghoul as a bargaining chip to gain his mother's freedom, but now that Daeryn saw Luther's sudden glee at the peril of a subordinate, his wisp of hope for a trade was utterly dashed.

"Upon occasion." The hybrid met the Víchí High Elder's hard gaze as he forged a single golden flame in the palm of his right hand. The assembled deadwalkers shrank back as its sudden light lit the gloom. "I am not interested in a war, Luther, but I will reclaim what is mine. You will release Marga and you will let the pair of us leave this place unharmed or I will scorch every deadwalker in your keeping."

Luther studied him again. Was that a hint of fear in the ancient vampire's eyes? The Víchí High Elder turned to the cyclops guard at his left. "Bring Marga to me now."

As the Turned giant bowed and lumbered off toward the dungeons, Luther peered at Daeryn again — studying him as the hybrid fireforger fought to sustain the small flame that was his only remaining ruse. Daeryn began to tremble as he heard his mother's muffled screams echo up the stone corridor. He watched in horror as the cyclops tossed Marga's bloody and bruised form at his feet. Quickly he extinguished the flame and bent to untie her gag. He held her swollen face in his hands.

"Mother? Mother! I'm here. All is well; I'm here."

"Daeryn?" Marga whispered as she slumped in her son's arms.

Luther sighed as though bored and motioned one of the hags standing along the wall to step forward. The Turned dryad set a curious green bottle and rag down on the floor beside Daeryn and backed away.

"Tend to your son, Marga," the vampire elder said. "Your lifemate's rage has nearly lost him his arm, and that simply will not do."

Without a word, Marga slowly sat upright and coated the rag with the pungent ichor from the proffered bottle. As she dabbed it along the gash on his arm, Daeryn felt instant relief from the throbbing pain that had been his constant companion for the past several months. In turn, Daeryn took the cloth and wiped it gently along his mother's injuries. She leaned close to him as he did so and whispered, "You should not have come! Flee this accursed place while you are still able! If you do not, he will use us against each other!"

Daeryn regarded her and shook his head. Then he looked up to find Luther watching them. "Release us now," he demanded.

"No."

"I will fire this place and every monster in it."

Luther's smile toward him was that of a predator. "No, you will not. Even healed, you lack the strength for it. You have overplayed your hand, Daeryn, and that will cost you."

Luther motioned to the archers stationed around the throne room and they took aim at the pair. What little color there was drained from Daeryn's pallid face and he began to tremble in fear. For the span of a single breath, Daeryn wished more than anything that Dayalan was with him now.

"What is your price for her freedom?" he asked Luther.

The Víchí High Elder shrugged. "Yours."

"Mine?"

Luther shrugged again. "Yours and one other's. You will either aid Curqak in retrieving the twelve Keystones which your mother has hidden from me all over the Sylvan Continent, or you will willingly take her place yourself as my captive and bring a certain being from the Sylvan Continent to me. Either of these tasks will satisfy my needs and gain Marga her freedom, so I will let you choose which you wish to undertake."

Daeryn looked into the pleading eyes of his mother. "Please, Daeryn, don't. Save yourself!" she whispered.

He gazed at her and fought back sudden tears. Then he chose what he hoped would be the least of two evils. "Very well, I will trade my own freedom and one other's for hers…"

*

The memory faded and Katja found herself in the Summersted mirror room once more.

And I am the one for trade, she thought.

Sorrow haunted Daeryn's crimson eyes. *Yes.*

What happened, then? What happened to you and your mother? she asked. She was shocked to find tears now standing in her own eyes.

Luther locked us both in a dungeon room with water chains encircling our hands and feet. He brought generous helpings of food to my mother and left me to starve, he replied, hatred and sadness flickering across his face. *My mother grew stronger as I grew weaker until at last Luther seemed to listen to her pleadings and brought me a horse from which to feed. The beast was just a half-dead, runt of a thing, but I didn't care. I was so deliriously hungry that I fed without question—gorging myself on his blood and killing him in the process. It was only after the feeding that I saw my white fangs turn to yellow and realized what I had done— that I had imbibed in the blood of a being not a beast. By the time I realized that the horse was actually a kelpie, it no longer mattered. He was dead and his life, through his blood, sang throughout my body—giving me a measure of strength that no beast could have ever bestowed. It is that strength that I have tried time and again to pass on to you, Katja.*

All whom Luther Turns are directly beholden to him because he is their immediate blood sire. And all whom are Turned by Luther's converts are, themselves, beholden to Luther as their ultimate blood sire. Yet no vampire's fangs have ever touched my veins. I Turned myself. Of all vampires, I alone exist outside of Luther's influence, which means that any being whom I Turn will be also be free of his Taint. Daeryn wrinkled his aquiline nose in disgust even as his eyes remained soft in sorrow. *My one regret in all of this is that my mother had to see her own son Turn into that which she most fears.*

He shook his head. *No one living can destroy Luther—not even you, not even Dayalan. Luther knows all of our weaknesses and is himself too strong to defeat without the strength gained from Turning. Deep in your soul, you know this to be true.*

No matter how she tried, Katja could not sense any deception in the vampire's thoughts and that fact unnerved the wraithwalker even more than his blade resting against her closest friend's neck.

You need what I offer you, Katja. Bond with me... Daeryn mentally whispered again and Katja felt the full strength of his seduction behind that mental plea. She felt her back paw's muscles waver with the uncertainty of a step toward the vampire as she regarded him.

"Daeryn, why do you just stand there? Destroy them!" Naraka hissed behind him. "I have enough of a task to undertake here without the added stress of their interference! The High Elder wants the mirrors mated and their connection will open soon!"

Daeryn snarled in frustration and abruptly cut his mental link to Katja. "Retreat now," he whispered in deadly voice.

"Never," Daya'lyn retorted, raising his sunsilver staff.

Fear and hatred ruled Daeryn's eyes as he regarded his brother's changed appearance. He held the dagger tighter against Lauraisha's throat and a small rivulet of blood seeped between the blade and her flesh—its coppery scent causing both twins' nostrils to flair and the pupils of their eyes to dilate. Unlike Daya'lyn, Daeryn did not hold the growth of his fangs in check at the sight and smell of the female's fresh blood. The yellowed points extended fully past his lips as he smiled—taunting his brother to act. Before Daya'lyn could, however, Katja stepped forward.

"I will come to you, Daeryn," Katja said.

XXIV
THRESHOLD SACRIFICES

Everyone stared at her in utter confusion. Daeryn was as wide-eyed as Daya'lyn. "What?"

"I will come to you," she said again.

Daeryn smiled in satisfaction. "So you finally see the wisdom in allying yourself with me?"

Katja shook her head. "I will trade my freedom for Lauraisha's just as you traded your freedom for your mother's." The smile slid from Daeryn's face as she spoke. "You have given me the same choice as Luther gave you, which proves that you are no better than he despite your claims to the contrary."

For a moment, Naraka stopped drinking and stared at Daeryn over Kyla's bloody neck. "Daeryn, what is she talking about?"

Daeryn glanced at her in apprehension. "Never you mind. Just open the threshold. Now!" He looked back at Katja with eyes as hard as stones. "Come then, changeling, and save your precious friend."

"Katja, no!" Felan gasped as the werecat put down her weapons and moved to the vampire's side. The werewolf tried to step forward, but Zahra restrained him—her eyes narrowing at Daeryn even while her mind remained open to Katja's. Despite both of their efforts, neither of the females could reach Lauraisha's enthralled mind; however, they had still been able to communicate their basic emotions with each other and so Zahra understood the fundamentals of Katja's plan.

Desperate hunger ruled Daeryn's eyes as he watched the werecat approach.

The Creator has not given me a soul full of fear...

As Katja neared him, she noticed that the sunsilver-and-bloodstone spear shard that she had taken from Daeryn was now hanging from a leather cord around the vampire's neck.

So Daeryn did manage to steal it back after our battle! she thought.

Between her claws and perhaps even one of Daeryn's own weapons, she hoped to distract the vampire long enough for Zahra to pull Lauraisha to safety and to steal the shard-imbedded spearhead tip away from him so he could never use it to harm her or her packmates again.

"Let her go, Daeryn. Now," Katja said in a voice far calmer than she expected as she stood before the pair.

His smile was full of fang as he reached for her with his injured hand. She stood just beyond his easy grasp. "Come close to me first, Katja," he purred.

When the werecat backed away a step, Daeryn snarled and tightened his grip on Lauraisha even more. A second trickle of blood began to flow from beneath the dagger.

Katja's eyes narrowed and she raised unsheathed claws to her own neck. "That is *not* how this game will play out. You will release her or I will slit my own throat." To emphasize her point, Katja caused a ruby trail of droplets to fall from her own neck. "Think carefully, Daeryn. You cannot hope to Turn me before the loss of blood from such a wound kills me—my packmates will make certain of that—and if I die, all of *your* hopes for an alliance between us with be destroyed."

Daeryn's fangs lengthened with his thirst for her even as utter fear gripped his crimson eyes. Slowly, he loosened his grip on Lauraisha.

"Daeryn, what are you doing!" Kyla cried. "If the werecat dies, she cannot harm the High Elder or any of the rest of us! Let her kill herself!"

But Daeryn continued to stare at the werecat in panic. "Please, you mustn't..."

Katja snarled in defiance and dug deeper into her own neck. The sluggish droplets turned into a steady stream.

"Release her, body and mind!"

Daeryn glanced behind him at Naraka. "Is it done?"

Naraka shook her head slightly even as she continued to drink. Naraka was fully ashen now and she had not moved since her last outburst. A strange darkness permeated the older vampire's crimson eyes and she sucked more ravenously now—straining desperately to gather every last drop of blood from the younger vampire's body.

Daeryn shuddered—whether in revulsion or excitement, Katja was unsure—and turned back to gaze at the werecat. "Am I so repulsive to you?"

She snarled at him.

With a low moan of anguish, Daeryn lowered his dagger from the princess's neck. Katja rushed forward to touch the blade wound with her paws and skinshifted it closed. As the laceration healed and comprehension began to flood back into Lauraisha's eyes, Katja and the Keystones were jerked backward into Daeryn's icy grip. Zahra leaped forward and pulled the groggy human away from Daeryn even as the vampire shoved the werecat's claws away from her own neck. With a shock, she felt his cool, moist tongue brush along her damp fur to clean her wound even as he pinned her arms behind her back.

"You will not leave me so easily," he whispered as her wounds knit themselves together, once again of their own accord.

She closed her eyes, bracing for the sharp pain when his fangs pierced her neck, but the agony did not come. She stared at him in utter confusion. But Daeryn was looking at the mirror now, not at her. Katja followed his gaze and witnessed the horror of Naraka standing before the Ott vre Cael, bloated and trembling from her recent feeding. With one hand, she gripped the desiccated body of King Kaylor. In the other, she held the drained body of Kyla. She shoved both bodies against the mirror's roiling surface with far more strength than a female her size should possess, and intoned: "Ancient portal of blood and bone, accept my sacrifices to renew your power. The essence of a king once living, now dead; the essence of a queen once living, now undead; and the essence of one princess, once undead, now destroyed, reside within me. Take us for your nourishment! Open wide the threshold forever!"

The mirror's crimson surface darkened as Naraka pushed Kaylor's and Kyla's bodies against it. As the bodies merged into the swirling reflections, Naraka bit her own wrists and pressed her bleeding hands hard against the mirror. Blood flowed into the Ott vre Cael's churning depths through her wounds and then a small point of ruddy light began to grow in the space between her outstretched arms. As it grew larger, Katja realized with growing horror that the light was actually a doorway leading into the same massive black throne room that Daeryn's memories had shown her. Assembled in that throne room and in the corridors beyond were thousands upon thousands of deadwalkers armed for battle. And there, at the head of his army, stood Luther—his fire-damaged wings raised in triumph even as he pressed his blood-smeared hands against the Ott vre Blaec's surface to expand the threshold between the two mirrors.

"It has begun," whispered Daeryn as he gripped the Keystones in his injured hand. He suddenly turned back toward Katja. "I must take you so that he does not," he hissed as he pushed his fangs against the werecat's neck—his eyes burning with a dangerous hunger and an even more desperate fear.

"No!" Felan howled. The great werewolf sprinted forward—his fangs and axe flashing in Daya'lyn's and Lauraisha's hastily kindled flames. Katja heard the distinct twang of Zahra's bow as the dryad let her vine arrows fly. Daeryn's sudden gust of conjured wind knocked the packmates from their feet and sent them and their weapons careening into the hard stone wall on the far side of the room even as he pulled himself and Katja out of harm's way. Vraelth alone remained rooted to the stone where he stood, his steady hum keeping him upright. Daeryn snarled and threw up a wall of solid cloud to blind the charmchanter before he too could interfere. As the sudden darkness enveloped the two of them, Daeryn pulled Katja tight against his hard body—his full fangs urgently seeking her neck.

"Wait," Katja whispered as his mouth brushed against her chin. She leaned forward and kissed him on the flat of his vile yellow fangs just as she had seen Lauraisha do to Daya'lyn. There was no ardent love in her action. Instead, she felt a sudden overwhelming compassion for this male who had lost so much and who was so damaged.

"I forgive you," the wraithwalker told him with her mouth and her mind, pouring truth into her action and her words.

Daeryn's breath caught in his throat and he stared at her in consternation. For a moment, his grip loosened and that was enough. Katja wrenched herself out of his icy grasp and swiped the spear shard and Keystone necklaces from him before rolling to safety under the blinding blanket of fog. The mist abruptly evaporated as Katja came to a shaky stand next to Vraelth and Felan. Daeryn pressed a black-clawed hand to his lips and gazed at her from across the room—his expression unreadable.

"Kyla!" Manasa screamed in anguish as the Ott vre Cael pulled Naraka, Kaylor, and Kyla into itself and gained its final nourishment from their corpses. The Tyglesean guards tightened their protective circle around her.

As the queen wailed, Felan howled in rage and charged Daeryn even as Lauraisha and Zahra began shooting fireballs and vine-tipped arrows at the vampire. Daeryn dove behind a wall of chests and carved stone benches to avoid their wrath.

"Destroy the mirror and protect the Keystones!" Daya'lyn yelled as the profane glass gave a final burst of red light and completed its connection with its mate in Blaecthull. Vraelth and Lauraisha's brothers began hacking at the Ott vre Cael with any and all weapons they possessed.

"Katja, help me destroy this thing!" Daya'lyn shouted as he ran toward the mirror.

As soon as Lauraisha relieved her of the Keystones' weight, the werecat retrieved her bone staff and sprinted toward the mirror—suddenly aware of the monstrous masses marching toward them from just beyond the crimson façade and of Luther strolling between the connecting thresholds toward her. None of the companions' weapons—sunsilver or otherwise—could damage the massive mirror. Its surface repelled every sharp edge and deflected every projectile.

Creator, keep us! We are too late!

She knew she had neither the strength nor the knowledge

to halt this terrible thing that had been set in motion, but she must try—even with her dying breath, she must try.

Creator, what should I do! What can I do!

She gripped her staff for comfort, feeling the slight yield of the bone cradled within her paws. In the distance, she heard Verdagon's roar of despair. He knew what was happening, but the mirror blocked him and his Pyrekin brethren from coming to the Sylvans' aid.

A flicker of dark movement caught the edge of Katja's vision and she turned to gape in horror at Daeryn as he emerged from behind one of the few intact stacks of furniture. Felan lay sprawled on the floor behind him—blood trickling slowly from a gash on the werewolf's neck. The vampire licked his bloody lips as the burns of his body began to heal using the skinshifter's strength.

"What have you done!" Katja screeched as she stared at the werewolf's still body.

"What I must," he retorted grimly.

Zahra screamed in rage and launched her attacks at the male anew.

"Katja!" Daya'lyn yelled. "Help us!"

She stared uncomprehending at the fireforger. Together Daya'lyn and Vraelth had constructed a wall of molten rock, which was pressed against the Ott vre Cael's seething surface. The two mages were straining to keep the flowing magma under control while it, in turn, held Luther and his army at bay within the confines of the mirrors' threshold. The fireforger and the charmchanter had bought the wraithwalker precious time, but to what end?

"*Sandrie!*" Lauraisha's panicked cry and thought pierced Katja's mind and heart.

In the moments that the werecat had been distracted by the mirror, Daeryn had knocked Zahra unconscious and grabbed Lauraisha's youngest brother. With his back against a wall, Daeryn held the seventeen winter-old in a headlock with his fangs poised over the youth's neck.

The cornered vampire snarled at the semicircle of Tygleseans surrounding him. "Give me the Keystones, Lauraisha!"

"No!" she screamed in defiance, clutching the necklace

of stones against her chest and holding her flaming sword protectively in front of her and the unconscious Zahra. The human fireforger's flames were barely golden now.

"I will bite him!" Daeryn hissed.

"I know," she whispered.

Daeryn snarled a curse of frustration and then ripped into the male's neck with his fangs. Sandor screamed as the vampire sucked a long draft of his blood before pulling away and carelessly letting the human's red life cascade down the front of his blue doublet.

Manasa's screams echoed Lauraisha's as Sandor's blood pooled on the floor.

"Think quickly, Lauraisha," the vampire hissed as he began to drag Sandor's body back along the wall with him toward the mirror. "I haven't Turned him yet. There may be time enough yet for Katja to staunch the wound and save him...if you toss me that necklace."

"I cannot!" she cried. Tears cascaded down her face as rapidly as the blood flowing down her brother's chest.

"Very well." He pulled Sandor close and lapped his fill from the gaping gash.

"Stop it! Stop it!" she screamed.

"Stones, Lauraisha!"

"Never!" she said even as the last of her fire died.

Daeryn hissed and threw Sandor's lifeless body into his brothers. With wings unfurled he launched himself at Lauraisha—tackling her and hoisting both of them into the vaulted ceiling under the labored power of his still healing wings.

"Lauraisha!" Daya'lyn roared. In his panic, the lava wall collapsed—spreading molten rock in every direction along the floor. As Daya'lyn spread his wings and flew after them, Vraelth, Manasa, and the guards sprinted wildly out of the way of the molten flow while Katja and Lauraisha's remaining brothers pulled Felan and Zahra out into the hallway to safety.

As Katja worked to skinshift Felan's fang wound closed, she stared back through the doorway to see the furniture all catch fire. Within moments, their flames began licking the wooden support beams of the vaulted roof. In the midst of it all, Daeryn and Lauraisha flew wildly toward the mirror with Daya'lyn flinging fireballs in mad pursuit. When the last of Lauraisha's flames extinguished, so had her strength. She watched Daya'lyn helplessly from her position within Daeryn's firm grasp as they both plunged into the mirror.

"Lauraisha!" The scream echoed from her packmates and family members alike as the pair disappeared into the depths of the mirror. Daya'lyn was forced to pull up short to keep out of the other deadwalkers' reach. Luther was standing behind the mirror's surface so that it shielded him from the lava. He had called a huge herd of zombies forward through the threshold and their shuffling progress covered Daeryn's escape.

"Move!" Luther commanded. The zombies advanced beyond the threshold—groaning as their ragged feet touched the pool of lava. One by one, they caught fire, but they kept moving toward the mirror room's entrance—toward the Keystones.

In one last act of defiance, Lauraisha had tugged open the necklace clasp in Daeryn's grip and scattered the Keystones along the lava-strewn floor just before the pair had plunged into the mirror. The sacred gems now lay sparkling amid the wavering heat.

"Daya'lyn, the stones!" Katja cried.

Luther snarled as the fireforger dove low and plucked the three sacred gems and the signet crest from the smoldering floor.

"Destroy him!" the First Turned screeched at his slaves. Zombies poured out of the mirror—trampling over the tops of their smoldering allies toward safe ground and the packmates.

Daya'lyn dodged high above their flailing arms and weapons—coughing and sputtering amid the smoke of the flaming roof as he held onto the Keystones. With a last desperate effort, he rammed his flaming sunsilver staff into a sagging section of roof. The force of his thrust was enough to cause the collapse not only that section but of most of the rest of the room's ceiling as well. Katja watched in horror as the fireforger and zombies alike were buried under the flaming rubble.

"Daya'lyn!"

"Katja, you must destroy that mirror!" Vraelth said from behind her.

The werecat turned to stare at the elf in shock. "But Lauraisha…"

"If you don't, we'll all die or be Turned and no one can help her then! Destroy it!"

"I don't know how!"

Vraelth frowned at her. "Of course you do! The others told me how you rebuilt the Ott vre Caerwyn from thousands of shattered pieces in a mere moment. Surely you could cause the reverse of that event if you wished."

"How?"

"Use the Caerwyn shards."

Katja looked down at the broken spear shards dangling on her chest and the Ott vre Caerwyn embedded within the two pieces. She felt the spear shards warm against her chest as she looked at them. A soft whisper met her ears: "Command us!"

"How do I destroy the Ott vre Cael?" she asked the shards.

"Such a mirror may only be destroyed by a wraithwalker in possession of sunsilver, a bloodstone, the blood of an Unturned being, and the bones of a dragon."

Katja stared at her bone staff and the bloodstone shards in sudden comprehension. "Tell me what to do!"

"Command us to reform ourselves and we will do so."

"Reform, then!"

As she held her and Daeryn's halves of the sunsilver spearhead together, the Ott vre Caerwyn shards embedded in their centers liquefied and then merged together into a single piece within the spearhead.

"What now?"

"Attach us to the end of your staff. When you are ready, prick your paw with the spearhead's tip and then strike the center of the Ott vre Cael's surface with us."

Katja stood on shaky legs and gripped the spear with a bleeding paw. Between her and the mirror lay the smoking rubble of the caved-in roof and the twitching bodies of burnt zombies. Luther was readying his second wave of invaders as she wove between the burning wreckage and charged the length of the room. What little color there was immediately drained from the Víchí Elder's scarred face as she approached. When she saw him, Katja gave voice to her defiance and her rage. Her roar caused even the mirror's surface to recoil.

"Stop her!" he hissed.

"Lauraisha, forgive me!" she said as she took aim and threw the shard-encrusted spear at the center of Ott vre Cael's undulating surface. The mirror bowed and rippled inward around the spearhead as the dragon-bone staff plunged beneath the Tainted reflection's surface. With the sound of a thousand simultaneous screams, the mirror shattered outward—spraying the room with its sharp shards. Instinctively, Katja dropped to the floor and covered her face and chest with her paws and arms. The force of the mirror's explosion knocked her backward into a nearby pile of debris— snapping her head back against something hard.

"Katja!" Felan roared.

Through her dimming vision, the bleeding werecat saw the werewolf as he desperately crawled through the splinters and shards toward her, his neck wrapped in one of Vraelth's shoddy tourniquets.

Tears formed in Katja's eyes when she realized that the werewolf was still alive.

"I love you," she whispered to him just before she lost consciousness.

* * *

Blackness pervaded Katja's senses for what seemed a long time. The darkness carried neither painful memories nor hideous nightmares, nor really any feeling at all. That numbness was a strange comfort to her. For a fleeting moment, she wondered if she were dead. But, no, this wasn't the Wraith Realm or the Dyvesé Realm or even the ruined place beyond Edgewater. And only when the darkness ended and her vision brightened to a scene unlike any that she had ever expected, did Katja realize that she was once again sharing another being's awareness...

*

The wraithwalker saw Luther and Daeryn standing in the middle of a dark cave—the likes of which she had never seen.

Luther was shrieking in rage as Daeryn stood bruised and bloody before him—his expression unreadable.

"...Not even one Keystone! You couldn't bring me one!" Luther snarled curses at him. His black claws suddenly encircled Daeryn's neck and dragged the younger male off of his feet. "You were supposed to bring the changeling wraithwalker to me! I wanted Kevros and Devra's daughter, not this useless Tyglesean brat!"

Daeryn stared at him in defiance even as he struggled for breath. "Lauraisha is Katja's dearest friend...the one she willingly tried to give...her own life to save..." Luther's grip loosened slightly so that Daeryn could speak. "As long as the princess remains a Blaecthull prisoner, the werecat will come for her, High Elder. She must."

The Víchí High Elder hissed "She had better!" into the other vampire's face before flicking him backward into a wall. Luther stalked out of the room, spitting obscenities.

Daeryn lay dazed against the wall for a long time, sputtering and coughing. When he was finally able to regain his feet, he strode purposely to the opposite side of the room. He stared down at Lauraisha as she sat bound in water chains, her mouth covered with a filthy rag. Silent tears streamed down her face and she rocked back and forth like an angry child. He frowned, bent down, and jerked the gag from her lips.

"He's not gone... He's not gone... He's not gone..." she muttered before he replaced the gag and stood again— absently licking his fangs as he watched her.

"Why did you bring her here, Daeryn?" a quiet voice asked from the shadows.

The male turned toward the far corner of the room, his expression softening into one of immeasurable sadness.

"Are you well?" he asked as he bent down in front of the human woman who was also bound in water chains.

The woman gave no reply, but watched him steadily until he finally answered. "Lauraisha is the key, Mother. Neither Katja nor Dayalan will be able to resist coming after Luther now that he has her. Luther believes that Katja is the fulfillment of prophesy...that she is the Discerner and the Daughter of the Manticore—that the two prophesies actually align." He frowned in thought. "If Luther is correct, what would be the connotations of that?"

She shook her head and looked over at Lauraisha. "Who exactly is she?"

"She is now the only surviving princess of Tyglesea. The last I knew, she is now fourth in line for the throne," Daeryn replied as he watched the young female.

"And is it true that you killed her brother?" Marga asked him.

Daeryn's crimson eyes widened in surprise.

"What?" Marga snapped at him. "Did you think that because she is gagged that she cannot communicate? She is a dreamdrifter mage as well as a fireforger, Daeryn. One of the more powerful I have seen. And not even this room with all its layered curses can dampen such a dreamdrifter's skills. We have shared dreams ever since she first arrived!"

Daeryn's sigh was weary. "I took the life of Prince Sandor while in combat, yes."

Marga gave him a knowing nod. "Don't lie to me; I saw how he died."

Daeryn hissed at her. "And I suppose you also saw the fact that your precious favored son is the Sylvans' new Inquisitor—now intent on slaughtering all of the vampires, including his own brother?"

Marga shook her head. "You have brought his wrath upon your own head by casting your lot with Luther. And I do not choose favorites."

"No, of course not. That would be my falíchí quisling of a birth father."

"How dare you disrespect your father! Caleb and I gave up everything to see to it that you and your brother were raised under protection from those who would harm you—or worse, use you! And this is how you repay us? By Turning? By murdering? By becoming one of the very monsters that we fought against for centuries?"

"I am not a monster!" Daeryn roared. He shut his eyes and breathed deeply for a few moments to regain control of his rage. "Am I not still loyal to you, Mother? Whether you would see it or not, I love you. I always have and I always will. I Turned myself because there was no other way I could protect you!"

Marga shook her head sadly. "No, son, you Turned yourself because you crave power above all else in this world—over honor, loyalty, or even love. You did not Turn to protect me, you used my imprisonment as an excuse to dabble with the darkness that so entices you. You have failed where your brother has succeeded. Despite his many faults, Dayalan knows true love. You once loved just as he, but now that ardent light has been all but smothered by the twisted shadow of your lust."

The sound of Daeryn's slap across Marga's jaw echoed across the small dungeon chamber. They stared at each other as Marga's cheek began to redden and swell. Daeryn swallowed hard and turned away—his yellow fangs lengthening and his black-clawed hands shaking as he shoved open the chamber's heavy iron door and strode out of the dungeon.

*

Katja awoke from the dream to find herself facing a nightmare of different proportions. She was lying on a thin mattress on the hard stone floor in between Daya'lyn and Felan. The three of their makeshift beds were lined up along the wall of a long, wide corridor with hundreds of other injured Sylvans. A sharp pain shot through the left side of her chest with each breath she took. The werecat frowned and felt that side of her body with her bandaged paw—hissing suddenly at the heightened pain.

"Katja, stop pressing on your broken ribs," Daya'lyn growled as he slowly sat upright and rubbed his haggard face.

The werecat squinted at him. "What happened?"

The male arched his white eyebrows at her. "From what I was told, you stopped the deadwalker invasion of Tyglesea... and nearly managed to kill yourself in the process. I am fairly certain that there were more shards of the Ott vre Cael lodged in your body than there were left in the rest of the bloody mirror chamber."

Katja stared at the bandage on her right paw. "Why did I not simply skinshift my wounds closed?"

"You were too injured. Felan did his best to stop some of the bleeding, but that was all he could manage before fainting.

Neither of you are in the best of health." Daya'lyn winced as he shifted his right arm in its bloody sling. "Nor am I."

"What happened to you?"

"I broke my left arm, wing, and clavicle when the roof collapsed." He shook his head. "I am just grateful the injuries weren't worse."

"Is Felan...?"

"Zahra told me that neither of you suffered serious cases of Taint infection." The dhampir shook his head. "I still have no idea how that is even possible. In any event, Felan should be fine with a few weeks' rest to mend the last of his broken bones, just as you will be.

"Zahra was less than pleased with him for crawling through all of the sharp debris to try to heal you after the mirror's explosion, though." Daya'lyn gazed at her for a long moment. When he spoke again, his voice was soft. "I told you he loved you."

Katja bit her lip at the sudden tears standing in the male's eyes. "I'm sorry, Daya'lyn. I failed. I tried to protect her and I failed."

He shook his head slowly. "We all failed her. Lauraisha did not deserve this...any of this. She did not deserve to see one sibling Turned or another die any more than you did. And now, Lauraisha is alone. She must bear her grief and her fear alone thanks to Daeryn..." The male snarled in sudden rage and frustration. "How I despise him!"

Katja cocked her head to one side and frowned as she watched him—remembering what Daeryn had shown her in the mirror room before his attempted Turning. "I don't."

He turned back to her. "Why?"

She told him of Daeryn's memories.

"They're lies!" he roared, loudly enough to wake Felan.

The startled werewolf sat up quickly and then, after realizing there was no immediate danger, laid gingerly back against his mat and growled at the two of them. "Daya'lyn, don't yell! I just about skinshifted in my sleep!"

"Sorry," the fireforger mumbled.

The werewolf held a paw out to Katja. "You're finally awake."

She took it and held it to her cheek, fighting back tears as she felt the warmth of his fur against her own. When Felan saw the sad smile on Daya'lyn's face, he gently cupped Katja's cheek and then pulled his paw away. "What were the two of you discussing, anyway?"

Katja repeated what she had learned from Daeryn and explained what happened while the others were blinded by Daeryn's fog bank.

Felan's expression grew more and more troubled as he listened. After a long silence, he asked, "Could you discern any falsehood in him?"

Katja shook her head. "There was none. He showed me the whole truth—at least, what he absolutely believes to be the truth, anyway. He kept nothing hidden from me." She shuddered. "It was beyond unnerving."

Daya'lyn scratched the pale stubble on his chin in thought. It was strange to see him unshaven and Katja wondered how long the three of them had stayed in this hall. She looked around, desperate to change the subject. "Where is Zahra?"

"Since she and Vraelth are in much better health than the three of us, they are helping with the war effort," Felan said quietly. "Vraelth has been aiding the masons in their repairs to Castle Summersted and to the city at large, while Zahra and Saldis have been busy combining their knowledge of herbal remedies and poultices to help heal the infirm. Queen Manasa and Prince Ashomocos have set the castle in order by surrendering to the besieging Sylvan Orders and drying out the castle's lower levels." The werewolf sighed. "Finally, Prince Tryntin is currently helping our allies round up every last deadwalker in the country. Any deadwalkers that they find are being incarcerated down in the dried-out Summersted dungeon pits with plenty of sunsilver-wielding guards to keep them contained. The queen awaits the time when Mage Inquisitor Daya'lyn is strong enough to hold a proper Witch Trial and execute them. I expect that it will be the first legitimate Witch Trial in Tyglesea in decades."

Daya'lyn nodded and then winced. "That will be a few days, I think."

Felan grunted. "More like a moon-cycle or two, my friend."

Katja looked around the hall and then down at her own

wounds. The number of broken bodies lying in that hallway was staggering, and they reminded her of the 194 werecats that she and her brother Kayten had laid to rest in the amphitheater of their own village after the Feliconas Massacre at the beginning of this horrific war. She squinted her eyes shut, suddenly overwhelmed by the amount of suffering. "Is this the only healing ward?"

The werewolf shook his head. "Zahra told me that Queen Manasa had to convert the entire wing of guest chambers into another area just like this one. They have Zahra and Saldis running ragged."

Hot tears trickled slowly through the werecat's golden fur. Felan put a paw over hers as the tears rolled down her cheeks. She wished more than anything that he could hold her in his arms, but both of them were far too injured for that.

"We have lost so much in the battle for our freedom," she whispered as she looked at Felan.

"And the war is far from over," Daya'lyn replied, as the males also shed their tears.

XXV

THE MANTICORE'S DAUGHTER

Katja stared over Castle Summersted's scarred battlements at the crumbled buildings of Kaylere. The once glorious merchant district had been reduced to rubble during the short deadwalker occupation and the subsequent siege by Sylvans. She shook her head at the devastation, angry once again at the dead King Kaylor for allowing such disaster to befall his country. The dead king's wife and sons had worn the indigo hues of mourning for most of the last moon-cycle and yet, as Ashomocos had once explained to her, they wore their dark doublets and sashes is a sign of sorrow more over the losses of Kyla and Sandor and possibly Lauraisha than for Kaylor.

Despite its outward devastation, the Tyglesean capital seemed a brighter and much happier place now that its tyrannical king was dead and gone. The Ott vre Cael's destruction had eliminated the threat of direct deadwalker invasion—either in small numbers as had first been the case through the initial experiments, or en masse thanks to Naraka and Kyla's later efforts.

With the last of the Asheken deadwalkers either destroyed or pushed east out of the country, Katja saw with a small smile that the merchants had set up temporary tents among the ruins even as masons and other craftsmen worked at the queen's command and out of the generosity of the royal treasury to rebuild their shops and stalls. Normalcy was slowly returning to the kingdom after almost forty winters of human and inhuman oppression.

This peace, however, had come at a steep price. Over three thousand Tygleseans and eight thousand Sylvans in total had given their lives to secure the country from the Tyglesean tyrant and his Asheken allies. The pyres aboard the funeral barges had lit up the night sea for a fortnight after the final siege at Summersted. Their acrid smoke had burned such an acute memory in Katja's mind that she had had to turn away a few days later when Sylvan Inquisitor Daya'lyn had pronounced his final judgment on the remaining captive deadwalkers and set fire to the barge imprisoning the screeching monsters.

"For you, Lauraisha," the male had whispered as they watched the smoldering wooden barge sink beneath the salty waves of the Westylere Sea.

Katja shook herself to clear her troubled thoughts, and moved away from her crouched position on the battlements to stand with her packmates as they discussed the business of the day.

"...There is still much work to be done," Ashomocos was saying. "The craftsmen tell me that it will take another month or two for the merchant district to be repaired to the point of complete functionality, even with the continued aid of those charmchanters who have elected to stay"—he nodded to Vraelth in gratefulness—"and help us with the reconstruction efforts.

"In the meantime, I have had to segregate all of the intact portions of the city to reduce the amount of racial conflicts. After decades of living with racial purity, my fellow Tygleseans are adjusting very poorly to the recent influx of Sylvan Order immigrants. Violence has been particularly bad toward the ogres and werewolves." The prince shook his head. "We are not Vihous, and therefore our minds cannot be opened to such diversity of thought and culture in a single month."

Katja snorted. "Mine was, and so was your youngest sister's."

Ashomocos frowned back her. "True, but the two of you had no choice in the matter. You either adapted or you died. Tygleseans largely feel that the danger posed by the deadwalkers has passed and, therefore, they see little need to continue their alliances with the other races."

Felan shook his head. "The danger hasn't passed. We may have crippled Luther's invasion plan and driven his forces toward the eastern side of the continent once again, but deadwalkers will continue to invade as long as the Sphinx's Gape remains open."

The Prince Regent nodded. "I know, which is why I will commit the best of the remaining Tyglesean troops to the cause as soon as my coronation ceremony is complete. In the meantime, my mother has granted temporary refuge in this city for all Sylvans who fought for our freedom regardless of race. I will see to it that one of my first acts as king will be to give permanence to that decree."

"The King's Council members will not approve of those decisions," Daya'lyn said.

"Bleed the council!" Ashomocos snapped, his eyes smoldering with sudden anger. "I'll not take part in another reign like my fa…like Kaylor's!"

"It is a wise resolution, Your Highness, not to be like him," Verdagon said as he perched upon the Summersted battlements with his barb-tipped tail curled around a half-ruined tower for added balance. "However, for the sake of diplomacy, I suggest that you begin your dealings with the advisors to the crown with a gentle touch. They are far too used to your father flippantly ignoring their guidance and reducing their status to that of mere figureheads instead of true patrons to their represented peoples. Therefore, if you genuinely consider their opinions, you will gain their trust and win their allegiance much more easily. Even at thirty-two winters, you are still young and you will need wise counsel to help govern your country. Why not use the councilors' considerable experience to your advantage?"

Ashomocos studied the dragon before inclining his head. "So be it, My Sir."

Zahra turned her gaze from Ashomocos to Verdagon. "Is there any way to close the Sphinx's Gape?"

Verdagon shook his massive head. "No, not with the Sphinx now dead. Canuche's visions, as shown to me through Lauraisha's and Katja's dreams, have proven that. The Race Founder's rotting corpse has made an unbroken bridge between the continents, one which must be burned away before we can hope to seal the isthmus again."

"What can be done to rescue Lauraisha?" Daya'lyn asked.

The dragon shook his head. "Without knowing her whereabouts for certain, there is little that we can do to recover her."

Katja frowned. The dream showing Daeryn's exchanges with Luther, Lauraisha, and Marga revisited her memory with such vivid detail that she realized she could not have imagined it. The dream had been real and yet the werecat wondered how she possibly could have witnessed events that had clearly occurred in Blaecthull. Had Lauraisha somehow dreamdrifted the memories to her? That seemed highly unlikely given the expansive distance between Luther's stronghold and Castle Summersted in Tyglesea. The werecat shook her head in confusion.

Verdagon was looking at her. "What is it, Katja?"

"I know where Lauraisha is, although I'm not sure how or why," she replied. Quickly she recounted the full dream to the others.

"So Lauraisha is grieving alone in a Blaecthull dungeon?" Ashomocos asked.

The werecat shook her head. "No, not alone. Marga is with her."

Vraelth frowned. "Yes, but will that fact offer either of them protection?"

Katja again recounted the memories that Daeryn had shared with her before he had tried to bite her in the mirror room.

"Do not believe a word my treacherous brother says, Katja," Daya'lyn snarled. "He was lying to gain your trust."

But the wraithwalker merely shook her head. "As I've told you before, Daya'lyn, I tested his soul and mind. There was no lie when he showed me those things. Your brother was noble and honorable once. Even though he has corrupted himself now, a small part of his loyalty still remains."

"If that is the case, then we have some hope left," Felan said. "Provided Marga can keep Daeryn in check."

Katja scratched her furry cheek in thought. "What did Daeryn mean when he said that I might fulfill and align two prophesies by being the Discerner as well as the Daughter of the Manticore? I know the prophecy about the Discerner being of integral importance in uniting the Keystones, but I don't remember ever hearing of a prophesy involving a 'Daughter of the Manticore.'"

"Nor have I," Daya'lyn said as Vraelth, Zahra, and Ashomocos all shook their heads.

"I have, Katja," Felan said.

The werecat turned sharply to stare at the werewolf from where he sat on the stone watching the others. Immediately she regretted the action as it tweaked her still sore ribs and neck. She held her throbbing ribs with one paw and hissed. Never in her life had she wished for a full moon to come as quickly as the one occurring tonight. She needed its light to strengthen her skinshifting ability so that she could finally heal the last of her wretched injuries and be free of this accursed pain.

Felan put a gentle paw on her shoulder. "I found a reference to a 'True Daughter of the Manticore' and a 'True Son of the Sphinx' while studying at the Mage Citadel on the Isle of Summons. It involves the prediction that two descendants of the Manticore and the Sphinx might one day breed true and that the True Daughter of the Manticore and the True Son of the Sphinx would help to finally overthrow Luther's domination."

The werecat frowned at him. "What do you mean breed true?"

Felan shook his head. "No one is quite certain. The general consensus among mage scholars is that there would be the birth of a werewolf who would possess the human-like head, wolf body, and eagle-like wings of our races' Sphinx ancestor, as well as a liopion or werecat who would possess the human head, lion-like body, and scorpion-tail characteristics of our races' Manticore ancestor."

Vraelth frowned at him. "Why would Luther think that Katja is the Daughter of the Manticore when she was born with neither of those features?"

"For the same reason that I do; she can skinshift," Felan replied. "There is a small contingent of mages who believe that the Daughter of the Manticore and the Son of the Sphinx could actually be a pair of skinshifters who were powerful enough to transform at will into a full Manticore and Sphinx rather than either actually being born as such. In fact, the belief is held by so few that I have seen only one such mention of it. It's actually in the book about skinshifting I gave to you before your journey here, Katja."

The werewolf's face grew from thoughtful to angry. "I discovered the reference on the night that Perefaris attacked Zahra and we had to destroy a pack of deadwalkers within the very halls of the Mage Citadel." He took a deep breath and let it out slowly. "I had thought little about the implications of that passage until a few moon-cycles ago, when, after seasons and seasons of perfected practice, my skinshifting routine suddenly changed."

He considered the werecat for a long moment before asking, "If I'm not mistaken, Katja, you have also experienced a full moon that caused you to skinshift into an odd combination of human and lioness."

She stared at him and slowly nodded, remembering her bizarre transformation while she, Lauraisha, and Daya'lyn had been camped beside Azuralle Lake in the naiads' territory. "I thought that it was a byproduct of the skinshifting madness," she said. "That perhaps Daeryn was attempting to gain control of my transformations for his own purposes."

Felan shook his head. "While he did likely manipulate you, I think the events also speak to something even deeper than that—especially since I too have been unable to control my own transformations."

"How do you explain it, then?"

The male frowned in thought and then looked up at Verdagon. The dragon gave a slight nod of his large, armored head.

Felan turned back to Katja. "If Luther is correct and you are the Daughter of the Manticore, then it would be reasonable to assume that you would physically manifest that fact in some way."

"Like skinshifting madness?"

"Not of the kind you experienced at the Citadel, Katja," Verdagon answered. "What happened to you then was caused by Daeryn breaking through your mental defenses when you were naturally vulnerable during your skinshift. That being said, I think Daeryn's mental presence during your recent skinshifts has done something to spur your transformations and this fact, in turn, has caused both you and Felan to experience a shift in prophesy that has driven your more powerful skinshifting abilities to the surface of your souls and minds. I have known for a while that neither of you had reached the height of your abilities, but what that apex is I cannot be sure."

Felan looked back at Katja. "Do you have the skinshifter book with you?"

She pulled the Mage Citadel library book out of her rucksack and gave it to the werewolf. He thumbed past the scrap of parchment marking the place where she'd stopped reading and flipped to a page at the back of the book.

The werewolf spoke: "'When I rise again, I will share my fire with my followers and bring devastation upon the bloodlines of Blaecthull through seven Keystone-wielding mages. You will meet your day of destruction when you see the red sun set and the blood moon rise behind the silhouettes of the Son of the Sphinx and the Daughter of the Manticore, Luther.'"

Aribem's prophetic words raised the hackles on Katja's neck.

"There is a note here explaining that this prophesy is actually a vow that Aribem supposedly made to Luther just before the First Fireforger committed Crawhmongue and split the Northern and Southern Continents with his fire."

"But do you really think that the last part of that prophesy refers to you and me, Felan?" the werecat asked.

Felan shrugged. "At the very least, Luther seems to think it refers to you, and that fact explains why he has been so desperate to capture you in the first place. Even if he had not realized that you were a skinshifter in the beginning, the fact that you were Kevros and Devra's daughter would have made him wary enough to want to destroy you and your siblings just to end that potential threat. In any event, if we can indeed transform into such powerful beings as a sphinx and a manticore instead of simply being two of the Founders' eventual offspring, I expect that the initial transformations would likely be too overwhelming for us to control—just as skinshifting was difficult to control when we first began to do it."

Katja groaned and flicked her ears. "I hope not. I've had a painful enough time trying to learn how to use the ability in the first place."

Felan nodded in sympathy. "As did I before my father mentored me. Nonetheless that seems to be what is happening. Our skinshifting is overwhelming our minds and manifesting its power in unpredictable transformations."

"So how do we remedy that?" the werecat asked.

Again Felan looked to Verdagon.

"For the present, I suggest sealing each of you inside one of the intact archery towers from dusk until dawn so that you can both skinshift in safety and seclusion until you can learn to once again master your skills," the dragon said. "I can be with you to help guard your minds against skinshifting madness while you experiment with your abilities, but it will ultimately be up to each of you to prove whether or not you are indeed the true Son of the Sphinx and Daughter of the Manticore."

"When do we begin?" asked Felan.

"When the full moon has reached its height in the sky tonight, you will be at your strongest. Attempt the changes, then."

Felan and Katja both nodded.

Verdagon sighed. "Ashomocos, will you see to the necessary preparations?"

The human bowed. "Of course, Your Excellency."

The dragon nodded and then turned to gaze at the early afternoon sun. "Good, let us continue our aid efforts until evening. Then we shall see what prophesies hold true."

Verdagon dismissed the companions who all returned to their allotted tasks: Ashomocos to his council meetings, Zahra to her herbal remedy making, Vraelth to his masonry, Felan and Daya'lyn to the continued training of new Castle Guard recruits, and Katja to her skinshifter's healing for those still injured from the recent battles.

* * *

That evening a great feast was held in the Great Hall. Katja and Felan, however, both shunned the festivities in favor of spending an evening alone together in the castle gardens. They had had so little time to themselves during Kaylor's downfall and the interim reconstruction of the Tyglesean capital city. There was always some responsibility that called their attention. But, finally, the pair took this quiet moment to sit together on the stone bench beside the central water fountain.

"Are you nervous about tonight?" Felan asked.

"A little. I wish you were able to be there with me."

Felan nodded. "I do too. Even so, I won't be far away."

"I know…"

They sat together in silence for a time until Felan finally turned to her. "What are you so worried about, Mith vil Perle?"

She looked at him with sudden tears in her eyes. "You."

The werewolf frowned.

"Felan, the night that the Clan Shamgar ogres adopted me, I dreamed of you and Zahra and Qenethala. I saw Zahra's near-death and the lengths that you went to while trying to save her."

"If you saw what happened, then you know that it was Vraelth and Verdagon who saved her, not me."

"Yes, but you told her that you loved her!"

The werewolf was still frowning. "Of course, I did because I do. Zahra is a closer sister to me than even my own flesh-and-blood sister, and she knows that."

Katja shook her head. "But she is still in love with you. She wants you as her lifemate."

Comprehension dawned in his eyes. "You're jealous."

A flash of sudden anger overwhelmed Katja's mind, and the reaction made her pause in consternation. *Am I?* When she finally nodded, a small smile creased the werewolf's lips.

"You needn't be."

"Why?"

He sighed. "Zahra has loved me a long time. She was beyond wounded when we annulled our betrothal in front of her mother before we left the Glen to guard you and Lauraisha during your journey to the Isle of Summons. I sent a letter explaining the annulment to my family and clan once

I began training on the isle. My father's reply was less than accepting of the decision. He and my mother were furious. A union between Zahra and me would have created an even more powerful alliance between the Zolaramie Tribe and the Geirgerd Clan and they couldn't fathom why I would quit such a match. Still I, in good conscience, couldn't choose Zahra as a lifemate when I didn't love her with the depth that a soulmate should."

"Do they know about your affections for me?" Katja asked.

He shook his head. "Not unless Zahra or Zahlathra have mentioned you to them. I doubt that has happened though. Zahra didn't even want to tell *me* about your talents as a skinshifter. As it turns out, she did see you as a potential rival for my affections. You are the being who completes me, not her. That realization pained her far more than I had ever understood. Our last night with Qenethala finally forced me realize it. She thought that my choosing you meant that she was losing me, even as a friend. If Vraelth hadn't been there to pull her out of the tree and out of her melancholy, I don't know what we would have done."

He sighed again. "It will take her a long time to recover from the grief of losing Qenethala, but at least Zahra has finally found her match and he has added some much needed joy back into her life."

He pointed a clawed finger across the castle grounds toward a pair of figures walking hand in hand in the waning daylight. Katja smiled as she saw Vraelth stop in the shadow of a wall and pull Zahra to him, stealing a kiss from her, before they walked on laughing and talking.

"Is he good for her?" Katja asked.

Felan nodded. "Vraelth is a good male—complicated, but good."

"That does not exactly set him apart from the rest of us."

"No, it does not. His sad story matches those of the rest of our pack well. He has spent most of his life being overlooked in favor of beings far less noble and far more self-important. Then Verdagon chose him as herald and he became a member of the Inquisition. Now strangers fawn over him." The werewolf sighed. "Both situations have been difficult for him to bear, but he has dealt with them graciously."

Katja watched the pair disappear around the corner of a building and then turned back to Felan with guilt and joy warring in her expression. "I am sorry for being jealous."

His expression was mischief itself as he smiled at her. "Thank you, but I find your jealousy over me intensely satisfying."

Katja grinned and then grew serious as she rested her head on Felan's broad shoulder. "These past moons have been a torment without you."

He slipped his arms around her as he nodded. "Yes, they have been, but no longer."

She leaned further into his soft, dark fur—slowly breathing in the precious scent of him as they cuddled. Felan kissed the top of her head before leaning back to study her with his magnificent emerald-azure eyes. "During your reading, did you ever find the special note that I left for you in the pages of your skinshifting book?"

She gazed at him. "I found a note that said, 'I love you.'"

His eyes twinkled. "Yes, that one."

"I love you too."

He smiled as he leaned down to brush her lips with his own. The contact made her giddy. She pressed her maw hard against his in response. She felt Felan's strong arms tighten around her even as she encircled his neck with her paws. Felan growled low as her strong, small body pressed against the hard muscles of his chest. Sudden passion flared between them as they kissed, causing each to remain oblivious to the sound of approaching footsteps along the cobblestone walkway leading to their section of the garden.

Ashomocos cleared his throat uncomfortably. "I am sorry to interrupt, but it is time."

With one last kiss, the two skinshifters stood together and followed him out of the castle gardens. As the sun began to dip toward the endless waves on the western horizon, Ashomocos led Katja and Felan up the steps of the outer ward wall. He led them to one of the towers and unlocked its massive door with a key from the ring on his belt.

"I had provisions laid out for each of you in your respective sequester chambers," he said after he swung open the door.

Katja stared past him into the small supply room, which was usually used to house shifts of archers while they protected the castle from besiegers. There was a small blanket-covered cot huddled against one round side of the tower opposite a pair of outward-facing arrow slits looking northeast over the city and the coastline. A large slab of raw meat sat on a platter atop a rough stone table built into the far side of the room close to a second pair of arrow-slit windows. A wooden stool stood on one side of the table and twin casks of mead and well water stood on the other. Pangs of sorrow and delight rushed through Katja as the provisions reminded her of the supplies found in the main den of her family home.

"I know it isn't much, but I hope it will suffice for the night," Ashomocos said as he handed her his lantern.

"It's perfect," she whispered and bowed low to the prince. "Thank you."

She turned to embrace Felan, who kissed her and held her tight for a moment before she stepped into the chamber.

"Just remember that Verdagon is on watch and I will be but a few bounds away if you have trouble," Felan said by way of farewell.

Katja smiled and arched an eyebrow. "And what will you do? Break down the door if I need you?"

Felan returned her smile. "Always."

When Ashomocos had locked and secured the tower door, Katja sighed. The werecat snuffed out the lantern flame so that its light would not interfere with the summer moon's glow and sat down at the table. The sun had set under the waters of the Westylere Sea by the time she had finished her evening eat.

As dusk turned to dark and the full moon finally won the heavens, Katja moved to sit on the soft blankets underneath the northern arrow slits. She felt the strength and will to skinshift unlock inside her soul. She stubbornly refused to allow herself to transform, however, and continued to wait as the moon climbed the sky. She could not see the moon from her place inside the tower, but she could feel its influence over her growing stronger. She gripped the mortared stones in front of her in an effort to stave off the change and then, when she could no longer resist it, she finally let herself skinshift.

The skinshifter lay back on top of the pile of blankets covering the cot and let the moonlight bathe her changing body. She gritted her fangs as her skin began to itch in a thousand places simultaneously, and then suddenly shed her fur all at once. Even as she wiped away the golden hair still clinging to her sweaty skin, she felt her flat nose bulge on her face and her rounded ears slide down the sides of her head. She wrapped a blanket around her trembling body even as she felt the sensitivity ebb from her nose, ears, and her golden-green eyes. Then her paws reformed into human hands and feet and then, strangely, reverted to clawed paws again just after the rest of her head became human.

Katja stared down at herself in the moonlight filtering through the arrow slits. Even though she was furless, she had kept her werecat form, including her prehensile tail. Her head was the only thing human about her. As she stared quizzically at her furless tail, the appendage began to ache. It throbbed dully at first, but then with an increasingly sharp intensity. Again Katja gritted her fangs—which had not changed—in agony as the base of her tail thickened and then flattened out. The pale skin hardened and darkened until it formed overlapping plates along the length of Katja's tail. Then the thickened skin plates spread up her spine and across her abdomen to the rest of her body. The skinshifter threw off her blanket wrap and stared in disbelief as her body took a form startlingly similar to the girtab Aria's. Thick coal-black plates covered every area of her body except for her human-like head. Katja stared slack-jawed at her tail as its segmented and curled up behind her. The tail's tip bulged and then tapered to form a scorpion's hooked stinger. As the final plates hardened into position, Katja felt a tickling sensation replace the pain. She watched as golden fur once again sprouted across the tops of her skin plates to cover her in warmth once more. As the moonlight bathed her, Katja's ears and nose changed once again—resuming their former positions and shapes. Finally her senses, which had been mercifully muted throughout the process, regained—and then surpassed—their former efficacy.

The full moon sat in the center of the sky when Katja finally finished her skinshift. She crouched on the blanket-covered cot and stared at her transformed body. Slowly, she put a clawed paw against her ribs. They no longer hurt. Although the change had left her exhausted, she no longer felt the ache of any of her half-healed wounds from the Ott vre Cael skirmish. Not only had her body's transformation healed the last of her injuries, it had made her stronger. Katja flexed the retractable claws of her paws and marveled at their sharpness.

At the sound of Felan's howl and Verdagon's bugle, the manticore smiled and then added her roaring voice to their chorus of triumph. She stood staring through the arrow slit out across the moonlit sea toward the north—the claws of her scared right paw digging deep gouges into the chiseled stone in front of her.

"*I am coming for you,*" the Manticore's Daughter purred with both mouth and mind.

* * *

In an underground dungeon on the Northern Continent far away from Katja's moonlit chamber, a human dreamdrifter ceased her endless troubled rocking. Ignoring the pain of her water chains, Lauraisha sat upright away from the slimy stone wall and cocked her head to one side, listening as a faint whisper broke the silence of her captivity.

* * *

In an opulent bedchamber several floors above the dreamdrifter, a vampire shade sat bolt upright on his silken sheets. He heard the manticore's words in the depths of his dreams just as Lauraisha did and the power of the wraithwalker's voice had caused cold beads of sweat to trace their way down the pale length of his spine.

* * *

In the same moment, Lauraisha and Daeryn answered Katja: "*I know.*"

CHARACTERS

PRONUNCIATION GUIDE AND GLOSSARY

Aaron (ĀR-on): Erdeken human; the only mage prophet to ever correctly predict that Aribem's fiery death would destroy a third of the deadwalker hordes and split the continents.

The Abomination (ah-BOM-i-nā-shuhn): Drosskin drake; a powerful Litkyn who rebelled against the Creator and was cast to the fringes of the Wraith Realm as punishment for his betrayal. He then enslaved a Pyrekin dragon and used his body to host the Darkkyn's own corrupted soul, thus creating the first Drosskin drake.

King Aedus (Ā-dus): Erdeken human; the king of Tyglesea at the time of the Tyglesean Uprisings. Kaylor slew King Aedus and his family when he usurped the Tyglesean throne.

Alqama (AL-kahm-ah): Asheken hag; a hag who was originally beholden to the powerful vampire Lothian, who died during the Second War of Ages. Alqama stole her Víchí master's bloodstone and used its magic to help her survive the deadwalker purges after the war. Eventually she was able to build the Hag's Nest island fortress in a secluded part of the River Ehud. She existed largely unharmed on the Southern Continent for several centuries until allied Sylvan forces destroyed her and her allies during the Third War of Ages.

The Arbitrator (AR-bi-trā-tor): Erdeken, unknown race;

one of the seven mages prophesied to bring about Luther's destruction through use of the Twelve Keystones.

Aria (AR-ee-ah): Erdeken girtab, also called a werescorpion; Daughter of Paraburus who lives at Caerwyn Castle under Caleb's protection. The venom from Aria's scorpion-like tail can be used to help mitigate the effects of Asheken Taint.

Aribem (ĀR-i-bem): Erdeken human; the first fireforger mage ever to exist. He taught his followers how to forge mage fire and use it to destroy deadwalkers. His sacrificial death during a fight with Luther caused the split of the Northern and Southern continents and the formation of the Nyghe sol Dyvesé Mountains.

Arlis (AR-lis): Erdeken human; King Aedus's valet who dies while helping the king's daughter Laura escape Castle Summersted during the Tyglesean Uprisings.

Ashomocos, Ash (ah-SHOH-moh-kohs): Erdeken human; nicknamed Ash by his siblings, Ashomocos is the first son and first-born child to King Kaylor and Queen Manasa of Tyglesea. He is sibling to Prince Tryntin, Princess Kyla, Prince Saldis, Prince Sandor, and Princess Lauraisha. He teaches Lauraisha how to ride a horse.

Aver'lyn (av-ER-lin): Erdeken elf; a dreamdrifter mage master from the Aevry Clan of Elves. He is the Mage Magistrate for the General Council of Mages and the Ring of Sorcerers on the Isle of Summons.

Azmar (AZ-mahr): Pyrekin unicorn; the Pyrekin beholden to the White Opal Keystone. He acts as Daya'lyn's main spiritual guide and guardian.

Borlag (BOR-lahg): Erdeken ogre; the father of Borgar, Borlag served as the Brute (leader) of the Shamgar Clan of ogres for many years before his son claimed the title.

Borgar (BOR-gar): Erdeken ogre; Borgar serves as the Brute (leader) of the Shamgar Clan of ogres. He is the son of Borlag, the lifemate to Kulgra, and father to Sorsha.

Bren (bren): Erdeling beast, wolf; a white wolf who is Dayalan's bloodmate. Bren can speak some of the tongues of beings, which is quite unusual for a beast. Bren dies while defending Katja and the other packmates from Daeryn, forcing Dayalan to take the horse Tyron as his new bloodmate.

Cabrica (KAH-breek-ah): Pyrekin Hayoth lioness; the Pyrekin beholden to the Chrysoberyl Cat's Eye Keystone, which is rumored to be in the possession of the Apotharni Clan of centaurs in the Sylvan city of Cheiron.

Calder (KAHL-der): Erdeken kelpie; originally mistaken as a nacken beast, this white horse-like being acts as Lauraisha's steed throughout most of their journey together from the Isle of Summons to the country of Vihous. Calder is a waterweaver mage.

Caleb, Calais Luthrial (KĀ-leb, KĀ-luhs LOOTH-ree-ahl): Erdeken dhampir; formerly an Asheken vampire; Caleb was originally a Toulouse Clan elf Turned by Luther into a vampire. Caleb is the only Redeemed Víchí in existence and terms himself a dhampir because he still carries some of the vampiric traits even though he is once again living. Caleb is the lifemate to Marga and the father of twin sons Dayalan and Daeryn. He is the master of Caerwyn Castle, a powerful shadowshaper, and a weak harmhealer mage.

Canuche (KAN-oo-cheh): Erdeken griffin; king of the Kirni griffin kingdom whose soul was inadvertently banished into a stone effigy by members of the Judas Coven of Víchí during the Second War of Ages. Canuche is a powerful dreamdrifter mage who helps Katja and Lauraisha at the beginning of their journey to the Isle of Summons.

The Creator (kree-Ā-tor): divine; the Creator is the eternal being who created everything else in existence.

Curqak, Solomos (SER-kak, sol-oh-mohs): Asheken ghoul; a servant of the Víchí High Elder Luther. Curqak is responsible for the death of Katja's parents as well as for the Feliconas Clan Massacre. Curqak was originally an elf named Solomos who was first Turned into a ghoul by the vampire Calais. When Calais was Redeemed and became the dhampir elf Caleb, Curqak became Luther's soul servant.

Cyrena (SĪ-ree-nah): Pyrekin sylph; she is the guardian for the altar gateways between the Erde Realm and the Wraith Realm. Vampires captured Cyrena's sister and used her transmuted corpse to help create the Ott vre Cael, the first of the three bloodstone mirrors.

King Daan (DAHN): Erdeken human; the king of Vihous, Daan is known as a wise and gentle king whose rule has been marked by generosity. Although open to trade with most Sylvans, Daan does keep tight border security, especially along the county's common border with Tyglesea. Although he is human, Daan took a dwarvish name during his coronation just as all of the kings of Vihous have before him in deference to the original dwarf inhabitants of Vihous.

Daeryn Calebson (DĀ-rin KĀ-leb-son): Asheken vampire; Daeryn is the son of Caleb the Redeemed and Marga Amerielle. He is the identical twin brother to Dayalan. As second-born, Daeryn is considered a steward of Caerwyn Castle, not its heir. He is a powerful shadowshaper mage and a very weak fireforger mage who looks very similar to a vampire. When he breaks his vow never to drink the blood of an Erdeken being, he is the first being to ever Turn himself into a vampire.

Damya (DAHM-yah): Pyrekin pyrefay or firesprite; the Pyrekin beholden to the Sapphire Keystone. Damya acts as Lauraisha's main spiritual guide and guardian.

Dayalan, Daya'lyn Calebson (DĀ-ah-lan, DĀ-ah-lin KĀ-leb-son): Erdeken hybrid, dhampir; Dayalan is the first-born son of Caleb the Redeemed and Marga Amerielle. As such, Dayalan is the heir of Caerwyn Castle, while his identical twin brother

Daeryn is its steward. Dayalan is a powerful fireforger mage who looks very similar to a vampire, but has sworn to only drink the blood of beasts rather than Erdeken beings. Dayalan is named the Sylvan Inquisitor by the Ring of Sorcerers after his renaming as mage Master Daya'lyn.

Deception (DEE-sep-shuhn): Darkkyn, race unknown; a powerful Darkkyn whose true name no one knows.

Devra Escari (DEV-rah es-KAR-ee): Erdeken werecat; Katja's mother and a member of the Feliconas Clan of werecats. Devra was long thought by others to be a weak harmhealer mage, but she is actually a different type of mage. She and Katja's father Kevros were killed in a rockslide when Katja has twelve winters of age.

The Discerner (DIS-sern-er): Erdeken, race unknown; one of the seven mages prophesied to bring about Luther's destruction through use of the Twelve Keystones.

Durhrigg (DOO-rig): Erdeken troll; a collector and hoarder of historical artifacts, weapons, and artwork who lives in the ancient dwarven ruins under Crown Canyon.

Eiriana (eer-ee-AH-nah): Erdeken pixie; Eiriana helps the members of the Inquisition journey through Vihous lands on their way to the country's capital city of Jorn.

Eliza (EE-li-zah): Erdeken dryad; Eliza is older sister to Ella and a sproutsinger mage. Together the sisters undertake the Initiation Quest in order to prove their bravery as warriors and gain the status of adults in their clan. When the dryads find the Agate Keystone, Eliza sacrifices herself to save Ella and to keep the sacred gem out of deadwalkers' possession. She is the aunt of Zahlathra and the great aunt of Zahra. The story of Ella and Eliza is one of the more famous in Sylvan history and is recounted in the book *The Dryad's Sacrifice*.

Ella (EL-lah): Erdeken dryad; Ella is the younger sister of Eliza and a sproutsinger mage. Together the sisters undertake the

Initiation Quest in order to prove their bravery as warriors and gain the status of adults in their clan. When the dryads find the Agate Keystone, Eliza sacrifices herself to save Ella and to keep the sacred gem out of deadwalkers' possession. Ella goes on to fight against the deadwalkers during the Second War of Ages alongside the famous griffins King Canuche and Nach. She is the mother of Zahlathra and the grandmother of Zahra. The story of Ella and Eliza is one of the more famous in Sylvan history and is recounted in the book *The Dryad's Sacrifice.*

Escos (ES-kohs): Erdeken human; commander in charge of the Fifth Falcon Regiment of Tyglesea. A close friend and ally to Queen Manasa, Escos decides to free Lauraisha and Katja when they are captured by his troops while trying to reach the Isle of Summons. Escos loses his life while battling the deadwalkers that hunt the females.

Eureshra (YUR-esh-rah): Erdeken naiad; a staunch ally of Chief Naya (naiad supreme ruler) Neamyntha, Eureshra is the leader of the naiads in the Ten Fang Marshes. She and her naiads help protect the members of the Inquisition as they pass through naiad territory.

Evita (Ee-vee-tah): see Naraka.

Federicos (FED-er-ee-kohs): Erdeken human; he is the son of Commander Escos and the Tyglesean Emissary to Vihous.

Felan Bardrick (fel-LAN BARD-rik): Erdeken werewolf; a member of the Geirgerd Clan of werewolves, Felan is the son of Chief Fenris and Vilda Bardrick. He is a powerful skinshifter mage and wielder of his family's distinctive sunsilver battle axe.

Fenris Bardrick (fin-RIS): Erdeken werewolf; Fenris is chief of the Geirgerd Clan of werewolves, Felan's father, and Vilda's lifemate. He is a powerful skinshifter mage.

Garret (GĀR-ret): Erdeken centaur; the mage initiate often paired with Katja for combat training. Garret finds Katja still in lioness form after her first bout of skinshifting madness and escorts her to Verdagon.

Glashtin (GLASH-tin): Erdeken kelpie; originally mistaken as a nacken beast, this white horse-like being acts as Katja's steed throughout most of their journey together from the Isle of Summons to the country of Vihous.

Gornash (GOR-nash): Erdeken ogre; Gornash serves as the Brute (leader) of the Barak Clan of ogres.

The Guardian (GAR-dee-an): Erdeken, race unknown; one of the seven mages prophesied to bring about Luther's destruction through use of the Twelve Keystones.

Helerha (he-LĀR-rah): Erdeken naiad; a staunch ally of Chief Naya Neamyntha, Helerha is the leader of the naiads of the Suuthe Marshes and Rerahept Trench. She is one of the naiads that the members of the Inquisition meet as they pass through naiad territory.

Hem'lyn (HEM-lin): Erdeken satyr; a sproutsinger mage and elder member of the General Council of Mages who raises strong objections to the appointment of a mage Inquisitor during the voting session.

Holis (HOL-is): Erdeken human; a journeyman shadowshaper mage and an important political figure in the kingdom of Vihous.

Ist'lynn (IST-lin): Erdeken human; a Tyglesean clergywoman and seer who prophesied that King Kaylor would meet his own death through an act of defiance by King Aedus's daughter and Kaylor's own daughter.

Joce'lynn, Jocelana (JOS-e-lin, JOS-e-lan-ah): Erdeken human; originally named Jocelana, Joce'lynn was originally a Tyglesean human. She is a member of and ruling judge for the Ring of Sorcerers, which governs the General Council of

Mages. A powerful wraithwalker mage, Joce'lynn is a war hero from the Second War of Ages and acts as one of Katja's main mentors.

Kapriel (KAP-ree-el): Pyrekin Hayoth lion; the Pyrekin guardian of the golden stairway leading from the Wraith Realm lands to the Dyvese Gateway.

Katja Kevrosa Escari (KAHT-yah KEV-rohs-ah es-KAR-ee): Erdeken werecat; a powerful skinshifter and wraithwalker mage, Katja is the youngest daughter to Devra and Kevros Escari and sibling to Kumos, Keepha, and Kayten. She is the sole survivor of the Feliconas Clan Massacre, which was perpetrated by deadwalkers at the beginning of the Third War of Ages. Katja is named a member of the Sylvan Inquisition by the Ring of Sorcerers.

Kaylor Ryhnus (KĀ-lor RĪ-nus): Erdeken human; the king of Tyglesea, Kaylor rules by general intimidation and through the scapegoating of mages. He is lifemate to Queen Manasa and the father to Prince Ashomocos, Prince Tryntin, Princess Kyla, Prince Saldis, Prince Sandor, and Princess Lauraisha.

Kayten Escari (KĀ-tin es-KAR-ee): Asheken nemean; he was the youngest son to Devra and Kevros Escari, and a sibling to Kumos, Keepha, and Katja. Once Daeryn becomes a vampire, Kayten is the first Sylvan that he Turns. Dayalan is forced to destroy Kayten with mage fire when Kayten attacks Katja.

Keepha Escari (KEE-fah es-KAR-ee): Erdeken werecat; she is the eldest daughter to Devra and Kevros Escari, and a sibling to Kumos, Kayten, and Katja. She and Kumos are brutally killed by deadwalkers during the Feliconas Clan Massacre.

Kevros Escari (KEV-rohs es-KAR-ee): Erdeken werecat; he is the lifemate to Devra and the father of Kumos, Keepha, Kayten, and Katja. A powerful wraithwalker mage, Kevros acted as the village discerner for the Feliconas Clan of werecats for many years until his death.

Kulgra (KUHL-grah): Erdeken ogress; the lifemate of Borgar and mother to Sorsha of Clan Shamgar.

Kumos Escari (KOO-mohs es-KAR-ee): Erdeken werecat; he is the eldest son to Devra and Kevros Escari, and a sibling to Keepha, Kayten, and Katja. He and Keepha are brutally killed by deadwalkers during the Feliconas Clan Massacre. Kumos acts as Katja's guide among the dead the first time that she walks in the Wraith Realm.

Kyla (KĪ-lah): Erdeken human, Asheken vampire; she is the first daughter and third-born child to King Kaylor and Queen Manasa of Tyglesea. She is sibling to Prince Ashomocos, Prince Tryntin, Prince Saldis, Prince Sandor, and Princess Lauraisha. Although Kyla secretly hates her father, she is still Kaylor's favorite child. As one of Naraka's earliest Tyglesean allies, Kyla is responsible for Naraka's introduction to the court at Castle Summersted.

Laura (LAR-rah): Erdeken human; King Aedus's youngest daughter and Tyglesean princess. Most believe that Laura died when Kaylor murdered the rest of her family with the fall of Castle Summersted during the Tyglesean Uprisings; however, a few beings suspect that she might have successfully escaped the country and sought sanctuary with the dryads at Mount Sol'ece.

Lauraisha of the House of Astraht'a (lah-RĀ-shah ah-STRAHT-ah): Erdeken human; she is the second daughter, sixth-born child, and youngest child of King Kaylor and Queen Manasa of Tyglesea. She is sibling to Prince Ashomocos, Prince Tryntin, Princess Kyla, Prince Saldis, and Prince Sandor. She is a powerful dreamdrifter and fireforger mage. Lauraisha is named a member of the Sylvan Inquisition by the Ring of Sorcerers.

Lothian (LOH-thee-an): Asheken vampire; the hag Alqama's former master. Lothian was destroyed during the Second War of Ages by Katja's father Kevros. When he died Alqama stole his bloodstone and used it to build the Hag's Nest fortress.

Luther, Luthrael (LOO-ther, LOOTH-rāl): Asheken vampire; necromancer mage; Luther was originally a Toulouse elf wraithwalker mage. When he was Turned by the Abomination, he became a necromancer and the first vampire ever to exist. Thus Luther is the sire of all Asheken deadwalker races. Among them, he is thus known as the Víchí High Elder and the ruler of the Northern Continent.

Mainmangi (MĀN-mahng-gee): Pyrekin ursa bear; Pyrekin beholden to the Ursa Agate Keystone. She is best known for her aid to Ella and Eliza at the beginning of the Second War of Ages.

Manasa of the House of Astraht'a (MAH-nah-sah ah-STRAHT-ah): Erdeken human; Kaylor's lifemate, the queen of Tyglesea, and the mother to Prince Ashomocos, Prince Tryntin, Princess Kyla, Prince Saldis, Prince Sandor, and Princess Lauraisha. Manasa is largely responsible for Lauraisha being safely smuggled out of Tyglesea after Kaylor hired a pair of assassins to kill the princess.

The Manticore (MAN-ti-kor): Erdeken manticore; he was one of the six Founders of all Sylvan races. The Sphinx and the Manticore's union produced the races of accipions, canis, giants, girtab, griffins, harpies, Tyglesean humans, liopions, ulfrions, werewolves, and, werecats like Katja that resemble lions.

The Manticore's Daughter (MAN-ti-kors DOT-ter): Erdeken, race unknown; before his death, Aribem prophesied that one day the Daughter of the Manticore and the Son of the Sphinx would help destroy Luther. Sylvan scholars have long debated the likely identity of these two beings.

Marga, Marg'lynn Amerielle (MAR-gah, MARG-lin, AH-mer-ī-el): Erdeken human; Caleb's lifemate and the mother of twin brothers Dayalan and Daeryn. Marg'lynn was once advisor to the Mage Council and the Ring of Sorcerers, but she fell into disfavor when she married Caleb. Once she was stripped of her mage rank and title, Marga retired from Isle of Summons politics and moved to Caerwyn Castle. She is presumed dead by all of her family and friends except Daeryn who insists that she is alive and a captive of Luther at his fortress at Blaecthull in the Northern Continent.

Mori'lyn (MOR-i-lin): Erdeken satyr; originally named Moricz, he is a dreamdrifter mage adept and Head of Archives for the Isle of Summons as well as an adviser to the Ring of Sorcerers. Under the influence of the deadwalker spy Perefaris, Mori'lyn betrays his fellow Sylvans by mentally assaulting Lauraisha and having her, Katja, Daya'lyn, Felan, and Zahra all imprisoned. Mori'lyn was later killed by Perefaris.

Nach (Noch): Erdeken griffin; a fierce Kirni griffin warrior and fireforger mage who is one of Ella's main allies during the Second War of Ages. Nach also assists Dayalan and Katja in the Wraith Realm during the Third War of Ages.

Naraka (NAR-ah-kah): Asheken vampire, shade; she is Luther's mate and one of his chief spies. Under the guise of a human named Evita, Naraka becomes a courtier at Castle Summersted in Tyglesea and quickly rises to prominence as King Kaylor's suasor (most trusted advisor).

Nascius (NĀ-shuhs): Erdeken human; a human of Vihous-ancestry, Nascius captains the boat that ferries the packmates through the Summons Lake for the funeral burial of the wolf Bren, and then ferries the Inquisition members across the Summons Lake at the beginning of their journey to Tyglesea.

Neamyntha (NEE-ah-min-thah): Erdeken naiad; the Chief Naya (naiad supreme ruler) and Mistress of Azuralle Lake's naiad community. Neamyntha helps the Inquisition members during their journey to Tyglesea.

Neha'lyn (ne-HĀ-lin): Erdeken elf; the harmhealer mage master in charge of the Isle of Summons Healing Ward. Despite his being a Toulouse Clan elf, Neha'lyn is highly respected by both clans of his people for his healing skills and gentle demeanor.

Nicho'lyn (NIK-oh-lin): Erdeken liopion; he is a fireforger mage master and member of the Ring of Sorcerers. Nicho'lyn acts as Dayalan's and Lauraisha's main fireforging mentor on the Isle of Summons.

Oeled (Oh-led): Erdeken elf; an Aevry Clan elf and apprentice harmhealer mage, Oeled works directly under Neha'lyn's tutelage and supervision in the Isle of Summons Healing Ward.

Onofré (on-OF-rā): Erdeken human; a Tyglesean human and Kaylor-loyalist who acts as Captain of the Guard for Summersted Castle in the Tyglesean capital city of Kaylere.

Otwenia (OT-wen-yah): Erkeken harpy; a harpy from the Clan Eerondus who brings news about her clan joining the fight at Reithrgar to Verdagon and Katja during their first flight together.

The Pariah (pe-rī-ah): Erdeken, race unknown; one of the seven mages prophesied to bring about Luther's destruction through use of the Twelve Keystones.

Peha'lyn (pe-HĀ-lin): Erdeken centaur; originally named Pehalius; sproutsinger mage master and member of the Ring of Sorcerers. He was bitten and Turned into the deadwalker spy and dullahan Perefaris.

Perefaris (PAHR-uh-fār-is): Asheken dullahan; see Peha'lyn.

Prisca, Pris'lynn (NAH-roo-lin): Erdeken centaur; a powerful centaur harmhealer who goes through the Naming Ritual to become a mage master together with Dayalan.

Qenethala Rahalazel (KEN-uh-thahl-ah ra-HAH-lah-zel): Erdeken dryad; she is Princess Zahra's younger half-sister and the chief messenger for Zahlathra. While she is an important member of her clan, Qenethala is not considered a dryad princess because she came out of Queen Mother Zahlathra's second marriage while Zahra came from the first.

The Renewed (REE-nood): Erdeken, race unknown; one of the seven mages prophesied to bring about Luther's destruction through use of the Twelve Keystones.

Rubero (roo-BEHR-oh): Erdeken brolaghan, greyman; brother of Ruthero, who was destroyed by Katja when she was ambushed by Curqak and his allies after the Feliconas Clan Massacre. Rubero is a powerful shadowshaper and waterweaver mage.

Runnel (ROON-nel): Erdeling beast, nacken; one of the nacken pack beasts that accompanies the Inquisition members on their journey across the Sylvan Continent from the Isle of Summons to Tyglesea.

Ruthero (roo-THEHR-oh): Asheken revenant; the revenant shade who darkens the skies for Curqak and his allies when they massacre the Feliconas Clan and hunt Katja Escari.

Saldis, Sal (SAHL-dis, SAHL): Erdeken human; nicknamed Sal by his siblings, Saldis is the third son and fourth-born child to King Kaylor and Queen Manasa. Saldis is sibling to Prince Ashomocos, Prince Tryntin, Princess Kyla, Prince Sandor, and Princess Lauraisha. Although he has no mage abilities of his own, Saldis is a great cook and medicine maker. Most of Lauraisha's extensive herb knowledge comes from him.

Sandor, Sandrie (SAN-dor, SAN-dree): Erdeken human; nicknamed Sandrie by his siblings, he is the fourth son and fifth-born child to King Kaylor and Queen Manasa of Tyglesea. Sandor is sibling to Prince Ashomocos, Prince Tryntin, Princess Kyla, Prince Saldis, and Princess Lauraisha. Of all of her siblings, Lauraisha shared Sandrie's dreams the most while they were growing up. He and Tryntin helped teach her how to hunt and fish.

The Seer (SEER): Erdeken, race unknown; one of the seven mages prophesied to bring about Luther's destruction through use of the Twelve Keystones.

Si'lyn (SĪ-lin): Erdeken dwarf; a charmchanter mage master, Si'lyn acts as Chief Counselor of the Ring of Sorcerers on the mage Isle of Summons. He occasionally acts as Vraelth's mentor.

Solomos (SOL-oh-mos): see Curqak.

Sora'lynn (SOHR-ah-lin): Erdeken harpy; a high-ranking official in Vihous and a harmhealer mage.

Sorbash (SOR-bash): Erdeken ogre; only surviving ogre harmhealer from the Hag's Nest Battle.

Sorsha (SOR-shah): Erdeken ogress; daughter of Borgar and Kulgra of the Clan Shamgar.

The Sower (Soh-er): Erdeken, race unknown; one of the seven mages prophesied to bring about Luther's destruction through use of the Twelve Keystones.

The Sphinx (sfeenks): Erdeken Sphinx; she was one of the six Founders of all Sylvan races. The Sphinx and the Manticore's union produced the races of accipions, canis, giants, girtab, griffins, harpies, Tyglesean humans, liopions, ulfrions, werewolves, and, werecats like Katja that resemble lions. The Sphinx was chosen by Aribem to guard the isthmus between the Northern and Southern continents once the two continents were divided. She faithfully protected southern-continent-dwelling Sylvans from the Northern hordes of Asheken deadwalkers until Daeryn slew her in battle at the beginning of the Third War of Ages.

The Sphinx's Son (sfeenks suhn): Erdeken, race unknown; before his death, Aribem prophesied that one day the Daughter of the Manticore and the Son of the Sphinx would help destroy Luther. Sylvan scholars have long debated the likely identity of these two beings.

Tristin (TRIS-tin): Erdeken human; Kaylor's younger brother and second in line for the Tyglesean throne once Kaylor usurps it; Tristin was Manasa's first husband who was killed in a horse-riding accident a month after their wedding.

Tryntin (TRIN-tin): Erdeken human; he is the second son and second-born child to King Kaylor and Queen Manasa of Tyglesea. He is sibling to Prince Ashomocos, Princess Kyla, Prince Saldis, Prince Sandor, and Princess Lauraisha. He and Sandrie helped teach Lauraisha how to hunt and fish.

Tylner (TIL-ner): Erdeken human; captain of the *Nedaleta Benefta* ship which takes Daya'lyn, Lauraisha, Katja, Federicos, and his entourage from Jorn and Kaylere via a seventeen-day voyage on the Westylere Sea

Tyron (TĪ-rohn): Erdeling beast, horse; Lauraisha's huge sorrel stallion who stands roughly eighteen paw-lengths tall at the shoulder by Katja's reckoning. Tyron becomes Dayalan's bloodmate after Bren dies.

Verdagon (VER-dah-gohn): Pyrekin dragon; The Pyrekin dragon beholden to the Emerald Keystone. He acts as Katja's main spiritual guide and protector.

Vilda Bardrick (VIL-dah BARD-rik): Erdeken werewolf; a member of the Geirgerd Clan of werewolves, Vilda is the lifemate to Chief Fenris and mother to Felan.

Vraelth Verd (vrālth verd): Erdeken elf; he is a charmchanter mage and an Aevry Clan elf.

Zahlathra Ellazel Etheal (ZAH-lath-rah EL-lah-zel EE-thee-ahl): Erdeken dryad; she is the dryad Queen Mother, leader of all dryad tribes, and the direct leader of the Zolaramie Tribe.

Zahra Zahlathrazel Etheal (ZĀR-rah ZAH-lahth-rah-zel EE-thee-ahl): Erdeken dryad; a powerful sproutsinger mage, Princess Zahra is one of Zahlathra's daughters through her first marriage and, therefore, in line to succeed Zahlathra as the dryad Queen Mother.

ACKNOWLEDGEMENTS

While there are many people who have my deepest gratitude for their help in the realization of this book and the furtherance of this incredible story, there is one who deserves my utmost praise: Jesus Christ. He is my hope and my savior, the being for whom I write every single day. I love you, My Sire, and I'm continually amazed by your willingness to sacrifice everything for me despite the Taint I hold in the depths of my soul. Thank you for the redemptive fire of your all-consuming love. Romans 10:9 now and always!

Thank you once again to my family members who have helped and supported me throughout life's trials. While the wounds that I've accumulated while writing this book have cut deep, the balm of your love has once again proven deeper. Matthew, your understanding and reassurance continually amaze me. Thank you for delighting in my goofy, weird antics...and adding to them daily! Mom and Dad, your encouragement and support mean so much to me! Thank you for always challenging me to do my best and to dig deeper in all that I do. Ian, I've dedicated this book to you because you are never afraid to be real with me even when reality hurts. Thank you for that and for being a true brother. Derek, I can't wait to meet you some day when my work here is finished. For now, I will continue pursuing the path that God has set before me.

To the band members of Fireflight, RED, and Skillet. As of this writing, you and I have never met, but I hope we do someday. I want to tell you face-to-face that your music has been absolutely essential to the creation of this book, this series, and in helping its author stay somewhat sane through some of the darkest slogs of my life. For now, let me take this space on a page to say thank you! You remind me daily that while I may be desperate, God knows my name and He weeps with my pain. He is my salvation, my hero, and the source of my rebirthing. Though life may leave me in pieces, I am not alone. God can and will breathe into me and rescue me from the fight inside of my darkest part.

Lorelei Logsdon, thank you once again for your encouragement and your expert editorial eye. I am so grateful that you are part of this project! To my beta readers and advance readers, you are all so amazing! Richard Barmore, David Gray, Paul Hostettler, Esther McIntyre, and Matt Sears, thank you especially for your hard work. This new chapter in Katja's story is once again the best that it can be because of you!

Finally, my dear readers, each and every one of you deserve a standing ovation for discovering and sharing in my characters' adventures. May we have many more together! I love you all!

ABOUT THE AUTHOR

Alycia Christine grew up near the dusty cotton fields of Lubbock, Texas, with a fearless mutt for a dog and a backyard trampoline that almost bounced her to the moon. She fell in love with fantasy and science fiction books when her father first read them to her at age ten. Her love of fiction writing blossomed during her time at Texas A&M University. Alycia's fiction has received wide praise for its unique characters and vivid storytelling. Her award-winning art photography has been featured in Times Square. When she isn't writing or shooting photos, Alycia enjoys long talks with her husband, drinking copious amounts of tea, and coaxing her skittish cat out from under the living room furniture. Find her at AlyciaChristine.com.

An excerpt from the upcoming adventure

FIREFORGER

BOOK THREE OF THE SYLVAN CYCLE SERIES

K atja, please?"

The werecat growled in frustration. "I don't know if it will do any good, but I'll try my best, Daya'lyn."

The fireforger nodded. "That is all I ask. Thank you."

"No, all you ask is a miracle," she muttered before moving to the center of the war-torn room to stand before the shattered Ott vre Cael mirror. "Stand well away from me. I'm not sure what might happen."

The dhampir nodded, and then he and Katja's other packmates stepped to the outskirts of the half-collapsed room with their weapons held at the ready. With a sigh of resignation, Katja crouched and retrieved one of the mirror's blackened shards from the half-melted floor. The glass reflected a swirling red darkness unlike anything in the gray stone room around it. As she watched, the shard's scene changed to show her own sunsilver-and-dragon-bone spear striking it. Then the shard seemed to pulse with sullen rage.

"So you do recognize me," she whispered to the pitch-colored glass.

"Destroyer," came the shard's answering hiss.

The wraithwalker's eyes narrowed at it.

"Reformer," she answered, and pricked her right palm with the sullen shard just above the crescent-shaped scar left from her first encounter with the Ott vre Caerwyn.

"And now my moon shall have a star," she murmured.

The shard greedily drank in her life's flow and then

seemed to spasm. "Manticore..." the shard's chorus of voices whispered even as its surface transformed to match the hue of her blood. "Command us!"

Katja took a deep breath and looked around the room at the mirror's other scattered shards. "Arise!" she intoned.

The packmates shrank back as pieces of the Ott vre Cael's black glass lifted from the floor and began to spiral around the werecat.

"Katja..." Felan said in consternation as the shards hissed.

"Katja!" Daya'lyn yelled in panic when they swirled closer.

"Now, fireforger!" she snarled. "Purify them!"

Daya'lyn's blue-white fire surrounded the werecat in twin walls of flame. She knelt as the flames touched and cleansed every spinning shard near her. The purifying flames then extinguished as quickly as they had been forged. With a sigh of relief, Katja stood once more amid the now silver shards and pointed her bloody paw toward the shattered mirror's frame.

"Reform!"

The shards flew to the ruined mirror and assembled themselves in perfect order inside its frame—piecing themselves back together with a proficiency that the skinshifter almost envied. With an effort, Katja expelled the shard's Taint from her paw and then skinshifted her wound closed. She grimaced at her newest magic-induced scar and then walked the length of the ruined room to the mirror while clutching the scarlet shard to her chest.

As the rest of the packmates kept a respectful distance, Daya'lyn joined her before the reformed Ott vre Cael.

"It worked!" He smiled.

She eyed the mirror warily. "We'll see."

"Command us, Katja Escari," the scarlet shard whispered after she had inserted it in its rightful place within the mirror's silver surface. As soon as the scarlet shard touched its fellows, the silver shards all seemed to melt and then reformed into a single solid reflection.

"Show me Caerwyn," she said as Daya'lyn stood beside her.

The mirror clouded and an image shimmered into view

of the red-carpeted room in Caerwyn Castle which housed the full-length mirror of Ott vre Caerwyn. The room looked just as it had the last time that Katja had set paw in it.

"Caleb! Hear me!" Katja spoke to the image of the empty room. "Daya'lyn and I must speak with you!"

A male's deep voice answered her then, but it was too warbled for her to understand its message. A chorused hiss shrieked from the mirror, then, and the image of Caerwyn vanished from its silver surface.

"What happened?" Daya'lyn asked.

She shook her head and kept her focus on the mirror. She moved to stand to one side as the fireforger took her place directly in front the mirror's center.

"Let Daya'lyn command you!" she told the mirror.

Daya'lyn told the mirror once again to show them Caerwyn and then they waited—staring intently at its dark visage. The surface swirled as if clouded by smoke and then a pale figure walked through the gloom toward them.

"Hello, brother," Daeryn said in a voice like honey-dipped knives.

Daya'lyn's twin's eyes were crimson with bloodlust and he bore no clothes save a leather loin cloth. As he stretched his drake-like wings fully behind his broad, muscular back, Katja shuddered and thanked the Creator that the male could not see her from where she stood.

"What do you want, Daeryn?" Daya'lyn snarled.

"To settle a question." Daeryn's smile toward Daya'lyn was full of fang. "Since Lauraisha now resides at Blaecthull, she and I have had the opportunity to spend time together. I have dreamed her dreams and shared in her memories, Dayalan." The smile curled into a snarl. "And what they taught me troubles me deeply."

Daya'lyn's eyes narrowed, but he said nothing.

"You were close, brother; so close to gratifying the Thirst and becoming even more powerful than me. I saw the lust in your eyes for her," the vampire continued. "And yet you exchanged the pleasure of the Thirst for a pithy flame instead. How long can you deny the instinct stirring inside of you? How long will you fight your need for her?"

"Silence, brigand!"

"You know you want her. You know she is willing. She wanted you and yet you would not take her for your own when you so easily could have. Why?"

Again Daya'lyn said nothing.

"Why, brother? Do you not know the strength that you could gain from her and she from you? Nothing could harm either of you ever again. Not even Luther could withstand you!"

"I will not be like you!" Daya'lyn's shout echoed off the half-tumbled rafters.

Daeryn glared at his twin a moment and then snarled. "You always did try to prove yourself the noble one. Very well. I will make a bargain with you, *Inquisitor*." He dropped his wings to show Lauraisha kneeling gagged and bound with water chains behind him. Daya'lyn's and Katja's wide-eyed shouts were incomprehensible.

"I am thirsty, brother, and unlike you I feel no qualms about satisfying my innate desires. So here is my arrangement with you: your blood or hers. I long to bite Lauraisha and gain her power, but I will let you choose whose precious fireforger blood I imbibe first." Daeryn's yellow fangs flashed as he smiled.

"You have not the strength to withstand either of our fire!" Daya'lyn snarled. "No vampire does!"

Daeryn tilted his head to one side, considering his twin with humorless laughter. "Did you not notice my body, Inquisitor? It bears no scars from the wrath of your hottest fire. You may have squandered your opportunity to be the first true immortal, but I will not waste mine."

He snarled at Daya'lyn and then peered at the bound female behind him. "If you come too late, I will drain and Turn Lauraisha, Dayalan, and your precious fireforger will greet you with the fanged kiss that you should have given her in the first place. But if you come now, I will gorge myself on your blood and your power instead." Daeryn smiled then, and turned to stare toward the side of the mirror, right into Katja's eyes. "And just before the last of your life ebbs from your veins, Daya'lyn, you will witness me Turn Katja."

WHAT WILL
ALYCIA CHRISTINE
WRITE NEXT?

From Thorn's newest exploits on the high seas to Katja and Ella's latest battles against the cursed deadwalkers, more pulse-pounding adventures are racing your way!

Fireforger
Book Three of the Sylvan Cycle series

The Vampire's Redemption
Second Novella of the Sylvan Prelude series

Sloop and Sword
Second Novella of the Tempest Maiden series
and more!

Can't wait to read what comes next?

Sign up for the **newsletter** to:

Get FREE books
Learn about the latest releases
Get access to exclusive content and more!

AlyciaChristine.com/news